Praise for

This book was just what I was hoping for and wickedly entertaining. The premise of this book is really well done. Parts are hard to read of course. This book is about a serial killer who targets mostly young teenagers. The book isn't very graphic, but it still breaks your heart in places. But there is also a sweet romance that helps to give the book a sense of hope. Mix that with some strong women, the creepiness of the paranormal factors, and the book balances out really well. There is a lot of potential with these characters and I'd love to see their stories continue. If you are a Hill fan, grab this.

-Lex Kent's Reviews, *goodreads*

Hill is a master writer, and this one is done in a way that I think will appeal to many readers. Don't just discount this one because it has a paranormal theme to it! I think that the majority of readers who love mystery novels with a romantic side twist will love this story.

-Bethany K., *goodreads*

It was suspenseful and so well written that it was anyone's guess what would happen next! The characters—all of them, as you'll learn, were perfectly written.

-Gayle T., *NetGalley*

Gerri Hill has written another action-packed thriller. The writing is excellent and the characters engaging. Wow!

-Jenna F., *NetGalley*

...is a phenomenal book! I wish I could give this more than five stars. Yes, there is a paranormal element, and a love story, and conflict, and danger. And it's all worth it. Thank you, Gerri Hill, for writing a brilliant masterpiece!

-Carolyn M., *NetGalley*

After the Summer Rain

...is a heartwarming, slow-burn romance that features two awesome women who are learning what it really means to live and love fully. They're also learning to let go of their turbulent pasts so that it doesn't ruin their future happiness. Gerri Hill has never failed to give me endearing characters who are struggling with heartbreaking issues and beautiful descriptions of the landscapes that surround them.

-The Lesbian Review

Gerri Hill is simply one of the best romance writers in the genre. This is an archetypal Hill, slightly unusual characters in a slightly unusual setting. The slow-burn romance, however, is a classic, trying not to fall in love, but unable to fight the pull.

-Lesbian Reading Room

After the Summer Rain is a wonderfully heartfelt romance that avoids all the angsty drama-filled tropes you often find in romances.

-C-Spot Reviews

Moonlight Avenue

Moonlight Avenue by Gerri Hill is a riveting, literary tapestry of mystery, suspense, thriller and romance. It is also a story about forgiveness, moving on with your life and opening your heart to love despite how daunting it may seem at first.

-The Lesbian Review

...is an excellent mystery novel, sheer class. Gerri Hill's writing is flawless, her story compelling and much more than a notch above others writing in this genre.

-Kitty Kat's Book Review Blog

The Locket

This became a real page-turner as the tension racked up. I couldn't put it down. Hill has a knack for combining strong characters, vulnerable and complex, with a situation that allows them to grow, while keeping us on our toes as the mystery unfolds. Definitely one of my favorite Gerri Hill thrillers, highly recommended.

-Lesbian Reading Room

The Neighbor

It's funny... Normally in the books I read I get why the characters would fall in love. Now on paper (excuse the pun), Cassidy and Laura should not work... but let me tell you, that's the reason they do. I actually loved this book so hard. ...Yes it's a slow burn but so beautifully written and worth the wait in every way.

-Les Rêveur

This is classic Gerri Hill at her very best, top of the pile of so many excellent books she has written, I genuinely loved this story and these two women. The growing friendship and hidden attraction between them is skillfully written and totally engaging.... This was a joy to read.

-Lesbian Reading Room

I have always found Hill's writing to be intriguing and stimulating. Whether she's writing a mystery or a sweet romance, she allows the reader to discover something about themselves along with her characters. This story has all the fun antics you would expect for a quality, low-stress, romantic comedy. Hill is wonderful in giving us characters that are intriguing and delightful that you never want to put the book down until the end.

-The Lesbian Review

The Stars at Night

Other Bella Books by Gerri Hill

About the Author

Gerri Hill has over thirty-eight published works, including the 2020 GCLS winner *After the Summer Rain*, the 2017 GCLS winner *Paradox Valley*, 2014 GCLS winner *The Midnight Moon*, 2011, 2012 and 2013 winners *Devil's Rock*, *Hell's Highway* and *Snow Falls*, and the 2009 GCLS winner *Partners*, the last book in the popular Hunter Series, as well as the 2013 Lambda finalist *At Seventeen*. Gerri lives in south-central Texas, only a few hours from the Gulf Coast, a place that has inspired many of her books. With her partner, Diane, they share their life with two Australian shepherds—Rylee and Mason—and a couple of furry felines. For more, visit her website at gerrihill.com.

Bella Books, Inc.
P.O. Box 10543
Tallahassee, FL 32302

Printed in the United States of America on acid-free paper.

First Bella Books Edition 2020

Editor: Medora MacDougall
Cover Designer: Sandy Knowles

ISBN: 978-1-64247-175-5

The Stars at Night

GERRI HILL

BELLA
BOOKS
2020

CHAPTER ONE

Kyler stood on her little back porch, leaning her shoulder against the cedar beam. The first birds to arrive at the feeder this morning were the goldfinches. Two lone pine siskens soon followed. She enjoyed watching them for the few months they hung around. By late February, the goldfinches and siskens would be heading back north, not to return again until October.

Her gaze lifted from the feeder to the sky. It was particularly red this morning, and she wished she'd driven up Skyline Drive to catch the sunrise, something she didn't do nearly enough. A rustling in the junipers brought her attention back to the feeders and a young doe stood staring back at her. She smiled.

"Good morning, Daisy," she said quietly.

The deer twitched her nose as if making sure it was her, then walked out into the open, finding the corn she'd tossed out earlier. She also threw some out in the evenings. She shouldn't feed them, she knew. They asked the campers in the state park not to feed the wildlife, yet here she was, disobeying the very signs she'd help put up. Daisy was the only deer who came by each morning. In the evenings, five or six would show up. She supposed if the javelinas found the corn, she'd have to stop. While they weren't animals that she feared, a javelina with young was as fierce as a momma bear guarding her babies. She'd found that out the hard way.

She smiled, remembering how she'd sprinted through the brush, screaming in panic as the herd of javelinas charged her. She'd literally leapt into the back of her work truck to escape them. Nope. She didn't want to lure them to her house. Of course, the corn was always gone by morning. For all she knew, they came during the night to eat without her knowing it.

The sun was now up, the red color fading from the sky. She knew she should go inside and get dressed for work. She was simply feeling too peaceful to move, though. When had this contentment with her life taken hold? The second year? The first? Before that? Hard to believe she hated it up here at first. The Davis Mountains— so far from the beaches of Mustang Island—were the last place she thought she'd be. Her own stupidity got her transferred to this remote state park in the first place. Funny how a colossal mistake could turn into the best move of her life.

Yeah. Because she loved it here.

With Daisy crunching on the corn and the birds fighting for space at the feeder, she turned and went inside her little cabin. One of the perks of being in such a remote place was the housing that the state park provided its rangers. The cabins were small and mostly clustered together, but they were surrounded by woodlands— piñons, junipers, and oaks. While at first she missed the sandy beach of her little rental cottage on the Gulf, she wouldn't trade this for anything now. Yeah, she'd missed the beach. And her friends. She didn't miss going out and bumping into Britney, though. Britney, with her silky blond hair and radiant smile.

Oh, let's don't forget the dark-haired beauty Britney had been dating the last time they'd bumped into each other. Britney had overplayed the whole thing, making Kyler wish she could have thrown up all over their sandal-clad feet.

But that would have been childish. She was over Britney by that time anyway.

"Right."

She rolled her eyes. Well, she was certainly over her now. However, one broken heart in her lifetime was enough. She didn't imagine she'd be so free with her heart from now on. Not that this remote area afforded her much opportunity. It didn't matter though. She loved it here. Whether there was opportunity to date or not wasn't a consideration.

With one last glance at Daisy, then the birds, she went inside. Her cell rang as she moved into her bedroom and she answered with a smile.

"Good morning, Tammy. Are you already at the office?"

"Kyler, good morning. No, no. Someone called the emergency number. I'm still at the ranch. But you've got maintenance this week, right?"

Her smile faded. "Now what?"

"Sorry, sweetie. The men's bathroom over by the tent area has a problem. A toilet is overflowing."

She groaned. "Okay. I'll get right to it."

CHAPTER TWO

"Move? You're going to *move*?"

Lexie watched as a bright red sports car sped past, then she pulled her gaze from the parking lot that was only partially obscured by tree branches. She turned to her best friend, who was still looking at her in shock.

"Trial run, Trish. That's all. Trial run." Those were her brother's words when he'd been cautioning her about the move. *Think of it as a trial run, sis.* Yes, it could simply be just a test. If she wanted it to be. Shockingly, she wasn't sure any longer. But she wouldn't tell Trish that. Not yet.

"You can't possibly consider leaving Austin. This is home. Your friends are here."

Lexie waved at her apartment, the place she had called home for the last three years. "I can't afford this place anymore. I can't afford Austin anymore."

"You can move in with me," Trish offered quickly.

Lexie shook her head. "As much as I love you, that would never work." She held her hand up when Trish would have protested. "I haven't had a job in eight months. I have no leads. Every job I apply for, there are a hundred others fighting for the position it seems. I'm thirty years old. Why pay me when they can hire someone fresh out of college for much less?"

"First of all, I can't believe you're thirty! Secondly, I *still* can't believe you got laid off. That's so unfair."

"You, my friend, will be thirty too in February! It's coming!" The smile left her face. "But yeah, we all thought it wasn't fair." She shrugged. "In a business acquisition like that, no one is safe. Those making the most are usually the first to get axed, especially if your job is considered redundant. Mine was."

"But they said they were going to rehire some of you, right?"

"I took the severance pay. I won't be one of them." She tucked her hair behind her ears with a sigh. "Point is, I can't afford to keep paying rent here, Trish. I'm draining my savings at an alarming rate."

"So you move seven hours away? Lexie, what do you know about running a motel?"

"It's a lodge. A rustic lodge."

Trish waved her hand dismissively. "Whatever. My point remains."

"I don't know anything about it," she agreed. "I'm sure I'll learn."

"That lodge thing was your parents' dream, not yours. They're out in the middle of nowhere. My God, Lexie, you've never even visited them out there! Now you want to *move* there?"

"I haven't visited them because—"

Because why? Well, yes, it *was* in the middle of nowhere. And yes, a seven-hour drive from Austin, at least. That was an excuse, really. She'd simply had no desire to go out there. Because there was nothing to do there. Trish was right. It was in the middle of nowhere and it was her parents' dream, not hers. She'd followed in her parents' footsteps when it came to her career—the tech industry was huge in Austin and she'd found a job easily after college. Her one and only job. She'd moved up the ranks quickly. She'd had a very nice salary. She'd been a project manager, the last two years with three teams under her. It was fast-paced, sometimes stressful—okay, most of the time stressful—and she'd loved it.

But then her parents were offered early retirement—voluntary separation is what their company called it. The severance package was too substantial to pass up, so they jumped at the offer. They took the money and bought an old rustic lodge and restaurant in the Davis Mountains, adjacent to the state park there. Lexie had seen pictures—it was lovely. Lexie had heard stories—they loved it there.

Lexie had never visited, however. She hadn't followed her parents there when they'd asked her to come aboard. She hadn't even considered it because at that time, seven years ago, she'd still loved her job. Her brother had gone to run the restaurant and he seemed genuinely happy, but Lexie had no intention of leaving Austin to join the family business. As Trish had said, Austin was home. But things change, don't they?

"I haven't visited because I haven't had time," she said lamely. "It's not like I don't see them. Mark comes to visit every summer in August when things are hot and slow there. And, you know, my parents come here every year after Christmas, during their dead month, as Mom calls it."

Trish shook her head. "No, that's not it. You haven't visited because you're a city girl and you like city things. From what you've told me, they're hundreds of miles from any city."

"It's two hundred and ten miles to El Paso, yes."

Trish stared at her blankly. "You're crazy to even consider this. You have a full life here, Lexie. We have group dinners, parties. You've got your fitness freaks from the gym you hang out with. We go dancing at the clubs on Saturday nights. Sunday morning brunches. You're *always* doing something. You can't just up and leave like this." She narrowed her eyes. "You never do anything on the spur of the moment. You always analyze and overthink everything to death. Why are you so quick to jump on this?"

"It's not quick. It's simply that I've not told you I've been considering it. My mother mentioned it to me at least a month ago, if not longer. And yes, I've been debating the pros and cons for weeks now." She waved her hand in the air. "You're right. I overthink things. I know that." She shrugged. "But it's what I do. And after careful consideration of all the facts—both pros and cons—I'm willing to give this a chance."

"But not now, Lexie! It's the holidays!"

"I know. That was both a pro and a con. I'll get to be with my family, but I won't be here like I'm used to. And all of it, yes, will be culture shock, I'm sure. I'll probably be bored out of my mind."

"Then why do it at all?"

"I told you—I don't have a job and unless I take a major cut in salary, I won't get one. This is an opportunity that I need to at least consider."

"It's just not you, Lexie. Can't you see that?"

"Oh, Trish. I know," she finally admitted. She met her gaze. "I'm…I'm depressed. I'm all out of sorts and nothing is going right for me. I need a change."

"Depressed? You don't seem depressed. Why, just last night—"

"I put on a happy face. I can't fake it anymore, Trish."

"So you want to do *this*? If you're depressed here, what will that be like?"

She went to the fridge and took out a water bottle, absently twisting off its cap as her mind reeled. Was Trish right? Would moving away make things worse, not better? Could she *really* be going to do this? Could she really be going to pack her car and head to far West Texas?

"I'm going there right after Thanksgiving. Leaving early Friday morning. I'm going to stay through the holidays. That will give me plenty of time to see if I can make it work. My lease is up here at the end of January. It's perfect timing."

Trish arched an eyebrow. "Are you doing this because of Crazy Cathy?"

Lexie rolled her eyes. "Oh, please. I threatened her with a restraining order. I haven't heard from her in months."

"And that's another thing! You'll be single forever! You're moving to the middle of nowhere! Who are you going to date?"

"I haven't recovered from Crazy Cathy yet. As I've told you—and everyone else these last six months—I have no desire to start dating again. None. I mean, I'm talking *years* yet."

Trish smiled at that. "I can't believe she stole your car."

"Stole my car? She drove it into the lake!"

They both laughed. Yeah, they could laugh about it now. It had been six months. To say that Cathy hadn't taken the breakup well was an understatement. However, the whole car incident was ruled a domestic dispute and Cathy was never charged. The only positive to come out of it was that she'd gotten a new car. A previously owned, new-to-her car, that is. Not having a job wasn't conducive to splurging on a new car.

Trish walked closer and hugged her. "You know I'm being totally selfish when I say I don't want you to go. We've been friends since we were freshmen in college."

Lexie hugged her tightly. "I know. But it's only a trial run, remember?" She felt a twinge of guilt for lying to her, but Trish would never understand her need to get away. "I may hate it there. In fact, I'm prepared to hate it there. As you said, it's in the middle of nowhere. Ft. Davis has a population of about twelve hundred people. I would imagine by the time Christmas rolls around—if I haven't lost my mind by then—I'll be racing to get back here."

"At least you're not going to miss Thanksgiving. The group dinner wouldn't be the same without you."

"I wouldn't miss it. It'll give me a chance to say goodbye to everyone."

"Last year we had over thirty people, I think. I can't believe how big it's gotten."

It started with a group of five college friends and had grown from there. "I know. It's the only time I get to see some of them." Yes, she'd miss her friends. Of course she would. She'd miss the groups she belonged to, the activities she'd gotten accustomed to. She would probably miss all of that.

She wouldn't miss the job hunting. She wouldn't miss the constant stress of her shrinking bank account. She wouldn't miss the badgering she took from friends who were determined to set her up on blind dates, despite her assertion that she was taking a long break from dating. She didn't have to remind herself that she met Cathy on a blind date.

Truth was, though, she was tired. Tired of going out every night, every weekend with one of her groups. Tired of her daily gym sessions. Tired of dinner dates with friends who always seemed to bring along a single woman who Lexie found herself sitting next to, attempting small talk with a stranger. Tired of strolling Sixth Street every Saturday night. Tired of the hustle and bustle. Tired of spending money as if she wasn't unemployed. She wanted to slow down, take a breath, and reevaluate her life.

She was thirty and in a rut. A deep rut. What did she want to do with the rest of her life? Get another job in the tech industry? So far that wasn't working out for her. Get a new career? She was too old for entry-level. Go back to college? She mentally rolled her eyes at that. *No way.* She wasn't *that* crazy! But was she? Was she crazy to consider this move? More than consider, really. After debating it for the last month, she'd talked herself into it. Trish obviously thought it was a bad idea. But her parents had made the offer. They hadn't pushed, but they'd offered. Mark hadn't pushed either—he knew her—but he thought it was worth a try on her part. Change of scenery, as he'd said. It would definitely be that.

She shook away her musings and smiled at Trish, hugging her again. "Gonna miss you the most. You've kept me sane these last six, eight months."

Trish met her gaze. "You say that as if you're not coming back. I mean, you *are* coming back, right?"

"Of course I am. I'll be back sometime in January, one way or another."

CHAPTER THREE

Kyler paused at the door, taking in the familiar scene of the Cottonwood Creek Bar and Grill. The patrons weren't always the same but after more than four years, she knew most of them by name. Tonight, Joe Bob Edwards and his wife, Shelly, were sitting in the first booth, both nursing longneck beers. Stuart Gilmer was sharing a table with the Mertz brothers, the three of them laughing at a joke Stuart had told. Tammy, who ran the office at the park, was having dinner with her husband, Phil. Mark was behind the bar, wiping a spot where Bill's Jack and Coke glass had sweated a ring. A few of the tables were occupied with strangers, either campers from the park or those staying at the lodge. Country music played in the background and Mark was bobbing his head to the beat.

Irene was delivering dinner to one of the tables. She looked up and smiled warmly at her. "Kyler," she said with a nod. "Brought you some cookies today."

She grinned at the older woman. "You spoil me." She then walked over to Tammy and Phil, holding her hand out to him in greeting. "Hey, Phil, how you doing?"

"Good, good. I was just telling Tammy that you haven't been out to the ranch in the last few weeks."

"That's because Tammy keeps me too busy out here."

"Well, that filly you've been riding misses you, I think. It's time to take her for a run."

She nodded. "How about I come out next week on one of my off days?"

"Sure. Make it afternoon and you can stay for dinner. Give me an excuse to fire up the old grill."

She laughed and clapped his shoulder affectionately. "Sounds good." She nodded at Tammy. "See you tomorrow."

Mark had a beer drawn for her by the time she made it to the bar.

"You're late."

"Oh, hell. One of the bathroom toilets overflowed this afternoon."

"Again? Didn't you do that the other morning?"

"I did."

"Damn shitty job you got there, Ky."

She laughed at that. Oh, yeah, it had been a shitty job. "It was my week to work the maintenance schedule. Stood to reason something like that would happen. You know how my luck runs."

"Men's bathroom again?"

"Yeah. And you guys are nasty." She took a large swallow of her beer. "My turn to bring food for Sunday's football party. What are you in the mood for?"

"Let's do steaks." He nodded in the direction of the Mertz brothers and pulled three beers from the cooler. "Be right back."

She wasn't a fan of steaks, but it was Mark's favorite and she usually went along with it. They had a standing date every Sunday, whether it was football season or not. He was a couple of years older than her and they'd become fast friends, a pleasant surprise considering she'd been essentially forced out here to the Davis Mountains.

She grimaced, remembering that episode. She could have let her boss fire her, she supposed, but then she'd have been blacklisted and her career as a park ranger would be over. She figured she could last up here a year—two tops—then request a transfer somewhere else, somewhere less remote. Somewhere closer to home. But two years, then three had breezed by, and now four were behind her. As she cruised into her fifth year, she felt no urge to move on. She'd fallen in love with this high mountain desert in the Trans Pecos region. It was far from her home along the coast, that was for sure, but she was happy here. She had no intention of leaving anytime soon.

"When are your off days next week?" he asked when he returned.

"Tuesday and Wednesday. Why?"

"You up for a shopping trip?"

"El Paso?"

"Oh, no. Not going that far. Over to Ft. Stockton. My mom's got a list for me. Thanksgiving stuff. Ride with me."

She nodded as she took a swallow from her beer. "Thanksgiving is right around the corner, isn't it?"

"Yeah, it is. And Lexie is coming up on that Friday."

She nodded. "That's right. You said your sister was coming for the holidays." She knew he went to visit her each summer in Austin, but other than that, he rarely talked about her or Austin, for that matter.

"She's never been up here before, right?"

"No. Lexie is…well, let's just say, a city girl." He picked up her beer and wiped under it. "She's staying until the New Year. Trial run, I call it."

"Your folks finally going to get that RV they've been talking about?"

"That's the plan. If they can talk Lexie into moving up here permanently and running the lodge for them, that is."

"How do you feel about that?"

He shook his head. "No, it's not that. I'd love for her to be up here with us. Hell, I've got my hands full here—I couldn't handle the lodge too. But Lexie works in the tech industry. Computers and stuff. Her company got bought out and she got laid off several months ago. That's why she's entertaining the idea of moving here." He shook his head again. "Out here—this is so not her. She'll never last. I mean, I hope she does, but…"

"It wasn't me either," she reminded him. "I grew up in Houston. Lived in Corpus. Worked down at the coast. I didn't know a piñon pine from an oak tree. Now? I love it here."

"You work for the Parks and Wildlife Department. Big difference. Her idea of parks and wildlife is going to Zilker Park and feeding the squirrels."

Without asking, he got another frosty mug from the freezer and filled it with beer, sliding it over to her. She nodded her thanks and picked it up.

"She married? Got a family?"

He laughed. "Lexie? No, no. She's single. Well, ever since Crazy Cathy took her car for a swim. I thought I told you." He leaned closer, his voice quiet. "My sister is gay."

Kyler's eyebrows shot up and she looked around conspiratorially. "Should I be alarmed?"

"Just sayin'."

She stared at him for a second, then quickly shook her head. "No. No, no, no. Don't even think about it."

"What?" he asked innocently.

She pointed her finger at him. "Do not try to set me up with your sister. That ain't happening. It would be creepy."

"That thought never even crossed my mind." He smiled then. "But she's cute. Really cute."

"All brothers think their sisters are cute. And have great personalities. And are super nice." She shook her head. "Nope. Not interested. At all. I don't care how cute she is."

"You haven't even met her yet."

"Still not interested. There's way too much drama involved in dating."

He laughed at that. "Screwing your boss's wife should not be considered dating! But what about that last one up here? What was her name? That gal from Marfa?"

She shuddered. "Heather. Don't remind me. And that wasn't dating. That was only a one-time hookup, nothing more."

"Had a pet pig in the house! That's so cool."

"Two pigs!" she corrected with a laugh.

He leaned forward, a smile on his face. "Remember that double date we went on with those twins?"

She laughed. "Oh, god. How could I forget? I should have known right away they wanted to do group sex!"

"Yeah, they were kinda odd." He wiggled his eyebrows. "We should have gone through with it."

"Yeah, every guy's dream—in bed with three women."

"Well, you're gay and my best friend. I wouldn't really count you."

She shook her head, but her smile remained. "I love you, buddy, but I don't want to see you naked. I certainly don't want to watch you have sex."

"Our prospects for meeting someone are slim up here anyway."

"Yeah, they are, but I love it here."

He eyed her affectionately. "You ever been in love, Ky?"

"Once. But I got my heart broken when I was twenty-five and I don't want to ever do that again. Ever. So I'm not worried about dating."

"You can't stop dating because of something like that."

"Why not? You don't date." She saw the cloud cross over his face.

"My reason is different than yours."

"I know. I'm sorry. My broken heart has healed."

"And mine never will." He slid a menu toward her, even though she knew the damn thing forward and backward by now. "I like hanging out with you. No complications that way."

A bell dinged behind him, signaling an order was ready and he spun around, hurrying over to the kitchen window. Yeah, that's what he usually said: he didn't want to complicate things by dating. She pushed him sometimes, though. Like the double date with the twins. She knew they weren't interested in dating any more than she was. She thought maybe it would be a good outlet for Mark—anonymous sex. As far as she knew, that was the one and only time he'd gone out with someone since he'd been there. He told her about his wife, but other than that, he didn't talk much about his life in Austin. In fact, like he rarely talked about his sister, he rarely mentioned anything from his past. Too many memories, she supposed.

She picked up the menu, even though she already knew she would order the hamburger steak with cream gravy and mashed potatoes. She'd tried pretty much everything on the menu and tended to alternate between four or five items. There was nothing at all healthy about any of her choices and she'd finally gotten over the fact that she couldn't get a meal with fresh fish. That was one thing she missed about living on the coast.

She glanced over the menu now, not really seeing the words there. She listened to the conversations going on around her, watching as Mark balanced three plates as he went to deliver them to Stuart and the Mertz brothers. She didn't know their names. She wondered if anyone did. They were simply The Mertz Brothers, like some kind of showbiz group. That's how she'd been introduced to them and she'd never seen one without the other. Both bachelors in their late fifties, she guessed, they owned a ranch a few miles up the road. Still lived at home with their mother.

She drank the last of her beer, then shoved the glass away. Two was her limit when she had to work the next day. Most nights she'd eat her dinner here, but occasionally she took it with her. She'd eat in solitude, then pour a little splash of whiskey into a tumbler and take it outside. During the cooler months, like now, she'd get a campfire going in the stone circle she'd built. She'd lean back in her chair, her gaze on the multitude of stars overhead. Stars so big and bright, you could almost touch them.

"Here's those cookies, Kyler."

"Thanks, Irene." She eyed the plastic bag. "What kind this time?"

"Cowboy cookies."

"Let's see. That's the oatmeal chocolate chip combo? Those are one of my favorites."

"I know. With walnuts." Irene patted her hand. "Come out to the house this week. The horses need exercise. And old Bo misses you."

She smiled at the mention of Irene's dog. Bo was barely a year old and way too much for Irene to handle. "I wish I could. Mark's got me going shopping with him one day and I promised Phil I'd go out there and ride that filly I was telling you about."

"The one that tossed you?"

"Yeah, that's the one. She's almost five and not gentle in the least. He didn't spend enough time with her, he says."

Irene snorted. "And now he wants you to tame her? Maybe you should wear a helmet when you ride. You come on out to my place. Those old mares barely get into a trot. Just our speed."

She chuckled as she walked off and Kyler smiled after her. Irene was almost eighty years old. Her hair still held some dark color mixed in the gray and her face was etched in wrinkles. She had been born and raised out here, marrying a boy she'd known since grade school. She'd worked the ranch alongside her husband for fifty years and then some. He dropped dead one day when they'd been putting up hay for the winter. Right before Thanksgiving, she thought Irene had said. Their only child—a daughter—had wanted Irene to sell the ranch and move to Dallas with her. Irene had refused. That was fifteen or so years ago. Since then, Irene had comforted her sister when her husband passed away. Then, five years ago—right before Kyler got there—she'd buried her sister too. She had no family left out here and her daughter had given up on getting her to move.

Like Kyler had been when she moved out here, Irene had been absorbed into other families. Tammy and Phil—whose ranch neighbored hers—hosted her for the holidays each year. And Mark's parents—even though Irene was technically employed by them—treated her like a grandmother. Kyler supposed she did too. Everyone tended to look out for Irene.

What most didn't know, Irene didn't need looking out for. She was one tough old gal. She still had the strength to saddle her own horse and Kyler enjoyed riding with her. Irene's ranch was one of the largest in the area and even though she now leased it for cattle grazing—having sold her husband's herd years ago—she still had the run of the place. She'd taken Kyler back in the hills, showing her the springs, taking her to where Limpia Creek flowed down from Mt. Livermore, and riding high up where the ponderosa pines outnumbered the junipers. It was quiet and peaceful, and you felt like there wasn't another soul for miles. Which, as it turns out, could possibly be true.

"You daydreaming?"

She smiled at Mark and nodded. "Yeah, I was. Irene wants me to come out and ride. So does Phil."

"I need to go with you sometime."

"Yeah, you do. Irene can run this place without you for a few hours."

He leaned closer. "Okay, truth is, I'm a little afraid of horses."

She laughed. "Like I didn't know that. You've made every excuse in the world."

He pointed at her mug. "You want another?"

She shouldn't. She should order dinner and go home. But it was still early. Better to sit here and chat with Mark and then go to her quiet little cabin. She met his gaze, knowing he'd be pleased if she stuck around to visit a little longer.

"Yeah, one more. You can tell me about your sister."

He smiled and opened the freezer for a mug. "Did I tell you she's cute?"

CHAPTER FOUR

It was a cold morning and Kyler's breath frosted around her as she walked from her Jeep to the ranger station. Before opening the door, she paused to glance at the bird feeders. A flock of house finches—the red feathers of the males streaked with brown—had already descended on the tray feeder. A lone woodpecker—a ladder-back—was hanging on the suet cage. She'd gotten pretty good with identifying the resident birds, but she was still learning.

"Good morning," Tammy greeted when she went inside.

"Morning." She headed straight to the coffeepot.

"How was your shopping trip?"

Kyler cocked an eyebrow. "Is there anything that happens around here that you don't know about?"

Tammy laughed. "No. As I hear it, the Waltons are prepping for *after* Thanksgiving. Their daughter is coming to stay for a bit. Trying to talk her into moving here and running the lodge."

"That's what you hear, huh?"

"Well, everyone knows that Dale and Susan have been talking about RVing for the last several years. So much so that I hear they even entertained the idea of selling the lodge."

"Selling? No, I don't think so. This is kinda their dream job up here." She added sugar to her black coffee. "Mark says his sister is a city girl, though. Doesn't think she'll stay long."

"Well, it does take a certain type to love it up here. When Phil dragged me out here, I came kicking and screaming. Now? I wouldn't dream of leaving."

Tammy was mid-fifties—fifty-six or -seven, she couldn't remember which—and childless. She and Phil had moved out here to Ft. Davis twenty-something years ago. Phil's grandfather had passed, and he'd come out to see about selling the ranch. Instead, he'd fallen in love with the wide-open spaces of the high desert mountains. Tammy claimed she'd contemplated divorce when he said he wanted to move here. She had been a vice president of a bank in Dallas, and was comfortable in heels and power suits, two things that did not fit out here. Tammy said she liked the ritzy neighborhood they lived in and *didn't* like the woods.

"So you wouldn't go back to the city?" She tasted her coffee, then added a little more sugar.

Tammy shook her head emphatically, her blond hair swinging back and forth. "No way. Besides, what's there for us now? We've lost touch with old friends. Both of our parents love coming out here to visit." She leaned closer and lowered her voice. "Phil's come a little more than we'd like, though. And they're all coming for Christmas again this year."

Kyler laughed, knowing that Tammy and Phil's mother butted heads over every little thing. "At least they visit. Mine only came the one time, as you know."

"Well, they came to see where you live. It's certainly not for everyone—this wild, remote wilderness that we have here. You were a little shocked at first too, weren't you?"

"Yeah, I was. Grew up in Houston. Then moved to Corpus. Worked on Mustang Island. It wasn't just being far from a city that was different. The land, the terrain, the weather. Night and day difference from where I came from."

"Oh, I know. But I've had longer to adjust." Her eyes softened a bit. "You ever going to tell me why you moved out here?"

"I did tell you."

"You needed a change. That's a little vague, don't you think?"

Kyler looked away from her stare. "It's kinda embarrassing... so..."

"Well, I don't guess it's any of my business. You're here and we love having you."

"Thank you. I've grown to love it here. And I had a great time on the ranch the other day. I need to get out there to ride more often."

"Phil enjoys it when you come. As he said, any excuse to cook on the grill. Now, what about Thanksgiving? Do you want to join us this year? The Millers are coming over with their daughter and grandkids. And Irene, of course."

"Thanks, Tammy, but I think Susan would be offended if I skipped on them. I know Mark would."

"They've kinda taken you into their family, haven't they? That's so nice."

"Yeah, they have. But you're right. Susan is more excited for Friday than Thanksgiving, I think. She's anxious for me to meet Lexie."

"That's the daughter?"

"Yeah. Mark said that Susan thinks if we become friends then she'll be more inclined to stay here." She shook her head. "Don't know that I'm going to have much of a bearing on it."

"How old is she?"

"Mark said she just turned thirty."

"And not married? Or is she divorced?"

Kyler smiled at Tammy's attempt to garner information on the mysterious Lexie Walton—a daughter and sister they'd only heard the occasional mention of. "I think she's single. Don't know much about her, really." Other than she was supposedly very cute and—according to Mark—Kyler would love her.

"Well, I suppose you'll find out soon enough."

Kyler topped off her travel mug with more coffee. "Guess I'll take a swing through the campgrounds. Are we full?"

"Pretty much. Totally booked come Thursday. When I first started working here, I couldn't imagine why people would come up here to go camping over Thanksgiving instead of staying home with family and feasting on turkey."

"A lot of people bring the feast with them."

"Yes. And a lot treat it like any other day." She waved her hand in the air. "To each his own."

"We were always booked at Mustang Island too," she said. "Of course, the weather down there was usually still warm enough for shorts. Certainly warm enough to go surf fishing." She glanced at Tammy. "I do miss that. The beach. The waves. The sounds of the gulls." She laughed. "The winter weather." She pulled her phone out of her pocket. "Let's see. It was thirty-four when I got up this morning. Down there? Ah, a balmy sixty-six." She looked up. "Gonna be over eighty today out on the beach. Yeah, I miss that weather."

"And you forget, come July, when we're only in the upper eighties and no humidity, you could be way down there along the coast, sweltering in one hundred degrees and ninety percent humidity!" She shook her finger at her. "Besides, we're going to be in the upper sixties today ourselves. You can't beat that for Thanksgiving weather."

"Oh, I know. It's really only January and February that get to me. We're slow and it's cold." She tapped the counter as she walked past. "Gonna go check the sites. Tell David I'll tend to the bird blinds this morning."

"Why haven't you made that your official job yet? You're the only one who truly loves filling the feeders."

"Yeah, well, don't tell anyone, but I've become a little bit of a birder. The winter birds are here, and I enjoy watching them." She waved a hand. "See you later."

"Oh, I almost forgot. Jim posted the holiday schedule yesterday afternoon. He's got you working a four-hour morning shift on Thanksgiving."

"Okay, good. Who drew the short straw for the afternoon?"

"David volunteered in exchange for Friday off. He's got family coming up for the weekend so they're not having their turkey dinner until Saturday."

"And I've got Sunday and Monday off?"

"Yes. And we'll start decorating for Christmas on Tuesday."

She left with a nod, not really caring what days off she had although she did enjoy the ritual of decorating the office for Christmas. And she knew Tammy was intentionally waiting until Tuesday so she could participate. Tammy went a bit overboard, but that was okay. Most of the decorations she put up at her cabin were from Tammy's discard pile.

She went to the white truck with the state parks' decal on the door. She paused to take a sip of coffee before getting inside. She started the truck, then put the heater on high. She saw Tammy watching her from the window and she gave her a smile before backing away.

She drove through the park—oaks and junipers lining the roadway. Colorful tents could be seen among the trees and smoke wafted about from some early morning campfires. She took the first loop of the campground, checking the permits as she went. Later, after it warmed, she'd go back through and clean up the sites where people had vacated—pick up any trash left and clean out the fire pits, sweep off the concrete slab around the picnic table and get it ready for the next campers to move in. It was mindless work and she found she liked it more than most. And as such, Jim assigned her to campground duty more than the others.

This week, she and Todd were on trail detail in the afternoons. Today they were going to hike up Skyline Drive—the trail that followed the road up to the highest peak in the park—and remove any limbs or obstacles along the way. It was one of her favorite trails, perhaps because it was the least popular one in the park—multiple switchbacks and a steady climb to the top. Most people avoided it. They stuck to the lower trails that meandered through the foothills. Since Skyline Drive was less populated, she could often hike it without encountering anything more than deer and squirrels. She could pull her small binoculars out discreetly then and watch birds in private.

She pulled into an empty campsite, her truck facing the rocky slope below Skyline Drive. She was in the full hook-up area—with water and electricity—with larger RVs and travel trailers. As she stared out past the junipers, she saw a flash of blue. She knew it was a scrub jay without having to grab the binoculars.

She was secretly embarrassed that she'd started watching birds. Down at the coast, she was pretty much indifferent to it, even though hordes of birders flocked there during migration season. Identifying the little shorebirds gave her fits—they all looked alike. When the spring warblers came through, however, she had better luck, even though she had to sneak out her warbler cheat sheet when no one was looking. Here? No, there weren't many rabid birders to stare at her and judge her lack of skills. She proudly—albeit in secret—brought out her bird book to learn the identity of the multitude of birds that called the Davis Mountains home and the migrants that came to stay during the winter months.

"I've turned into a damn birder," she murmured with a shake of her head. Who would have thought?

CHAPTER FIVE

"My God...where the hell am I?"

Six hours into her seven-hour-plus drive found Lexie getting gas at the first place she'd seen in Ft. Stockton. A place that apparently everyone else—perhaps desperate for gas like she'd been—stopped. She'd had to wait more than ten minutes before a spot opened up at the pump. As she filled her tank she looked around, a vast expanse of a brown, lifeless landscape meeting her gaze in all directions. A cold wind blew and she shivered, watching as the gallons—and dollars—ticked by. She filled the tank, even adding more after the nozzle had clicked off. Even though her parents had told her they weren't *really* that isolated, she wanted to be prepared in case she was hundreds of miles from another gas station. After all, she'd just driven hours and hours along I-10, heading west into nothingness.

"In the middle of freakin' nowhere. God, I must be crazy," she murmured, pulling her coat tighter around her as she put the cap back on her gas tank.

Crazy, yes. She didn't have many alternatives though, she reminded herself. Even if she didn't stay—as each mile passed she was having second and third thoughts—she'd still have to give up her expensive apartment. Trish's offer had been sincere, she knew, but she and Trish—while the best of friends—were too different to consider living together. Sharing a dorm room in college had told her that. She was a bit of a neat freak. Trish was not. She was gay. Trish dated four guys at once. She was a gym rat. Trish's idea of exercise was walking down Sixth Street on a Saturday night, barhopping.

She met her glance in the rearview mirror. Yeah, she'd probably miss that, she supposed. Since she'd ended things with Cathy— several months too late—joining Trish and her friends on Sixth Street was a stress-free alternative to dating. Trish's friends were all straight and no one ever tried to set her up. She was free to tag along with them without the stress of a date. She could relax at dinner on West Sixth, then mingle with the crowds as they hit the bars and music venues on Old Sixth—or Dirty Sixth as the locals called it.

She let out a heavy sigh as she pulled back onto I-10, merging with the huge eighteen-wheelers that had dominated the roadway ever since she'd passed San Antonio. Yeah, her life pretty much sucked, didn't it? It wasn't an exaggeration to say she was in a rut. She'd grown weary of her job, but she'd been making too much money to consider quitting. So when she'd gotten laid off, she thought perhaps it was a blessing in disguise.

Turns out, no, it wasn't. Her skillset wasn't that specialized and moving to another company would be like starting over. She'd slipped from her twenties to thirty during this unemployment phase and she'd convinced herself that she was too old for an entry-level position with entry-level pay. Of course, after a few months, she was forced to apply for those entry-level positions anyway. Yes, she applied and was told more often than not that she was over-qualified. As more and more jobs passed her by, it was harder and harder to maintain a cheerful persona during interviews. In reality, she was sinking into a pit of despair.

Then her relationship with Cathy turned sour and she knew she needed to end it. When she finally had had enough of Cathy's jealousy—Cathy had accused her of having an affair with Trish— and told her they were through, an argument escalated to the point of items being thrown against walls. Nearly all her dishes had ended up smashed. A week later, her car was stolen. Since Cathy had a key to it, the police were hesitant to call it "stolen" even when it was found submerged in Town Lake.

She slowly shook her head. What a hell of a summer it had been. Eight months without a job, six months of dealing with her crazy ex, and then a rapidly dwindling savings account had her on the road to the Davis Mountains, of all places.

She sighed once again, trying not to think about what she'd left behind. The holidays were her favorite time of year. The group dinner for Thanksgiving had been fun and not nearly as emotional as she'd expected it to be. She hadn't made a big announcement about her leaving, mainly because she knew most of their attitudes would be like Trish's had been. Besides, she *was* going back in January. The dinner, though, kicked off the season every year, and nearly each weekend someone was having a holiday party of some sort. Even though her parents and brother were no longer in Austin, she never felt cheated. Trish and her family included her in all their Christmas activities and then her parents would come for two weeks after the first of the year. It was a pattern that had held true since her parents had owned the lodge.

But not this year. No. She was going on a trial run. She would have her own room—Mark's old apartment—rent free. She could eat at the restaurant—also free—or eat with her parents. And she'd get a salary for running the lodge. A small salary, but with free room and board, it was more than she could turn down. At least for now. She'd stay through the holidays. Her lease wasn't up until the end of January. She had time to consider her options, as limited as they were. She would do as she planned. She'd evaluate her life and her future. She would take a break. She would slow down. She would exhale and give this thing a chance. Keep an open mind.

Yes, she would. This was a choice she'd made, but it wasn't written in stone. If, after the New Year, she found herself going totally stir-crazy out here, she'd simply head back to Austin, swallow her pride, and apply for any and every job she qualified for and some she didn't. She would start over. She was only thirty. She wasn't *that* old.

Before long, the exit for Balmorhea appeared. She felt a little bit of apprehension hit as she turned off the highway. Balmorhea was a tiny desert town whose claim to fame was a spring-fed pool. The San Solomon Springs dumped clean, clear water into the pool and canal that ran through town, supplying farmers in the area with free irrigation. She only knew that because Mark had sent her several links to the area's attractions for her to check out. The Balmorhea pool was about twenty miles from Ft. Davis. Which was about five miles from the state park and lodge. Which was in the middle of nowhere.

"This is so crazy."

CHAPTER SIX

Kyler rushed over when she saw Susan Walton struggling with the fifty-pound bag of birdseed.

"Let me help."

"Oh, Kyler, you're a godsend."

"I told you to call me when the feeders need filling. I talked you into this bird garden. The least I can do is help."

Susan waved her protest away. "You have your own job and own bird feeders to tend to." She paused to rest. "The feeders seem to empty every other day now."

"The winter birds are here. They're going through the suet like crazy."

"Oh, yes. Thank you for those suet feeders you brought over. The guests love them. So unique. Of course, the birds do too."

"Thank you."

She'd made two for the park. She'd found a dead-standing juniper tree that had fallen along Limpia Creek. She and Todd had taken the chainsaw with them to move it and she'd salvaged several slabs. She'd drilled diagonal holes on both sides and then—with a paint scraper—shoved suet into the holes. She'd hung the feeders among the trees in the bird blinds and the birds loved it. So she'd gone back to the tree and cut a couple more slabs and had given them to Susan as a gift.

She lifted the birdseed bag now, storing it in the garage where Susan kept her bins and other supplies. "I can fill them for you. I don't mind."

Susan patted her arm. "You secretly love it, don't you?"

"Don't tell anyone. Especially Mark, but yeah, I've kinda gotten into the birding thing."

She laughed. "Yes, Mark would tease you, I'm certain of it. Well, if you're sure you don't mind, I think I will take you up on your offer. I have a million things to do still. Lexie should be here within the hour. Are you coming for dinner?"

"Oh, I don't know. I'm sure you guys want some family time."

"Don't be silly. You're family too. Besides, I can't wait for you to meet Lexie."

She held her hand up. "Look, I already told Mark and I'll tell you—do not try to set us up. I am not interested, so don't even think about it."

"Set you up?" Susan laughed again. "I wouldn't dream of it. You and Lexie are complete opposites. That would never work. I was going to ask, however, if maybe you could try to draw her out some, show her around the park. She's coming up here with a closed mind, I just know it. If she would give it a chance, I think she could learn to love it up here." She pointed at her. "Look at you. When you first came here, you were—"

"It was culture shock."

"Exactly! I think for the first six months, you threatened to leave nearly once a week."

Kyler laughed at the memory. "Yeah, I did."

"But now you love it."

"I wouldn't think of leaving."

"See? Maybe you could make friends with her, show her around." She moved closer and linked arms with her. "She thinks she's moving into the middle of nowhere—which she is—and will go batshit crazy—her words, not mine. So maybe you could show her around, take her places." Her eyes widened. "What about taking her down to Big Bend?"

"Is she into hiking?"

"No, I don't think so. So Big Bend is out."

"I could take her to see the Marfa lights," she suggested.

"Oh, yes! If they show themselves. The last two times we've gone—nothing."

"I've seen them three or four times."

Susan squeezed her shoulder. "You have? Great! You have luck then! Plan on taking her there."

"McDonald Observatory? Is she into stars?"

Susan's brows drew together. "I don't know. I'm going to guess not. But up here, the stars are—"

"Incredible. The observatory is best in January, after the holiday crowds are gone. I've got a little telescope. If she's interested, I could set it up for her one night."

"You're so sweet, Kyler. I knew I could count on you." She leaned closer and kissed her cheek. "Dinner is at seven, as usual. Nothing fancy—a casserole. Just need to pop it in the oven. After the big Thanksgiving meal yesterday, I wasn't up for cooking." She turned, then stopped. "We're decorating for Christmas too, you know."

"Yeah, I noticed you'd already started on the lodge."

"That's an all-day affair that I'll tackle over the weekend. But we'll be trimming the tree at our place, so plan to stay after dinner, won't you?"

She nodded. "You know I love doing that."

"I know you do. Good family time." Then Susan's expression softened. "I wish your parents—"

"It's okay, Susan. This isn't their thing, up here. I've accepted it."

Susan stared at her a beat longer, then leaned closer and kissed her cheek once again, then left her.

Kyler smiled as she scooped birdseed into the bucket. Yeah, she loved it up here. The Waltons always made her feel like part of a family. Even that very first year, they'd included her during the holidays.

Her smile faltered a little. Her own family had made the effort to come see her exactly one time. They weren't into camping, so she'd booked a room here at the lodge for them. Unfortunately, to her mother that was only a very tiny notch above what she perceived camping to be. Their planned weeklong visit lasted four days. They hadn't been back since and she hadn't been to Houston to see them either. She frowned. Actually, the whole time she worked on Mustang Island, they'd come to visit her only once too. A quick overnight stay—at an expensive hotel in Corpus with a view of the bay. They had treated her to a fancy dinner, though.

Her parents were both from the city, both well educated, both in the medical profession. Her mother was a doctor, her father a pharmacist. Her becoming a park ranger was probably the farthest thing from their minds when they were planning her future. Hers too, for that matter. She'd been a biology major with aspirations of medical school. Her mother had been thrilled, of course. But she'd switched to environmental sciences after one year, still not knowing what she wanted to do. A college buddy had put the idea of working as a park ranger in her head and the more she researched it, the more she fell in love with the idea.

Her parents had never warmed to it, to say the least, and their focus had turned to her younger sister. Kinley hadn't disappointed them. She'd zipped through college and gone on to med school in the blink of an eye. She'd married a nice man, ten years her senior. He, too, was a doctor. They had a family practice in The Woodlands, north of Houston. Kinley juggled all of that and a baby. A girl. Her parents were beyond proud. Kyler supposed she was nothing more than an afterthought now. They had their perfect little world down there, a world that Kyler simply didn't fit into.

It didn't matter. As she'd told Susan, she'd accepted the relationship she had with her parents. She was happy up here. Maybe if she'd stayed at the coast—a couple of hours from Houston—she and her parents would be closer. Maybe. But she wasn't at the coast, was she?

She thought back to the reason she was even up here in the first place. Damn stupid thing to do. But she'd been lonely and Tina had been really, really persuasive.

"And married, let's don't forget," she muttered as she filled the first feeder.

Oh, yeah. Married to her boss. Their affair was uncovered a mere two months after it started. And then she was basically screwed. Bart had wanted to fire her on the spot. He had no cause, though. Well, no work-related one. He'd made her life hell for three weeks instead. She got *all* the shitty jobs. Then he'd offered a compromise. Transfer out, somewhere far, far away. Or quit. Or be stuck with the shitty jobs until she broke...and quit anyway.

His idea of far, far away had been different than hers. She'd applied at parks within a few hours' drive. He refused to give her an endorsement. He sent her an email a few days later telling her he'd given a glowing recommendation to Jim Turner, the superintendent at Davis Mountains State Park. Seeing the writing on the wall, two weeks after that she'd packed her Jeep and made the trip out, her first and only venture to far West Texas.

She paused as two white-winged doves landed under one of the hanging feeders. She listened, hearing the chatter of the tiny bushtits in the trees as they foraged for spiders and insects. She'd learned to recognize other bird sounds as well: the black-crested titmouse, the mountain chickadee, the house finches. The trees seemed to be full of birds, as if they were all waiting for her to fill the feeders and then get out of their way. She smiled contentedly, feeling a peacefulness settle over her. Yeah, she'd had a bumpy road to get out here, but she'd fallen in love with the place as surely as Mark and his family had. It was home now.

Her mother had told her—after they'd come for their one short visit—that she wouldn't last a year. Who in their right mind would want to live in such a remote place? she'd asked. Maybe it was only defiance on her part, but Kyler had wanted to prove her mother wrong. Now? It was that very remoteness that drew her. The wide-open spaces. The quiet. Dark, dark skies that offered an unparalleled view of the stars at night. The dry air, the cool breeze—and, yeah, the birds and wildlife. She'd grown to love it all.

She moved on, chasing the doves away as she lifted the feeder from the hook. She refilled it quickly, then hung it again. She went about the chore absentmindedly, filling all seven feeders to the brim. The suet feeders still had enough to last the day, so she'd let Susan tend to them tomorrow. She hauled the bucket back to the bin and latched it, turning to watch as the two doves returned, joined by a group of chipping sparrows.

She was still smiling as she walked away. It wasn't so bad being a birder. There were worse hobbies to be had.

CHAPTER SEVEN

Lexie paused at the intersection, glancing quickly at her GPS, making sure she was still on track. Left would take her into the tiny town of Ft. Davis. Right would take her up the mountain to the lodge. There was no traffic behind her—she hadn't seen another vehicle since she'd left Balmorhea. She peeked around the curve to the left, seeing a few buildings that seemed to indicate that there was indeed a town there amongst the rocks and the smattering of trees.

"Yes. Population twelve hundred. I've lost my damn mind coming here."

With a sigh, she turned to the right, winding her way around the mountain, steadily climbing. The terrain changed suddenly. Rocks—boulders really—lined the edges of the roadway and trees similar to the cedars she knew from Austin took hold, replacing the barren landscape she'd just traveled through. She had to admit, it was quite pretty. Of course, after where she'd just been, *any* sort of tree would be pretty.

Three miles up, she saw the sign for the state park. She automatically slowed, glancing to the left at the entrance, then sped up again. Her mother said the lodge entrance was three miles past the park. A lovely, hand-painted sign—she knew that because her mother had told her so—directed her to turn left for Cottonwood Creek Lodge. The trees seemed thicker now and she saw no indication that the lodge was nearby. She kept going, minding the "slow down" sign as the road curved to the right, then cut through the trees again. Up ahead she saw the reflection of cars in a parking lot and finally she came to a clearing and got her first view of the two-story lodge. Off-white adobe siding with natural log beams, it blended in beautifully with the landscape.

She followed the signs to the office, remembering her mother said to park up front instead of going around back to where the little apartment was. She got out, feeling a bit of excitement hit her at the prospect of seeing her parents again. And Mark, of course. She'd missed them all. The wind wasn't nearly as blustery up here and she assumed the trees helped to temper it. She didn't bother with her jacket as the bright sunshine seemed to warm the air. The sweatshirt she'd slipped on in Ft. Stockton was enough.

"Home sweet home," she whispered under her breath as she made her way up the rock steps to the office. It, too, was two-stories tall, with the office downstairs and her parents' living quarters upstairs. She paused, seeing her mother tidying the front counter. She recognized the nervousness of her actions and she smiled, feeling a rush of something—relief, maybe?—at the sight. The tension she'd felt from the drive out here, the stress of being unemployed, and the constant worrying over her future all seemed to fade away as she watched her mother. She smiled—yes, it was relief—and tapped on the glass. Her mother looked up sharply, then grinned at her before rushing over.

The door was jerked open and she found herself in a tight hug, being bent side-to-side by her mother's exuberance. She held on to her, still smiling, knowing her mother would release her when she saw fit.

"You made it finally!" Her mother held her at arm's length. "Oh, my. You look lovely, Lexie." She touched her hair. "You've let it grow. And wasn't it blond when we saw you in January?"

"It was. I got tired of coloring it." The reality was, she'd skipped her last two appointments because she couldn't justify the cost. "Do you like it?"

"I love it. You look like you with your light brown hair again."
She hugged her once more. "So good to see you, honey."

"Good to see you too, Mom. I've missed you."

"We're so happy you're here. We haven't all spent the holidays together in forever. How long has it been?"

"This would have been seven years."

"Can't believe we've been here that long already." She stepped back. "Come in, come in. This is the office, obviously."

She looked around, seeing a neat and tidy desk behind the check-in counter. A rack of brochures was next to the wall and a cute wooden bear—chainsaw art, she guessed—stood guard. On one side wall were shelves selling T-shirts and books, coffee mugs, and other trinkets.

"Where's Dad?"

"Tinkering with one of the hot water heaters last I saw him." Her mother drew her behind the counter and motioned to a chair. "You want some coffee?"

"It's four o'clock in the afternoon. I'm way past coffee."

"You and your brother are just alike. I swear, he won't touch the stuff after ten. Me? I drink it all day long." She was about to pour a cup, then stopped. "Do you want to see your apartment? Unpack a few things? Relax for a bit?"

Her mother seemed nervous and fidgety and that surprised her. "What's your plan?"

"Well, Mark said I was to bring you over as soon as you got here. He's anxious to see you, obviously. Nothing fancy for dinner. After yesterday's big meal, I was all cooked out. Just a simple casserole. We'll trim the tree tonight and celebrate you being here." She paused. "Oh, and our friend Kyler will join us too."

Lexie nodded. "Yes, you've mentioned him before. Mark's drinking buddy or something or other."

Her mother frowned. "Him? No, no. Kyler's a woman. She's a park ranger here. Just the sweetest thing. We love her to death."

"Her?" She shrugged. "Okay. The way Mark talked—oh, or are they dating then? That would be wonderful. Mark—"

"Mark still doesn't date, no." Then her mother gave a short laugh. "But Kyler? No, honey. If she were going to date someone in the family, it would be you, not Mark."

Lexie closed her eyes and took a deep breath. "Oh, no. Absolutely not."

"No, what?"

She shook her head firmly and held a hand up. "No, Mom. Don't even think about it."

"If you're implying that I'm trying to set you up or something, you're way off base. Kyler thought the same thing. And as I told her, you two are the complete opposite of each other. There is no way you could date," she said with a laugh. "But as you said, she and Mark are good friends. She's around a lot so I'm sure you'll see her. She's close to your age, I think. Younger than Mark." She linked arms with her. "So no, not trying to set you up at all, but she would make a good friend. I know that was one of your hesitations about coming up here."

"One of about fifty," she reminded her.

"Well, now you're down to forty-nine," she teased. "So? What will it be? Want to see your room first or go see Mark?"

"I think I'll take a few bags in and freshen up a bit. Thirty minutes?"

"That's fine. I'll ride with you and show you around to the back. You've got a little patio and a wonderful view of the bird garden. You can walk to the restaurant from there."

Lexie went outside with her mother, wondering what a bird garden was. They drove around the side of the office, past the "private drive" sign. The road narrowed to one lane and meandered around to the back of the office building. Her father's truck was parked there, and she pulled up beside it. There were two doors on the back of the building. From what she remembered from her mother's explanation, one was for the office—and the backstairs that went up to their suite— and the other was for Mark's old apartment, the place she would call home for the next two months. At least.

"There's the patio. Mark built it the first year we were here." Her mother paused as they got out. "And there's the bird garden," she pointed. "Lots of our guests come for birdwatching. They love the garden. The Montezuma quail is our big draw up here."

The patio was a square shape at the edge of the building. A small round table and two chairs made it look inviting. Across from where they were parked was the bird garden. Several feeders were hanging among the trees—six or eight, at least. She heard the sound of running water but saw none.

"What is a bird garden?"

"Oh, that's what Kyler calls it. She cleared the underbrush around the trees and set up all these different feeders."

"Is there a stream nearby?"

"Oh, no. Cottonwood Creek is dry this time of year. And Limpia Creek is on the other side of the lodge, at the state park boundary. That's the waterfall you hear. I'll show you later. Mark and Kyler built it for me there in the bird garden. They hauled rocks and stone in and even poured concrete pillars. It's so dry and arid up here, the birds love it. So do the deer."

Lexie opened the trunk and took out one of her bags, handing it to her mother, and she took another one. "I can get the rest later."

"Doesn't look like you brought much."

"Jeans and sweaters and such. Enough, I think."

Her mother opened the door to the apartment, then stood back, letting her enter first.

"I've had the windows open on and off as the weather allows. Mark hasn't lived in here in three years, so it's been closed up."

The living room was small, but she'd been expecting that. Mark had given her a layout of the apartment already. The kitchen area was little more than what you'd find in a motel kitchenette—small fridge, microwave, and a two-burner stove. What looked like a brand-new Keurig was on the counter, however. Her mother must have seen where her glance landed.

"Your dad's idea, since you don't drink coffee by the pot like we do."

"That was nice of him. I almost brought my own from home."

"There's not much to the kitchen, I know."

"It'll be fine."

"You can share meals with us anytime and of course use the restaurant at will. I know you're used to going out for lunch and dinner. I'm sorry. That's going to be a huge change for you."

"Yes, it will. I'm sure I'll adjust."

She went past the sofa and into the bedroom. A queen bed, at least, she noted as she put her bag on it. No windows.

"You hate it, don't you?"

She turned around. "It's fine, Mom. Quit worrying. I don't hate it."

Her mother sighed. "I just want you to be comfortable and feel at home. And I can see by the look on your face that you're disappointed. Honey, we can—"

She held her hand up. "Mom, really, it's fine."

Her mother blew out a frustrated breath. "I should have listened to Mark. He said you would hate it up here."

"I don't hate it," she said again. "It's different than what I'm used to, that's all. Let me unpack and relax for a bit. I'll meet you back at the office."

Her mother came closer and hugged her. "You make me feel like we forced you into this."

"You did not force me, Mom. I weighed all my options. And being up here—trial run, remember?—has both pros and cons. But you did not force me." She smiled at her mother. "I needed a change, and this is certainly it. And yes, Mark gave me fair warning. It's remote. There aren't a lot of activities like I'm used to. It's quiet. It's slow. So let's take it a day at a time and we'll see where it ends up."

"I want you to be happy, honey. I don't want you to stay up here because you think it'll disappoint us if you don't."

"I know. And like I told you on the phone the other day, I needed a break from my life—from everything. I think this might be good for me."

"I hope so. It'll be so nice for us all to be together again. Especially for Christmas. It's still so hard for Mark." Her mother pulled at the neck of her sweater. "Is it hot in here to you? Your father must have left the heater on," her mother fussed as she went to inspect the thermostat. "It's stifling all of a sudden."

Lexie smiled. "Hot flash?"

Her mother went to the door and opened it, fanning herself. "God, menopause is going to be the death of me. It's been four years and I'm *still* having hot flashes!"

Lexie laughed. "Then take your sweater off."

"Oh, it'll pass." She smiled at her. "I'll let you get unpacked. Come find me when you're done, and we'll go see Mark at the restaurant."

"Okay. Fifteen minutes, half hour tops."

She glanced around the living room quickly, then went into the bedroom. Instead of unpacking, though, she lay down and stared at the ceiling. Was this a mistake? Nothing felt *right* about it. Of course, this was what she was expecting, wasn't it? She'd all but convinced herself that she would hate it, that she *should* hate it.

She sighed and sat up. No. She'd told herself she'd keep an open mind and that's what she would do. This trial run was two months. She could do anything for two months. She'd have a chance to be around her family again, for one thing. She would look at it as an extended vacation. Yes, that's what she would do. A Christmas vacation.

And, as an added bonus, it was a vacation that didn't have to end if she didn't want it to. There was no job to get back to. Surprisingly, that thought didn't bring its usual sense of dread along with it. She had a job if she wanted it.

Running a lodge.

Outside of Ft. Davis, Texas.

A million miles from anywhere.

CHAPTER EIGHT

Lexie followed her mother's directions, walking around the lodge then taking a stone pathway through the trees. It was short—thirty or forty feet—and it ended at the edge of a parking lot. She paused, admiring the log cabin-style building, complete with a large covered front porch. A sign below the eave proclaimed the Cottonwood Creek Bar and Grill and a neon Open sign hung in one window. Before heading up the steps, she looked around, noting only three cars in the parking lot. Beyond the lot was a paved road, heading away from the lodge. A brown sign—Davis Mountains State Park—was partially obscured by the trees.

A bell jingled when she opened the door. She looked around, finding her brother behind the bar, wiping the top methodically, his head bobbing quietly to the country song that played in the background. He glanced up, a smile lighting his handsome face when he saw her.

"There's my favorite sister!"

He hurried around the bar and she went to him, accepting his tight hug with one of her own.

"Damn good to see you, sis."

"You too." She touched his face affectionately. "I've missed you." He nodded and kissed her cheek. "Me too." He took her hand and tugged her toward the bar. "You want a beer?"

"Show me around first."

He motioned around them. "This is it. Eight tables. Six booths. The bar." He jerked his thumb behind him. "Kitchen back there." She sat down at a barstool and took one of the menus that were tucked between a napkin dispenser and salt and pepper shakers.

"Don't judge." He opened a cooler and took out a frozen mug. "You won't find anything healthy on there."

"My god...everything is fried! Who eats this crap?"

"Not everything is fried," he countered. "Grilled cheese sandwich."

"Dripping in butter, no doubt. Might as well be fried." She closed the menu. "You seriously need an upgrade."

"You think so? This is pretty much the same menu they had when Mom and Dad bought the place." He motioned to the kitchen. "Same cooks too. The locals that come here, this is what they're used to."

She took a sip of the cold beer. It tasted refreshing. "And those staying at the lodge?"

"Well, we do get some requests for grilled chicken sometimes." He shrugged. "Now that you're here, maybe you can overhaul the menu."

She smiled at him. "I know nothing about running a lodge and only slightly more about restaurants. And that's only because I eat out at nearly every meal."

"I warned you about that. There's a barbeque place in town and a Mexican café that's only open for lunch. That's it. There's a little country tavern down in Marfa that does decent steaks and fried chicken. And a Mexican restaurant that's pretty good. Or so I've been told."

"And Marfa is where?"

"About twenty-five miles southwest of here."

She frowned. "I didn't think there were any towns nearby."

"Marfa is only a little bigger than Ft. Davis. Fifteen or sixteen hundred people, maybe. Now Alpine is decent size. College town. Probably six thousand people there. It's about thirty miles southeast of here."

"So six thousand people. There's shopping. Restaurants. That's a relief. You and Mom made it sound like you were totally isolated up here."

"Well, yeah. Kinda is. Ft. Davis, Marfa, and Alpine make a little triangle. You'll find burger chains and stuff in Alpine. McDonalds. Burger King and the like. Not much else. If we need real shopping, we have to go to Ft. Stockton. That's more than an hour and a half drive from here."

"That's where I stopped to get gas."

"It's different than what you're used to, that's for sure. If it's something I need that I can't find at Potters or at the hardware store, I just order it online." He shrugged. "You get used to it."

"So you say."

"Having second thoughts?"

She shook her head. "I'm going to give it a try. I think two months ought to be enough to know if I can make this work."

"But you've got to go back anyway, right? Your apartment?"

"Yes. I'll need to be moved out by the end of January, one way or another."

"I can help, you know. After the holidays, things slow down a lot. Irene can handle it here for a few days and I can go with you. I can probably talk Kyler into going too. She never takes her vacation days. She's got weeks piled up."

She nodded. "For some reason, I thought Kyler was a guy. Mom said you two are good friends."

"The best. We hang out on weekends. Watch football. Grill out a lot. I credit her for keeping me sane." He smiled. "And vice versa. You're going to love her. She's really nice." He wiggled his eyebrows. "And cute too."

She shook her head. "I'll tell you like I told Mom. No. Don't even think about it."

"Just sayin'."

"Nope. I am *so* not interested."

"You're both so stubborn, I swear."

"No, Mark. It's not happening. Ever."

"Okay, okay." He held his hands up. "She wasn't interested either."

"Why? What's wrong with her?"

"Nothing's wrong with her. I told you, she's cute." He grinned. "Well, she's got bad taste, that's for sure. Had an affair with her boss's wife. Got caught. That's why she came out here to begin with. Then there was the woman with the pigs."

"Pigs?"

"She had pet pigs. Two of them. In the house."

She wrinkled up her nose.

"Ah. But then the twins. They were cute."

"She dated twins?"

He laughed. "No, not really dated. They wanted to have sex." He grinned. "She brought me along. Kinda a group thing."

"Oh my god! You did not!"

"No. We both thought it was creepy."

"Where did you find twins?"

"Kyler met them in Marfa. Well, she met one of them. Jessa and Tessa. We went out to dinner and we never could tell them apart. One was an artist."

"Well, at least you date. You rarely talk about going out."

"No, sis. I don't date. Kyler made me go with her, that's all."

She reached across the bar and squeezed his hand. "I miss her too."

"Yeah. She was the best." He returned her squeeze, then pulled his hand away. "I feel like I'm cheating on her if I go out."

"Oh, Mark, no. Mia would never want you to be alone."

He shrugged. "I'm happy, sis. Really. I've grown to love it up here. Kyler—she keeps me grounded. We're buddies. That's all I need."

"Does she know about Mia?"

"I told her, but we don't talk about it. I...I never want to bring it up. Mom and Dad—we don't talk about her, so..."

No. They wouldn't. Her mother loved Mia like a daughter and her death had hit them all hard. Their plans for buying the lodge had already been put in motion when she'd been killed. Mark never came out and said it, but she assumed—when he'd jumped at the chance to join them up here—that it was his way of running from Mia's memory. Mia and his unborn son.

"Maybe you should. It might do you good to talk about it with someone other than me. I mean, it's been—"

"Seven years. But what is there to say? I don't want to relive it all again. Especially this time of year." He tapped his chest. "She's still in here. I haven't forgotten about her, Lexie. So I don't need to date. I'm not ready for that. I may not ever be."

She smiled at him. "I miss her white chocolate chip cookies." He met her gaze and she saw tears welling there.

"I gave you her recipe."

"There was obviously a secret ingredient. They're not the same."

He leaned on the counter. "I miss her Sunday brunches."

"Yes. Blueberry pancakes."

He stared at her. "I haven't been on a bike since that day. She so loved to ride."

"You both did."

"Kyler rides. Mountain bike. She's been bugging me to get one and ride with her."

She tilted her head. "Maybe you should."

He smiled. "I told her I didn't know how."

Lexie rolled her eyes. "Who doesn't know how to ride a bike?"

He laughed. "Yeah. She said the same thing."

She leaned closer. "Are you *sure* y'all aren't dating?"

He laughed again. "If she was straight, I would be tempted." His face turned serious. "I think you're gonna love her. She's hard not to like."

"No, thanks. I'm not interested in dating. At all."

He wiggled his eyebrows. "She loves Christmas time as much as you do."

"So did Crazy Cathy. You see where that got me." She slid her empty beer mug over to him. "Why are you pushing her so much?"

"Because you two are my most favorite people in the world."

She smiled at that. "Well, thanks for the sentiment. But really, it's culture shock enough being up here. I'll say emphatically that I'm not dating. But I wouldn't mind making a friend."

He nodded. "You're going to love her."

CHAPTER NINE

"Is she here yet?"

Mark grinned at her. "See! You *are* anxious to meet her."

Kyler flicked her eyes at him and shook her head. "You all but threatened me if I didn't show up."

He filled a frosty mug from the tap. "You missed her, though. She just left. But you're going over to the folks' place for dinner, right?"

"We're trimming the tree. Yeah," she said as if it was obvious.

"Lexie loves decorating the tree. Always has."

"And your mom is making one of her casseroles. I hope it's that Mexican taco one."

"Mom loves making that. Lexie will pretend to like it but push it around on her plate. Watch her."

She gave an audible "ah" as she took a swallow of the cold beer. "Why doesn't she like it?"

"She's more into fish and tofu and stuff. Chicken occasionally. Definitely not beef."

Kyler wrinkled her nose. "Tofu?" She rolled her eyes. "No, she will so not fit in up here. I don't think you can buy tofu within a hundred miles."

Mark nodded. "She looks good, though. When I went to see her in July, she was dealing with Crazy Cathy and the lack of a job was still fresh. She was totally frazzled and stressed out."

"Yeah, a crazy ex will do that to you."

His eyebrows shot up. "Is this the broken heart ex or—?"

"No."

"So?"

"It was right after college. She liked to get high. I wasn't really into that, so—" she shrugged. "When I broke up with her, she went nuts and trashed the apartment." She grinned. "It was her apartment, not mine. I had already gotten my things out. I mean, she went *nuts*. Police showed up. There were drugs there. She got arrested. The whole thing."

"Man. It's a wonder they didn't haul your ass in too."

"It was quite obvious which of us the drugs belonged to."

"You see her after that?"

"Yeah. It's why I ran away to Corpus."

"So you have a Crazy Cathy in your life too. Cathy trashed the apartment, only it was Lexie's place."

She finished her beer. "That's another reason I'm not interested in dating. After her—Micha was her name. After Micha, then it was the broken heart. Britney. So I don't date."

"Your boss's wife?"

"That wasn't dating! That was sex."

"That's just crazy," he said with a laugh. "You're lucky he didn't kill you."

"When he caught us, I think if he'd had a gun…"

They looked at each other, both smiling. "If we don't find you a date soon, you and me, ten years from now…"

"Yeah, we'll be sitting here drinking beer, wondering where the time went." She smiled when she said it, but it was probably the truth. Four-plus years had already buzzed by. She wasn't really concerned, though. She was happy. Content. Her days were full. Her life felt full. The people here had adopted her as one of their own. She certainly wasn't lonely. That thought never even crossed her mind. Boring, maybe. She supposed she had become boring.

"Maybe we should get a dog."

She arched an eyebrow. "We?"

"Well, you. I can visit him when I come over."

"If I got a pet, it would be a cat."

"A cat? I don't see you as a cat person. A dog. A black lab, maybe."

She considered it. "Maybe. A hiking partner." She slid her empty glass toward him. "So? How was she?"

"Lexie?" He laughed. "Culture shock, like you when you first walked in here." He refilled her mug. "You asked me where you could get a one-way ticket out of town. Remember?"

She laughed. "I'd been here three days before I found out there was a bar up here. That's the only reason I came in."

"Yeah, to drown your sorrows." He smiled broadly. "And then you met me, and all was right with the world again."

She rolled her eyes. "So what about your sister?"

He shrugged. "She stayed for a beer. We chatted. She's terrified, I think. Like a fish out of water, you know. She had a lot of friends, was always busy, always going out, doing stuff."

"So maybe she'll take up hiking."

"She went to the gym every day. She's a beast on the treadmill."

"Why run inside when you can run outside?"

"Spin classes. Weight machines. Some fancy rowing something or other." He picked up her glass and wiped under it. "I told her the closest gym was in Alpine."

"Alpine is a college town. She could probably make some friends there."

"She'd probably come closer to making friends in Marfa. You know, artists and old hippies and such. Marfa has more of an Austin vibe than Alpine. Besides, she's thirty. Kinda old to hang out with college kids."

"Well, you shouldn't worry about it. She'll either fit in or she won't. She'll stay or she'll go. Your mother seems to think she's already got her mind made up anyway."

"I don't know. Lexie wants to make it work, I think. I mean, in her mind, she wants to give it a go. Said she needed a change." He shrugged. "But you should have seen her face when she walked in here."

"Was she expecting a five-star restaurant or something?"

"We're not much more than a roadside diner. Greasy spoon." He laughed. "Then she read the menu."

"No tofu."

"She was like, 'Everything is fried! Who eats like that?'"

"Maybe she can help with the menu then. You've been talking about putting in one of those indoor grills. You could do real steaks, grilled chicken. Grilled fish," she added hopefully.

"I know. We'll see."

She glanced at the clock above the bar. "We're going over at six thirty, like usual?"

"Yeah, Irene can handle it." He leaned on the bar. "I'm anxious for you to meet Lexie."

"Oh, Mark, don't push it so much. I told you—"

He laughed. "She looked really good. I think you're going to like her. In fact, she's—oh, speak of the devil," he said when his phone rang.

"Hey, sis." He nodded. "Okay, I won't forget. We'll bring them." Then he smiled at her. "Kyler's having a beer with me." He paused. "She's not a big wine drinker." He nodded. "So you should tell her. Just like you should tell her you don't like the greasy, meaty, cheesy casserole, tell her you don't like wine." He paused again. "Okay. I'll bring a bottle of bourbon. Yes, and some Coke too." He ended the call.

"What was that about?"

"Dinner rolls. Don't let me forget. I took them out of the freezer earlier to thaw."

"And wine?"

"She said Mom had three bottles of wine out. Lexie wanted to know what kind you drink."

"So she's not a wine drinker either. I would have guessed she was. You know, the tofu and fish thing."

"My sister likes bourbon. And then she dilutes it with Coke like you do."

"My kind of gal."

"See? I told you. And she's cute."

Kyler shook her head. "She may be cute and she likes bourbon, but I don't do tofu."

"You've never had it, have you?"

"No."

"It's not bad. Whenever I go see her, she takes me out to a vegan restaurant at least once." He looked past her and nodded. "Be right back."

She stared into the mirror behind the bar, absently watching as he took beer bottles over to a table. She didn't know why, but she was a little nervous about the prospect of meeting Lexie. She didn't care one way or the other if she liked the sister or not. Or vice versa. It wouldn't affect her life. And based on the little she'd learned about Lexie, she would probably be leaving and heading back to Austin after the holidays. As Tammy had said, it takes a certain person to embrace the remoteness that they had up here.

"We're not that busy tonight. Irene told me to go already. You want to head over?"

She nodded and finished off her beer. "Don't forget the bourbon and dinner rolls."

* * *

They went around to the back door of the office and took the stairs up to the Waltons' suite. She smiled at that thought. That's what Susan always called it—their suite. It was larger than an apartment, though. They'd gutted the whole upstairs when they bought the lodge. It had been cramped with three bedrooms—the previous owners had four kids—and a small kitchen and living area. Susan and Dale had opened it up—bright and airy—and enclosed only a master bedroom for them. Everything else was open, with thick wooden pillars spaced throughout. The white sheetrock walls were replaced with cedar planks and a bank of windows displayed the rocky hillside of junipers and oaks. It was warm and inviting and Kyler felt right at home there.

She took a deep breath as Mark tapped his knuckles against the door before going inside. She paused only a second, then went in after him. At first glance, everything seemed normal. The flames in the fireplace were dancing, a candle was lit on the mantel, and quiet music—a Christmas tune—played in the background. The enticing smell of dinner wafted about.

Then her gaze was drawn toward the kitchen. A young woman was at the sink, washing dishes. Light brown hair, silky and shiny, not quite shoulder length, was tucked behind both ears. She caught a twinkle of diamond from an earring. The woman turned and Kyler felt her breath catch. Mark hadn't been lying—his sister *was* damn cute. Her hair was parted slightly off center and part of it feathered across her right eyebrow. An eyebrow that was dark and thick and arched slightly as Kyler stared. She smiled then, meeting eyes that were…what? Green? Blue?

"Kyler, come in," Susan beckoned. "Meet my daughter, Lexie."

The eyes were blue, she decided.

"Nice to meet you." Lexie held up wet hands. "I'd offer to shake, but…"

No. The eyes were green. *Say something.* She swallowed.

"Hi. I'm…Kyler."

The blue or green eyes blinked at her. "Yes, I kinda assumed as much."

She stumbled to think of something—anything—to say when Mark elbowed her.

"Told you she was cute."

CHAPTER TEN

"Open whatever wine y'all want."

"I brought bourbon."

Lexie feigned surprise. "You did? I think I'll have that instead of wine." She smiled at her mother. "You don't mind, do you?"

"No, honey. Have what you want. Kyler? What about you?"

"You know, I think I'll have bourbon with them."

Lexie was surprised when her mother playfully pinched Kyler's cheek. "I know you only humor me when you join me for wine. I know you would rather have a cocktail with the guys."

She watched as a very lovely blush covered Kyler's face. Oh, Mark hadn't been fibbing. In fact, he hadn't been generous enough in his description of his friend. Her hair was dark and thick and wavy, reaching just past the collar of her shirt. Smooth, tan skin— she looked almost handsome.

"Yeah. Mark's a bad influence on me."

"Sure. Blame me." He sat the bottle of Crown on the countertop. "Where's Dad?"

"In the shower. He finally got that hot water heater working. Took him all afternoon."

Lexie twisted off the cap. "Cocktail or straight up?"

"I'll have a cocktail. Kyler and I found this sipping whiskey that is to die for. Pecan praline. It's like candy. That's the only thing I'll drink straight now."

"So you two hang out a lot, huh?" She didn't ask the question to either of them in particular, but Kyler was the one to answer.

"When I first moved up here, I was completely lost. Everything was foreign to me. I came from down at the coast—Corpus Christi. I went into the bar and there this handsome fella was."

Mark blushed. "Yeah. Remember when Tammy tried to set us up?"

"Who is Tammy?"

"She's a clerk in the office at the park." Kyler took the glass she offered her. "Thanks. She and her husband have become friends of mine. They have a ranch and I go out and do some riding."

"Horses?"

"Yeah. Their property backs up to Mount Livermore so there are some great trails." She raised her eyebrows. "Do you ride?"

"Me?" Lexie shook her head. "No. I've never even been near a horse."

"Oh, then Kyler should take you," her mother offered.

Lexie gave her mother a fake smile. "That's okay. I'm sure you'll have plenty to keep me busy."

"Don't be silly. Other than working on our new online registration system, you're going to have plenty of time on your hands."

"What online registration? I thought you already installed one."

"Oh, we have one, but it's not totally what we wanted. We couldn't decide which software we liked the most, so we got the one that fit us best. Dale thought we could just write our own, taking bits and pieces of everything we liked, but he stays so busy." She added wine to her glass. "Frankly, I'm scared to even try it. I haven't written code in over seven years. We thought we would talk you into taking a look at it. Maybe tweak the one we've got."

"Me? I don't know the first thing about a reservation system."

"But you know all about building programs."

"I know about managing projects to build programs. Big difference."

Susan waved her protest away. "You were better at it than both me and your father. I can't believe you couldn't get another job."

"I could have gotten a job, Mom. Just not at the salary I was used to and not as a manager." Lexie turned to Kyler. "The company I worked for got bought out," she explained. "My department was absorbed and we were deemed redundant."

Kyler nodded. "I'm sure that was tough."

Lexie cocked an eyebrow. "You already knew that." She turned to Mark. "You have to tell her everything?"

"Surprisingly, I've told her very little about you. But I was explaining why you were coming up here."

Kyler held her hand up. "Really. He rarely talks about you. Well, he did tell me about Crazy Cathy."

"Oh my god! You told her about *that*?" She glared at Mark. "Really?"

"What's the big deal?"

"I never did like Cathy," her mother chimed in, on cue. "I told you that from the very beginning."

Lexie rubbed her forehead. "You had a dream she set my car on fire. I know."

"You were *in* the car at the time."

Lexie held her hand up. "Mom…I know. Thankfully, your dream did not come true."

"How long were you dating?"

Lexie turned to Kyler. "About two months too long."

"About two *years* too long," her mother added.

Lexie took a large swallow from her drink. "Shouldn't we start on the tree?"

* * *

Earlier when Lexie had inspected the tree, she'd been shocked to find that it was a real tree. As long as she could remember, her parents always had an artificial Christmas tree. This one smelled wonderful and when her father plugged the lights in, the room was transformed into holiday goodness. Oh, her mother had already put out a few Christmasy knickknacks, but it wasn't until the tree was lit that the room became festive.

She quickly found out that Kyler was an ornament hog. She also found out that Kyler was right at home with her family. She was also quite familiar with their tradition of making note of each ornament that was hung.

"Oh, this is the one that Phil made a few years ago."

"He's such a talented wood carver," her mother added. "Can't believe it's only a hobby of his."

"Who is Phil?" she asked as she pulled a small ceramic owl from the box.

"Phil is Tammy's husband," Mark supplied. "She's the one who works at the state park."

"Runs the office," Kyler interjected as she nudged Lexie out of the way to grab another ornament. "When we go riding at their ranch. I'll introduce you to Phil. He's got a great collection of carvings."

"I'm not going riding," she said a little too forcefully as she hung her owl on the tree. "I don't remember where this came from."

"I got that owl in El Paso at a garage sale, of all places," her mother said.

"You have a lot of new ornaments. I don't recognize them."

"Yes, I suppose we do. When we were in Austin, our tree was a little more fancy, always a theme and matching ornaments. Our theme has become a little more nature-oriented up here." She held up a little squirrel with a tiny red scarf around its neck. "Picked this up at a shop in Marfa. We'll need to go by there during the holidays. They've got so much neat stuff."

Her father was in his recliner, watching them. His hair was showing gray now, but he was still as thin and fit as always. "Lexie, there's a deer in there. Put him over on the right, toward the bottom. Got a good spot for him."

Mark found the deer and handed it to her. Kyler had pulled out a bright red cardinal, sitting on a snow-covered log.

"One of my favorites."

"You got that for us that very first Christmas you were here." Her mother laughed and turned away. "Which reminds me—I have a gift for you." She produced a small box wrapped in red and green paper. Kyler took it and weighed it in her hand as if trying to determine what it was.

"An ornament, I'd guess."

"Yes, it is. For your tree, not this one. Open it," her mother urged.

Kyler ripped into it, then a blush covered her face as she grinned at her. Her mother in turn laughed out loud.

"I couldn't resist!"

Kyler held up the ornament—a bright blue bird with exaggerated feet and bill, holding binoculars up to its eyes. Bird Watcher was stamped across his breast.

Mark laughed too and slapped her shoulder. "Busted!"

Lexie frowned, feeling left out of the obvious joke between them.

"Well, for your information, I love it. Because I'm starting a new theme on my tree. All birds." Kyler glanced at her, seeming to recognize the distance Lexie felt. "I'm a closeted birdwatcher. I knew your mother had a clue, but I didn't think Mark knew."

"How could I not know? You made me put a bird feeder up at my house so we could see it from the deck."

Lexie saw the genuine affection between them as they smiled at each other. "So what is it that you do? As a birdwatcher," she clarified. "I mean, other than watch them."

"Well, you identify them. Using a bird book. And then you put them on your life list." Again, a slight blush lit her face. "Sounds kinda lame when I say it out loud." They all laughed, including Kyler. "It's a hobby, that's all. I only wish I'd started it when I worked on Mustang Island. Tons of birds down there."

"Well, if you ever got off this mountain and took a vacation, you could go visit. I'm sure your parents would love to see you," her mother said.

Kyler and her mother exchanged glances and Lexie recognized the gentle nudging of her mother's words. It was obvious that Kyler was a part of the family. At that moment, Lexie felt like an outsider and Kyler seemed much more like the daughter than she was. Her father seemed to sense her withdrawal and he called to her.

"Lexie, come tell me about your drive out."

"It was uneventful," she said, her words a bit clipped.

She still held the deer in her hands, and she moved to the tree, finding a spot on the side for him. She was feeling out of sorts all of a sudden. Like she didn't belong. Like she was a stranger. Like—

"I have to work tomorrow, but I'm off on Sunday. Why don't I show you around?"

Lexie blinked at Kyler, then shook her head. "No, thanks. I'm sure my mother will have stuff for me to do. I'll need to start learning the ropes sooner or later."

"Oh, no, honey. It's Sunday. You go with her," her mother insisted. "It'll be good for you to get out."

She turned pleading eyes to Mark, but he only gave her a subtle wink. "It'll be more fun with Kyler showing you around than me."

"But—"

"You'll be back by noon," he said. "I've never known Kyler to miss kickoff."

"What's on the menu?" Kyler asked.

"I'm doing wings and nachos." He turned to her. "You'll come too, of course. It's an all-day affair when Kyler has Sunday off."

She let out a sigh. She supposed it wouldn't be so bad. Kyler was obviously a part of their group and would be around a lot, by the sound of it. She might as well get to know her. Besides, she loved football.

"Okay. Look forward to it."

"Great. I'll pick you up early. Set your alarm."

She frowned. "How early?"

"Before sunrise. Still dark. I'll pick you up about six thirty. So get to bed early."

"No. That's insane."

"Oh, you're taking her up Skyline Drive?" Her mother patted her arm. "That's a wonderful idea, Kyler."

At her blank stare, Kyler explained. "To see the sunrise."

"The sunrise," she repeated dryly. "Umm, no. Not happening."

"Yes. You'll love it."

"I don't think so."

Kyler only smiled at her. "Six thirty."

CHAPTER ELEVEN

Kyler drove the familiar winding road between the state park and the lodge. From what she'd learned from Tammy, the road in the park originally ended just past the picnic area where Cottonwood Creek dumped into Limpia Creek. The owners of the lodge at the time struck a deal with the park service. They'd pay to extend the road onto their property, thus giving the campers and staff access to the restaurant and bar without having to drive outside the park and take the main road up the mountain. It was only a handful of miles as it was, but with the road extended, their business at the restaurant nearly doubled. And the park was able to afford to add more hiking trails around the creek. That was some sixty years ago or more. The park service maintained the road now and there was no evidence that it had once been a dead end.

She slowed as she saw movement on the side of the road. Two deer darted across, flashing through her headlights. She paused, waiting, and sure enough, two more followed. She knew the curves well after making this trip almost daily. If she wasn't going to the bar, she was going to Mark's house. At first, it was to his tiny apartment, although they tended to hang out at her place more often back then. Once he built his cabin, they took turns hosting dinner and get-togethers, but his place—which was up the hill from the lodge—afforded them more privacy—and a large deck—than her state park cabin did.

As she wound her way around the lodge and to the back, she wondered at her offer to show Lexie around. It had been made without much consideration on her part. Lexie had had such a forlorn look on her face—a look that said she felt terribly out of place. Part of that was her fault, she knew. She should have declined Susan's offer and let them have some family time. It was Lexie's first night there. Kyler shouldn't have interfered. But she did, so she felt somewhat responsible. Showing her around—and getting to know her—seemed like the least she could do.

She parked beside an unfamiliar car that she assumed was Lexie's. A dark Honda, four-door. Charcoal or black. It was hard to tell, even with the porch light on. She got out of her Jeep and went to the door, knocking loudly.

"Rise and shine," she called.

The door was jerked open and a sleepy-eyed Lexie Walton glared at her. "This so better be worth it."

"I told you to go to bed early."

"I've been unemployed." She covered her mouth as she yawned. "I'm used to staying up well after midnight and sleeping in." Lexie closed the door, then paused. "Do I need anything?"

Kyler glanced over the hooded sweatshirt she wore and jacket that was slung across her arm. "No. The hoodie should be enough. After the sunrise, we'll swing back down here and get some coffee from Mark, then I'll take you on a scenic tour. You'll love it."

"Can't wait," she mumbled.

Kyler laughed. "I had your same attitude when I first got here. I wanted to be anywhere but here. Mark got tired of my whining and took me on an all-day trip. Ended up down in Big Bend. Slept in back of his truck after we tried to kill off a bottle of tequila." She shuddered. "I can't drink the stuff to this day." She politely opened the passenger door and stepped back. "It was fantastic, though. We were serenaded by coyotes most of the night." She closed the door when Lexie got in and she hurried to her side. Oh, yeah. Lexie Walton was a cutie—sleepy eyes and all.

"You warm enough?" she asked when they pulled away.

"Yes. It doesn't seem that cold."

"No. Low forties. Gonna be a nice day. Near seventy. Mark puts the TV out on the deck."

"So you can watch birds and football at the same time?" Her tone was teasing, and Kyler nodded.

"To be honest, I'm a little embarrassed by my hobby. But, I mean, I love it."

"Why embarrassed?"

"Birdwatchers are stereotyped. Older. Geeky. Social misfits. Wear funny hats."

Lexie laughed quietly. "You don't seem to fit any of those. Or do you have a hat hidden away?"

"No. But I did buy a harness for my binoculars. I don't dare put it on, though, until I'm down the trail and out of sight."

Lexie leaned back against the seat. "So, what's this Skyline Drive?"

"Highest peak in the park. Panoramic view."

"So both sunrise and sunset?"

"Yep. And it's spectacular for star watching. And you've got to take in the moonrise from up here. Fantastic." She turned to her, realizing her exuberance was showing. "Have you noticed the stars yet?"

Lexie glanced out her window to do just that, but they were in the trees now. "I guess I haven't. I live in the city so I'm not used to looking skyward, I guess."

"Austin's right there at the Hill Country. You never get out? Tons of state parks there."

"I'm not really into camping or anything like that."

"No? You ever been?"

She shook her head. "Can't say that I have."

"It's…it's quiet. Peaceful. Reflective. Just being outside, away from people and city sounds. I tried to get transferred to the Hill Country. Enchanted Rock. Pedernales Falls. Blanco State Park. None were hiring."

"You're an awfully long way from the coast."

"Oh, yeah. I grew up in Houston. Got my first job at Goose Island State Park in Rockport. Then moved down the coast a little way to Mustang Island."

"So how'd you end up here?"

Kyler shook her head. "That's a story for another time."

"Oh, so it has nothing to do with an affair with your boss's wife?"

Kyler felt a blush light her face and was glad for the darkness. "I swear, that boy can gossip."

Lexie laughed. "Yeah, he can." She motioned to her right. "There's one of the campgrounds. This one is for tents. No RVs allowed. Used to be, you had mostly tent campers and a few RVs. Now? Just the opposite. Most parks had to scramble to enlarge the sites and put in hookups."

"Hookups?"

"Water and electricity. We have one loop of RV spots that also has sewage hookups. Saves you having to dump your tanks on the way out of the park. People who stay four, five days—a week—they use those."

"And do a lot of people camp over the holidays?"

"Oh, yeah. We're full. Even Christmas, we're booked. Through the New Year. January and February are the dead months. Also the coldest. Even then, it's not like brutally cold. Well, compared to down at the coast, yeah, it's cold. I mean, we're at six thousand feet here. Seven at the observatory."

"What's that?"

"McDonald Observatory. They've got several huge telescopes. It's a research place. Part of the University of Texas." She glanced over at her. "It's open to the public, if you're interested."

"For…?"

"Stargazing." She turned right and headed up Skyline Drive. "When we get to the top, it won't be dark enough still to get the full effect, but you'll get an idea how incredible the stars are."

She drove a little faster than normal as she saw a red tint beginning to show in the east. She loved this time of morning. The sky was crystal clear, the air dry. No clouds, no haze, no fog. And no light pollution. The stars filled the sky, so close they were right on top of you.

As expected, they were the only ones up there. Sunset was a different story as more of the campers took advantage of the view. But cold, frosty mornings usually meant she had the place to herself.

She reached into the backseat and took out a blanket. "To sit on," she explained. She also grabbed her binoculars.

The wind was still, but up this high the air was cold, so she put her own hood over her head and pulled it tight. Lexie did the same, then put on her jacket. There were several wooden benches, but she headed past them, going up a little trail to an outcropping of rocks. To the east, a red glow rimmed the horizon, but to their west, it was still black dark.

"Turn this way," she said, turning Lexie away from the approaching sunrise. "Look up."

"Oh my god," Lexie murmured. "There's like…thousands of them."

"That's good. Most people would say there are millions of stars in the sky. And yeah, sure. I mean, it's infinite. But really, we can only see around two thousand in the nighttime sky. We're seeing far less than that now since the sky is starting to lighten."

"Birdwatcher *and* stargazer?"

"An amateur at both, I admit."

Lexie was still staring overhead. "It's beautiful." She pointed to a bright star. "What's that? A planet?"

"I don't think so. You want to see planets, we'll have to come up here after sunset. Venus and Jupiter were both out last night, bright as can be." She tugged her around a piñon pine. "There. See the crescent moon? That's called a waning crescent moon. Look to the right of it. That's Mars." She looked through her binoculars for a bit, then passed them to Lexie. "Take a look."

"Okay. This will sound silly, but I've never used them before."

"Not silly." She took Lexie's finger, showing her the focus wheel. "Turn that to focus in on it."

Kyler could hear Lexie's soft breathing as she looked through the binoculars. She looked to the sky too for a second, then brought her gaze back to Lexie. There wasn't enough light to make out her features—the tiny crescent moon did little to cut the darkness. When she lowered the binoculars, Lexie turned to look at her.

"What's a waning moon?"

"Oh, that's when the moon is getting smaller. Like when you have a new moon, you can't see it. It's out during the day, usually in line with the sun, so you can't see it. Then you have the little crescent moon—like today—only it would be opposite." She pointed to the west. "It would be like this, only you'd see it after sunset. That's called a waxing moon—it's getting bigger."

"Uh-huh."

"Yeah." She moved toward the large rock where she normally sat and placed the blanket there that she'd still been holding. "This moon, it probably rose about—I don't know, three thirty or four this morning. And in a day or two, you won't be able to see it at all. It's getting smaller. Then we'll have the new moon. Those are the best stargazing nights because there's no moon in the sky."

She sat down, wondering why she was blabbering on so about the damn moon phases. Lexie probably thought she was some goofy birdwatching, stargazing nerd. She smiled to herself. And maybe she was. So what?

"It's lovely out here." Lexie sat down beside her. "I've never given much thought to things like this. The moon is either in the sky or it's not. The sun rises, but I haven't seen many of them. I have enjoyed some sunsets over Lake Travis, though."

"Down at the coast, there were some awesome sunrises. Sunsets were harder to come by. When I worked at Goose Island, we had a view of both. Sunrise over Aransas Bay and sunset over Copano Bay."

"Do you miss it?"

"Not enough that I'd want to go back. Not anymore. I guess maybe I miss the vibe down there. Port Aransas is the only town on Mustang Island and it's, you know, a beach town. Just a laid-back, slow-moving beach town. Rockport was the same. I loved it there. I did. But up here, what I hated at first, I now love."

"What's that?"

"The remoteness. The quiet. No people." She laughed. "Don't get me wrong, I don't hate people. Working at a campground down there—it's noisy and boisterous. Spring Break will test your patience. Up here, it's quiet. People are respectful of nature. You don't have loud music blasting from campsites. People go to the beach to let loose, have fun. People come up here for different reasons. Not to say they don't have fun, just different. More hiking, more solitude. Quiet. Reflective. Peaceful."

"Judging from my mother's comments the other night, you haven't been back."

"No. And I should, I know. I'm not real close with my family." She shrugged. "We've kinda drifted apart. And my old friends? I keep in touch. Sort of. But it's not the same. I'm into year five now up here." The sky was brightening, the deep red was turning to orange. "Besides, I couldn't go back to Mustang Island, even for a quick visit. He'd probably shoot me on sight."

Lexie laughed quietly beside her. "I don't know you from Adam, of course, but I don't picture you the type to have an affair with a straight married woman." She paused. "I'm assuming she was straight."

She sighed. "Oh, Tina didn't really know what she was. Her husband was eighteen years older than her, and let's just say, I wasn't her first. Considering what his reaction was, I'm probably the first one who got caught though." She pointed out ahead of them. "See the glow? It's about to pop up."

Lexie looked above them. "The stars have mostly disappeared."

"It happens quick."

"The times seem different here. I mean, sunrise...sunset."

"It's because we're so far west and we're at the edge of the time zone. I think in the summer, the sun sets about thirty-five or forty minutes later than it did at the coast." She felt anticipation as the very tip of the sun—a deep red—showed itself. "There."

It only took a matter of seconds before the red and orange spread out before them, like slender fingers painting the sky one line at a time. Then the colors seemed to explode in all directions as the red orb crept above the horizon. She always felt like time stood still. There was no sound. No wind to rustle the trees. No birds. No people. Just her own heartbeat, her own breath as she was swallowed by colors shooting across the sky.

"Wow. It's gorgeous."

The softly whispered words reminded her that she wasn't alone. Whispered, because even though Lexie didn't make a habit of this, it seemed she knew—intuitively, perhaps—not to disturb the beautiful silence with words.

She didn't reply. She sat still, her shoulder inches away from Lexie's. She'd shared this rock with a few others. Mark, a couple of times. Susan had come up with her a few times too. It felt different this time.

It didn't last. It never did. A slight breeze kissed her face. A white-winged dove, one the earliest of risers, cooed from down below them. A raven soared past, into the canyon, heading toward the campgrounds. The red and orange faded into a shimmering yellow and the sun lost its gentle shine. A new day was upon them.

"As much as I was dreading this—my alarm went off at five thirty—I'm very glad I came."

She turned, smiling. "Five thirty?"

"Shower. Two cups of coffee. Internet surfing."

"Ah."

"You?"

"Oh, I usually get up at five every morning."

"Good lord, why?"

She stood, taking one last glance at the rising sun. "I work the morning shift. Seven to three. I—"

What? How did she explain? She did a quick workout of bodyweight exercises and kettle balls. She took a shower. She drank coffee. She made breakfast. She went out with a flashlight and filled the bird feeders. She flipped through the pages of her latest astronomy book—most of the information over her head. She read the online birding page where people logged their finds. She got out an old-fashioned paper map and planned quick daytrips for her days off. She sat on her deck until sunrise, waiting for the first birds to arrive.

"I sit around and drink coffee."

Lexie eyed her, her head tilted. Kyler wanted to turn away in case Lexie suspected the truth. Because how pathetic and nerdy did her morning routine sound?

But Lexie didn't say anything. She smiled. A smile that—at least in Kyler's imagination—said that she guessed exactly what it was Kyler did each morning and she didn't think it was nerdy in the least. Or that's what she hoped she thought.

"Speaking of coffee, I could use a cup right about now."

"Yeah. Come on. Let's go see your brother."

CHAPTER TWELVE

"What time does he open?"

"Daybreak. Which is earlier in the summer than winter, obviously."

"Why on earth so early?"

"Guests from the lodge go over early. Especially those who take daytrips. Like to Big Bend. Some of the locals come by for breakfast and just to sit around and drink coffee and shoot the shit."

Lexie shook her head, trying to picture her brother in that atmosphere. She turned to Kyler. "Do you know what Mark did before he moved out here?"

"Did? Like work? Yeah, he said he worked for an investment firm. Suit and tie."

"Yes. So I'm having a hard time seeing him sitting around drinking coffee with old-timers, gossiping about their neighbors."

"I've only known him like this, so he seems to fit right in. I am curious about his time in Austin, though."

"What do you mean?"

"Mark and I are friends. We talk about everything. Except that. He's always evasive, doesn't elaborate." Kyler shrugged. "I haven't pushed. I mean, he obviously doesn't want to talk about it. He told me about his wife, briefly, so I assume that's it."

She nodded. "Yes."

"It's none of my business, I guess. Our friendship is new."

Though she was sure Kyler tried to hide it, Lexie thought her words sounded a bit wounded. And why not? Kyler had been here going on five years. Is that still considered new?

"He told me he doesn't talk about it because he doesn't want to relive it. I told him maybe it would do him good to talk about it."

Kyler turned, eyebrows raised.

"She was six months pregnant when she was killed. They were cycling, like they did a lot. A woman failed to stop at an intersection."

"Oh my god."

"It hit us all hard. Mia was…well, the sister I never had. She was a second daughter to my parents. It hit us all very hard. Mark—I wasn't certain he was going to recover from it. My parents were already in negotiations to buy this place when it happened. Mark jumped at the chance to come up here with them."

"I knew he was still heartbroken over his wife. I had no idea she was pregnant." Kyler pounded the steering wheel. "Damn. I hate that I push him sometimes to date."

"Like with the twins?"

Kyler whipped her head around. "He *told* you?"

"He told me you were the one who backed out."

Kyler laughed. "Yeah. I'm not quite that adventurous. Maybe ten years ago I would have done it. But no, he ran as fast as I did!"

Kyler's smile remained when she turned into the parking lot at the restaurant. There were three other cars there. Lexie could see her brother moving about inside, delivering plates of food to a table.

"He's got his Christmas tree up. Yesterday?"

"Yes. I helped decorate." She stared at the twinkling lights that she'd framed the inside windows with. It looked pretty and festive. "What do you call this place?"

"What do you mean?"

"My mother calls it the restaurant. Mark calls it the bar. What do the locals call it?"

"Oh. Most call it Cottonwood. Like, going over to Cottonwood for a beer. Or, heading to Cottonwood for dinner. Like that."

"And you?"

"It depends, I guess. If I say it out loud, like to Tammy or somebody, I'll say Cottonwood. If I'm thinking it, it's usually the bar. Because that's where I always sit and have dinner. Up at the bar." She turned to her when she cut the engine. "Why?"

"I don't know. Restaurant seemed too formal. When Mark talks about it to me, he usually says the bar or the grill. I don't think he's ever referred to it as the restaurant."

Kyler opened her door and Lexie did the same. "More of a local diner than a restaurant anyway. Mark calls it a greasy spoon."

"And that it is. Mark's old apartment doesn't have a kitchen, as I'm sure you know. My eating options appear to be here or with my parents."

"So add some healthy stuff to the menu. Fair warning, though. I doubt anyone will order tofu."

She laughed. "So he told you I have a fondness for tofu, huh?"

"He did. And fish. And he said you'd push the food around on your plate if you didn't like it. Which is what you did the other night."

She paused at the door. "I'm not a big meat eater. I don't eat beef at all, so it was kinda hard to pick it out of that casserole. I have chicken occasionally. I suppose that will change."

"Fish and tofu are hard to come by up here." Kyler pushed the door open. "Down at the coast I had fish nearly every day. That was one of the biggest changes when I moved up here."

Mark was at the bar, already pouring two cups of coffee for them. She followed Kyler over and sat down beside her.

"What did you think, sis?"

"It was beautiful and well worth going to bed by ten," she conceded. "How often do you do it?"

"Only when Kyler drags my ass up there."

"Which she's going to do here in a couple of weeks." Kyler took a cup and stirred sugar into it. "Meteor shower."

"You're going to make me get up in the middle of the night again, aren't you?"

"Two in the morning is peak viewing."

"I'll probably skip it this year. But Lexie…"

When Kyler looked at her, she held up her hand. "Oh, no. Don't even think about it. No."

"It is pretty cool," Mark said. "Shooting stars all over the place."

"At two in the morning? I don't think so."

"Sit out for an hour or so, watch the stars, go back to bed." Kyler smiled at her. "You'll be glad you did."

Lexie looked at her skeptically. "We'll see."

"So where are you taking her today?"

"Thought I'd do the loop. Swing by the observatory. Go to the overlook."

"Don't do the whole loop. She'll be bored on the part in the desert. Stay up here in the mountains."

Lexie sipped her coffee, thinking she'd be bored silly regardless of what route Kyler took.

"The place looks nice, by the way. Very Christmasy."

"Lexie did most of it. Got more lights up than I did last year."

"You do your house yet?"

"No. Gonna make you two help me today."

"Not a chore. I love it."

Lexie nodded. "Me too. Now, when it comes time to take everything down, you're on your own."

CHAPTER THIRTEEN

"Are you sure?"

"Of course. You go and enjoy yourself. Irene works the office for us on Sundays."

"She's the one who helps Mark too?"

"Yes. We'd be lost without her. She sort of came with the place when we bought it," her mother said with a laugh. "She lives alone in an old ranch house about six miles up the road. Her husband died years ago, and she only has one daughter, who lives in the Dallas area. Poor thing hardly ever gets to see her grandkids. Well, great-grandkids now too."

"Did you have her over for Thanksgiving dinner?"

"No, she usually has Thanksgiving with the Stensons. That's Tammy and Phil. They're neighbors."

She nodded. "Tammy works at the park and Phil is the woodcarver."

Her mother smiled. "See? You're learning people already." Her mother opened the fridge and took out a jar of pickles. "Now, how was your tour? You weren't gone as long as I expected."

"It was fun, actually. Very scenic. Kyler makes a good tour guide. We didn't do the whole loop, though. Something about the desert. She turned around at some picnic area."

Her mother nodded. "Once you get on the south side of the loop, it's pretty barren. About the only thing exciting to see is if a herd of pronghorns come close."

She smiled. "That's exactly what Kyler said."

Her mother sliced the pickle lengthwise. "You like her?"

"Yes. She's very nice." Then she held her hand up. "No, Mom. Don't get any ideas. That will never happen."

"I told you, you and Kyler are too opposite. I don't see it."

"You think so?"

"Yes. Kyler is a tree hugger. You're a city girl."

"Well, this city girl actually hugged a tree today." She stole one of the pickle strips and popped it into her mouth.

Her mother held the knife suspended, her eyes wide. "You? You hugged a tree?" Then she smiled. "Let me guess. One of those big ponderosa pines up by the observatory?"

"That would be the ones." Then she smiled too. "I refused, of course. But she was hugging it and saying how it smelled like vanilla so…"

"And what did you think?"

"I thought it was more butterscotch than vanilla."

Her mother laughed. "I'm trying to picture you with your nose stuck into the bark of a tree."

"I know." She shrugged. "I had a good time. It was relaxing."

"Different?"

"Yes. Quiet." She pointed to the pickle that she was now mincing. "What's up with that?"

"Oh, I'm making my homemade relish to put in my potato salad later. Your father is going to grill burgers this afternoon."

"Sounds like fun." If they were veggie burgers, she added silently, wondering if she would ever get one of those again.

"Mark will have a spread. They always do. What did he say this time? Nachos and wings?"

"Yes, I think so. I feel like I should bring something."

"Well, maybe during the week, I'll take you to Potters and you can shop. Make something you'd like and take it next Sunday."

"So this is an every Sunday thing?"

"During football season, yes. And whenever Kyler drags him away from the restaurant."

"What will you do today?"

"Oh, I've got a few more Christmas decorations to put out. Your father will be in his recliner watching games all day. That is, unless something comes up."

"So tomorrow you'll start my training?"

"Yes. And within a week, you will be an expert. There's nothing to it." She waved the knife in the air. "Now, you should get going. I'm sure Kyler is already there."

"Actually, Mark never gave me directions. Which road do I take?"

"Road? Oh, we always walk there."

"Walk? How close is he?"

"Oh, up the hill. Not far. There's a path through the woods. He and Kyler made it. It's past the bird garden. You can't miss it."

"Okay. I guess I'll find it." She stole another pickle. "See you later, Mom."

"Have fun," her mother called after her.

She went into her little apartment for a jacket, thinking it would be late—and cooler—when she made the trip back home. Now, though, it was a beautiful, sunny day and the temperature was quite pleasant. She draped the jacket across her arm and headed to the bird garden.

She paused there, spying the bird feeders hanging from limbs. There was a wooden wall on one side with cutouts for viewing. What people called a blind, she assumed. She walked slowly and quietly, easing behind the wall. The birds that were there didn't pay her any mind and she wondered if perhaps they were used to people by now.

She, of course, had no idea what the birds were. There were some cute little brown and red ones. And there was a black and white bird that she guessed was a woodpecker of some sort. It had a red spot on its head. Doves. She knew that, but she didn't know the species. A small gray bird with a dark crest landed on the feeder, stole a sunflower seed, and flew off.

Kyler would know the names, no doubt. She smiled, remembering the binoculars that had been pressed into her hands, Kyler urging her to look at a hawk. A red-tailed hawk, Kyler had said. It was quite majestic as it soared, and she found she loved watching it.

As she'd told her mother, she had enjoyed the whole trip. Besides coffee, Mark had given them tacos to take along for breakfast. Eggs and potatoes—he'd left the bacon off hers—in a flour tortilla that one of the cooks makes from scratch each morning. It was smothered in a spicy green sauce and was so good, she wished she'd had two. In fact, it was so good, she could envision going there for breakfast every morning. She could also envision herself gaining ten pounds in the blink of an eye!

She realized she was still standing there, watching the birds. Not really watching them, no. She didn't watch birds. With a shake of her head, she moved on around the blind, looking for the trail that would take her to Mark's cabin. She saw the sign before she found the trail.

"Private Residence. No Entry."

Yes, it did look like a hiking trail, thus the need for a sign. The path appeared well-used and she assumed that Mark walked this way each day to the restaurant. How wonderful that must be. She paused, wondering where that thought came from. It was most likely dark and cold when he made the trip down each morning.

But it wasn't far. Uphill, yes, but not far. She spotted the cabin through the trees. It felt good to do some exercise. She would miss her gym access, that's for sure. It had become a daily ritual to head over there right after work. She'd made lots of friends there. After a good workout, there was always someone willing to grab a smoothie with her and sometimes even dinner.

Well, before Cathy, that is. Once Cathy came into her life, she was expected home. They'd then usually go out together for a meal or on the rare occasion, stay in and cook something. She enjoyed cooking. Cathy, on the other hand, would rather eat out. She shook that thought away. She certainly didn't want to think about Crazy Cathy.

No, she didn't. She did wonder, though, how things were going with her friends. Trish had texted her pictures from their night out on Sixth Street. It had looked like the usual fun—crowds of people walking the sidewalks under flashing neon signs, going from bar to bar, only stopping when the music inside met everyone's approval. There was no regret on her part for missing out, though. She hadn't seen the text until morning. She'd been sound asleep when Trish had sent them. Sound asleep by ten and up at five thirty. Would any of her friends have believed that?

She paused at the edge of the clearing, wondering why she was so out of breath. It hadn't even been a week since her last—and final—trip to the gym. Surely she wasn't getting out of shape that quickly. Probably the altitude. Maybe she should take up jogging. It would be vastly different to run outside compared to her treadmill sessions. And in lieu of her spin class, she could take up cycling. She remembered Mark saying that Kyler biked. And while he didn't want to join her, perhaps Kyler would extend the invitation to her.

"Hey. You're about to miss kickoff."

She looked up, finding Kyler leaning against the deck railing. She appeared to be holding a beer.

"Catching my breath."

Kyler nodded. "Altitude."

She headed up the steps. "Good. I was afraid I was getting out of shape already." She smiled at her, then looked around. Yes, Mark had indeed brought a TV outside. It was against the wall of the cabin and three chairs were arranged around it.

"He's getting the wings marinated. You want a beer?"

"Is it even noon?"

Kyler grinned. "Somewhere." She looked at the black sports watch on her wrist. "Eleven fifty. Is that close enough?"

Kyler had already opened a cooler and pulled out a beer bottle from beneath the ice. She recognized the dark bottle with the gold label. The Shiner Bock was shoved into a koozie with a zipper. A Dallas Cowboys koozie.

"Is that who we're watching?"

"The Cowboys? They don't play until three."

"Then why the urgency for a noon kickoff?"

"Because Mark has satellite TV and he gets every game. So we pick one we want to watch or flip around between them."

"I didn't realize Mark enjoyed football that much. He usually bailed on me and Dad when the games were on."

Kyler shrugged and gave an almost apologetic smile. "Excuse to drink beer at noon."

The beer was cold and smooth and she nodded. "Good. Thank you. I'll be better prepared next time and bring my own."

"No problem."

She sat down beside Kyler. The sound was muted on the TV and it looked like the game hadn't yet started. She nudged Kyler's arm with her elbow.

"I had a really good time today. I never in a million years would have thought that it would be fun. But it was and I enjoyed it."

"Did you? Good. Like I said, we'll need to make a trip to the observatory one night. In January when there are no crowds is the best time to go. It's totally awesome seeing the planets through those telescopes. It's what got me hooked on it."

"Do you have your own telescope?"

"I do. Nothing too fancy but it's enough for me." The smile Kyler gave again had a bit of embarrassment in it, she thought. "It was all I could afford. Maybe someday I'll get a bigger one."

Mark came out then, carrying a tray with chips and some sort of sour cream dip. "Spinach?" she guessed, remembering the dip Mia used to make.

"It is." He met her gaze and nodded. "And yes, I made it myself." He looked at the TV. "Which game are we watching?"

"I don't know, but I want a tour of your house first."

"Sure. Come on in." He pointed at Kyler. "Pick a game. And not the Patriots."

* * *

Kyler was both surprised and pleased that not only did Lexie like football, she was also well versed in it. She had screamed out "That was holding!" even before the referee tossed his yellow flag. She also learned that Lexie liked beer and it made her giggly. And in turn, Kyler found herself getting giggly as well. Which was so not her.

"You like her, don't you?"

She turned her head, having been caught staring as Lexie went inside to put Mark's wings in the oven. "Yeah. She's nice."

"Come on. You know what I mean."

"Okay, okay. I like her. She's different than what I expected. You made her sound like a snobbish bore."

His eyes widened. "I did?"

"You know, city girl. Tofu. Won't fit in. But she's...fun." She shrugged. "We could be friends." She nodded. "Yeah, we could be friends. She does fit in. She's knows football way better than you."

He laughed. "I will admit, I wasn't that much of a fan until I moved out here."

"Yeah? More free time up here than when you were in Austin?"

She saw a shadow cross his face and she wondered if she'd simply missed it before. He didn't talk much about his past life and she didn't question it. Their friendship was based on the here and now, and neither of their pasts mattered. Should she tell him she knew about his wife? That she'd been pregnant? Was it any of her business?

"I didn't watch much football when I lived in Austin. We used to cycle all the time. Every Saturday and Sunday. Any free time we had, we were on bikes."

She raised her eyebrows. "And you said you didn't know how."

He smiled. "Yeah. That was a silly excuse."

She nodded. "Your wife was killed on the bike. You had said she died, but you never said how."

He raised his eyebrows. "Lexie told you?"

"Yes."

He let out a heavy sigh. "I figured she would eventually. I didn't think it would be the first day."

"If you want or need to talk about stuff, Mark, I'm—" Then she held her hand up. "No. It's none of my business. If you don't want to talk about it, that's fine." She met his gaze. "I love you."

"Oh, man." He stood and turned away, but not before she saw tears in his eyes. "I don't think I would have made it without you, Ky."

"You were here almost two years before I got here," she reminded him.

"Yeah. And I was miserable. Lonely. Still wallowing in grief. And when you walked into the bar that first day, you had the same lost look in your eyes that I saw in mine every morning in the mirror." He smiled at her. "I knew at that very moment that we were going to be friends."

She nodded. "I think I did too."

He sat down again, then nudged her arm. "I love you too."

She grinned. "We're a pair, huh?"

"Yeah, we are." He motioned toward the house. "So, you like my sister?"

She laughed. "I do."

"Told you she was cute."

"Yeah, you weren't lying about that."

"Told you you'd like her."

"I like her as a *friend*. Nothing more. She's not really my type."

"What's your type?"

"Well, that's not true. If I were still down at the coast, she'd probably be exactly my type. But I've changed. Up here, I've changed. I've become—yeah, a damn tree hugger. Being outside, in nature, that's become important to me. If I ever were to date someone again, it'd have to be someone who loved all this as much as I do." She met his gaze. "Britney. She kinda reminds me of Britney."

"The one who broke your heart?"

"Yeah. I can see myself having a crush on your sister, much like I had on Britney. But I'm not twenty-five-years-old anymore. I need more than sexual infatuation."

He leaned closer. "So you're saying that you're sexually infatuated with my sister?"

"I'm saying, yeah, she's cute and kinda flirty and fun to be around." She arched an eyebrow. "What? Do you want me and your sister to have sex? Because that would probably be all it is."

"Because she's not your type."

"Right."

He closed his eyes for a moment, then held his hand up. "Okay, I really don't want to think about you and Lexie having sex."

She laughed. "Then quit bringing it up!" They both turned when the back door to the cabin opened and Lexie came back outside. She looked between them, eyebrows raised.

"What did I miss?"

CHAPTER FOURTEEN

"I'll drop you off on my way."

Lexie was thankful for the offer. It was dark by the time the game was over and they'd cleaned up the deck and kitchen. Dark and cold. Even though Mark had a propane heater on the deck—one that mimicked a campfire—it had gotten quite chilly once the sun went down.

She kissed Mark's cheek. "I had a great time. Thanks for including me."

"Well, you know, it's a thing now. Every Sunday."

She turned to Kyler. "So it's at your place next week?"

"No. We take turns if we're doing a regular dinner, but Sunday football is always here."

"Okay. I'll be better prepared next week. I'll contribute something to the meal and bring my own beer."

She smiled as Kyler and Mark embraced. "Had fun. See you at the bar."

"Yeah. See ya."

"I'll come over tomorrow evening to finish decorating," Lexie told him.

"Thanks."

He stood on the porch until they got into Kyler's Jeep, then waved one last time before going inside. Kyler put the heater on, then backed out of the driveway. "That was fun."

"Yes. I hope I wasn't in the way."

"Not at all. As I told Mark, you know football better than he does."

"You and Mark are really close, huh?"

"Yes. He's the best." Kyler glanced at her quickly. "He's an all-around good guy and I can't imagine what my life would be like without him. We just clicked and fell into such an easy friendship. It was like we'd known each other for years."

"Which was why it surprised me that he hasn't talked to you about Mia."

"We talked a little today, actually. He finally told me they used to cycle on the weekends, so he wasn't that much of a football fan." Kyler glanced at her again. "I told him that I knew Mia had been killed on the bike. I like to ride around the park. There are some trails that are suitable for mountain bikes and it's loads of fun. Couldn't talk him into going, though, no matter how hard I tried. When he brought up cycling today, I told him I knew."

"Did he tell you she was pregnant?"

"No. And I didn't mention it."

"He doesn't ever talk about it to us, either. But speaking of cycling, if you'd like a partner, I would love to join you. My experience is mostly spin class, but I think I'd like riding out here."

"Oh, yeah, sure. That'd be great."

"I'll have to get a bike first."

"Alpine. They've got a bike shop. I got mine there. Used. A lot of the college kids sell their bikes back when they leave." She paused, then continued. "I'm off tomorrow. I'll take you down there if you want."

"Maybe. I'm supposed to start my training tomorrow with Mom."

"Okay. Well, let me know."

When Kyler pulled into the parking spot next to her car, Lexie asked a question she'd been curious about.

"Why aren't you dating anyone?"

Kyler seemed surprised. "I don't know. I could use the excuse that there aren't a lot of lesbians in the area, but that's not really it.

Marfa, for its size, actually has a fairly large gay population. Artists and old hippies, Mark likes to say. And Alpine is a college town." Then she grinned. "Of course, I'm over thirty now. That would be creepy to hang out there." She raised her eyebrows. "Why?"

"Curious, that's all. You're nice. You're attractive. I haven't noticed any glaring flaws," she added with a smile.

Kyler leaned closer, her voice low. "So you think I'm attractive, do you?"

Lexie held her hand up. "Hey, no. No, no, no. I'm not hitting on you. At all." She shook her head. "And no offense to you, but I'm not even a little bit interested. Sorry." The porch light cast enough light into the Jeep to see Kyler's face. She was smiling.

"I think you're attractive too."

She sighed. "Please say this isn't going to be an issue. Because I had fun today. I'd like to be friends. I don't want to have to keep my distance because you—"

"No, no." It was Kyler's turn to hold a hand up. "I think we can be friends. You're not really my type, so you don't have to worry about that. If you ever think I'm flirting with you, remember that. It'll just be teasing. Because you're not my type."

Lexie let out a relieved breath. "Okay, good. Thank you. Because you're not anywhere near my type either."

"Oh, yeah, I suppose not. Mark and Susan both say we're complete opposites." Kyler gave her a lopsided smile. "Besides, I'm a weird birdwatcher. Who would want to date someone like that?"

Lexie smiled, thankful that she and Kyler were on the same page. It would make it so much easier to form a friendship without them worrying that the other might want more out of it. "Well, I don't think you're strange, but I've yet to see your funny hat," she teased. "Thanks for dropping me off."

"No problem. Let me know if you want to go shopping tomorrow."

"I will. Goodnight."

Kyler gave her a quick wave as she pulled away. Lexie stared after her for a moment, watching the red Jeep disappear into the night. She turned, but before going inside her little apartment, she walked out into the parking lot, away from the porch light. She looked up, again amazed at the clarity of the sky. The stars were right on top of her, twinkling—dancing—overhead. She was smiling as she watched, her eyes moving across the sky slowly. She wondered if Kyler knew the constellations. She spotted a couple of bright stars and thought they must be planets. Kyler had mentioned Jupiter and Venus being out at night. She wished she'd thought to ask her before she left.

But no. Stargazing—like birdwatching—was Kyler's passion, not hers. That wasn't something she was interested in. She turned and went to her apartment, pausing again to glance up once more before opening the door.

Maybe she shouldn't have mentioned cycling. She liked Kyler. She did. As both Mark and her mother had said, Kyler was nice. She took off her jacket and hung it on one of the pegs on the coatrack on the wall beside the door. Yes, Kyler was nice. And she was attractive. And if they spent too much time together…well, then things might change.

No. Because I'm not interested in her and she's not interested in me.

"Thankfully," she murmured.

She didn't want any drama in her life. She didn't care how cute she was or how nice she was. She simply wasn't interested in anything other than friendship with her. She was glad Kyler felt the same way.

And it wasn't because Crazy Cathy had wreaked havoc on her life. Yes, she had vowed to take a break—a very long break—before dating again. But truthfully, she didn't feel she had the energy to devote to dating. She didn't want any complications or added stress to her life. Moving out here in the middle of freakin' nowhere was enough on her plate.

Now, a friend? Yes, she could use a friend. Someone to hang out with and do stuff with. That would make this transition much easier. And after today, she assumed that Mark and Kyler would welcome her into their little group. And if she and Kyler could go cycling occasionally, that would be a bonus. Since she wouldn't have a gym close by, she needed some form of exercise.

So, if her mother would allow her a few hours off, she'd take Kyler up on her offer to shop for a bike. And then they could start this friendship in earnest.

Yes. That was a good plan.

CHAPTER FIFTEEN

"And you need to check this at least twice a day," her mother repeated.

Lexie rubbed her forehead. "It shouldn't be this complicated. You have an online reservation system. Why do you have to manually assign the rooms?"

"Because this particular system doesn't do that. And it would be helpful, yes." Her mother patted her hand. "Maybe this is something you could tinker with."

Yes. If this was going to be her baby to run, then that would be one of the first things she did. "You have online checkout?"

"No."

"Why not?"

Her mother waved her hand. "That's so impersonal. We like to interact with the guests. Ask how their stay was. Get a feel as to whether they'll be back. That sort of thing."

"But the system is capable?"

"Oh, yes. We disabled that bit."

"Mom, you offer Wi-Fi. You should at least *offer* online checkout. What about those that leave early in the mornings?"

"We have a drop box for keys, of course. Even if we had online checkout, they'd still need to bring their keys by."

"Keycards?"

"We did talk about it. But the cost to upgrade was too much to justify." Her mother filled her coffee cup again. "This is an old, rustic lodge. Not some fancy hotel. Keep that in mind."

"Okay. You're right. I guess keycards would be out of place here."

An alert sounded and her mother clapped her hands lightly. "Got another reservation!" She pointed to the small box that had popped up on the bottom right corner. "Click that. It'll bring up a snapshot of the reservation."

She did. Margaret Seymore had booked four nights in April. Margaret had requested room number twelve.

"Oh, that's Maggie. They come every year. They're from Lubbock. Sweet couple."

"And what do they do here?"

"Do? Oh, honey, not everyone needs to be constantly entertained, you know. Maggie and her husband love hiking. That's one of the benefits to being connected to the state park. There are miles of hiking trails. They also take a day trip down to Big Bend each year."

"Kyler mentioned Big Bend. What is that?"

"That's the national park that borders Mexico. It's vast. And you think we're in the middle of nowhere? That place is an hour and a half in all directions from civilization," she said with a laugh. "But beautiful. Worth the trip." She paused. "Maybe Kyler would take you sometime."

"How did Kyler get stuck showing me around? Mark hasn't even offered."

"Mark is at the restaurant every day. The only time that boy gets away is when he'd visit you in Austin. Or when Kyler makes him take a break on her days off. Irene is plenty capable of handling things there. Now that you're here, I hope he'll get away more and do things."

"Does he ever talk about Mia?"

"Oh, no. Never."

"That can't be healthy, Mom."

"Oh, that's not to say that I don't bring her up from time to time. In passing, sometimes, a memory of her will come up." She sighed. "That was such a tragic time in our lives."

"Yes, it was."

"Mark handled it the way he wanted to. We have to respect that."

"I know."

Her mother leaned against the desk, a wistful look on her face as she sipped her coffee. "My only chance at a grandchild, I guess."

"Oh, Mom…"

Her mother gave her a sad smile. "I remember when you were in high school. You were adamant that you were never having babies. I assumed you would grow out of it. Then, well, when you told us you were gay, well…"

"Mom, being gay has nothing to do with not wanting a baby. I simply have no desire to be a mom. I don't have that gene, I guess," she said with a smile, hoping to lighten her mother's mood.

"I know, honey. I didn't mean to make you feel uncomfortable. I just wish Mark would meet someone and get over Mia."

"He'd known her since the second grade. I don't think he'll ever get over it." She shook her head. "Plus the fact that he was there when it happened. I'm sure that scene is replayed in his mind far more than he'd like. Replayed, wishing for a different outcome, wishing he'd done something, wishing they'd taken a different route."

"You sound like you've replayed it too."

"I guess I have. They hadn't taken Mia away yet when I got there. It was all still so fresh." She shook her head again, hoping to clear the image away. "Anyway, I think we need to accept that it scarred Mark more than he lets on."

Her mother put her cup down, then bent down to hug her. "I'm so happy you're here, Lexie. You'll be good for him, I think."

"Kyler's good for him."

"Oh, yes, she is." Her mother's smile was genuine and warm. "Kyler is like one of the family now."

"Yes, I can tell."

"I hope you'll be friends too."

"I think we will. Speaking of that, she's offered to take me to Alpine to buy a bike. I asked if I could ride with her out here in the park."

"That would be wonderful! I had no idea you rode. After the thing with Mia, I doubt Mark will ever get on a bike again."

"He might. Mountain bike, not a road bike like they used. But no, I don't really ride, Mom. I rode with them a few times, but like Mark, I got rid of the bike after the accident. The only bike I've been on since is at the gym. But I think it might be fun."

"So when are you going?"

"Well, she's off today."

Her mother threw her arms up. "So what are you doing here?"

"I *am* supposed to be in training, aren't I?"

"Well, then let's hurry it up so you can go."

"Then let's do."

She turned her attention back to the reservation system, trying to remember what it was they'd been doing. Oh, yes. Maggie Seymore booked room number twelve. The search box her mother had shown her was by either date or room number. "Is there a calendar view?"

"Yes. You can look by week or by month." Her mother leaned over her shoulder and pointed. "Click the dropdown there."

"Okay, good. This is better." She pulled up the month of December, able to see the entire month at once, noting that most of the rooms were booked throughout the month.

"You think so? I don't use it much. A lot of our guests are repeats and they usually request a particular room."

"Aren't the rooms all the same?"

"Different views. Some prefer upstairs, some down. Some have king beds, others have two doubles, things like that. We have four rooms that are larger and have a refrigerator and a small microwave. Those are the most popular rooms."

"If those are your most popular, why not upgrade more rooms like that? I'm assuming you charge more for them."

"Yes, we do. But really, your father wanted to keep it rustic. It was all I could do to get those upgraded." She sat down again. "Now, if this works out and we start traveling, then I'm sure he'll be receptive to any changes you want to make. Within reason," she added quickly.

"What about the cleaning crew?"

"Oh, we have four ladies. I need to introduce you to them."

"Only four?"

"That's one of the benefits of being as remote as we are. People usually stay three, four nights, at least. We don't change sheets or clean the rooms during their stay. We switch out towels and take their trash, and that's only if they request it," she explained. "We have these cute little signs for them to put out if they want service."

"I suppose that makes sense." She opened the online reservation listing, finding Maggie Seymore now at the top of the list. "Okay, so I now add her manually to room twelve on these dates?"

"Yes. And should there be a conflict with rooms, I always email them and offer the closest room or, of course, give them the choice to choose another."

"So a really smart online system would check room availability before the person books."

"Yes, but we couldn't see paying that much more for a system like that when we only have thirty rooms. It's not that difficult to sort through. And most of our repeat customers make reservations months in advance. It's rare for an issue to come up."

"I'm not complaining about how much manual entry and maintenance you have to do. I'm simply used to programs that run themselves."

"Like I said, tinker with it if you want."

She leaned back in her chair. "What's the occupancy rate? I mean, on average."

"Oh, it depends on the season. We're full over Thanksgiving and the two weeks around Christmas and New Year's. April and May are pretty much full too. The Spring Break weeks in March are full. In the summer, we run about sixty to seventy percent, I'd guess. August is pretty quiet. It's hot and school has started. October picks up again for people wanting cooler weather after the summer heat."

"So January and February are the dead months?"

"Oh, yes. We've gone a week before without a single guest. A couple of years ago we had a brutal winter. The last two weeks in January and the first week of February, not a single guest showed up."

She motioned to the laptop. "So this doesn't take a whole lot of your time. What do you do all day?"

"I'm certainly not tied to the computer, that's for sure. But running the lodge isn't all bookings. There's payroll. There's quarterly taxes to do. There's inventory and ordering supplies." Her mother motioned to the front desk. "I make sure all the brochures are stocked. I fill in with maid service if one of the girls can't make it. In the spring and summer, I plant flowers out front and around the lodge. There's always something to do. I certainly don't get bored if that's what you're asking."

"What about the restaurant? Is that separate?"

"Yes, thank goodness. Mark handles everything over there. I'm not sure that your father and I could have managed it all if Mark hadn't come up here with us. Your father is a one-man show when it comes to maintenance and with thirty rooms and a lodge this old, there's always something that needs his attention." She went to refill her coffee cup again. "We'll have to see about having someone on call, of course, if you take over. Once we get our RV—*if* we get it—we plan to be gone months at a time. If something should break, I doubt you and Mark could fix it like your father does."

"Surely there's someone in town who you could call if, say, a hot water heater went out."

"Not in Ft. Davis, no. At least not for that. Alpine, yes. But their solution would be to install a new unit. Your father may tinker with it all day and get it going again. That's the difference." She took a sip of her coffee. "Some of them do need to be replaced, I know, but we can't afford it right now. When we bought this place, all the rooms had window AC units and ancient furnaces for heat. It was a major, major expense—including some remodeling—to upgrade the HVAC in all of that."

"I remember you telling me about it. You had to close off several rooms at a time while you had the new ventilation system installed."

"Yes. It was nearly a yearlong project. Needless to say, there was a lot more money going out than was coming in." She smiled almost reassuringly. "That's not to say we aren't profitable. We are. I don't want you to worry about that. But that project took a huge chunk out of our savings that we're just now catching up on."

"Mom, I feel bad taking a salary then. I mean—"

"Don't be silly. There's money in our operating budget. We try to keep that constant and now that we've nearly gotten our money back, I won't have to be so frugal on some things. When I show you the books, you'll get an idea."

"So I shouldn't worry?"

"You shouldn't worry. This little lodge has already paid for itself and we're only in year seven. It was a wonderful investment for us and we're both happy here. Of course, having Mark with us helped at the beginning. Now that you're here, everything feels complete."

"No pressure there, Mom," she said with a smile.

"Oh, I know, honey. Trial run. I haven't ordered you a nameplate yet," she teased. "But I so hope you'll stay. It's such a wonderful life up here. A slow, peaceful life. You have time to breathe. Time to smell the roses, as they say."

"I understand what you're saying, Mom. And maybe for you at your age. But I'm only thirty. I still enjoy going out to dinner, grabbing lunch with friends. Hitting Sixth Street on Saturday nights." She let her shoulders slump. "Going to the gym. Getting a green smoothie. Eating at a taco truck vendor. Starbucks," she said wistfully. She leaned her head on the desk. Four days. She'd been here four days. Was she homesick already?

Her mother pulled her chair closer and sat down beside her. "Would you believe me if I said I felt the same way when we moved up here? I think it was the second week. I was tired. I missed my friends and I was lonely. All I wanted to do was order a dang pizza, curl up on the couch, and watch an old movie that I'd seen a hundred times."

"What did you do?"

"I cried. There was no pizza delivery and my favorite DVDs that I'd brought with me were still packed in a box somewhere and there was no online streaming. Your father and Mark didn't quite know what to do with me." She smiled and patted her leg. "Mark drove all the way to Alpine where there was a Pizza Hut and your father found a movie on the satellite. *Pretty Woman*. So the three of us sat on the floor and ate pizza and drank beer and watched a movie."

Lexie smiled, picturing the scene. She had a pang of sadness, though. She should have been there too.

"The next morning, I called Debra. You remember Debra, don't you? I worked with her for years."

"Yes."

"So, we chatted, and I got caught up on all the office gossip and when I hung up, I realized I didn't really miss it as much as I thought I did."

"You're saying I need to give it time?"

"Yes. And you need to keep things in perspective. It's different here than there. You can't really duplicate things, but you can replace them with something else. I've made new friends, I have new hobbies and interests, and frankly, my marriage is as strong and fulfilling as it's ever been."

Lexie held her hand up quickly. "We're not going to talk about sex, are we?"

Her mother laughed. "I'll draw the line there." Then she winked. "I never knew the stress of our jobs back then was such a downer on our sex life. We're like brand-new people up here."

"Okay. I get it," she said quickly. "You don't have to spell it out." She was certain she was blushing, and she was also certain this was the very first time her mother had mentioned having a sex life. She also hoped it would be the last.

"We don't girl talk much, do we?"

"No, we don't. Let's keep it that way, shall we?"

Her mother stood, still smiling. "Oh, Lexie, you always were so embarrassed about things like that. In high school you would never talk to me about your personal life."

"Because I was gay, and I was afraid to tell you."

"And I'll tell you now like I told you then. I already knew." She bent down and kissed her cheek. "And I loved you then and I will always love you. No matter how many Crazy Cathies come into your life."

"God, let's hope that was my one and only."

"Yes, let's hope. Now, don't forget to add in Maggie's reservation. When you're done, call Kyler and go get you a bike."

"Okay. Thanks, Mom. I love you too."

Her mother went down the short hallway to the back and she watched her go, amazed how her mother could cheer her up with only a few words. Yes, she would miss getting a green smoothie after her workout, but that was only because it was a habit. Her routine. So, she'd have to find something different, as her mother suggested.

A bike ride would be different. With Kyler.

That would be different.

CHAPTER SIXTEEN

Kyler looked at her cell, not recognizing the number. As a rule—mostly to avoid telemarketers—she rarely answered a call she didn't know. But this was an Austin number. She smiled.

"Kyler here."

"Hey. It's me. Lexie. What are you doing?"

Well, "Waiting on you to call" didn't seem like the appropriate response. However, saying she was sitting on her little porch watching the house finches seemed almost worse. She could make up something, she supposed. Chopping wood? Training for a marathon? Finishing her Christmas decorations? Working on her six-pack abs? *Right*. Maybe she could—

"Kyler?"

"Yeah. I'm—nothing, really. Just relaxing. What's up?"

A quiet laugh. "Are you watching birds at your bird feeder?"

She rolled her eyes and sighed. "Yes. Guilty."

Another laugh. "Why were you afraid to tell me?"

"Because it makes me seem perfectly boring."

"Kyler, that's your thing. That doesn't make you boring. What if my thing was something like paint by numbers? How boring does that sound if you're not into that?"

"Do they still sell that?"

"I have no idea. So, what birds are at your feeder right now?"

"House finches."

"What do they look like?"

She slid her gaze to the feeder, smiling as she tried to think of a way to describe them. "They are kinda brown with streaks on their wings and back. The males have pinkish red color on their heads and throat and on their rump. The females don't have any red on them."

"I saw them! Yesterday when I was walking to Mark's. They were at the feeders there in Mom's bird garden."

"Yeah. They're common up here."

"There was some sort of a woodpecker there too. Black and white. Had a red spot on his head."

"Probably a ladder-backed woodpecker. They have white, horizontal stripes on their backs."

"Where do you live anyway?"

"Oh, the park provides cabins for us. It's over on the north side, away from the campgrounds."

"So you're close."

"I am. You want to go shopping for a bike?"

"Can we?"

"Sure. Now?"

"My mother has dismissed me, yes. If you haven't had lunch, maybe we could stop somewhere?" She paused. "I'm having Mexican food withdrawals."

"Then I know just the place. I'll be right over."

* * *

"I don't come here much, no." She loaded up a chip with red salsa. "I feel like I'm cheating on Mark if I do."

"So you live off of that stuff at the bar? How do you stay fit with all that fried food?"

"I'm very active. If I didn't have the kind of job I do, I could never eat like that." She took another chip. "You'll need to revamp his menu. To be honest, I only alternate through four or five things and I'm pretty sick of them."

"I'm sure you are. Right now, my options are baked potatoes and steamed veggies. I think I'm going to see if he'll do some sort of pasta dish with veggies." Lexie leaned her elbows on the table. "Will anyone order it?"

"Not sure. People go on vacation to splurge, normally. You probably won't have people searching for the healthiest items on a menu in a place like that. The locals don't even look at the menu when they come. They know what they want." She dipped another chip into the salsa. "He's mentioned getting one of those indoor grills so he can grill steaks and chicken instead of frying everything. I'm pushing him hard for that."

"It's called a bar and grill. You mean there isn't a grill?"

"Nope."

"Okay. Then I'm definitely on board with him getting an indoor grill."

She grinned. "I have ulterior motives. Grilled fish. God, I miss grilled fish. When I lived in Rockport, there was this little fish market, about a block from the harbor. My favorite was snapper, but you'd have to get there early, or they'd sell out. Grouper was my second favorite. Or flounder." She spread her hands out. "They had these two huge coolers on each side of the room, filled with crushed ice. They'd lay the fish fillets on top of the ice on one side and shrimp would be on the other side. And the place smelled something awful," she said, wrinkling up her nose. "They had this glass window where you could see in the back. The guys would be back there sorting through stuff they'd just bought off the boat. If you wanted to order shrimp with the heads on, she'd go back there and grab some. Oh, and oyster season? They had this pile of oyster shells outside. It grew and grew and grew as the season went on. It was huge. As tall as the building." She smiled at Lexie. "I hate oysters, by the way. Now shrimp? Fried shrimp—I could eat my weight in them. Grilled too. But fish? I liked grilled fish best."

"You sound like you miss it there."

"Oh, just memories. Like anything, your memory is grander than the real thing. If I went back to visit, I'd hit up my old favorite spots and order my old favorites, but I doubt it would taste as good as I remember."

Lexie nodded. "I suppose you're right."

"If you went to your favorite Mexican food place, what would you order?"

"Hmmm. Brunch would be cheesy migas and fried potatoes. This one place—Jalisco's—makes a spinach and mushroom quesadilla with grilled onions and peppers and they have a creamy potato cheese sauce to dip it in." Lexie closed her eyes and moaned. "It was to die for."

"Potato cheese sauce?"

"Yes. It's not real cheese. No dairy. They actually spell it with a 'z' instead of 's' and yes, it is made with potatoes."

"Sounds yummy. Not."

Lexie laughed. "I'd bet you ten bucks you couldn't tell it wasn't real cheese."

"I'll take your word for it."

"I have the recipe."

"For this potato cheese stuff?"

"Uh-huh. I'll bring it to one of our next football parties."

"Can't wait," she said dryly.

Lexie snapped a chip in half before dipping it into the salsa. "Why your boss's wife?"

Kyler raised her eyebrows, wondering at the question.

"Were you in love with her?"

"God, no. It wasn't like that." She waved her hand dismissively. "It was a stupid thing to do, yeah. Obviously. She initiated it, not me. Of course, I could have said no." She sighed. "She was cute and flirty and one rainy afternoon I found myself alone with her in the office. She was relentless in her flirting and...and I gave in."

"You must be easy," Lexie said with a smile. "Or very weak."

"Or crazy." Actually, she had still been sulking after her breakup with Britney. So yeah, maybe she had been weak. She wasn't going to tell Lexie all that, though. Instead, she smiled back at her. "Speaking of crazy—tell me about Cathy."

Lexie groaned. "Do I have to?"

"Was she really crazy?"

"In the clinical sense? No. At first, she was infatuated with me to the point of being neurotic about it. She was...very possessive."

"Abusive?"

"Physically, no. Verbally, yes. Certainly emotionally." Lexie took another chip, pausing before dipping it into the salsa. "Mom was right. I ended it two years too late."

"Still loved her?"

Lexie met her gaze. "No. It was one of those situations where you're dating and the next thing you know, you're living together.

And it wasn't like it was a horrible relationship or anything. At least, not at first. She was always jealous of anyone who talked to me. Always. And where I thought it was kinda cute at the beginning, it got annoying very quickly. We got into so many arguments about it—it was exhausting."

"So why didn't you end it?"

She sighed heavily. "Because I think I knew she really would do something crazy, so it was easier to tolerate her." She leaned her elbows on the table again. "Honestly, I tried to be such a bitch to her, hoping she'd get tired of me and leave."

"Were you still having sex with her?" As Lexie's eyebrows shot up, she smiled. "What? Too personal?"

Lexie shook her head. "No. I refused to sleep with her."

"So you were a bitch and you were withholding sex and she still wouldn't leave?"

"Right."

"Wow. She must have really loved you."

"Not loved. Obsessed."

"So how you'd get away?"

"Trish and I—Trish is my best friend—we both took off work one day, packed all her things and left them outside the apartment door."

"This is when she went crazy and broke all your dishes?"

"I see my brother has filled you in on all the highlights."

"Why did you let her inside?"

"Because she came home before I could get the locks changed."

"Ah. So all of that came before or after she stole your car?"

"Before." Lexie held her hand up. "And that's enough about Crazy Cathy."

"Really? But I have a bunch more questions."

Lexie laughed. "Sorry. It's too depressing to think about, much less talk about. I was such an idiot to get trapped in that relationship. I'm usually over-cautious and think things to death before I do them. Like I said, one minute we were dating, the next, she'd moved in. So I would rather not talk about it anymore." She pointed behind her. "Besides, I think our order is here."

Kyler turned, seeing Ana bringing over a tray with their food. "Looks good, Ana."

"Thank you, Kyler. You should come by more often." She slid a plate in front of her. "I put extra peppers for you this time."

"Thanks." She looked at her heaping plate of enchiladas and then at the huge rice and bean burrito on Lexie's plate. She assumed they'd both be taking leftovers home.

"Wow. It's big."

Ana smiled at Lexie. "Since you didn't want chicken or beef, I put some vegetables in there. Mushrooms and onions. I hope that's okay, yes?"

"Of course. Thank you."

"Enjoy," Ana said with a slight bow, then left them.

"That was nice of her. I didn't even think to ask."

"Everything is made from scratch and to order. She's very accommodating."

Lexie cut her burrito in half, revealing a tortilla stuffed with rice, black beans, and veggies. "You come here often?"

"Not really. A couple of times a month, I guess. I sometimes stop for lunch when I'm in town doing my shopping." She used her fork to cut the enchiladas—chicken smothered in a sour cream sauce. "I don't cook much so there's not a lot of shopping to do." She took one bite and moaned. "Delicious."

"Mine too. Very spicy. I love it."

Kyler took a drink of her tea, the extra peppers making her mouth burn in a wonderful way. "Tell me about your job," she asked before picking her fork up again. "Or is that off limits too?"

"Not off limits, no. I loved my job. I was a little bored there at the end, but I loved the company and the people I worked with." She ate another bite before continuing. "We developed intrusion detection software. We monitor various companies' network traffic, both incoming and outgoing. We can spot malware or any suspicious activity, really. Anyway, I was a project manager. The signatures must always be updated because threats are constantly changing. We were trying to stay one step ahead of the bad guys."

She took another bite, then paused. "Our little company was too successful. We got bought out. I got a 'thank you for your service' and a very nice severance payment." She shrugged. "I tried to look at it as an opportunity to perhaps get a better job, something a little different but yet the same." She shook her head. "The job market is very competitive in Austin and my skillset is not that specialized.

There was no better job, I found out. That was depressing to realize." She paused to take a swallow of her tea. "Long story short, I couldn't afford the rent at my apartment any longer and my lease is up at the end of January. My parents made me an offer I couldn't turn down. At least on a trial-run basis. After the holidays, I'll have to decide if this is something I want to do long-term."

"I guess I don't have to tell you how excited your mother is that you're here."

"I know. And really, it's good to be here. I missed them. With Mark living here with them, I felt like I was missing out on family time."

"Yet you never came to visit."

"Are you trying to make me feel guilty? Because it's working."

"No, no. Just a statement. I know how far away we are up here. It's not like you can hop on a plane to get here."

"I know, but that's an excuse. I should have made the time. But when you've got a busy life—and I certainly did—it's hard to squeeze in a week when it takes a whole freakin' day to drive out here," she finished with a laugh.

Kyler stared. Lexie's laughter had transformed her face from serious to playful in a split second. Oh, she could see why Crazy Cathy was obsessed with her. She was beyond pretty. Smooth, fresh skin. The tiniest bit of makeup. Eyes that were bright and alive.

"Green or blue?" she found herself asking.

"Excuse me?"

"Your eyes."

"Oh. In between, I guess. Mostly greenish. If I wear something that is blue, then they change."

"Mark has brown eyes."

"Yes. My dad's eyes are hazel. His mother has blue eyes and his dad green."

"Are they still alive? Your grandparents?"

"Yes. Both sides. And both live in Florida. My dad's parents moved first. They bought a condo after they retired and love it there. My mom's parents then bought a place just a few blocks from them—walking distance." She smiled, a sweet smile that showed her affection for her grandparents. "They've been best friends forever. My mom and dad have known each other their whole lives."

"Do you see them much?"

Lexie laughed and embarrassment showed on her face. "Okay, yes. You *can* hop on a plane to Tampa. At least once a year. Sometimes twice."

"So you like the beach?" She raised an eyebrow. "Bikini?"

Lexie blushed. "Oh, no, you're not."

"Picturing you in a bikini?" Kyler was sure she must be blushing too. "Of course not. You're Mark's sister. I would never do that." She shoved her plate away. "Lunch for tomorrow."

"I agree. There's no way I could eat this whole thing."

Kyler turned, finding Ana watching. She held up two fingers and Ana nodded, quickly bringing over two white Styrofoam containers.

"Delicious lunch, Ana. Thank you."

"My pleasure." She turned to Lexie. "You enjoyed? Yes?"

"Oh, yes. Very good. I'll definitely be back."

"Good! You come back."

Kyler took a couple of bills from her pocket—a twenty and a ten—and handed them to Ana. "Keep the change."

"Always so generous, Kyler. See you next time."

"Thanks."

They went out into the sunshine, the wind making it feel cooler than it was. "Cold front coming tonight. Feels like it may already be here. I think the winds have shifted."

"That's what Mom said. Twenties in the morning?"

Kyler opened the Jeep door for her. "Yeah, but it'll warm up. Back into the sixties in a couple of days."

When she got behind the wheel, Lexie touched her arm lightly. "Thanks for lunch. I certainly didn't expect you to pay for it, though."

Kyler smiled at her before starting the Jeep. "You have a bike to pay for. I don't."

CHAPTER SEVENTEEN

Lexie felt like a kid at Christmas as she rode around the lodge's parking lot on her new mountain bike. Well, new to her. But really, had they not told her it was used, she wouldn't have known. It was all shiny and clean and way more expensive than she thought a used bike should be. Kyler had assured her it was a good price, and judging by how much the new ones were, she finally conceded.

It was her first time to ride a mountain bike and she wanted to get familiar with it before taking it on the park road. Back when Mark and Mia rode, she would sometimes join them, but they all had road bikes. After the accident, she'd gotten rid of her bike almost as quickly as Mark had. Since then, her time spent on a bike was at the gym on their NordicTrack or sweating it out in an hour-long spin class.

But this? Oh, what freedom! She buzzed around the office to the back, a smile—a grin—on her face. Surrounded by the fragrant smells of the junipers, the deep blue sky, the cool breeze…and yes, the sounds of birds as they flitted in and out of the bird garden, all made her senses come alive. This was so not a gym class. She stopped near the bird garden, making a mental note to ask Kyler what those huge doves were. She took a deep breath of the cool air, looking around her, seeing the trail that went up the hill to Mark's cabin.

Austin was littered with greenbelts and hike and bike trails. Why had she never considered getting a mountain bike before? Because she did her exercising in a gym, not out of it. She ran on a treadmill, not on the streets or a hike and bike trail. This was going to be so much better.

That thought made her pause. Was it going to be better? She could be out of her little apartment door and into the woods in a matter of seconds. Kyler had said the hiking trail that started at the picnic area on Limpia Creek was suitable for bikes. And the picnic area was right down the road from the restaurant.

She spun around and peddled over to her apartment, then wheeled the bike inside. She took off her helmet and strapped it to the handlebars. Yes, this was just what she needed. She wished she could go out right now, but it was already late afternoon. She didn't think she'd get very far before twilight approached. Besides, she wasn't familiar with the park. Kyler went back to work tomorrow but told her she usually finished at three each day. Lexie was to call her if she wanted to ride one afternoon. Probably not tomorrow, though. The temps wouldn't get out of the forties, or so Kyler had said. Back into the upper sixties by Thursday. That was the day she was shooting for. If she could wait that long. For some reason, she was itching to get out on the trails.

She was here to work, she reminded herself as she walked down the hallway to the office. Her mother was at the desk, flipping through a magazine, the ever-present cup of coffee sitting within reach.

"You're back already?"

"Already? It's after four." She sat down across from her. "Did I miss anything exciting?"

Her mother smiled at her. "Well, if you call Mrs. Barry getting locked in her bathroom exciting, then yes."

"Really? What happened?"

"Should have been a comedy show. Her husband drove into Ft. Davis for gas. They're heading out early in the morning, so they're going to do their checkout today. Anyway, she was taking a shower. Thank goodness she had her phone in there with her."

"So she's locked inside. Let me guess. No clothes. Dad goes to let her out."

Her mother laughed. "Oh, yes. I went along too. I'm so glad I did. It was hysterical." She laughed again. "Mrs. Barry isn't a small woman. Our towels aren't exactly extra-large. You can imagine the scene."

Lexie found herself laughing along with her mother. "What did Dad do?"

"He nearly knocked me over in his haste to get out of there. He had no idea how the lock jammed. He'll look at it tomorrow after they leave." She fanned herself. "Oh, Lexie. The look on both their faces! It was so funny. Mrs. Barry was tiptoeing around, trying to keep the little towel over her and she's right there in front of the mirror! There was no hiding for her, poor thing!"

"That is funny. And I'm *so* glad I wasn't here."

"Yes. Be thankful." She took her coffee cup to the small sink and rinsed it out. "Now tell me about your trip. You got a bike?"

"I did. We had lunch too."

"Oh?" Her mother nodded. "Kyler is so sweet, isn't she? She'll do anything for you."

"Yes, she is. We had Mexican food."

"In Alpine?"

"No, here in Ft. Davis. Ana's."

"Oh, yes. I've been there. She makes everything right there in the kitchen. So good."

"Ft. Davis is a cute little town."

"Did Kyler show you around?"

"She pointed out the grocery store—Potters. And a hardware store."

Her mother nodded. "Gilmore's Farm and Ranch. I love going in there. Both the Gilmores and Potters have been living in this area for generations and both their stores have served the area for decades on end. The Gilmores have had that store for nearly a hundred years. You should go in sometimes, just to walk around. So much history there."

"Yes, Kyler said the place was full of old photos."

Her mother sat down again. "So, when is she taking you out on your new bike?"

"Maybe Thursday afternoon, if it's warmer. She gets off work around three, she said."

"Well, you go whenever you need to. Don't worry about the office. I've got a handle on it."

"Mom, I came here to learn the ropes, remember? Not take a vacation."

"Who says it can't be both? Honey, I want you to be comfortable up here. And what better way than to have a friend, someone you can do stuff with. I know how active you were in Austin. I know you left a lot of friends behind. I don't want you to feel like you're so isolated here. Kyler—"

"Kyler is very nice, but I don't want to use her for my entertainment purposes. We're becoming friends. She's really easy to talk to."

"I think the reason it took her a while to adjust was because she didn't have anyone. She and Mark are good friends, but Mark doesn't do a lot of the things she likes."

"Like ride? Hike?" She smiled at her mother. "I don't do those either."

"You bought a bike."

"Yes. To take the place of gym class. Actually, I rode it around the parking lot. I think I'm going to love it. I can't wait to take it out."

"After this little cold front, I think we have a few days of warmer weather. You should take advantage of it. There's a big front coming after that and it'll stay cold for several days."

"Does it rain much, Mom?"

"No. We're very dry. Arid. Our rainy season is June through August and even then, if we get an inch or more, it's considered a major event," she said with a laugh. "We usually get snow every winter. Not much. A dusting a few times. Just enough to make it all wintery for a day or two." She pointed at the laptop. "Want to learn payroll? Friday is payday for the staff."

"Sure. Let's get to work."

CHAPTER EIGHTEEN

Kyler watched as Lexie pulled her hair into a ponytail before strapping on her helmet. The strands closest to her face weren't long enough to be contained and she tucked them behind her ears. Lexie turned, meeting her gaze, and Kyler looked away quickly.

"Ready?"

Lexie nodded. "Anxious."

"Why anxious?"

She'd brought her own bike over on her Jeep, so they headed out between the lodge and the restaurant, taking the road back into the state park.

"It's a bit different than a stationary bike. Or a road bike."

"Better than a road bike. Fat tires." She lifted her hands from the handlebars. "Better balance."

"Show off."

Kyler laughed, then slowed, letting Lexie come up beside her. "How about we stay on the road. I'll take you through some of the park. On the way back, we'll hit a trail and see if you're comfortable."

"Okay. Deal." She pointed to the No Entry Without Permit sign. "Is that directed at guests from the lodge?"

"Mostly. Your mom has a sign at the front desk letting people know that they have to go around to the park headquarters for entry permits. Occasionally we'll find someone cruising the park without one but not too often. I mean, it's only six bucks a person for day use."

"So how does one get into being a park ranger?"

"You mean what was my motivation?"

"Yes. Lifelong dream?"

Kyler shook her head. "Not even close. My parents aren't really the outdoorsy types. I'd never stepped foot in a state park before, actually."

"Then why?"

"I was taking a lot of biology classes and stuff. I was planning for medical school."

"Really? A doctor?" Lexie smiled. "I don't see it."

"I know. My parents pushed me in that direction, and I didn't have a clue as to what I really wanted to do. I went to college in Corpus—Texas A&M. After the first year—and talking to people—I knew the medical field wasn't for me. I switched to environmental science with a plan to get my master's in marine biology." She pointed to her left. "There's the picnic area. The creek flows through it. There's a little bridge—'cause it's a little creek—that goes to the other side. The trail is over there. We'll come out that way later."

Lexie nodded. "Go on. Marine biology."

"Oh. Well, living in Corpus, being at the coast, marine biology was a popular degree. Then one of my buddies told me about the park service. I began researching it and actually started going to some state parks. I was twenty, I think, when I went on my first camping trip." She smiled. "Fell in love with it. Pretty much every weekend after that I was out at some park or other. Anyway, my grades were good, so I was able to get into their Fast Track program."

"That's where you take graduate courses while you're still an undergrad?"

"Yeah. And they count toward both. I took full loads during the summers, so I got both my undergrad and master's degrees in four years plus one semester."

"And you were exhausted!"

Kyler laughed. "I was. So much so that I took four months off before I got a job."

"You hung out on the beach?"

"I did. And I got to know the superintendent at Goose Island and that's where I landed my first job."

"And the boss's wife?"

"Mustang Island. Port Aransas. Hindsight at the time had me kicking myself for ever leaving Goose Island in the first place, but Mustang Island is like thirty minutes from Corpus. That was the draw for me." She pointed to a road to their left. "That will take you to the amphitheater. It's built right into the rocks. Really cool."

"And what do you do there?"

"In the summer, we'll do slideshows at night. Showing the different animals in the park, stuff like that. It's also where we meet for ranger-led hikes. And we do stuff for kids there. And when I get a little better, I'll start leading birdwatching tours." She laughed at that. "There's a lady from town who leads them now, but I'm a little—okay, a lot—intimidated by her. She can hear a bird flying over or in the trees and say, 'Oh, that's a MacGillivray's warbler, probably a juvenile,' and I feel really stupid because I couldn't ID the bird even by sight, much less sound."

"And I'd guess she probably has years and years more experience than you do."

"Oh, sure. I know. And I've gotten better. I have. I know pretty much all the resident birds by sound now. Even those that stay the winter. Spring and fall are the hardest when the migrants come through. I'm usually lost and stay off the trails when real birders are around."

She slowed as they approached the first cluster of campsites. "There's one of the birding blinds that I keep up. We have three in the park."

"So Mom's bird garden—you modeled it after these?"

"Yeah. Pretty much the same. Lots of feeders and running water. Cottonwood Creek only has water for a month or two a year and that's on a good year. Limpia Creek usually has some water all year long—it's spring-fed—but during the dry months, it's no more than a trickle."

She pulled into the parking lot and stopped. "Do you want to take a look? See what's about?"

"Sure."

They leaned their bikes against a tree, and she moved slowly toward the blind. There were four cutouts for viewing and a larger one for those who liked to set up tripods for their cameras.

"What's that white stuff smeared on that one feeder?"

"Oh, that's suet. We buy it in a big tub, but they sell it in smaller cakes."

"What is suet?"

"It's mostly fat and they put birdseed and cracked corn in there. Some will have fruit. I'll put the stuff out with fruit in the spring to catch the orioles that come through."

"Oh, what's that blue bird?" Lexie asked quietly.

"That's a scrub jay. They're kinda bossy. We also have Steller's jays here. They're a brilliant blue with a black crest."

Lexie's eyes widened. "Steller's jay? Are they mean?"

"Mean? No. A little bossy with the little birds but not mean. Why?"

"I read a book where a Steller's jay was—well, he wasn't really a bird, I guess. He was a spirit that took over the bird. And he controlled this serial killer and there was a psychic—" She shook her head. "Never mind. But if we see one, point him out to me."

"Okay, sure. They're pretty." There were the normal house finches clustered on the tray feeder and four doves were on the ground. "Those are white-winged doves."

"I've seen them before. I was going to ask what they were."

"Collared doves are big like them, but they have this black neck ring," she said, making a circle around Lexie's neck. "And no white on the wings. They're usually here too."

Lexie smiled at her. "You don't give yourself enough credit, I think. You seem pretty well versed to me."

"That's because you don't know any real birders. Come on. I'll take you through part of the campground, then we'll hit the trail."

* * *

Lexie wasn't as nervous as she thought she'd be as she followed Kyler from the pavement onto the hiking trail. As Kyler had said, riding through the park got her accustomed to—and a little more familiar with—her new bike. However, it didn't take long for the nice, easy path to turn rocky.

"It narrows up here," Kyler called over her shoulder. Lexie felt her hands tighten their grip and she slowed as she approached the curve, which nearly caused her to fall when she hit a rock the size of a softball. She sped up again, her eyes watching the trail and not the scenery that buzzed by.

"Down there is the biggest canyon in the park. This is the best view of it."

"I'll have to take your word for it, lest I fall into said canyon," she managed as she never took her eyes from the trail.

Kyler laughed. "I'd rescue you, of course."

"I would hope so."

"There's a little overlook. We'll stop."

Half a minute later, Kyler slowed and pulled to the left. Lexie braked a bit too suddenly and nearly threw herself into a juniper. She rested both feet on the ground, trying to catch her breath.

"Fun?"

"I think I'm too scared for it to be fun."

Kyler took her helmet off and ran a hand through her hair. Lexie found herself watching, noting her tanned complexion, her outdoorsy look. Her cheeks were flushed with color, her forehead damp with sweat, her hair tangled. Kyler looked at her, capturing her gaze for a second before Lexie looked away.

"You're in good shape. Strong. You'll pick this up in no time."

"I hope you're right." Lexie looked past her, enjoying the view across the rocky and nearly barren canyon. "Are there other trails suitable for bikes?"

"Here around the campground area, this is the only one that bikes are allowed on, other than a really short one over by the tent area. Now, across the road—the main road that you drove up here on—there are two trails there. If you take the loop, it's a good ten miles in and back. Great views. Nice little canyons where Limpia Creek flows."

"You ride there?"

"I do. It's steep and challenging."

Lexie followed her to a smooth ledge that had a log fence barrier. "Oh, that's pretty. That's the creek?"

"Yeah. Hard to believe that little creek carved this out." She touched Lexie's arm. "Look. Deer. He doesn't think we can see him."

The buck was behind a small shrub of some kind, his ears twitching as he watched them. Lexie relaxed, breathing deeply of the fresh air. The only sound was that of the wind as it passed through the junipers. She absorbed the quiet, smiling as she took her gaze from the deer and back to the canyon. Yes. Quiet. Peaceful. She turned, feeling Kyler watching her. She widened her smile. "I love it."

She realized that statement could pertain to a lot of different things. The trail. The bike ride. The deer. The view. But Kyler simply nodded, not needing an explanation apparently. Her declaration of loving it surprised her, though. She'd had her doubts that she would find anything about this remote area attractive, much less find something she could love about it.

"You ready to head out? If we linger too long, dusk will catch us."

She nodded. "Yes." Then she paused. "Thank you, Kyler. For the tour, for…for making me feel welcome here."

"My pleasure. Thank you for riding with me. It's always more fun with company."

Whether for her benefit or not, Kyler seemed to slow her pace a little and Lexie had no problems keeping up. All too soon she saw the picnic tables and knew their off-road trek was nearly finished. The trail took them to a little bridge that crossed the creek and in a blink of an eye, they were back on pavement, heading to the lodge.

As Kyler was lifting her bike onto the rack that covered the spare tire, Lexie took in her attire. Not colorful, skintight, curve-hugging spandex but a looser version, black and comfortable looking. She had no such option and she'd worn a pair of her exercise tights under sweatpants.

"What kind of biking pants are those?"

"Yeah, these are almost too hot for today's weather. They're windproof, fleece-lined." She pulled the elastic waistband down, showing her. "Very comfortable, though. I've got another pair that are windproof only, not lined. I should have worn them today. The wind is not that bad and it was what? Fifty degrees?"

"I'm plenty warm enough too, but if I plan to ride, I should really get the proper clothing," she said, pointing at her dark gray sweats.

"I got these online. There's tons of choices so don't drive yourself crazy shopping." Kyler leaned an arm across the spare tire. "I'm heading over to the bar for a beer. Want to come?"

Lexie tilted her head slightly. "I usually have a green smoothie or a protein shake after a workout." Then she smiled, remembering her mother's words—find something to replace what she was used to. "A beer does sound good. Should we change or…"

"No, we're fine. We'll just walk over."

She quickly put her bike inside her apartment, leaving Kyler standing outside. She locked the door, then stuck her head inside the office.

"Mom? I'm back. We're heading over to see Mark."

Her mother came down the hallway, smiling. "Fun? No mishaps?"

"Yes, it was great fun. And as a bonus, I didn't fall, not even once."

"Good for you." Her mother turned her gaze to Kyler. "I'm making a big pan of lasagna on Saturday. Come for dinner?"

Kyler nodded with a smile. "I'll never turn down your lasagna, Susan. Thanks."

Her mother then looked at her. "I'm actually making a new recipe. A vegetarian one. How is it I didn't know that you don't eat meat?"

Lexie shrugged. "I guess because we only saw each other a couple of weeks each year. Our phone calls really didn't revolve around food. And I do eat chicken occasionally. But Mom, you should make the one that everyone likes. I can pick around what I don't eat."

"Yes, I know. You've been picking around nearly every meal I've served you. So I want to make something that you can eat too." She waved them away. "Go see Mark. Tell him about dinner on Saturday."

"That was nice of her," Kyler commented as they walked around the lodge.

"Yeah, but I'm sorry I ruined dinner for you." It was nearly dark, but she noticed that Kyler checked out the bird garden as they went past it. "Anything still there?"

Kyler smiled a bit sheepishly. "Habit."

Lexie bumped her shoulder with her own. "Don't apologize."

The lights on the back side of the lodge were plenty for them to see by. The crunching of their footsteps was the only sound as they crossed the rocks on the trail before hitting the restaurant's parking lot. There were five or six vehicles and she saw Mark through the window, chatting with someone at a table. The Christmas lights were blinking in every window, and behind Mark, she saw the tree, lit up as well. It made for a pretty scene.

"The decorations look nice," Kyler commented, as if reading her thoughts. "I don't think he had this many last year."

"I think I put up every light he had."

Kyler held the door open for her and she nodded her thanks as she went inside. She could sense everyone turning to stare at them. A few called greetings to Kyler and Kyler returned them. They sat at the bar—the same stools they'd used the other morning. Their eyes met in the mirror that hung behind the bar. Kyler smiled first and Lexie matched it.

She couldn't believe how quickly—and easily—she had made friends with Kyler. She had envisioned herself leading a lonely, solitary life up here, with only Mark and her parents for company. Yet, here she was, about to share a beer—and perhaps dinner— with a very pretty woman. She raised an eyebrow as their eyes still held. Could she call Kyler pretty? She was a bit too outdoorsy for that. Cute, attractive, certainly. But "pretty" conjured up a more feminine image and—

"What?"

She turned, meeting Kyler's gaze close up instead of in the mirror. She smiled again. "I like you. And you're attractive." The words were out before she realized how they sounded, but she couldn't take them back.

One eyebrow arched at her. "Are you flirting with me?"

"God, no!"

"Are you sure?"

"Of course I'm sure! I don't care what you look like one way or the other. I told you, I'm not interested in anything like that."

"Okay." Then she smiled. "Sure seemed like you were flirting, though."

"I was not!" she hissed as quietly as she could when Mark came over.

"So how was the bike ride?" he asked as he pulled two mugs from the freezer.

Lexie playfully kicked Kyler's leg, hoping to get in the last word on *that* subject.

CHAPTER NINETEEN

Kyler paused at the back door, seeing her reflection in the glass. She was glad she'd gone back inside her cabin to change, but it put her behind and now she was running late. For some reason, instead of wearing a regular pair of jeans, she'd put on her best pair—black ones. And instead of a T-shirt with a sweatshirt over the top, she put on a real shirt—buttons and collar and she'd even ironed it. And she'd even put on a sweater—a charcoal gray one. She looked nice. And then she panicked. Why in the world was she dressing that way? Mark would notice. Probably Susan too. She in no way wanted them to think that it had anything to do with wanting to look nice for Lexie. Because it did not. So she'd quickly changed and now she looked like she always did. Only it wasn't a plain old blue sweatshirt. No, she'd opted for one with the park's logo.

With a sigh, she went inside the back door. So she liked the woman. What wasn't to like? She was cute. She had an easy smile and she used it frequently. She was normal. No pet pigs. Kyler smiled a bit as she headed up the stairs. She was *cute* and she liked to bike. They seemed to have things in common. She paused at the door. Lexie wasn't her type, though, was she? No, she wasn't. None of that mattered. She and Lexie were becoming friends, which is what they'd agreed upon. So it didn't matter what she looked like. Wasn't that what Lexie had said of her? Friends. Lexie wanted to be friends. Nothing more.

She took a quick, deep breath, then knocked on the door. She heard a "come on in, Kyler" and she opened it. She absently looked around, her gaze settling on Lexie, finding her staring back. The smile she was getting used to was there and Lexie beckoned her over.

"You're late."

"Yeah, sorry."

"Toilet again?" Mark asked.

"No. With that front coming, we had some pipes to tend to. Out by the corrals."

"They say we'll be in the low teens tomorrow night," Susan said. "What would you like to drink? Cocktail?"

"I can get it, Susan."

"Sit down and visit. I'll fix it up. I'm fixing one for Dale too."

"You have corrals?" Lexie asked, patting the cushion beside her.

"Yeah. People bring their horses up here to ride." She sat down, taking care to leave a safe distance between them. "That trail I was telling you about across the road, that's a horse trail too. They've got a camping area up by the creek for those who want to stay overnight out there."

She could tell Mark was grinning at her and she finally looked his way. He smiled more broadly but said nothing. He didn't have to. She knew what he was thinking.

"You guys made your bike ride sound like such fun, it made me want to join you."

"Why don't you?" Lexie leaned forward to look at him. "It's nothing like being on the road in Austin."

He shrugged. "I don't know. I'll think about it."

"You should," Kyler said. "Get you out of the bar for some exercise. You keep eating that food, you're going to get fat."

"Yeah, but I hear my sister is going to overhaul the menu."

Kyler turned to Lexie. "Are you? Do I get any input?"

Lexie smiled sweetly at her. "Want fish on the menu?"

"If you could swing fish *and* shrimp, that would be super."

"You don't ask for much, do you? We're like a thousand miles from fish and shrimp."

Kyler grinned. "I'll make it worth your while."

Lexie met her gaze, still smiling. "Dare I ask what I'd get out of that deal?"

Kyler leaned closer. "I'll let you play with my telescope." She lowered her voice. "Stars at night—incredible. I'll give you a tour of the planets."

Mark cleared his throat. "Really? You're going to flirt with my sister right in front of me."

Kyler leaned back, away from Lexie. "I wasn't flirting with her. Just offering my services."

"Who's flirting with who?" Susan asked as she handed Kyler her drink. "You two?"

"No!" they said in unison.

"Yeah, they were."

"How sweet!"

"Mom…no. We were not. We were just…kidding around." Lexie looked at Kyler. "You know that, right? I was just—"

"Yeah, of course. I know. Me, too. God, I told you. Us? No way. You're not my type." She turned to Mark and tried to glare at him, but he was still smiling. When she looked back at Lexie, those green eyes—yes, green, not blue tonight—met hers. The eyes seemed to be smiling, much as her lips were. What did it mean? She returned the smile. At that moment, she didn't care what it meant. She only knew it made her feel good. Inside. Way down deep inside, Lexie's smile made her feel good. She didn't remember the last time someone's smile made her stomach roll quite like it was.

Oh god no.

She looked away, staring at the wall, letting that thought settle. Feel good? Inside? No. No, no, no. Lexie wasn't her type. She was too much like Britney and she didn't want to *ever* be attracted to someone like Britney again.

Dale came in, rubbing his hands together. "Front just blew in. The wind is vicious tonight."

The spell was broken, thankfully. When she glanced at Lexie, she was looking at her mother. The conversation turned to the weather and Kyler relaxed, leaning back against the sofa, feeling at home here with these people. Lexie went to help her mother and she and Mark chatted with Dale. Dinner was over all too soon, with Susan's new lasagna recipe getting praise from all of them.

The evening didn't end then, though. Mark was the one to suggest a card game. Dale bowed out, choosing to relax by the TV instead. The four of them settled on a game of Spades with she and Mark being partners. They beat Susan and Lexie three games straight and between the laughter and accusations of cheating, they played a fourth game. Susan and Lexie were finally victorious.

"See. You finally had to play without cheating and we beat your ass!" Lexie teased.

"We *let* you win," Mark countered. "All that bitching and moaning you two were doing. Geez."

Kyler wasn't sure whose side to take in that fight, so she kept quiet. Susan smiled at her across the table.

"It's so nice to have everyone together. We used to play cards all the time when they were still living at home."

"And he cheated then too!"

Mark laughed. "You just hate to admit that I'm better than you. Tell her, Ky."

Kyler held her hands up. "Nope. Keep me out of it." She pushed away from the table. "I should get going anyway. Susan, can I help in the kitchen?"

"I think that's what I'm here for." Lexie put the cards up. "Fun night."

"Yes, it was."

"Are we doing football tomorrow?" Mark asked.

"Yeah, but inside by the fireplace, not on the deck." She stood up. "I'll need to run by Potters. Anyone have a preference for snacks?"

"I'm actually bringing something." Lexie wiggled her eyebrows. "Cauliflower buffalo wings."

Mark groaned.

"Sounds...awful," Kyler admitted.

Lexie didn't seem offended. "They're delicious. And I'm making a spicy tofu ranch sauce for dipping. You'll love it."

"Where in the world did you find tofu?" she asked.

"Amazon is my friend. Two-day delivery. When I went down to Potters, the girl there didn't even know what tofu was. I mean, who doesn't know what tofu is?"

Mark put his arm around Kyler's shoulders and squeezed. "Kyler here has never eaten tofu before. This ought to be interesting."

Lexie shook her head. "A ranch dipping sauce is not really *eating* tofu. I promise, you won't be able to tell that it's not dairy." She walked closer to them, smiling in what Kyler swore was a flirty manner. "Now, if you want to lend me your kitchen, I'll be happy to make a dish with tofu for you. Expand your palate some. I'm not a great cook, but I do a pretty mean tofu stir-fry with lots of veggies and spice."

"Of course. You can use my kitchen whenever you want."

Mark laughed and squeezed her shoulder one more time. "I give it two weeks."

Kyler frowned. "Two weeks for what?"

"Before you're sleeping together."

Lexie gasped and Kyler felt her face turn beet red. Susan laughed from the kitchen and she even heard Dale chuckle behind them.

"You're out of your mind," Lexie said. "First of all, we hardly know each other. Secondly, she's your best friend. That would be... be weird." Lexie took a step away from them. "Besides, after Crazy Cathy, I'm taking a break. A long break." She looked at Kyler. "No offense."

"I don't want to sleep with you either." Was that a lie? She punched Mark in the arm. "Troublemaker." She turned her attention to Susan. "Thank you again for dinner, Susan. It was delicious."

"You're always welcome, Kyler." Susan winked at her and Kyler found herself smiling.

"Goodnight, everyone." She glanced at Mark. "See you about noon." Then to Lexie. "Can't wait to taste your cauliflower and tofu stuff."

Lexie smiled at her too. "You're going to love it."

"That remains to be seen, but I'll try anything once." She looked again at Mark. "I'll get something fattening and unhealthy at Potters for us."

"Get some of their frozen pizzas. And some chips."

She held her hand up as she went out the door. "See you tomorrow."

She went down the stairs, still smiling. Cauliflower buffalo wings? What in the hell was that going to taste like? Didn't matter. She was looking forward to the day. She always enjoyed their Sunday outings, but since Lexie had started joining them, it was a little more fun than usual.

Thoughts of Sunday football were blown away as soon as she stepped outside. The wind was brutal, and she was glad she had on the thick sweatshirt instead of the sweater. She pulled on her jacket before getting inside the Jeep. It was as cold on the inside as out and she turned the heat on full blast, then closed the vents as near arctic air blew on her. She shivered all the way home, not even the image of Lexie's flirty smile being able to warm her.

Well, it did a little, she conceded as she pulled into her driveway.

CHAPTER TWENTY

"Oh, that was so pass interference!"

Kyler shook her head. "My guy barely touched him."

"He practically mauled him!"

Kyler's mouth twitched as she tried to contain her smile. She apparently gave up. "You're right. He mauled him. Shame the ref didn't see it. Would have been a first down too. Instead, you have to punt."

"Don't count your money just yet, honey. We have the whole second half to go."

"I had no idea you liked football this much," Mark said as he handed her another beer. "I guess Dad's love of the game wore off on you."

"I guess. I will admit, I'm a bit of a rabid Cowboys fan. And this one," she said, pointing at Kyler, "has the audacity to root for the Packers."

Mark and Kyler exchanged glances, then they both laughed. Lexie narrowed her eyes. "What?"

"You're so bad," Mark told Kyler. "How are you pulling that off?"

"What are you talking about?" Lexie demanded.

"Lift up your sweatshirt."

"I will not," Kyler said, but the smile was still on her face. "So, how are those cauliflower things coming along. I'm starving."

"They're in the oven." She looked at her watch. "Four more minutes. What about your pizza?"

"Yeah, it needs to go in pretty soon."

When Kyler got up to add a log to the fire, Lexie grabbed the bottom of her sweatshirt and yanked it up. Her eyes widened in surprise as she saw a dark blue T-shirt with the star on the front.

"You are so busted!"

Kyler laughed. "Hey, you bet me ten bucks. The Packers are picked to win by seven. It was a no-brainer."

"You have a freakin' Cowboys shirt on!"

"Yeah. Diehard fan."

Lexie threw up her hands. "You're insane. A true Cowboys fan would *never* do that."

"Hey, ten bucks is ten bucks."

Lexie shook her head. "You're amazing."

"Oh, thank you. I think you're pretty amazing too."

Mark laughed as Lexie stuck her tongue out at Kyler. "I'm going to go check on my cauliflower."

"Put the pizza in the oven," Kyler called after her.

"Rooting for the Packers," she muttered under her breath. But she was smiling as she pulled the cauliflower wings from the oven. What fun the first half had been. Kyler was like a breath of fresh air, wasn't she?

She paused, thinking back to the handful of football parties she'd attended. Most of her friends weren't fans of the game or if they were it was only casual. Some of her workout buddies from the gym enjoyed football and that's where she'd normally go if there was a big game on. She'd usually find herself in front of the TV with the husbands as the girls hung out in the kitchen drinking wine. More often than not, she spent Sundays alone during the season.

Then there was Cathy. She hated football. Cathy hated sports, period. She flicked her eyes to the ceiling and shook her head. What in the world had she *ever* seen in Cathy? Yes, she was attractive. And charming, at least at the beginning. But what drew her? They had nothing in common. She'd known that after the first few weeks of dating. Why had she let it go on?

Loneliness? Boredom? Or was it that she'd been approaching twenty-eight years of age—which was damn close to thirty—and she'd heard the whisperings of her friends? Lexie must be difficult, why else would she *still* be single. Lexie must be horrible in bed—they never stick around. Lexie apparently is hard to get along with, she can't seem to keep a girlfriend for longer than a few months. Or her favorite—Lexie is just *too* picky.

Why was it considered "picky" when she knew it wasn't what she wanted? Was it so bad wanting to wait for that perfect someone who would sweep her off her feet? Someone she would fall madly in love with? She knew now—like she'd most likely known then—that twenty-eight was way too young to settle for less than what she wanted, settle for something that wasn't great, but good enough. Because, as it turned out, it wasn't good enough. Not by a long shot.

"Hey."

She turned her head, finding Kyler leaning against the breakfast bar. Warm brown eyes looked back at her, one eyebrow cocked questioningly. She answered the unspoken question honestly.

"Lost in thought. Thinking back to other football Sundays."

"Ah. More fun than this, huh?"

Lexie smiled at her. "Quite the opposite, actually." She motioned to the container of buffalo sauce. "Come help."

Kyler did as she asked, opening the lid and taking a sniff. "Oh, yeah. That'll open up the sinuses."

"It's a secret concoction so don't ask for the recipe."

Kyler peered over her shoulder. "So those are cauliflower wings. Looks interesting."

She elbowed her playfully. "You're going to love them. Drizzle some of that sauce on them. Then ten more minutes in the oven."

"What kind of batter is that?"

"It's a buttermilk batter. I normally use soy milk, but Potters was not accommodating."

"Had to use the real thing then?" Kyler teased as she spooned buffalo sauce. "How liberally?"

"A little more than that."

As Kyler finished the wings, Lexie took one of the frozen pizzas from the freezer. "Or do you want both of them?"

"We'll start with one. Because these things do look kinda good."
As Lexie absently opened the box and took out the pizza, she
watched Kyler meticulously coat each wing with sauce.

"Diehard fan? Really?"

"Yep." Kyler paused. "Well, I wasn't really into football growing
up. My dad was only a casual fan of the game. When I went to
college, I started watching college games. Loved it. A couple of
the guys I hung out with were from Dallas and got me hooked.
Sundays during football season were the highlight of each week."
She grinned. "I never used to drink beer until I met those guys."

"Hey...second half is about to start," Mark called from the
living room.

Kyler glanced at her and winked. "I hope I lose the ten bucks."

Lexie laughed. "Me too."

CHAPTER TWENTY-ONE

"I had so much fun." Lexie hugged Mark and kissed his cheek. "Thank you for including me."

"It was fun. And your cauliflower things were good. Not as good as chicken wings, mind you, but pretty good."

"Yeah, they were just okay," Kyler added as she put on her coat.

Lexie laughed. "Right. You ate like twelve of them." She pointed at Mark. "So did you!"

"Come on, I'll give you a lift down the hill," Kyler offered. She picked up the bag that Lexie had put by the door. "Not that it'll be warm, but it'll save you from fighting the wind."

"When will it warm up again?"

"Tuesday. In the fifties."

"Bike ride?"

Kyler nodded without hesitation. "Sure. I'll swing down after I get off work." She glanced back at Mark, trying to ignore his exaggerated smile. "See you tomorrow."

"Goodnight, girls."

The wind blew against them as they walked off the deck. With heads down, they hurried to the Jeep. The seats felt like ice and Kyler turned the heat to high.

"Sorry, but by the time I get you home, it'll still be freezing in here."

"Still beats walking." Lexie pulled gloves on, then flipped the collar up around her ears. "I need one of those caps."

Kyler adjusted her knit hat lower on her ears. "Yes. They come in handy." She pointed at the console as she drove off. "Already eighteen. Gonna be frigid in the morning."

"You don't have to work, do you?"

"No. I'm off."

"Do you have a fireplace?"

"I do. It's very small. I have a propane heater, though, that keeps the cabin pretty warm." A few turns down the bumpy road had them at the lodge and she pulled in beside Lexie's car. "Here you go."

Lexie lifted her hand to open the door, then paused. A long second, two. Maybe longer as the wind beat against the Jeep. Kyler thought that perhaps she was studying her. What for, she didn't know.

"Thank you, Kyler. As I said earlier, it was a fun day."

"Yes, it was."

Lexie again seemed to hesitate, then she surprised her by leaning across the console and giving her a quick hug. "Bike ride on Tuesday?"

"You got it."

Kyler waited until Lexie went inside her apartment before pulling away. She was smiling and she felt like humming. All from a tiny, brief, one-armed hug. What in the world was wrong with her?

By the time she wound her way through the park and onto the little road that would take her home, the Jeep finally showed signs of warming. She parked beside her cabin and hurried to her door, her head ducked against the onslaught of wind. She closed the door and leaned against it, the quiet pronounced in the dark, the wind relegated to the background.

She plugged the Christmas tree lights in, watching the colors twinkle for a moment before going to the corner where the propane heater was. She turned the flame up, then held her hands out to it, warming them.

Yeah, it had been a good day. Not to say that she didn't always enjoy Sundays with Mark. But it was different with Lexie there. A little more fun, a little more laughter. It was certainly more fun watching football with Lexie. She knew the game and she had a team. It just so happened to be *her* team too. Mark was too laid back to care much about who was winning or losing. It was simply an excuse to get together and drink a few beers and splurge on wings and pizza and the like.

"And cauliflower wings," she said with a shake of her head. They were damn good. And spicy enough to make her eyes water. And yeah, she'd eaten twelve or more, dunking them in the tofu ranch sauce that—as Lexie had predicted—she couldn't tell wasn't *real* ranch dressing.

She turned her back to the heater, now facing the tree. There was something about staring at the lights of a Christmas tree that made her feel peaceful. It was quiet inside. Still. The room dark. And warm. Her gaze slid to the empty sofa. She could see Lexie sitting there, smiling or laughing at something she'd said. Lexie would—

"God, what is *wrong* with you?" she muttered.

She moved away from the heater and turned on some lights, chasing Lexie away. Did she have a crush on her or something? No. She was thirty-one years old. *That's too old to have a crush.* So she ate cauliflower wings dipped into tofu sauce? She would have tried that for any other friend, not just Lexie. Yeah, they were friends and she could see them getting to be good friends.

But a crush?

The last time she'd had a so-called crush—Britney—she'd jumped in headfirst. And she crashed hard when Britney broke up with her. There'd been no signs that Britney wasn't happy. It had come right out of left field and Kyler remembered being speechless as Britney was telling her she didn't love her. And she remembered crying over her first—and only—broken heart.

That was years ago, though. In hindsight, Britney had been right, of course. They weren't destined to live happily ever after. They hadn't had enough in common. Even then. Now? No. She'd changed so much, Britney probably wouldn't even recognize her.

Lexie was like Britney, wasn't she? Cute and a little flirty, fun to be around. Lexie could be someone she could have a fling with, nothing more. If she wasn't Mark's sister, she might even pursue it. She was going to be here a couple of months, at least. A little

Christmas fling might be fun. But Lexie wasn't interested in that with her, so it was really a moot point.

Crush or no crush, Lexie wasn't interested in her and probably wouldn't be interested in a fling either. With a sigh, she pushed that thought away. They were friends. That was enough.

CHAPTER TWENTY-TWO

Lexie sorted through the brochures that had come in the mail, restocking the rack and putting out the new ones her mother had ordered. She looked at one of them, wondering what the Marfa Lights were. As she stacked them neatly on the rack, another caught her eye. Davis Mountains Scenic Loop. It was where Kyler had taken her on her tour of the area after the sunrise. She realized she was smiling as she put the brochure in its proper place.

It had been a rather slow morning, though. Only one guest had checked out. A nice couple. Eric and Darla, from San Antonio. They'd told her it had become an annual trip for them, although next year, they planned to come during the Thanksgiving week. They'd made reservations while they were here, and she booked them into their favorite room—twenty-three.

There were two guests scheduled to arrive that afternoon. They only had four vacant rooms, but even so, everything seemed quiet. There were no people milling about, none passing through, asking for directions or inquiring about nearby attractions. Not that she could help with either of those things. Well, she could hand them a brochure.

With a sigh, she went back to the desk and sat down. Her mother was in town, doing her weekly grocery shopping. Her father was in his workshop "tinkering" with something. She updated the reservation screen, hoping to find a new one, something to occupy her time. She'd already done enough research on the software that they ran to know that she'd not be able to tweak it for what her mother wanted. They did have the capability to upload files, meant for the purpose of populating personal data from a questionnaire that her parents weren't using. The questionnaire was fluid and could be changed easily. She thought she might be able to use that to her advantage. Dump the reservation file, populate the reworked questionnaire, then upload it back into the system, populating all the fields that they were manually doing now.

Granted, now that she was here and poking around, it wasn't that big of a chore. In fact, it wasn't a chore at all to do it manually. But if she could get the files working, set them to download and upload on a schedule, then the reservation system would basically run itself. It was already set up to send out confirmation emails and reminders.

"Then what will I do all day?"

A smile lit her face. Well, she could go bike riding with Kyler. She rested her chin on her palm, picturing the other woman. Kyler wasn't really like any of her friends. Like most people, she had different groups of friends. Trish and a handful of others in one group. Her work friends who she'd shared many a happy hour with. Her gym friends, some she'd known for years now. They intermingled only rarely.

She couldn't think of a one that Kyler reminded her of. The gym friends were just that—gym rats. They rarely exercised outside the confines of the club. Not the ones she'd gotten to know, anyway. Her work friends were a combination of geeky computer nerds and intellectual snobs. Her old college friends—Trish included— were in professional jobs, most of them married or partnered up, some with kids. She was the outlier. Which was why, after her relationship with Cathy fizzled, most of them tried to fix her up with someone in one way or another.

Oh, but Kyler was different, wasn't she? She was fun. She was pleasant. She was cute. She was easy to flirt with and she flirted back. And flirting was something Lexie should not be doing.

She didn't want to send her mixed signals, for one thing. And two, you don't flirt with friends. She needed a friend, she knew that. Someone other than her family. Kyler could be that person, couldn't she?

She was fun, and she was nice, and she was cute. Of course, the cute part shouldn't factor into whether they should be friends or not.

The bell on the front door jingled and she looked up, surprised—and pleased—to find the woman who had been invading her thoughts walking through the door. A smile lit her face and she got up, going to the counter.

"What brings you around?"

Kyler held up a paper bag. "Lunch."

Lexie's smile widened. "You brought me lunch?"

"I heard you were holding down the fort."

Kyler walked around the counter to the office like she'd done it a hundred times before. She scooted a chair up to the desk and plopped down.

Lexie arched an eyebrow as she sat down again. "What'd you bring?"

"Veggie burger."

Lexie's eyes widened. "Where in the world did you find a veggie burger?"

"Potters."

"Oh, my god! The little grocery store in town sells veggie burgers?" She took the offered sandwich that was wrapped in a paper towel. It was still warm. "How did you manage this?"

"I took the frozen burgers over to Mark and had them make one up for you." She held up another. "I got the real thing."

"You are too sweet."

Kyler blushed slightly as she unwrapped her burger. "You may have a kindred spirit in town. Bobby said they ordered them for Mary Rudolph. She's got heart disease and she read some book about changing her diet. Gave them a list of stuff she wanted."

"Really? That's good to know. Maybe they can order me some tofu."

Kyler bit into her burger and nodded. "Mine's good. How's yours?"

Lexie took a bite too, and yes, it was delicious. The only thing that would have made it better would have been a whole wheat bun instead of white, but she kept that comment to herself.

"Fabulous. This was so thoughtful of you."

"Well, I saw them when I was getting the pizza for our football party."

"And here I was all prepared not to like you."

Kyler looked up at her. "Why?"

"Well, not you specifically." She paused. "Maybe. I mean, I wanted to like it up here, but I was prepared not to. And when my mother first mentioned you, I assumed they were going to try to play matchmaker and I convinced myself that I wouldn't like you. At all. I mean, you were Mark's friend and all."

"But I'm irresistible?"

Lexie gave a quick laugh. "I like you. I wouldn't say you're irresistible."

"I like you too. And give it time. I'll grow on you."

Lexie took another bite of her burger. "You're not my type, Kyler. And I think you already said I wasn't yours."

Kyler put her burger down and wiped her mouth. "So, the wind shifted."

"Okay." So that was an odd changing of the subject. "The wind shifted. That's a good thing?"

Kyler nodded. "South."

"That means what?"

"It's gonna be warmer tonight. And tomorrow, we're supposed to hit low sixties."

"Oh." She smiled then. "For our bike ride?"

"Yep. We're still on?"

"Yes. I'm looking forward to it. Where are you going to take me?"

"Where do you want to go?"

"A tour of the whole park."

Kyler nodded. "We can do that. Although I think we should skip going up Skyline Drive. But you used to do spin class. Your thighs are probably in good shape." She smiled quickly. "Are they?"

"I've seen Skyline Drive in your Jeep and, no, I'm not ready to tackle it on a bike. It's straight uphill." Then she smiled too. "But yes, my thighs are in good shape. I think."

Kyler nodded. "Did you order some biking pants?"

"Oh, I did. And shorts too. I should get them today."

"Shorts? Gonna stay around for shorts weather?"

Lexie put her burger down, pausing to gather her thoughts. Kyler was someone she could talk to. From that very first morning when they'd watched the sunrise, she knew that. Kyler was watching her now, an eyebrow raised questioningly.

"As I said, I was prepared to not like it here. I find it a little shocking that I actually do." She met her gaze. "You are a part of the reasons why, as you've probably guessed. I was dreading not knowing anyone other than my parents and Mark. I was dreading not having any friends. Part of me was convinced that by Christmas, I'd be counting down the days—hours—until I could get the hell out of here."

"So you find yourself liking it...yet what?"

She sighed and leaned back in her chair. "I'm thirty. I fear I'll get stagnant. Running a lodge wasn't ever something I thought I'd be doing. I'm afraid I'll lose whatever technical skills I still cling to—I mean, I haven't worked in nine months now, almost ten—and if I eventually go back, I'll never get a job."

"Ah. So you think if you stay, then you'll be stuck here forever."

"Yes. Mom and Dad want to get an RV, they want to travel. They're counting on me staying to run things while they do that."

"You can't base your decision to stay or go on that, Lexie. You still have a choice."

"I know. But do I really have a choice? I've got to be out of my apartment by the end of January. There is no job to go back to. And it's not like I hate it here. As I said, surprisingly, I like it up here. I feel comfortable. There's certainly not any stress." She pointed at the laptop. "This thing can run the whole lodge by itself."

"Can it fix hot water heaters and change lightbulbs?"

"That's another thing! If Dad is gone, who's going to fix stuff? Mark?"

"I'm pretty handy."

"You already have a job."

"Stuff doesn't really break that often. Your dad just likes to fiddle with things. 'Tinker,' as Susan calls it. If he's gone and you have a major issue with an appliance or something, then you might have to get someone from Alpine to come up. If you have plumbing issues, there's a guy in town to call." Kyler finished off her burger. "I happen to be pretty good with plumbing too. I do it in the park all the time. And believe it or not, Mark is pretty handy too."

"So I shouldn't use that as an excuse?"

"No. But I understand what you're saying. Your parents know it too. This is not Austin. It takes a certain kind of person to love it up here. Yes, we're in a remote place in a very sparsely populated area of the state." She shrugged. "You get used to it. If there's something you need that you can't buy locally, you go to Ft. Stockton. Or you order online."

Lexie folded her hands together and rested her chin there. "Do you miss going out? Nightlife? Dinners?"

"Honestly, no. At first, I think I may have. It's hard to remember now. You find different things to do. My nightlife is watching the stars. Going out means I get on my bike or I go over to Irene's or Tammy and Phil's ranch and ride horses. And dinner?" She smiled at her. "Well, I'm hoping you get that menu redone so that I can get fish now."

"Do you think Mark is serious about that? I mean, I don't want to get into his business."

"From what he said, the menu is pretty much exactly like it was when he got here. If he got a grill, then there are so many things you could add."

"I liked those breakfast tacos. I had one this morning."

"Yeah, that's new. Maria has worked here for years and one day she made those for me and Mark. There were no customers and she brought those out for us, and Mark was like, why haven't you made this before? The next week, they were on the menu."

"Okay. I guess I'll talk to him then. If he's serious, then I'll get with the cooks and see what we can change."

Kyler held her hand up. "Not so much 'change.' 'Add to.' Take baby steps. Mark will say baby steps."

She nodded. "Yes. Change is hard. I should know."

Kyler wadded up her napkin and tossed it into the bag. "I guess I should go. I have laundry to do."

"Do you have a washer and dryer at your cabin?"

"No. They've got a little laundry room for us at the maintenance shed. I'll start it, then go fill the bird feeders while it washes."

"So you tend to the bird blinds even on your day off?"

"I don't mind. If I asked one of the guys to do it, they would, but it's kinda become my thing."

Lexie walked her to the door. "Thank you for lunch. That was very sweet of you."

"Sure. If you want another tomorrow, I left the box with Mark. There are three left."

"Thank you."

They stood staring at each other, smiling. Kyler finally nodded. "See you tomorrow."

"Bye, Kyler."

She closed the door, then stood at the window, watching as Kyler got in her Jeep and drove off. She was still smiling when she went back to the desk. She cleaned up the remnants of their lunch, tossing a napkin and the paper bag into the trash. So, she'd made a new friend. She was becoming very fond of Kyler, wasn't she? She hadn't even known her two weeks yet—was that even possible?

She decided it was.

CHAPTER TWENTY-THREE

The sun was bright, the sky was clear, and the wind was nothing more than a lazy, gentle breeze. Perfect for a ride. She lifted the bike from the rack and leaned it against the Jeep. She found herself whistling a Christmas tune—"Frosty the Snowman"—as she went to Lexie's door. Before she could knock, it opened, and Lexie greeted her with a smile.

"Hey. I thought I heard you drive up."

Kyler grinned as she looked her over, her gaze sliding over black biking pants with a bright yellow stripe on the side of each leg. "Wow. Nice pants." She wiggled her eyebrows teasingly. "Tight."

Lexie came outside, posing for her. "You like them?"

"I love them."

Lexie slapped the back of her butt. "Got one with extra padding."

"Were you sore last time?"

"A little." Lexie looked her over. "Your pants don't look padded."

"Not the pants, no. I've got cycling shorts on underneath."

Lexie's bike was leaning against the wall, her helmet hanging by the strap on the handlebars. Kyler watched as she pulled her hair into a ponytail again before putting on her helmet. Kyler simply ran a hand through her hair, brushing it back before slipping on her own helmet.

They headed out, passing by the restaurant before hitting the park road.

"Oh, yeah. These pants make all the difference," Lexie said. "I have several pairs of cycling tights back at my apartment in Austin that I used in spin class. I never once thought to bring them along."

"So you were gym all the way? No outdoor running or anything?"

"No. I fell into a routine, I guess. I ran, but always on a treadmill. I used to bike with Mark and Mia some but not often enough to warrant the money I spent on that bike. Then after Mia's accident, I got rid of it. I had no desire to get back on the road."

"This is different."

"Night and day, yes. They would hit the road and ride for thirty miles. I like this much better. It was fun on the trail the other day."

Kyler nodded. "We can take the trail first if you want. We can get out where we started last time, or we can stay on it. It comes out near the entrance, close to the tent camping area."

"That's fine with me."

When they got to the picnic area, Kyler rode across the little bridge and took the trail along Limpia Creek. She didn't look behind her—she could hear Lexie following. She relaxed, slowing her pace just a little, giving herself—and Lexie—time to enjoy their surroundings. They weren't racing, she reminded herself.

The trees were a little less dense here along the creek and canyon, allowing for more of a view. Some people might call this land barren, and in parts, it was. Below four thousand feet, the woodland trees gave way to thorny brush and below that it was a desert landscape with Chihuahuan scrub bush, creosote bush, and mesquite more prevalent. Up here though, piñon pines mixed with the fragrant junipers, and several species of oaks competed for what little moisture there was. Near Mt. Livermore, where Irene's ranch was and where Tammy and Phil lived, ponderosa pines and even stands of quaking aspens could be found—the terrain more like the Rocky Mountains than the Trans Pecos.

And she loved it all. She took a deep breath, enjoying the now familiar scents. Sure, she'd loved being at the coast and she'd enjoyed the smell of the salt air, but this was different. She'd found a peace up here that she didn't know she'd even been searching for.

The wide-open spaces, the endless sky—both day and night—the slow, unhurried pace of living and the sense of community had all been missing in her life.

What was missing then and was still missing now was having love in her life. After having her heart ripped out by Britney, she wasn't sure she wanted to give it a try again. Maybe she'd be like Mark, hanging on to old memories instead of making new ones.

No, she couldn't compare herself to Mark. He'd been truly, deeply in love with his wife and her death had devastated him. She'd only thought she'd been in love with Britney. No, that wasn't true either. She *was* in love with her. The person she was back then was in love with her. Who she was now? No. If she met Britney today, there's no way she'd fall for her.

Then why was she attracted to Lexie Walton? Didn't she tell Mark that Lexie reminded her of Britney? Did she really? Britney had been fun and flirty, yes. So was Lexie. They were both more comfortable in a city than out of it. Is that where the comparisons ended? Would Britney have ever ventured out on a mountain bike with her? No. She couldn't see it. Lexie, however, seemed to be enjoying it immensely.

"Can we stop at the overlook?"

Kyler shook her thoughts away and pulled over to the right, the same place they'd stopped the other day.

"Need a break?"

Lexie pulled her bike up beside her and gave her a beaming smile. "Not a break, no. I feel great. But I want to take a picture."

Kyler hadn't even noticed the small fanny pack Lexie had strapped to her waist. From inside she pulled out her phone and, without warning, snapped a picture of Kyler.

"You didn't give me time to primp," she complained.

"You're gorgeous as you are. You don't need to primp."

Lexie leaned her bike against Kyler as she moved to the edge where the wooden fence stopped her progress. Kyler watched as she took several shots from different directions.

Gorgeous? Kyler smiled but shook her head. No, so not gorgeous. She had on a biking helmet, for god's sake. She *knew* what she looked like with a biking helmet on.

Lexie turned around to face her, her gaze questioning. Kyler looked back at her with an equally questioning gaze, she assumed.

"Am I in your space?"

Kyler shook her head. "No. Why?"

Lexie moved closer. "You're used to doing this alone. I've run on the treadmill so long—alone—lost in my own thoughts or music, I wouldn't know how to act if I ran outside with someone. Especially a chatty someone."

"I wouldn't exactly call you chatty. But yes, I am used to doing this by myself. That's not to say I don't enjoy company. If you see something beautiful"—she motioned to the canyon—"you want to share that with someone. Late last spring, I was riding the loop across the road. I came upon a doe and her twins. I stopped and watched, probably twenty minutes or more. They got used to me. The twins nursed. It was a beautiful sight." She shrugged. "It would have been more special if someone had been there to share it with me." She smiled then. "When I told Mark what I'd seen, he wasn't nearly as impressed by it as I was."

"Well, if I'm getting into your space, I hope you'll tell me. If you don't want me to ride with you all the time, tell me no. I can go by myself. I doubt I'll get lost."

"Okay, fair enough. But I like you being around. Besides, if you're out here by yourself, I'll have to ticket you."

"Ticket me?"

"I don't believe you purchased a day permit."

Lexie laughed. "Well, hanging out with you does have its perks then. Saves me six bucks each time."

"Or you could buy a yearly pass."

"I suppose I could. It's more fun sneaking in with you, though. Certainly cheaper," she teased as she got back on her bike. "By the way, how was work today?"

"Pretty slow. That cold snap ran off the few campers we had. There are two RVs still here."

"Is it always slow this time of year?"

She nodded. "Depends on the weather. Christmas and then up to New Year's we'll be almost full, I think."

"We are too. I don't understand it. Don't people want to be home for the holidays?"

Kyler balanced on her bike, holding on to a tree with one hand. "Well, not everyone celebrates, for one thing. And some people have this time off from work, so they take advantage of that." She shrugged. "You have retired couples who are childless.

They'll come up in their RV and stay the whole two weeks. I think for some, it's a chance to escape the reminder that they're alone. There's enough decorations in the park to give them the feeling of Christmas without having it shoved down their throats."

"So they come up here to be a little less lonely? I guess I get that." She studied her. "What about you?"

"Am I lonely? Not really. Your family always includes me. And if they didn't, Tammy and Phil would."

"Do you miss *your* family?"

Kyler hesitated. Did she? She didn't give it much thought anymore, really. They hadn't been close in so many years, it had become the norm. Did she miss them though? Did she miss having a relationship with them? With her sister? Could the occasional text message be called a relationship?

"Honestly, I feel closer to your mom than my own. Strange, since I've only known Susan a handful of years." She shrugged and moved her bike away from Lexie. "My mom will call around Christmas. If she thinks about it."

"You could call her."

"I do sometimes. I always feel like I'm interrupting their life." She pushed off, heading down the trail. "We don't have a lot to talk about anyway. They're not too impressed with my job."

That was the excuse she used for not calling. It was easier to stomach than thinking her parents didn't want to talk to her, didn't want to know what was going on in her life. She stared at the trail but wasn't seeing it. No, she was trying to picture her mother, her dad. Her sister. She was so far removed from them, it was like they didn't exist—and she didn't exist.

A random text message from Kinley, a picture now and then of her kid. She got a family portrait—her parents included—at Easter. And a shot of her parents having dinner with them at some swanky restaurant. She wondered why Kinley had chosen those photos to send. Well, what else was she going to send? Changing the kid's diaper?

"Kyler?"

"Yeah?"

"I'm sorry."

She glanced at Lexie over her shoulder. "Oh, hell. Don't be sorry. It is what it is."

She sped up a little, not wanting to talk about it. Truth was, yeah it did bother her that she wasn't close with her family. She blamed herself. She was the one who had changed, not them. Maybe she should take Susan's advice and use some of her vacation days to go see them, try to reconnect or something. The prospect of spending a week in Houston nearly made her cringe, though.

When they got to the trail intersection where they'd gotten on last time, she kept going, taking Lexie through the woods that separated the tent sites from one of the RV sections. The tent area was still empty. When they got to the end of the campground, instead of continuing on the trail, she slowed and took a side lane that would put them back on the road.

"I'll take you to the office."

Lexie pulled up beside her. "That was fun. Was that the whole trail?"

"No. It goes on a little way yet. It stops by the full hookup sites. If you were using this trail for hiking, that's where it meets up with Skyline Trail. Bikes can't make it, though, so they get out there and take the road." She pointed up ahead. "That's the office. And the entrance to the park. You want to meet Tammy?"

"Sure."

She stopped by the side door and leaned her bike against the wall. Lexie did the same. She took her helmet off and ran her fingers through her hair. She was certain it was an unruly mess and she chanced a glance into the window, seeing her reflection. She groaned.

"It looks no worse than mine."

Kyler stared at Lexie, her light brown hair still confined in its ponytail, a few stray strands dancing across her face. Before she could stop herself, she reached out to tame the strands, tucking them behind her ear. Their eyes met and she smiled, then lowered her hand.

"Your hair looks like it did before the helmet. How do you pull that off?"

"My hair is thin. Yours," she said, touching it lightly with her hand, "is very thick." Again, their eyes met. "I like it."

They were standing close, too close. Kyler let her gaze lower to Lexie's lips, seeing a smile forming. A flirty smile that she was beginning to recognize was more teasing than serious.

"Come on. I'll introduce you to Tammy."

Lexie stopped her with a touch on her arm. "Kyler?"

"Hmm?"

"Would today be a good day to catch the sunset?"

She had a hand on the doorknob, but before she turned it, she glanced again at Lexie. "It'll be a perfect day. You want to?"

"Yes. Please."

"Okay. We'll take the road back to the lodge instead of the trail. Should get back in plenty of time."

Tammy was waiting when they went inside. A big smile greeted them.

"You must be Lexie Walton." Tammy held her hand out and Lexie shook it. "So nice to meet you. You're as pretty as Irene said you were."

"Thank you. And you must be Tammy. My mother speaks highly of you."

Tammy was nearly beaming, and Kyler was afraid the smile would break her face. "I took her on a bike ride," she offered. "Thought we'd pop in and say hello."

"I'm so glad you did. Things are downright boring around here. Not a single camper came in today." Tammy turned her attention to Lexie. "So, how do you like it here?"

"Better than I thought I would." Lexie flicked her gaze at her and smiled. "Kyler has helped."

"As I told Kyler, it takes a certain kind to embrace this life out here. Especially coming from a city with all its amenities."

"Did you?"

"Oh, yes. I lived in Dallas, worked in a high-rise in downtown, fought traffic, rushed through life as if it was a race." She waved her hand in the air. "Then Phil had his mind made up to move out here. Since divorcing the man I loved wasn't an option, I had to change my mindset. Instead of focusing on all my preconceived negatives about the place—and all the things I would miss in my former life—I started looking at the positives."

"Such as?"

"No rush hour traffic. I didn't realize how much stress my commute to and from work put on me. And the quiet. And the friendly people. Oh, and the stars! Have you taken a good look at the stars?"

Lexie smiled at her. "Kyler took me for a sunrise. We got a glimpse of them. She's promised to let me play with her telescope sometime."

Kyler laughed. "I'll trade you a telescope session if you'll cook dinner for me one night."

"Deal."

"It's so nice the two of you have become friends. It's not often young people move here. At least, not up here in Ft. Davis. As I understand it, Marfa is more of a draw." Tammy looked at her. "Didn't you meet some twins there once?"

Lexie laughed and Kyler felt a blush creep up her face. "I did. Turns out we didn't have anything in common."

"But you and Lexie seem to. So happy you've found someone to bike ride with."

"Me too." She made a show of looking at her watch. "Speaking of, we should get going."

"Well, thank you for bringing Lexie by." Tammy shook Lexie's hand again. "Nice to meet you."

"Yes, it was. Thank you."

"You'll need to bring her out to the ranch sometime, Kyler. Take her riding."

"Oh, I'm not sure I'm up for horses," Lexie said quickly. "I'm just getting used to the bike."

"Nonsense. Kyler can saddle one of the older mares for you." Tammy turned to her. "Bring her on one of your days off. Phil will cook on the grill for us."

"I'll try to talk her into it."

"Okay, dear. See you tomorrow."

As soon as the door closed, Lexie turned to her. "You're going to make me go riding, aren't you?"

Kyler smiled. "Make you? Do I have that power?"

"You can be persuasive. Anyone who can drag Mark out during the middle of the night to watch a meteor shower must be."

They put their helmets back on and pushed their bikes away from the building. "I drag his ass out every once in a while to break up his routine."

"And his routine is being at the bar every day, every night?"

"Yeah. Except for our occasional dinner dates on Saturday and football season on Sundays." They peddled away from the office, keeping to the park road as they headed back toward the campgrounds. "He must have loved her very much."

"He likes to say he fell in love with her in the second grade, which is when they met. I can't really think of a time in my life where Mia wasn't around. By the time they were in high school, I think everyone—her parents included—knew they'd get married."

"Do you think he'll ever get over it? Maybe date again?"

"I hope so, but honestly, it wouldn't surprise me if he didn't. He lives with his memories. I think it would take someone very special to break that hold she has on him."

"It can't be healthy for him. Mentally, I mean."

"No. Mentally. Emotionally. On the outside, he seems perfectly fine. And I think he really is okay. He's just not ready to let her go. That's something only he can decide."

They peddled back down the road, toward the campgrounds. "That's the real reason he's here then?"

"Yes. When Mom and Dad bought this place, like me, Mark had no intention of joining them. After the accident, Mom made the offer to him. I think she knew he needed to get away from Austin. Much like she made me an offer, I guess."

"Because you needed to get away?"

"I was slipping into a pit of depression, yes. I didn't realize how deflating it would be to interview for jobs only to be continually passed over. My life had become stagnant. I can see that now. But I always kept so busy, was always doing something. It didn't occur to me how empty my life was." Lexie glanced at her. "Do you know what I mean? I had a full life, yet…something was missing."

Did she know what she meant? Could she relate? Her life felt full. She loved her job. She had a few friends. And she had Mark. She had some hobbies that kept her entertained. She wouldn't call it empty by any means. Yet, sometimes, alone at night…yes, something felt missing.

"So you've been here a couple of weeks. You miss your friends?"

"I'm not sure." Then Lexie gave a guarded laugh. "That sounds selfish, doesn't it? I didn't mean it that way. I *thought* I would miss my friends. Especially Trish. We saw each other several times during the week. Lunch once or twice. Dinner on the weekends. Barhopping on Saturday nights. I really don't miss that at all."

"Barhopping?"

"It's a must-do when you're in college. Sixth Street. And for a lot of people, it carries on after college. The group that goes—they're Trish's friends, really. Mine only by default. Most of them are single. Those that are married go less frequently. I joined them before Cathy. And we would go together occasionally. After I ended it with her, I started going routinely again. It was exhausting, really."

"What? Staying out until two when the bars close?"

"Yeah. Then you'd feel like crap the next day, wishing you hadn't agreed to meet for brunch and a Bloody Mary."

"So why did you do it?"

"I don't know. To keep busy, I guess."

"To keep from being alone on a Saturday night?"

"Yes. And I know what you're thinking. I must be terribly insecure if I can't manage that."

"You don't seem insecure."

"I'll admit, my self-esteem took a hit after losing my job and then not being able to find another one. Then being single and friends trying to set you up with the *wrong* person. You start thinking maybe it's you, not them." Lexie lifted one hand from the handlebars and waved it at her. "Let's change the subject. This one is depressing."

"Okay. So…what? Should I change it to something exciting like birdwatching?"

"Yeah. And so that's *your* insecurity! It's something you love, yet you're embarrassed about it. I don't understand why."

"Because I'm not very good."

"Oh, Kyler. That's relative, isn't it? To me, you're an expert. Because I know nothing."

She nodded, knowing Lexie had hit on the truth. "Yes. It is relative. And when I'm by myself, observing, I think I'm pretty capable. But when out with others—and god forbid there are *real* birders there—I freeze up."

"There's nothing wrong with being a *new* birder, is there? I mean, even your so-called experts were new at one time."

"I know. I guess I feel like, in my profession, I should be better already. And I wasted years down at the coast where I could have learned, but I wasn't really into it down there. Those birders down there are fanatical. Funny hats and all," she added with a laugh.

"And they intimidate you?"

"Yes, they do. So it was easier to pretend I didn't know a damn thing than to acknowledge I knew a little."

They rounded the last curve and the picnic area came into sight. She glanced to the sky, figuring they had at least forty-five minutes before the sunset colors would begin. An hour before it set.

"Do I have time to change?"

"Yeah. It'll get cold once the sun sets. We can swing by my place before heading up the mountain. I'll change too."

Lexie flashed her a grin. "Good. I've wanted to see where you live."

CHAPTER TWENTY-FOUR

Lexie was trying to snoop without it being obvious. The cabin was small but certainly larger than her own little apartment. It at least had a kitchen. The room was tidy but not sterile. A couple of wildlife photos hung on one wall and a colorful blanket with a classic Mexican flavor adorned the side wall by the door. A sofa separated the kitchen and the living room. A coffee table had four or five books on it, and she peeked through them—an assortment of bird books and ones on stargazing. She smiled and put them back the way she'd found them. A large TV was against the wall and a cute fireplace was in one corner. The other corner was crowded with a Christmas tree, decorated to the hilt. She saw the birdwatching ornament that her mother had given Kyler and this, too, made her smile.

She slid her gaze to the kitchen, which was against the opposite wall. The appliances were simple and white, the counter space taken up by a coffeemaker and a toaster. A small, square table was shoved against the wall and three chairs were slid against it. She wondered where the fourth had gone.

"Planning a meal?"

She turned, finding Kyler in jeans and a sweatshirt. "Snooping around. I like it. It's cozy. And your tree is lovely."

"Thank you. I start a fire and turn all the lights off. Just the Christmas tree lights are on and the glow from the fire. It's as relaxing as a bubble bath."

She laughed lightly. "I can't picture you taking a bubble bath."

"Well, seeing as how I only have a shower here, no." She glanced at her watch. "Ready?"

"Yes. We won't be late, will we?"

"No. There's a service road that comes out near Skyline Drive. We'll take that instead of the road through the campground."

Back in Kyler's Jeep, instead of retracing their route, she turned left onto a small, dirt road with a Park Personnel Only sign.

"How many cabins are there?"

"Six."

"But you have more employees than that?"

"We've got eight. Actually, two of the cabins are vacant. Todd moved into Ft. Davis last year when he got married. The other one, one of the clerks lived there for a while. She doesn't work here anymore."

"Eight employees doesn't sound like very many."

"Our allocation is based on traffic in the park, not the size. Actually, eight is pretty decent. When I worked at Goose Island, we had fifteen or sixteen, I think. That park gets the most traffic in that region, and it's relatively small—acreage wise."

The dirt road hit pavement and Lexie was completely turned around as to where they were. Kyler turned left on to Skyline Drive.

"Oh. Now I see. We came from that direction the last time."

"Yes. The campgrounds are down that road."

As they climbed higher, Lexie could tell the colors were starting to change. She could also feel the wind as it rattled the Jeep doors.

"It wasn't really windy when we were riding."

"Not too much. The trees help block a lot of it. Plus, we're kinda in a bowl there. The Mt. Livermore area blocks winds coming from the west and this one blocks the north." Kyler pointed to their right. "Red-tailed hawk making a final hunt before dark."

Lexie glanced just in time to see the hawk disappear below them into the canyon. When they got to the top, Kyler drove to the opposite side from where they'd watched the sunrise. Which, of course, made sense as they were now watching the sunset.

"Do you want to get out or watch from in here?"

The old Lexie, the one who preferred her sunsets to be viewed from the comfort of a restaurant deck above Lake Travis—sipping a margarita—would have been content to stay right where she was. But to get the full effect of it—like the sunrise—she needed to be out in it. Not merely observing but experiencing the sunset.

She turned to Kyler. "Let's get out."

The quick smile on Kyler's face told her she'd made the right choice. However, the wind was quite a bit stronger than she'd anticipated. She put her jacket on and Kyler did as well. Then Kyler took the same blanket as before and led her around to a rock pile where a lone juniper tree grew.

"This is the best spot."

"We've got the place to ourselves," she noted.

Kyler put the blanket across the rocks. "I've found most people are really indifferent to the sunrise or sunset. If they happen to think about it and they have nothing else to do, they might make the drive up here. Of course, on busy weekends and holidays, there are more people around."

"Then you have to share your space? Or do you stay away?"

"I catch more sunrises than sunsets. It's rare that I have company in the early mornings." She smiled quickly. "I used to not be a morning person. I always volunteered for the late shifts when I was down at the coast. Getting up at five a.m. was for crazy people."

Lexie nodded. "I know. When I was working, I'd get up in time for a quick shower, a cup of coffee to take with me on my drive. I'd get breakfast on the way, eat at my desk. Out to lunch. Gym after work. Oftentimes dinner or drinks in the evenings. If I got to bed by midnight, it was a good day."

"I haven't seen midnight in years."

"Not even New Year's Eve?"

"Not even. The park is open every day. If it's not your day off, it's just another day."

Lexie leaned a little closer, letting her shoulder touch with Kyler's. "I haven't seen midnight since I've been here. Eleven a couple of nights. Mostly, by ten I'm heading to bed."

"You said you don't miss barhopping on Saturday nights. What about other nightlife?"

"I don't think so, no. There was a women's bar that I'd go to a couple of times a month." She shrugged. "Missing that hasn't even crossed my mind. Dinner dates, a movie." She shrugged again. "Like I said before, I thought I'd miss it, but I really don't."

She stared out as the sun sank lower, the bright shine of earlier settling down now as the day was drawing to a close. "I think I've realized that a lot of my going out was to compensate for my family being gone. I hung out with Mark and Mia a lot. We had family dinners, much like we do now. After Mia's accident and then their move, my life essentially changed."

"They've been up here seven years, right?"

"Yes." She leaned closer again. "It's getting close."

"The real colors will come after it sets. The sky will be a reddish purple from rim to rim."

She felt the pressure of Kyler's shoulder against hers and she stayed where she was. In these few short weeks, she felt more comfortable with Kyler than she'd ever felt with Cathy. She didn't remember *talking* with Cathy. How had they stayed together two years?

And why had her mother said that she and Kyler were complete opposites? There was no awkwardness between them. Complete opposites shouldn't have anything to talk about, should they?

The sun hung just above the horizon, the orangey glow turning red as it crept lower. The only sound was the wind as it sailed through the tree branches. She felt Kyler move, felt her hand squeeze her thigh as the top of the sun disappeared from view. As Kyler had predicted, the sky turned a beautiful deep red with only a hint of purple, stretching across north to south. Instead of disappearing with the sun, the colors seemed to grow, reaching higher into the sky, painting the mountain around them. It was one of the most picturesque things she'd ever witnessed in person.

"I'm not sure I've ever seen a more beautiful sight." She spoke the words softly so as not to disturb the silence. Kyler gave her thigh one last squeeze, then removed her hand.

"I never tire of that." Kyler leaned back a little, looking overhead. "The stars will be out in a little while. If you're not too cold, we could hang around to see Venus. It'll be a little toward the south. As soon as it gets a little darker, it'll pop out."

"Yes," she answered simply. She leaned closer again, letting her head rest on Kyler's shoulder. "I like you a lot." She could sense Kyler smiling and she jerked her head away. "I mean, I needed a friend and I didn't think I'd find one up here. Not this quickly."

Kyler shifted beside her, turning. "I like you too."

Kyler's gaze dropped to her lips for only a brief second, but long enough for Lexie to imagine what a kiss would feel like. That disturbed her. Since when did she visualize kissing friends?

Kyler met her gaze again as the shadows began to settle around them. Then she turned back to the fading sunset and Lexie did too. They sat there quietly, neither speaking, as the sky darkened. They sat there quietly, yes, but their shoulders were touching and the gentle pressure against her own was comforting. After a while, Kyler stood.

"Let's find Venus, then I'll get you back home. It's getting cold."

Lexie nodded, letting herself be pulled to her feet. They stood together, a foot or so apart, the big sky holding onto only a sliver of red in the west, offering just enough light to make out Kyler's features. Her dark eyes seemed to draw her, and Lexie didn't pull away. If Kyler had leaned in to kiss her right then, she would have offered no protest. Which was crazy, of course. She wanted nothing of the sort from Kyler. She only wanted friendship and that was growing each time they saw each other.

Something else was growing too, wasn't it? God, she hated to admit it, but damn it all—she wasn't blind to the attraction. Kyler was attractive and charming and fun to be around. They'd fallen into such an easy friendship, it was like she'd known her months and months, not mere weeks. Yet as they stood there looking at each other in the dwindling light, she felt like she was under a spell.

"Are you afraid I'm going to try to turn this into something else?"

Lexie let her breath out. Was she afraid of that very thing? Or was she afraid *she'd* be the one to turn their friendship into more? She shook her head and forced a smile to her face.

"I'm not your type, remember? I think we're safe."

She didn't think now—out here with the remnants of the sunset around them—was the right time to be talking about this, though. Not when they were about to go stand under Venus' light. Or maybe that was the spell that had her. The glorious sunset, the pull of Venus, the goddess of love. No, no, no. It was getting to be too much.

So she turned away from Kyler, looking overhead. She forgot about Venus' spell as her eyes widened in awe. "Oh my god," she whispered. "Okay, I know you said we could only see a couple of thousand, but there are like a million stars up there."

Kyler laughed quietly, then took her hand, tugging her along a dark path. How she could see, Lexie didn't know, but Kyler maneuvered them around rocks and scrubs to the flat area where they'd watched the sunrise the other week.

Now that they were facing east, away from the twilight that was quickly disappearing, the stars were twinkling all around them in the dark, dark sky. Kyler waved her arm out around them.

"No city lights for hundreds of miles. You sit out here during a meteor shower and it's—well, it's too magnificent to even describe. Shooting stars that seem so close, you want to duck your head when they fall."

"Will you take me?" she asked without thinking.

"Yes. The Geminids. I think it's on the thirteenth or fourteenth." She pointed to a bright star. "There's Venus." Then she turned slightly and pointed again. "And there's Jupiter."

Lexie followed her gaze, seeing the two bright stars among the multitude of others. There seemed to be so many stars in the sky, she didn't know where to look.

"Show me a constellation."

"Okay, let's see." Kyler looked around, scanning the sky. "Here's an easy one. Orion, the hunter. See the three bright stars in a row? That's his belt." She turned again. "Pleiades. The seven sisters. That's the cluster of stars there. You can see them much better with binoculars." She smiled. "And, of course, the telescope."

Kyler again took her hand, leading her farther along the trail. It was full dark now and the wind had died down to nothing more than a gentle breeze. It didn't feel overly cold although she assumed the temperature had dropped into the forties.

"Ursa Minor, which actually means 'little bear' in Latin, but we call it the Little Dipper." A gentle hand moved her head slightly. "There. See the bright star at the end of the handle? That's the North Star."

Kyler's voice was quiet, soothing. The fingers that still held her hand were warm, gentle. God, why were they holding hands? She closed her eyes to the night sky, trying to fight her attraction to this woman. It was simply all too romantic—the beautiful sunset, the allure of Venus, the glittering stars that seemed to be dancing above their heads. She opened her eyes again, feeling so at peace with her world she didn't quite know what to do with it. For the last eight, nine months, her world had been topsy-turvy, and she'd been drifting about, trying to make sense of it all.

Who would have thought that up here, in this remote region of West Texas, she'd find peace?

"Lexie?"

She turned to the sound of her name, surprised to feel a shiver run up her spine. She tightened her fingers around Kyler's, loving the contact with her. It was too dark to see her eyes, to read her expression, but she thought she felt her tremble. She pulled her hand away, tucking both of them safely beneath her arms.

"I was thinking how peaceful it is. How peaceful I feel," she clarified. "I haven't felt this in a very long time. If ever." She turned to her. "Thank you for sharing this with me."

"Anytime." Kyler took a step away from her. "Are you ready to head back?"

"I guess." She paused a beat. They should go their separate ways, yes. But she was feeling too peaceful to want to part from her company. "Let me buy you dinner?"

Kyler nodded in the darkness. "Sure. Dinner sounds good."

Yes. They were friends. Friends shared dinner.

CHAPTER TWENTY-FIVE

Kyler stood with her back to the propane heater, her gaze on the Christmas tree lights but her thoughts on Lexie Walton. Thoughts that made her feel all warm and fuzzy inside. She smiled at that, but the feelings didn't go away. No, the feelings didn't go away and that scared her.

She moved away from the heater, going to turn on some lights and break the spell she seemed to be under. She twisted the cap off a water bottle and sat down on the sofa, her gaze again going to the tree. She remembered holding hands with Lexie as they stared at the stars. That warm, fuzzy feeling came back. Why in the hell were they holding hands? It was her fault. She'd taken her hand and hadn't let go.

The sunset. The stars. The shadows. Only the two of them up there on Skyline Drive. Sitting close. Holding hands. She could admit it now. She had wanted to kiss her. So much so that she'd felt herself tremble at the thought. Lexie must have felt it too because she'd pulled away. What the hell kind of game were they playing? They had a budding friendship starting, yes, but friends didn't hold hands. A budding friendship didn't involve subtle flirting. She'd been around Lexie enough to know that she was playful, teasing—and, yes, they flirted. Like at the Sunday football parties, their impromptu dinner at the bar was no different. Lexie flashed that flirty smile time and again. Then other things—their knees touching against the bar, out of Mark's sight, quick squeezes of fingers while talking, lingering glances. They were both guilty. But perhaps they felt safe at the bar, with people around, with Mark there.

If she had driven Lexie home, she could imagine a hot and heavy kiss in her Jeep. The heat—the electricity—between them was sizzling by the time the evening came to an end. At least in her mind. Perhaps Lexie felt it too. She had stood, her gaze holding Kyler's for a long moment. What she was trying to find there, Kyler didn't know. Then Lexie had touched her shoulder, squeezing it gently before smiling and wishing her a goodnight.

Mark had teased her. "Oh, yeah, sexual infatuation."

She could have denied it, but hell, Mark was her best friend. "I'm attracted to her, yes. A little crush."

"But she's not your type."

"Are you patronizing me?"

"Just repeating your words."

He had poured a splash of whiskey in two glasses—the pecan praline they liked—and touched her glass in a silent toast, his eyes twinkling as he'd smiled at her.

She turned and stretched out on the sofa, resting her head on her hands as she watched the lights on the tree. She suddenly felt lonely. Her little cabin felt empty. She closed her eyes, wondering at the emotion that was relatively foreign to her. She had a best friend in Mark. She had an adopted family in Susan and Dale. Even Tammy and Phil treated her like family. Irene was more of a grandmother than her own had been. And now she had a new friendship with Lexie. Why did she feel lonely?

She sat up and rested her elbows on her thighs. Her phone was on the table beside the sofa and she reached for it. She had Lexie's number. She could call. Make plans for another bike ride or something. Could she convince Lexie to get on a horse?

She put the phone down, though, and picked up the remote instead. The TV sprang to life and with a sigh she proceeded to browse through the channels. Nothing held her attention for long, but it at least distracted her. Somewhat.

CHAPTER TWENTY-SIX

"Do you mind company?"

Mark smiled at her and motioned her to sit. "The lunch crowd is gone. You want to talk about the char-broil grill I picked out? Or did you change your mind on that one?"

Lexie sat down on a barstool. "No, no. It's great. I've actually started researching a few things we can add to the menu." She held up her hand. "And I know you said baby steps and nothing too radical. Adding a grilled chicken burger is not drastic and I don't think it'll shock your regulars. Grilled fish on a bed of seasoned rice with grilled asparagus might."

"I promise you, you and Kyler will be the only two who order fish. But if I can add real grilled steaks to the menu—and advertise in town—I'll get a lot of the traffic that normally goes to the steakhouse in Alpine."

"What about veggie fajitas?"

"We don't even offer regular fajitas."

"You could now."

"Again, you'll be the only one who would order veggie fajitas."

"I think people want to eat healthier. Why not give them a choice?"

He shrugged. "I suppose we could try it." He wiped at the already clean bar. "So what's up?"

She leaned her elbows on the table. "Can I get a beer?"

"Mom let you off work?"

"What work? There's nothing to do. Only five rooms are occupied. I think there'll be twelve for the weekend."

"The two weeks around Christmas are full, aren't they?" He filled a mug from the tap and slid it to her.

"Yes. Totally booked. Then after the New Year, nothing. And I mean *nothing*."

"Yeah. January and February are dead. The campground is pretty empty too."

"Do you stay open regular hours?"

"No. We close on Sunday and Monday those months."

"I can't believe you're open seven days a week as it is." She looked around at the nearly empty room. A man and woman sat at a booth, looking at their phones and not each other. "Of course, it is after three. Did you have much of a lunch crowd?"

"I wouldn't call it a crowd, no, but we served a few. What's wrong? Are you bored already?"

"Not bored, no. I should have gone on a bike ride or something. The weather is so nice."

"So do it. I'm sure Kyler would love to go."

"I don't want to call Kyler. I feel like I'm pestering her. She didn't ask for this job of keeping me entertained." She took a swallow of the cold beer.

"I don't think she minds."

"I see enough of her. I should buy one of those park passes so I can go out alone."

He frowned. "Are you avoiding her?"

She looked up sharply. "Why would you think that?"

"Why else wouldn't you want to go on a bike ride with her?"

She held her hand up. "I know what you're thinking."

He smiled. "Yeah. I told you you'd like her."

"No. I do not like her. I mean, yes, obviously I like her. But you've got to get it out of your mind that something romantic is going to happen with us. It's not. Neither of us are interested in that, Mark. We're too different."

"Then why are you avoiding her?"

"I'm not avoiding her," she said a little louder than she intended. Damn, why had she brought it up in the first place? Yes, of course she was avoiding her. That was obvious. She didn't know why, really. Well, she *knew* why. It was the sunset. It was—damn, it was *Venus*. It was all of that. She was attracted to her. Yes, she could admit that. She didn't want to be attracted to her, though. So, what better way to quell that than to avoid her. She hadn't seen her in three days. She'd intentionally stayed away from the bar, choosing to have dinner with her parents each night, knowing that Kyler would most likely be here. And that's why she came over now— at three in the afternoon—knowing she didn't normally pop over until after five.

"Speak of the devil." He motioned with his head to the door.

Instead of turning around, she looked in the mirror, seeing the familiar red Jeep pull to a stop. *Damn.*

"She's here early."

He shook his head. "No. This is her normal time on Fridays. Chicken fried steak is the special tonight. It's usually our biggest crowd."

"I see. So she comes early to beat the crowd?"

"It gets noisy. She comes to visit and drink a few beers while it's quiet, yeah. The Mertz brothers will come before four. Stuart gets here by four thirty. They'll drink beer until six, then order dinner. Same thing every day."

"Then I should go. Give you two some privacy before your regulars come."

Mark frowned at her. "What is wrong with you? You're acting weird."

The bell jingled as she finished her beer and she avoided looking in the mirror. Yeah, she was acting weird. She wasn't prepared to see Kyler. Which was ridiculous. They were friends.

"Hey, Lexie."

She turned as Kyler sat down beside her. "Hi." Thoughts of leaving vanished as soon as Kyler smiled at her. Oh, the hell with it. She returned her smile. "How was your week?"

"It was nice. I had campground duty this week. Not a lot of campers so I had free time."

Lexie playfully bumped her shoulder. "Do a little bird watching, did you?"

Kyler smiled easily at her teasing. "I did." She nodded a thank-you at Mark when he slid a beer toward her. "I took a couple of leisurely hikes and had the trail to myself."

Mark took Lexie's empty mug and refilled it before she could protest.

"It's three in the afternoon and I'm sitting at a bar drinking beer," she said with a shake of her head. "I should at least call Mom and let her know I'm not coming back to work."

"It's three forty-five and she knows Kyler's routine. I'm sure she assumes you're over here with us."

She took her phone out and sent a quick text anyway. She was technically shirking her duties. Her mother responded quickly with two words and a winking smiley face. "Have fun." Okay, but why winking? What did that mean? She put her phone facedown on the bar and took a swallow of the fresh beer Mark had placed there. She knew what it meant, of course. Her mother thought she was over here because Kyler was here. Her mother—despite saying she and Kyler were complete opposites—was playing matchmaker.

"The weather has been nice. I kept expecting you to call so we could take our bikes out."

Lexie bit the corner of her lower lip. "I…I was really busy this week."

"I thought the lodge was almost empty," Mark supplied. "You said there was nothing to do."

"Training. Payroll. Stuff like that." She glared at him. "Busy stuff."

"I see."

She turned to Kyler then. She couldn't possibly continue to avoid her. "How about tomorrow?"

"Can't. I have to work until five."

"Oh."

The bell jingled and Lexie looked in the mirror, seeing two men come inside. The Mertz brothers, she assumed. She then looked at Kyler, meeting her eyes in the mirror. That proved to be a mistake. Try as she might, she couldn't look away. She was aware of Mark getting two beer bottles from the cooler, seeing him walk away.

"I missed you this week."

Lexie finally turned to meet Kyler's eyes in person. She nodded. "Yes. Me too." And she had. She was avoiding her, yes, but she'd missed her. Maybe that's why the words were out before she could consider them fully. "You want to have dinner tomorrow?"

Kyler's right eyebrow arched questioningly.

"Well, I don't really have a kitchen, as you know, so it would have to be at your place."

Kyler nodded. "Okay. Sure."

"Good. I'll bring everything. It'll be fun to cook again."

"Yeah, well, don't tell Mark, but it'll be nice to eat something other than off his menu."

Lexie relaxed, feeling the tension—self-induced tension, she knew—dissipate. This was just Kyler, her new friend. There was no need to avoid her.

"The weather has been nice though. I'd love to get out."

Kyler nodded. "How about a hike?"

"A hike? Okay, I'm not really a hiker, but I'm game. When?"

"Sunday morning?"

"Sure."

"Early."

"Okay."

"Daybreak."

She groaned. "What's with you and daybreak?"

"Best time of the day. Besides, we have a football party at noon."

"Oh, yeah. Okay. So where will you take me?"

"Let's take the trail up to Skyline Drive."

She frowned. "It's going to be strenuous, isn't it?"

"It'll be a good workout, yes."

"Okay. I'm in. Daybreak. Sunday."

"I swear, the Mertz brothers can talk. Get them and Stuart together and it's never-ending," Mark said, wiping at the water spot under Kyler's glass. "You going to eat here?"

Kyler nodded. "I am. Got fish on the menu yet?"

"Funny. But I hear it's coming." He looked at her. "The new grill should be here late next week."

"Oh good. So when you place your next order for food, I'll have a few things to include."

He pointed at her. "We're going slow, remember?"

"I know, I know. Grilled fish, grilled chicken, and fajitas. That's not drastic."

"Fajitas? That'd be good. Something different." Kyler pointed at her mug. "I'll have another."

Mark glanced at Lexie. "You?"

"No. I should probably go." She stood and touched Kyler's shoulder. "So? Tomorrow?"

Kyler nodded. "Sure. Looking forward to it."

"I'll be over a little after five. Or is that too early?"

"No. I'll try to knock off early. I'll be home."

"Okay." She gave a short wave to Mark. "Thanks for the beer."

She was smiling as she heard Mark grilling Kyler. "Tomorrow what? You got a date or something?" Lexie shook her head. Between Mark and their mother, it would be a miracle if she and Kyler made it through this unscathed.

CHAPTER TWENTY-SEVEN

Lexie heard the familiar ringtone and snatched up her phone with a smile. "Hey, Trish!"

"So you are still alive? That's a relief."

"I've texted you several times."

"I thought you would have called by now."

She heard traffic noise. "Where are you?"

"Stuck on MoPac. I swear, it's freaking Saturday morning and you'd think it was rush hour or something."

"I don't miss that," she said truthfully. "But where are you going? I probably miss that."

"Brunch at Trudy's."

She groaned. "You're going to order the cheesy migas, aren't you?"

"Yes. And one of their famous Bloody Marys. Jealous?"

She paused. Was she? While it did sound like fun—the eating and drinking part—the thought of being stuck in traffic on MoPac kinda took some of the pleasure out of it. "Surprisingly, no."

"Do you miss Austin at all?"

She closed her eyes for a moment. "I miss you, of course," she said quickly. "But no, I haven't fallen into a fit of depression being away."

"God, I thought you'd already be going crazy. I mean, it's what? Two weeks?"

"Two weeks yesterday, actually." She moved to the door of her apartment and opened it. "Seems longer," she murmured.

"I imagine so."

She smiled. "I actually meant that in a good way. I've been keeping busy. Mom's got me running the lodge pretty much on my own. I've had to hone my customer service skills. I haven't had a job dealing with the public since I worked at Whataburger in high school," she said with a laugh. "And Mark has a friend who has taken me bike riding a few times."

Trish gasped. "Really? I thought after Mia that you'd never ride again."

"Mountain bike. We ride the trails in the park. It's been fun." She watched as a flock of finches flew into the bird garden and a smile lit her face. "We've become friends. She's someone to have dinner with, grab a beer with. And Sunday football parties—that's apparently a weekly thing during the season."

"She? *Oh?*"

"We're just friends," she said quickly, not sure if it was herself she was trying to convince or Trish.

"I know you were worried about that."

"I was. And it's been great to be around Mark and my parents again. Everything is all Christmasy, but the weather has been surprisingly pleasant. Well, we had a couple of really cold days, but that's it. Sunny nearly every day." She stepped out into the sunshine now. "I actually kinda love it so far," she admitted.

"Wow. Never thought I'd hear you say that. I expected you to say you couldn't *wait* to get back."

"I know. There's nothing up here that resembles my former life. Nothing. Yet, I'm adjusting. My mom made a veggie lasagna for a group dinner. I ordered tofu from Amazon. There is no fish to be found, even frozen. Mark's going to order some for the restaurant, though, as soon as he gets the indoor grill set up. And I'll have to resort to eating more chicken than I'm used to, I suppose." She didn't add that her plans for dinner tonight with Kyler included chicken. "It is remote, although not as sparse as I imagined. Everyone's been very nice so far. Oh, and I have a hiking date tomorrow morning before our football party."

"*Hiking*? Do you hike?"

"No. It'll be a first, but I'm looking forward to it." She didn't add she was mostly looking forward to being with Kyler. "I've been on the mountain bike on some of the trails and this hike is pretty much straight up to Skyline Drive. I've been up there in Kyler's Jeep for a sunrise and a sunset, but this will be my first hike."

"Kyler?"

"That's Mark's friend. Well, my friend too."

"So you've replaced me already?"

"No, of course not! She's very different than you. Different than anyone I know in Austin." She stared at the bird garden, seeing two doves land there. What had Kyler called them? Collared doves? Or were these the white-winged? "She's very outdoorsy. Kind of earthy, I'd call her. Into birdwatching and stuff."

"Birdwatching? God, she sounds positively boring," Trish groaned. "What do you have in common with her?"

Boring? No, Kyler was the opposite of boring. "She's actually quite fun. She enjoys football as much as I do."

"Football? You like football?"

"I do. And she's teaching me about the birds up here. My mother has a bunch of feeders that I tend to. The bird garden."

"Oh my god. What have you turned into? Would I even recognize this side of you?"

Trish tempered her statement with a laugh, but Lexie knew by her tone that she wasn't teasing. Would Trish—or any of her friends—recognize her? She didn't feel like she'd changed. Who changes in a mere two weeks?

But she had, hadn't she? She found pleasure in the small things that she once overlooked or considered boring, as Trish had said. Sunrise? Who got up early enough to catch one of those? Sunset? Sure, she'd made a point to catch a few—margarita in hand. Staring at thousands of stars on a chilly December night in a crystal-clear sky? No people, no sound, no city lights—just the stars at night and an attractive woman to share them with. And watching birds? She smiled, picturing Kyler pointing out the red-tailed hawk to her. Little things. Yet she felt so much richer for them, didn't she?

"Maybe you wouldn't recognize me," she finally said. "I'm usually in bed by ten, up by five thirty."

"Oh my god, Lexie, really? You're thirty. Have you turned into your mother already?"

She smiled, knowing her mother—with her coffee habit—rarely went to bed before midnight. And she got up in time to shower and stumble downstairs and into the office by eight, where Lexie had already been working for at least an hour.

"I have changed my routine, that's for sure."

"So no nightlife?"

"No nightlife. And I don't miss it."

"Oh, come on. Surely you miss hanging out on Sixth Street on Saturday nights?"

"I don't. I certainly don't miss the Sunday morning headache from too much drinking."

"Oh, come on. That's part of it! That's what Sunday brunch and a Bloody Mary is for."

"Well, I'll have to make do with Mark's bar, I guess," she said a little more curtly than she'd intended.

"So what about tonight? It's Saturday. Are you saying you're doing *nothing*?"

"I'm actually going over to Kyler's and cooking dinner. My apartment here doesn't have a kitchen to speak of."

"The birdwatcher? You're having dinner? What in the world do you talk about?" She paused. "Oh my god, are you *dating* her?"

"No, we're not dating!"

"Oh, finally! We're creeping up to thirty miles per hour!"

"Glad it's you and not me stuck on MoPac."

"But seriously. What do you talk about with a birdwatcher?"

"I don't know. We just clicked. There haven't been any lulls in conversation." She paused. "I like her."

Trish paused too. "But you're only friends, right? Because if something romantic was happening—with a freakin' birdwatcher!—I'd wonder about your sanity," she said with a laugh.

"We're new friends, yes," she said carefully. "She's my age, so that's a plus." She blew out her breath. "But, no. We're not dating. She's not my type at all. And I'm not hers. Like I said, she's kinda earthy, outdoorsy. She's a park ranger here at the state park. Not my type."

"No, definitely not your type." She laughed. "A birdwatcher? I'm trying to picture you dating a birdwatcher!"

"I know, right."

"So you're still going to stay until January?"

"I think so, yes. I feel about as good as I have in a very, very long time. I'm in a good place, mentally. Emotionally, too. I feel good, Trish. Things are slow and stress-free and I'm not constantly thinking about being unemployed. In fact, that hasn't crossed my mind in days."

"I know that was getting you down."

She looked up into the sky. "It was. That weight I was carrying around has slipped away, thankfully." And it had. The constant worrying about her future had taken its toll, practically zapping the life out of her, but it seemed to have disappeared. Right now, right this minute, she actually had a rosy outlook on life, something that had been missing for many months. She moved to the patio on the corner and sat down. "So, who are you meeting for brunch? Tell me some gossip."

They talked for exactly thirteen more minutes, until Trish reached the parking lot of Trudy's. They said their hurried goodbyes with Lexie promising to call more often.

She set her phone on the patio table and leaned back, her gaze going to the bird garden. The sun was bright and felt warm on her arms. Yes, whatever depression she'd been feeling was gone. She smiled more, she laughed more. Part of it was being around her family—it was heartening knowing they were right here and not six hundred miles away.

Part of it was Kyler, too. She'd taken her out of her comfort zone from the very first. An early sunrise, a scenic tour in a Jeep, bike rides. A sunset. A hike tomorrow. She watched as two doves landed under the feeders, scattering some little birds that had been there, making her sigh contentedly. Who would have thought she'd find peace on this remote desert mountaintop?

CHAPTER TWENTY-EIGHT

Kyler tidied the already clean cabin, shifting her books into a more orderly pile, then picking them up altogether, looking around for another place to put them.

"You're being ridiculous."

She put them back down. Lexie had already seen her house.

As five o'clock approached, it brought the impending dusk along with it. She went to the Christmas tree and turned the lights on, pausing to watch them twinkle for a few moments. She glanced to the fireplace. It had been another nice day—fifties and sunshine—but it would cool off quickly once the sun set. She already had the fire ready to go but wouldn't light it until later.

She turned the living room light off, leaving on the overhead in the kitchen. She stood there, restless, her gaze going from the lights of the tree to the front door and back again. Why was she feeling so nervous?

Well, because they would be alone. And the last time they were alone, they'd held hands. The last time they'd been alone, she'd wanted to kiss her. Because she was sexually infatuated with her.

She looked to the ceiling and shook her head. A damn crush. At her age.

She chanced a glance up to the mistletoe that was hung on the ceiling fan. Maybe she should take it down. She didn't want Lexie to think she put it there for a purpose. She rolled her eyes. Mistletoe was a part of the holiday tradition. Yeah, it was. That didn't mean she wanted to drag Lexie under the damn thing. *Yeah you do.*

She'd found the mistletoe just last week and had hung it up with, yes, visions of perhaps kissing someone. That someone being Lexie.

She heard a car door slam and she moved to the window, seeing Lexie getting some bags from the backseat. She went out to help.

"Hi. Need some help?"

"Oh, good. Yes. I have four bags."

"What all did you bring?"

"I didn't know what kind of pots and pans you had so I raided Mom's kitchen."

"I don't have much, really. I guess I should have warned you."

"Mom did." She handed her another bag. "And of course a shopping trip to Potter's. They actually had everything I needed."

They had all of Lexie's loot spread out on the table and she was surprised to find chicken on the menu. Before long, she was helping to chop and dice a mixture of onions, red and yellow bell peppers, mushrooms, and garlic. An iPad was propped up against the coffeepot and she glanced over to see what they were making. She cocked an eyebrow.

"What is 'Kinda Chicken Primavera' and where did you find a 'kinda' recipe?"

Lexie elbowed her playfully. "It's a healthier version. No heavy cream. And I 'kinda' made it up after combining three different recipes. Thus the name."

"You know, you threatened me with a tofu stir-fry one time. Why chicken?"

"I'm not averse to eating chicken." She paused in her chopping. "I have it a couple of times a week. I mean, I did back in Austin when I went out, which was often. I have resigned myself that it will become my staple since—other than stir-fry—I'm not great with tofu dishes. Besides, I don't really have a kitchen. And as much as I love fish, I would imagine I'd get tired of grilled fish every day."

"Hmm. Wonder if I will? I've got a lot of years to make up for."

The chicken was seasoned and put in the oven on a low bake, then Lexie left the veggies out on the counter. "We've got about thirty minutes before I'll need to sauté these."

"How about a drink?"

Lexie nodded. "I'd love one."

"I've also got a fire ready to go."

"That'd be nice. There's not one in my little apartment, but I enjoy sitting by my parents' fireplace." She sighed. "I try not to stay up there too much, though. I don't want to get in the way of their routine."

Kyler poured bourbon into two glasses. "Do you think you are?"

"Maybe. I don't want them to feel like they have to entertain me. Same with you."

"Me?" She poured Coke into the glasses. "Is that what you think?"

"I don't want you to feel like your free time has to be spent with me. On a bike or like tomorrow—a hike."

"Lexie, those are things I love doing. Sharing two of my passions with someone—you—isn't a hindrance. It's a benefit, if anything."

"You're used to doing them alone."

"Yeah. So it's nice to have company."

Lexie met her gaze. "Okay."

"Is that why you were avoiding me these last few days?"

"Was I?"

"Weren't you?" She tilted her head. "Or were you avoiding me because of what happened the other night?"

"No. The other night was fun." Then she shook her head. "Okay, maybe. I felt like we were—well, like we were getting close to that line."

She arched an eyebrow. "Is there a line?"

"Isn't there?"

"Does there have to be?"

"Oh, Kyler, you surely can't be serious. We've already had this discussion. We are so not each other's type."

"No, we're not. That doesn't mean I'm not attracted to you." Lexie seemed surprised by her admission and a bit uncomfortable about the topic. She decided to lighten things up a little. "Maybe because you're normal. You know my choices are women with pigs as pets and the twins."

"Mark mentioned the pig lady."

"She was nice enough, I guess, if you could get past the two pigs roaming the house."

She started the fire and they sat on the sofa, watching the flames for a moment. She assumed their conversation would shift to less personal topics, so Lexie's question startled her.

"Why don't you date? And I don't mean the pig lady or the twins. Or the excuse that you can't meet someone up here. What's the *real* reason?"

Kyler twirled the glass between her hands. What was the real reason? Bad luck? Poor decisions? Britney?

"Part of it is that there's not a lot of opportunity to date. That's only part of it. I haven't actually tried very hard."

"Why not?"

"At first, I was still reeling over the thing with my boss's wife. That was a huge mistake. I knew it was wrong and it was a damn stupid thing to do. It upended my life. Got me sent a thousand miles away." She took a swallow of the drink. "As you know, I don't have a relationship with my parents. Part of me blames that on being up here, so far away. And I'm up here because I made a bad choice." She glanced at her quickly. "Don't get me wrong, I love it up here now. I don't want to leave. If I finish my career and retire up here, I'd be happy."

"But you miss your family?"

"Sometimes, yeah. I told you they weren't crazy about my career choice. They kinda let me drift away on my own after that and they turned all their attention to my sister. We didn't see each other all that much anymore."

"Were you and your sister ever close?"

She leaned back with a sigh. "Close like you and Mark? No, I wouldn't say that. She's a few years younger than me. We never shared a room growing up, so we missed that closeness. We didn't have any mutual friends. We lived in the same house, that was about it." She turned to look at Lexie. "My parents aren't like yours. They're more clinical. Everything was always straightforward. Regimented, almost. Your mom and my mom? Complete opposites. My mom is cold where yours is warm. Susan is affectionate. My mom? I can count on one hand the number of times she's hugged me."

"That's so sad, Kyler."

"Yes, it is. That's why I love your mother so much. She makes me feel…included." She felt Lexie's hand touch her arm and squeeze it. "You're very lucky to have had her."

"My mother loves you too."

She nodded. "Yes, I know. That's not something I have to doubt."

"But you do with your parents?"

"Yes. They've never told me."

Lexie's hand squeezed harder. "You're kidding?"

"No. Actually, the first person to tell me they loved me was Britney."

"Who was Britney?"

She took a sip of her drink, wondering why she'd brought up her old flame. "It was love at first sight, I guess. For me, anyway." She shrugged. "I was twenty-four when I met her, and I went all in. Happiest time of my life…or so I thought. I was head over heels in love with that woman. For one whole year. There was no drama, no cheating, no big breakup scene either. I was twenty-five and we were having dinner one night and she said we needed to talk. She said she didn't love me anymore. She said she wasn't sure that she was ever in love with me. She said we were friends and we should have left it like that." She took a larger swallow of her drink, surprised how those words still smarted. "It was all so very calm and civilized. I was speechless. I don't think I said a single word to her."

"You were in shock, I imagine."

"Yes. Two days later, she had completely moved her things out and I was still in shock."

"Was there someone else?"

Kyler shook her head. "I think maybe it would have been better if there had been. Then I could have been angry. It was a month or so before I heard she'd started dating again. And then I'd bump into her from time to time."

Lexie reached a hand out to touch her arm again. "Are you not over it? I mean, are you still in love with her?"

Kyler jerked her head up. "Oh, no. I mean, yeah, it took a while for the hurt to go away, but I rarely even think about her anymore. I'm certainly not in love with her. Love blinds you, as everyone knows. After it was over, I saw her in a different light, I guess. She was right to end things. We didn't have enough in common to sustain a relationship. Especially now. I've changed so much since then. She's not anything like the person I'd want to spend my life with."

"So you just don't date at all? Your boss's wife?"

"That wasn't dating. I knew it wouldn't ever go anywhere." She shook her head. "But in my stupidity, I never considered how I was going to end things with her and still keep my job."

"And that only lasted a couple of months?" Lexie laughed. "Was she at least good in bed?"

"Honestly, I was so concerned with getting caught, it wasn't really enjoyable."

"And *did* you get caught?"

Kyler felt a blush light her face, something which prompted Lexie to laugh again.

"I see you did."

"We were in the supply closet at the headquarters. She worked as the clerk. Like Tammy does here. Anyway, he had radioed that he was riding with one of the guys to check out the beach picnic area. I was working the check-in booth that day. She called me. Told me to put the self-pay sign up." She shook her head. "And, like a fool, I did."

"He set you up?"

"Yeah. He suspected something, but he didn't know it was me. He thought it was Scott, one of the young maintenance guys."

"And he caught you in the supply closet? How bad was it?"

"We were still fully clothed. Well, mostly."

"She blamed you?"

"Of course she did. Said I forced her. And he wanted to fire me. Then he wanted me to quit. We compromised. I got sent far, far away—here—and promised never to step foot in the park down there again."

"And did she try to contact you?"

"No. Thankfully. I got up here and tried to put all that behind me. I love it here now, as you know. I made a poor decision, had a huge lapse in judgment, and it turned out to be the best thing that ever happened to me. This place, this area, it's like I was meant to be here. I feel at peace up here. Like my world is right where it's supposed to be."

Lexie nodded. "I was having those thoughts the other night when we were watching the sunset. How peaceful I felt." She smiled at her. "I don't know if it was the sunset or being with you. You're very different from the friends I left behind." She tilted her head a bit. "You're introspective. You get enjoyment out of little things, out of what nature provides. Most of my friends were all so career-oriented, ambitious to a fault, some. There was no downtime. No idle time. Their life existed only through social media, as mine did. My phone was for texting and Facebook, checking Twitter, Instagram. Actual phone calls were rare."

"I remember. I'm a millennial too, you know."

Lexie laughed lightly. "I would *never* describe you as a millennial. Never."

Kyler laughed too. "I know. They'd think I was giving them a bad name. I don't do Twitter. I don't do Instagram. I have a Facebook account, but I can't remember the last time I was on there. I just kinda do my own thing and don't worry about all that mess."

"How freeing that must be. I still feel compelled to check mine. I haven't posted anything, though. I mean, since I've been up here. No picture of the lodge or anything."

"Why not?"

Lexie looked at her thoughtfully. "I don't know, really. I think at first, it was why make a big announcement that I'm here if it's only going to be for six weeks or so. I mean, my closest friends all knew, but I felt uncomfortable sharing that with everyone." The timer on Lexie's phone signaled it was time to start the veggies and she stood. "I think I should. Post something, I mean."

"How about a picture of you on our hike tomorrow?"

"That's a good idea." She went into the kitchen, then paused. "Can we have a campfire later?"

"Outside? Sure. It's one of my favorite things to do."

CHAPTER TWENTY-NINE

Lexie sat beside the campfire ring, watching as Kyler layered twigs on top of the newspaper she'd wadded up.

"Did you make this?"

"Yes. All of the campsites have these metal rings with a dropdown grate for grilling. I brought one of the old frames over—minus the grate—and then put rocks around it with mortar and everything so you can't see the frame anymore."

"You're pretty handy, aren't you? Mom's bird garden, the waterfall…a campfire ring. Would you believe me if I said I'd never had a campfire before?"

Kyler nodded. "You live in the city and you've never been camping, so yeah, I'd believe you."

A loud rustling in the brush caused her to whip her head around. "What's that?" she whispered urgently.

Kyler lit the fire, then stood, shining her flashlight into the woods. "Let's hope it's a raccoon and not a javelina."

"What's a javelina?"

"Like a mean little pig." Kyler turned the light off again, apparently not seeing anything. "I throw out corn for the deer.

They might come during the night to eat if there's any left. I haven't seen any around here, though."

"Will they like…attack?"

"As a rule, no. But if they have babies and we get too close, they'd probably charge. The fire will keep them away." Kyler sat down in the chair next to her. "I haven't seen any at the cabins. Now the campsites, yeah. Even though we post signs to lock food up, people don't. Or they throw birdseed out on the ground. The javelinas come during the night to clean up." She leaned closer to the fire, adding a few small limbs to the flames. "I enjoy watching them. From a distance. They chased me one time."

"Really? What were you doing?"

"Oh, I was clearing some brush on a trail. It was early morning. They hadn't settled down for the day yet and I came upon a group with young ones. The whole damn herd charged me." She laughed. "And yeah, I screamed like a girl as I ran back to the truck. I jumped on the back in one leap with them nipping at my heels."

"How funny. I mean, probably not so funny at the time."

"No. I about pissed my pants. Maybe you'll get to see one. They don't come out during the day very often. If it's a dreary, overcast day—which is rare up here—a lot of the nighttime animals stay out longer. Those are the best days to be out in the woods. You see all kinds of stuff."

"So this is nice," Lexie said, scooting her chair closer to the fire. "It's safe to sit out here, right?"

"Yes. Whatever critters are out there, they'll stay away from the fire."

Kyler moved her chair to the other side of her, away from the smoke.

"Where's your bird feeder?"

Kyler turned the flashlight back on and aimed it into the trees, finding the hanging feeder. "I sit on the little back porch there in the mornings with my coffee. I throw corn out right before daybreak. There's this deer that comes by, a young doe. I call her Daisy."

Lexie leaned forward, holding her hands out to the flames. "You are probably the sweetest person I've ever met."

"Sweet?"

"Kind. Kind*hearted*," she clarified. She turned to her. "You named a deer. You wake up and come out here to watch everything else wake up too. I'm not sure something like that has ever occurred to me before. Certainly not anything I would have considered doing. But now? I go out of my apartment and I immediately turn my attention to the bird garden. And I've taken to having my morning coffee on Mark's little patio and I listen and I watch."

"Do you feel like a stranger?"

"Somewhat. Like, who is that person looking back at me in the mirror?" She gave a quick laugh. "No, not a stranger really. But I did talk to Trish today." Lexie glanced at Kyler. "Trish is my best friend. And I've only been here a few weeks and I feel us growing apart. I think she could sense it too."

"What do you mean? You didn't have anything to talk about?"

"Not really that. She doesn't understand how I could possibly like it up here. I think she thought I would be on the road back by now. She was quick to belittle this place, *you*."

"Me?"

"I told her a little about you. How I'd made a friend. She couldn't imagine that you and I would have anything in common." Lexie turned to her. "But we do, don't we? I don't feel like we're so completely opposite that we have nothing to talk about. In fact, my conversations with you are so much more meaningful than any I've had in, well, a long time."

"Maybe being up here is allowing you to see a side of yourself that you didn't know existed." Kyler held her hand out to the warmth of the fire. "I'm not the same person I was when I moved up here. My whole outlook on life is different. It's not only that I've taken up birdwatching and stargazing that's changed. Those are two byproducts of being where we are. The altitude, the atmosphere, the remoteness—it's a stargazer's paradise. That's why the observatory is located up here. Down at the coast, it's often foggy, cloudy. City lights. It would be futile. It never once crossed my mind."

"What got you started?"

"Irene. She had me over for riding and she cooked a meal for us. It was getting dark as I was leaving. She walked out with me and the sun had set but the sky still had that red glow. She looked over to the east and the moon was rising. She pointed at a faint star and told me it was Jupiter." She smiled at the memory. "I stared at it—the moon and Jupiter—and something clicked inside. I had been up here a couple of months by then and, sure, I'd noticed how clear the sky was, how bright the stars were, but I hadn't really given it much thought. That night, when I got home, I pulled a chair out. Right in this spot, actually. And I sat and watched the sky for hours." Kyler bent her head back to look at the stars now. "That was the first time I felt at peace. I didn't feel lonely anymore or out of place. I didn't feel like I needed to simply get through each day, each week, each month, all with an end date in sight so I could leave here and go back down. I had a sense of renewal, I think. I was living my life, but not really, you know? It was like I was on the fringes, looking in but not really *being*." Kyler turned to her. "Does that make sense?"

"Being present?"

"Yeah. I was present physically, but I never embraced it. I never was a part of it. Now I feel like I'm an integral part of everything around me. The earth, the sky, the birds, the critters that hide in the dark—I'm aware of all of that now. I'm a part of it." She glanced at Lexie and gave a quick smile. "I'm sounding like a weird tree hugger now, aren't I?"

Lexie shook her head. "You sound like you are at peace with yourself and everything around you. That's not weird, Kyler. That's something to envy." She looked overhead at the stars. "Trish asked me if I missed it there, if I missed the nightlife. She expected me to say yes. She expected me to say I couldn't wait to get back home." Lexie turned to her. "Truth is, I don't miss it. I can feel myself changing. I can see it. You're a big part of that. If I hadn't met you, I'm not sure I would be as content as I am. I feel like you're teaching me how to be me."

"Maybe you're finally allowing yourself to be you."

"I'm certainly different. I feel more whole. I realize how much I'd missed out on. All the little everyday things that some people take for granted. I spent exactly one week a year with Mark and two weeks with my parents. Every year. That's it. That's not nearly enough."

"When everyone still lived in Austin, you saw them more?"

"Oh, yes. When Mia was alive, I was at their place all the time. And we had a family dinner every Wednesday night. It was rare that either Mark or I missed. So yeah, when they all moved, I had this huge void in my life. But I filled it. And I filled it with all these trivial things that I convinced myself were important. I didn't miss my family as much because nearly every hour of every day was filled with something."

"That had to be exhausting."

"It was. Physically *and* mentally. But I think it was like you said. I was living on the fringes, just skimming the surface. It was like life or death if I missed a gym session. Dinner dates, brunch, barhopping. There was no downtime, no quiet time. No *me* time." She sighed. "Then I no longer had a job and I ended things with Cathy and all of a sudden, I had time on my hands, and I didn't know what to do with it. That's when it became glaringly obvious to me how truly empty my life was." She stood and turned her back to the fire. "Empty in that there was nothing meaningful. I had no job, I had no partner." She waved her hand. "So I tried to fill all the empty space with something. But still, at the end of the day, it was meaningless. It was as if I was trying to kill time."

"Time is too precious to kill."

"Exactly! So when my mother offered this to me, I was actually shocked that I was considering it. My first inclination was to say no, absolutely not. I loved my life. I loved all the stuff I did. I loved the freedom I had." She looked at Kyler. "I was lying to myself. I hated what my life had become. I hated all the stuff I'd started doing to fill my hours. So when I took a step back and took stock of my life, I was surprised at how unhappy I truly was. I did the pros and cons of moving up here and sure, I had a list of cons, but most of them were based on my current lifestyle."

"Do you still have cons?"

"Yes. I mean, it's only been a few weeks. I can't throw all my hesitations out the window after a couple of weeks. But they're not quite so prevalent now. And some of the cons were things I thought I'd miss, thought I *should* miss. Like Sixth Street on Saturday nights. And meeting friends for dinner or lunch. And the gym and spin class." She sat down again. "I feel surprisingly happy being here. But it's too soon to say I'm going to stay. I'd told myself I'd take at least six weeks, then decide."

"That's probably the wisest thing to do."

"I know. I have to look at it long-term. Maybe a change like this is something I need right now. But what about in a couple of years?

Five years? Ten? Will I wake up when I'm forty and wonder where the time went? And think it's then too late to escape?"

"Has your mother been pushing you to make a decision already?"

"No, not at all. Although she did mention that they want to take a couple of days off and go to El Paso to shop for an RV. And I overheard her on the phone with my grandparents. She was telling them that if I stay, they'd head out to Florida in February and spend a couple of months down there with them."

"So you're feeling pressured?"

"A little. I don't want to disappoint them."

"You've got to do what's best for you. Your mother will respect your decision."

"I know." She leaned her elbows on her knees, turning her head to look at her. "It's too soon to be sure, isn't it?"

Kyler nodded. "I think so. You'll know when you're sure. One way or the other."

Lexie looked at her thoughtfully. "Why do you call yourself weird? Weird birdwatcher. Now a weird tree hugger. Why?"

Kyler shrugged. "I guess because in my former jobs, I thought those people were weird—strange."

Lexie nodded. "I guess to the outside world, yes. They're different." She smiled then. "You seem perfectly normal. Different, yes, than my friends in Austin. A good different." She leaned closer to her. "Thank you for being my friend, Kyler. Thank you for giving me an outlet to voice my feelings, my concerns. Mark is a good listener, but I think he wants me to stay too badly to be objective."

"What makes you think I don't want you to stay?"

"Do you?"

Lexie felt a charge between them—they were too close. The flickering light from the fire seemed to be blanketing them, bathing them in its soft glow. Their eyes held and Kyler felt it too, she could see. Kyler's gaze dropped to her lips and Lexie felt her breath catch. Would they kiss? Now? Where everything was soft and romantic all of a sudden?

"I do."

No. She didn't want them to kiss. If they kissed, it would change things and she wasn't ready for things to change. No. So she leaned back, away from her. Kyler turned away too and stared into the flames, making Lexie wonder what she was thinking.

"Thank you for the campfire," Lexie said quietly as she stood. "But I think I should go."

Kyler stood too, taking a step away from the fire. "It was a nice evening. Thank you again for dinner. It was really good."

"You're welcome."

Lexie paused for a moment, wondering if she should say something else. Kyler was looking at the stars and Lexie followed her gaze, finding the Little Dipper. She stared at it for a long moment, then made herself move.

She went back inside to pack her things, gathering up the dishes and pans they'd washed earlier and shoving them into bags. She heard Kyler come inside too, and she turned to her. They weren't in the shadowed light of the campfire any longer. The bright kitchen light allowed her to see Kyler's eyes clearly.

She didn't know who moved first. She didn't care. Like two magnets snapping together—their kiss wasn't soft and gentle. Quite the opposite. Kyler's hands cupped her face, holding her as their mouths opened, moans filling the kitchen as they pressed close together.

Oh, dear lord, this was so not supposed to happen. She pushed that thought aside as her hands rested at Kyler's hips. The brush of Kyler's tongue against her own caused her to grip Kyler's hips tighter, pulling them toward her in an almost desperate motion. The jolt that shot through her body at the contact caused her heart to jump into her throat, nearly choking her.

She pulled away, her eyes wide as she backed up.

"No, no, no," she said, shaking her head. "We did *not* just do that."

Kyler had a smile on her mouth. "I think we did, yes."

Lexie held her hand up. "No. We can't do this." She took another step away from her. "Let's just pretend we didn't do that. Okay?"

"No."

"*No?* Kyler, you said yourself, I'm not your type." She shook her head almost fiercely. "We're friends. We should *not* be kissing."

Kyler took a step away from her too. "Okay. We probably should not be kissing. You're right."

"I know I am."

"So we'll pretend it didn't happen," Kyler said unconvincingly.

"Yes, we will." She grabbed the two bags she'd managed to pack. "I should go."

"We've got a hike in the morning, remember?"

She paused. "Maybe we should skip that."

"Lexie, it was just a little kiss. Don't overreact."

She let out a breath. "You're right. Hiking. Daybreak." She motioned to the counter. "I'll get the rest of this later."

Kyler didn't follow her out to her car, and she was thankful. She put the two bags she'd packed into the backseat, then got inside. She thought she saw Kyler watching from the window but wasn't sure. She backed away, her mind buzzing. What the *hell* just happened?

"Oh, don't be stupid," she murmured out loud. She knew exactly what had happened.

Yeah, she knew. But what the *hell* were they thinking? *Kissing?* No, no, no. Friends did *not* kiss!

CHAPTER THIRTY

She'd been awake since five and she was on her third cup of coffee. She was feeling a little anxious this morning. Okay, a lot anxious. Because she knew that she should not see Kyler this morning. They should not be alone.

It's a hike. What could possibly happen on a hike?

Right. It was only a hike. Hopefully, a strenuous hike that would have her laboring and out of breath. There would be no time to think about kissing.

"That was a stupid thing to do," she muttered to herself.

She should have left sooner. She shouldn't have gone back inside the house. But she had and so had Kyler. And as she replayed the scene in her mind, she was convinced that it was Kyler who had moved first, not her. But why?

They'd already talked about it. She thought they were on the same page. She wasn't Kyler's type. Kyler certainly wasn't her type. Why in the world did they kiss?

"Friends don't freakin' kiss," she said out loud.

* * *

Kyler felt sluggish this morning and after a fitful night's sleep, why not? It was the damn kiss. She'd woken up numerous times, worrying over it, wondering how it would change things between them. She didn't want things to change. She liked them the way they were. Lexie was fun and she enjoyed her company. She enjoyed having her along on bike rides. She was looking forward to the hike.

She shouldn't have followed Lexie inside last night. She should have let Lexie leave. That's what she should have done. Because she could feel the energy between them. Sitting around the campfire, she could feel it. So had Lexie. Why else had she tried to leave so abruptly? But no. She'd gone inside. She was going to help her pack, thank her for dinner—which had been delicious—and bid her a good night. No, that didn't happen. One look. That's all it took. Lexie had moved first, of that she was certain.

And now they'd kissed. Not a little kiss, as she'd claimed. A full body touching-in-all-sorts-of-places kind of kiss. A kiss that had stolen her breath away. A kiss that promised so much more.

There wouldn't be more, though, would it? They were going to forget about it. They weren't going to mention it. Lexie wanted to pretend it didn't happen. They'd go on a hike, they'd act like everything was normal, then they'd go to Mark's for football.

They'd pretend they hadn't kissed. They'd tease and laugh, and Lexie would flirt with her in that subtle way of hers and then she'd think about the damn kiss all over again.

Her head snapped up when she heard a car door close. Lexie was here. Her heart beat a little bit faster than it should and she went to the door, opening it before Lexie could knock.

They looked at each other and she saw a wariness in Lexie's eyes.

"Good morning. Am I too early?"

"No, no. I'm ready. Let me get my backpack."

CHAPTER THIRTY-ONE

"So when did you get hiking boots?"

Lexie held one foot up as they stood next to Kyler's Jeep. "Like I said, Amazon is my friend. I ordered them, like, the third day I was here."

"First time to have them on?"

"No, I've been wearing them some, trying to break them in." She eyed Kyler's hiking stick. "Where'd you get that?"

Kyler tapped it on the rocks a couple of times. "I made it. Pretty cool, huh?"

"Tell me." They started up the trail, which was in a little ravine between the interpretive center—and one of the bird blinds—and the RV camping sites, where three white RVs were parked.

"When we trim juniper limbs—either around the campground or sometimes along hiking trails—I keep the bigger ones. Well, those that are nice and straight. All I did with this one is sand it down to get the bark off and bring out the color. Except here around the handle." Kyler stopped, showing it to her. The bark around the handle seemed almost red. "Put a cedar stain on it, then a nice varnish and that's all it took." Kyler smiled at her. "You want me to make you one?"

"Would you?"

"Sure." She surprised her by offering the stick to her now. "Try it out. See if you like it."

Lexie took the hiking stick, not really sure how to use it. But as they walked on, she found it helped with her balance when going over rocks—and gave her something to lean on to catch her breath.

"How long does it take to get to the top?"

Kyler laughed. "You tired already?"

"No, but hiking on rocks—uphill—is way different than strolling from the lodge over to the restaurant."

"Different than a gym workout too."

"Yes, it is." She stopped walking and Kyler glanced at her, then stopped too. "I was talking about that with Mark the other day. Austin is full of outdoor opportunities. A huge greenbelt, lots of hike and bike trails, yet I never used them. I ran on a treadmill in the gym, not outside. I was stuck in spin class when I could have taken a mountain bike out on the trails."

"Why?"

"I'm not sure. I guess I never met anyone who did those things. The closest I ever got to getting outside for a workout was when Mark and Mia would go cycling and I'd join them. But like I said, it was a road bike and they wanted to do thirty miles or more." She shook her head. "That wasn't my thing." She grinned. "My ass hurt after fifteen miles."

"I was going to ask if you ever went to the greenbelt—Barton Springs Greenbelt. I've been on it a couple of times."

"You have?"

They started walking again and the trail smoothed out, the large rocks of the ravine replaced with a gravel-like surface now. The trail narrowed some, but it was still plenty wide for two to walk side-by-side.

"The first time, I was in college. I didn't have my own bike, so I rented one at a shop there. It was a blast. We'd ride for a while, then stop and swim, then back on the bike. I was used to Corpus and the beach so getting to be in the woods and ride along a crystal-clear creek was pretty awesome."

"And the second time?"

"It was about a year before I came up here. I went with two guys who were damn near pros on a mountain bike." Kyler laughed. "They left me behind pretty quick. So I had a leisurely ride and like before, I'd find a nice swimming hole and hop in for a bit, then ride on again. That was why—when I needed to find a new job—I looked at the parks around Austin."

"Are there creeks here that you can swim in? Limpia Creek?"

"Not here in the park, no. Enough to splash in and get your feet wet, that's about all. Of course, Balmorhea has the spring-fed pool but that's way too crowded for me. But up at Irene's ranch, Limpia Creek flows there, and she's got some nice holes." Kyler glanced at her and smiled. "You can only get to them by horseback."

"Determined to get me on a horse, aren't you?"

"It's fun. It's freeing. You get to see places that you wouldn't otherwise. And the views up there near Mt. Livermore are incredible."

"I do like to swim." Of course, that too was done at the gym. Had she ever been in water that wasn't chlorinated?

"Bikini?" Their eyes met and Kyler shook her head. "No. Don't answer that."

Lexie smiled as Kyler turned away and kept walking. So that was the closest they'd come to mentioning the kiss without mentioning it, of course. All of her earlier trepidation was unwarranted, apparently. Things had been friendly and normal between them. The tension that she'd arrived with had dissipated almost as soon as she got there.

Kyler stopped suddenly, her head cocked as she stared into the brush beside them. Lexie stopped too, hearing a rustling there. What was it? A herd of javelinas about to attack? A mountain lion?

Kyler held a finger to her lips to indicate she should stay quiet. Then she squatted down, beckoning Lexie to do the same. She did, her gaze going where Kyler pointed. Six birds foraged among the leaves under the branches of a bush. She had no idea what they were, but one had a pretty black and white face—clown-like almost in appearance. Short, squatty birds. Quail? One looked up in his task, seeming to look right at them. But the birds didn't panic. They moved on slowly, still scratching in the leaves. Then, quick as lightning, they ran, scurrying away in a straight line, one behind the other, their short legs flashing as they disappeared into the brush.

Kyler stood up, a bright smile on her face. "Montezuma quail. A pair with four young. Well, not so young anymore but their offspring from this year."

"The black and white face?"

"That was the male. They call it a harlequin pattern. He's beautiful, isn't he?"

She nodded. "Yes. Very." Then she smiled. "All that noise they were making, I thought we were going to be attacked by something."

Kyler started walking again. "A lot of birders come here to try to find the quail. You don't often see them this close, although in the evenings, they'll come to the bird blinds if it's quiet."

They walked on now in silence, the sun having finally crested the peak behind them. Lexie enjoyed the quiet, letting in sounds that had been in the background—birds in the trees, the gentle rustle of leaves, the crunching of their boots as they moved over the rocks. She paused once, tilting her face toward the sun, letting it warm her skin. She was conscious of the smile on her face and she opened her eyes, finding Kyler watching her.

"I love it here."

Kyler smiled but said nothing.

"I feel like I've missed out on so much." She looked around them, pointing the hiking stick at a thorny bush with a few red berries clinging to it. "I don't know the names of things—the plants, the birds, the trees."

"That's an agarita. It blooms in February. Yellow flowers. Very fragrant. The birds love the red berries in the fall." Kyler pointed at the tree behind the shrub. "Piñon pine. And why would you know the names? I didn't learn them until I moved here."

"I'm talking about everything. When we saw the birds, I didn't even know what they were. I guessed some sort of quail, but that was only a wild guess. I mean, there's so much to explore, yet I never did. My exploring was going up and down Sixth Street on Saturday nights or trying different restaurants or braving the climbing wall at the gym for something different." She shook her head. "We get into ruts, don't we?"

"We tend to stay in our comfort zone, yes."

"Mark said it was the company I kept. I wasn't friends with anyone who enjoyed the outdoors. That's an excuse, I think."

"As much as Susan and Dale love it up here, did you not go to parks and stuff when you were a kid?"

"City parks. We never went camping."

"What made them buy this place and come out here?"

"They'd always talked about wanting to own, like, some resort cabins on a river or some vacation place. I don't think this setting crossed their minds at the time. When they were looking to buy, they came out here and, like you, fell in love with the place. I remember my mom saying how quiet it was, how peaceful. How slow everything was." She smiled and shook her head. "And I thought how perfectly boring it sounded." She leaned on the hiking stick. "Because we never did things like this, went places like this. Once my grandparents moved, vacations were always spent in Florida, at the beach." She smiled at those childhood memories. "No complaints from me, of course."

Kyler nodded. "I can see if you were never exposed to this," she said, spreading her arms out, "that you wouldn't have any inclination to get out in nature and explore. I was the same way. I told you, a buddy took me camping for the first time when I was in college. I didn't have a clue as to what to expect."

"You fell in love with it."

"Yes. It was definitely a turning point in my life." She spread her hands out again. "Here I am now. I feel like I'm the luckiest person alive sometimes. I get to work out here. This is my *job*." She smiled. "I get paid to hike these trails. How many people can simultaneously work and enjoy their hobby at the very same time?"

"Birdwatching?"

"Yeah."

Kyler took a deep breath and Lexie found herself doing the same, breathing in the fragrance of the woods. Then Kyler moved on. She watched her for a moment, her jeans faded and worn, her hiking boots well used.

"Do you wear a uniform?" she asked unexpectedly.

Kyler glanced back at her. "Yeah, I do. Why?"

"Was it like the one Tammy wore?"

"Khaki pants, olive green top—yeah. Don't tell anyone, but in the heat of summer, when I'm out doing maintenance on the trails, I take my top off and just wear a tank."

"Do you get to wear shorts during the summer?"

"It depends on what I'm assigned to. Working the trails, no. Too thorny and brushy. But on the weeks when it's campground maintenance, I do."

"What's that?"

"Cleaning up sites after people leave. Get them ready for the next set of campers. Cleaning out the fire pits, picking up any trash, sweeping off the slab around the picnic table, things like that."

"And what else to you do? Trail maintenance? What else?"

"Restroom duty. I hate that. Invariably, a toilet will clog or something when it's my week for that. Because we're a small staff, we take turns with a lot of the stuff. In larger parks—larger, meaning more staff—they have specific duties. I like this better. It's never boring."

"And the bird blinds? The feeders?"

"I mostly do that. I'm trying to talk Jim into letting me build another blind. He says we spend too much on birdseed as it is."

"Jim is your boss?"

"He's the superintendent here, yes. Good guy."

"And does he have a wife?" she teased.

Kyler laughed. "He does. She's the grandmotherly type."

"Bet that was a relief."

"Oh, I won't make that mistake again."

They were quiet as they walked on, and the trail turned sharply and began to climb. Her breathing was a little labored, which surprised her. She could do six miles on the treadmill without a problem. She could make it through spin class without gasping for air. But now? Her thighs were burning, much like her lungs. It occurred to her then that her cardio work in the gym wasn't applicable to real life. She wondered if she ran the park road for six miles, would it be as effortless as the treadmill had become?

Their conversation was sparse as they climbed higher—an occasional comment from Kyler as she pointed out a particular bush or tree, or when they startled a rabbit from its daytime hiding place. She did little more than give her an "uh-huh," but Kyler didn't seem to notice that she was laboring.

"Here's the outcropping. Be careful on this part. The rocks are loose."

The rocks were numerous here, the landscape more open, fewer trees than down below. To their right was a drop-off into a canyon. A small railing—posts with one board across—blocked the trail from a dive into the canyon.

"That's not Limpia Creek, is it?"

"No. That's a dry creek. It's called Quail Gulch."

She was thankful for the hiking stick as they picked their way across the boulder field. Thirty or forty steps later, they were back on solid ground. She paused to rest, looking back where they had come. From this angle, the view into the canyon was better with the sun hitting the opposite side. She turned to Kyler, finding her watching. Beyond her, the trail curved to the left, climbing again. She nodded, indicating she was ready to push on.

"We're getting close," Kyler said after a while.

"Good," she managed.

Kyler smiled at her. "Different from the gym, huh?"

"How did you know I was thinking that?"

"A guess. You've been awfully quiet. Not enjoying the hike?"

"I'm loving the hike." She finally stopped. "I'm too winded to carry on a conversation. How sad is that? I was at the gym nearly every day working on my cardio."

"It's the altitude and we've been steadily climbing."

"You're not winded."

Kyler shrugged. "A little."

"Liar."

She laughed. "I hike a lot. I'm used to the altitude."

Lexie was leaning on Kyler's hiking stick, glad to have it. "You'll really make me one of these?"

"Sure. We've got all the stuff in the maintenance shed. I can do it this week." Kyler pointed behind them. "Look there. You can see the RVs. That's how far we've come."

She turned, her eyes widening. The RVs were mere white specks, it seemed. "No wonder my thighs hurt. That looks straight uphill."

"Mostly is. And on the way back down, your hamstrings and knees will be screaming." She moved again. "Come on. We're almost there. We'll sit and have a snack before heading back. Got football on the agenda, remember?"

"I do. And I didn't have a chance to make anything. What's on the menu today?"

"I think Mark is doing chicken wings and nachos again. Sorry."

"Oh, I'll get him to do some nachos without the beef for me. And wings? I guess I'll be forced to eat a few." She smiled. "I'm thinking a beer is gonna go down good."

"Or three."

"What kind of snacks did you bring?" She was suddenly getting hungry as she eyed Kyler's backpack.

"Peanut butter and crackers. A couple of bananas and an apple that we can fight over."

"Oh. Healthy stuff."

Kyler laughed. "What were you hoping for? Those cheesy breakfast tacos from the bar?"

"Yeah. That. I don't know what's wrong with me. I can't seem to find my usual desire for tofu and healthy food."

"Maybe because the things you're used to eating are not readily available."

"Maybe. Or maybe I really missed chicken and bar food like wings and nachos."

Only a few moments later, they crested the peak, but nothing looked familiar to her. She paused, looking overhead, trying to get her bearings.

"We're on the northwest side," Kyler supplied. "We can go to the rocks where we watched the sunset if you'd like to sit for a bit."

"Yes, please."

Once they got a little higher, she could see the road and the circle parking area at the top. She saw the piñon pine tree where Kyler had parked, and they headed in that direction. Before long, the large rocks of the outcropping came into view and she nearly collapsed on them.

"God...that was harder than I thought." She groaned. "And we have to go back down."

Kyler sat beside her and nudged her arm. "It's all downhill. Piece of cake."

"The next time I ask for a hike, let's do something a little tamer."

Kyler handed her a banana. "There's a short hike down where the campgrounds end. It follows a dry creek bed. One mile in, one mile out. Easy."

"And this one?" she asked as she peeled her banana.

"Almost six miles total."

She took a bite of the banana, realizing as she did how hungry she was. "This was fun. A little more than I bargained for, but fun." She took the crackers from Kyler. "Thank you."

They ate in silence, passing a water bottle between them occasionally. She noticed that Kyler's gaze was on the landscape around them, her eyes moving as things caught her attention. She had a satisfied look on her face, and Lexie finally understood how utterly at peace Kyler was in her surroundings, in her life, in her own skin. She was what she was, who she was, and she didn't apologize for it. She smiled then. Well, she sometimes apologized for being a birdwatcher, but Lexie imagined that would fade with time too.

She leaned closer, touching her shoulder. "Thank you for being my friend."

Kyler turned to her and smiled. "Yeah. It's been really tough. You're so difficult to get along with."

She turned to face her, smiling at her teasing words. "I've said this before, but I really like you. It's so refreshing to be around you. There's no drama, no games, no pretenses. You are who you are, and I can be who I am without having to worry about perceptions."

"And have you had to do that?"

"I think so, yes. To some extent, anyway. Especially when you have different groups of friends. I would find myself acting differently depending on who I was around. I don't think anyone would recognize me now."

"Have you changed that much?"

"Maybe not changed. Maybe I'm simply allowing me to be me."

"No one to impress up here, huh?"

She laughed. "That's the beauty of you, Kyler. You don't expect me to be anything other than what you see. When I was with Trish and her friends, it was…make sure you had the right clothes on, makeup done perfectly, and so on. My work friends, well, I was the boss so there was that. I always had to be a little bit reserved around them."

"And the gym?"

"Oh, the gym was mostly a competition. Friendly competition, for the most part, but still. I didn't often see them outside of the gym unless it was to go get a smoothie or something after a workout. I would occasionally grab dinner with someone, but mostly our interaction was at the gym."

She turned back, letting her gaze travel over the rocks and trees, the canyons below them. "I know now that I wasn't happy with all of that. I told myself I was in a rut because of my job and Cathy, but that wasn't really it. There wasn't any part of my life that I was truly happy with." She sighed. "How sad to realize I wasted so much time and didn't even know I was wasting it."

She turned to Kyler and offered a smile. "Sorry. I didn't mean to get so reflective with you. It's something about being out here, being with you, that makes me want to open up, to bare my soul."

Their eyes held and she knew Kyler was thinking about last night and their kiss. She'd almost forgotten about it. Things had been so natural between them—it hadn't been at the forefront of her thoughts. Now, though, as she looked into Kyler's eyes, she couldn't help but remember the kiss and how it had felt.

Instead of fighting over the apple, they shared it. Lexie thought it had to be the very first time she shared an apple with someone. They finished off the peanut butter and crackers, then Kyler stood and shouldered her backpack.

"Ready to head down?"

Lexie met her eyes again, then nodded. "Ready."

CHAPTER THIRTY-TWO

"How was your hike?"

"It was fun." Lexie stole a pickle from her mother's cutting board. "Making potato salad again?"

"Oh, it's like a beautiful fall day out, isn't it? Your father wants to grill steaks later, but I wasn't in the mood for baked potatoes again. We had them last night."

She leaned a hip against the counter. "Just so you know, I love it here."

Her mother smiled at her. "After you'd convinced yourself that you wouldn't? Are you finding a new side of yourself?"

"I am." She took another pickle. "I told Kyler that very thing. I'm not sure my friends would recognize me. Truth is, Mom, I'm loving everything about being up here. Meeting Kyler, getting to know her, that's part of it, but also being with you and Dad, with Mark—I didn't know how much I missed our family time." She waved a hand in air. "And that's not only it either. I find I actually *love* the place. The quiet. The simplicity of everything. I feel more alive than I have in years. And yes, I'm finding a new side of myself that I didn't know was hiding."

"Yet you still have reservations?"

"I haven't even been here three weeks yet. Maybe it's only the newness of it all. Maybe it's the upcoming holidays. Christmas will be here in less than two weeks."

"Twelve days, to be exact," her mother interjected.

"Then the New Year. I don't suppose I'll really get a feel for the place until after that. And you and Mark have already told me that January is a dead month. Maybe I'll go stir crazy then."

"At least you've made a friend. Kyler is one of the best people you'll ever meet."

"I'm seeing that, yes." She pushed away from the counter. "Anyway, the hike was fun, but it was nearly all uphill. I think I was a bit ambitious when I suggested it. Coming down was a breeze, though."

"And you have football today?"

"Yes." She looked at her watch. It was nearly eleven thirty. "I guess I should go and see if Mark needs help with anything." She paused. "Mom, do you think I could live here long term and be happy?"

"Only you can answer that, honey."

"What if I make the wrong decision?"

"Lexie, go have fun. Enjoy your day. Don't worry so much."

"You know me. I'm a worrier."

"Yes, you always analyzed everything to death, even when you were young." She waved the knife in the air. "Free yourself, Lexie."

"Free myself?"

"Yes. Free yourself. Get out of this prison that you've locked yourself in. Live free. Life is so much more rewarding when you don't worry about every little thing."

Lexie tilted her head a bit, studying her mother. Was she right? Had she locked herself up tightly, worrying over every detail in her life, so much so that she hadn't even realized how limited— how narrow—her life had become? How could that be? She'd kept so busy. She was always doing something, wasn't she? That wasn't being limited. She had tons of friends. Her life didn't feel restricted.

But was it? Everything was measured, everything was routine. Her friends, her gym sessions, her lunch dates with Trish, Saturday nights on Sixth Street, brunch every Sunday. The same safe routine. Repetitive and dull.

When she'd told Kyler that she hadn't been happy in her life, she hadn't really known the reason. Could this be it? Could this be why she felt like she was in a rut? There was no spark, no spontaneity in her life. Is that why being with Kyler felt like a breath of fresh air? Kyler was taking her out of her comfort zone and making her *do* things. Kyler was making her live life, not just meander through it in her usual, habitual way.

She smiled at her mother and nodded. "You could be right. Thanks, Mom."

CHAPTER THIRTY-THREE

Kyler plopped down in one of the deck chairs after helping Mark bring the TV outside. "Can't believe it's going to be in the seventies today. It's so gorgeous. And so not Christmas weather."

"I overheard the Mertz brothers talking about how dry everything is out at their place. You still allowing campfires in the park?"

She nodded. "Fire danger is high, yeah, but Jim hasn't prohibited campfires. This time of year, when the nights are cold, a campfire is like a rite of passage when you're out camping." She grinned. "We had one last night."

"Oh, that's right. Lexie made you dinner." He wiggled his eyebrows. "How'd that turn out?"

She met his gaze, then looked away. "We…we kissed." Both his eyebrows popped up.

"Oh? And how did that work out for you?"

"She freaked out." She met his gaze again. "She started it. Well, maybe I did. I don't really know. But she wants to pretend it didn't happen and not talk about it."

"That's crazy."

She shrugged. "It's probably best. Having a fling with your sister could turn out to be disastrous. We're friends. I should just leave it like that. Right?"

He shrugged too. "I don't know, Ky. I think that was one of Lexie's main concerns—that she'd not have any friends." He pulled a chair closer and sat down. "You like her? I'm not teasing now. You like her?"

She nodded. "I do. When I said she reminded me of Britney— the more I'm around her, I realize that's not true."

"But she's still not your type?"

"Oh, hell, Mark. I don't even know what my type is. I only know Britney wasn't it and Lexie—"

"You thought she was Britney 2.0?"

"Yeah. But now I think—" Her phone interrupted, and she recognized Jim's ringtone. "It's the boss," she said before pulling her phone from her pocket. "Hey, Jim."

"Kyler, I'm sorry. I hate to do this to you on your day off. I know you and Mark generally have plans for football."

She sighed quietly, hoping he didn't want her to cover for someone today. "That's okay. What's up?"

"Got a couple of missing kids. Young. Eight and four. The parents said the kids were playing by the short loop there around the interpretive center while they packed up. Disappeared on them. They're a little shook up."

She stood, meeting Mark's curious gaze. "Okay, sure. You want me to hike the loop?"

"I think the parents already have."

"The kids probably took one of those cutoffs between there and the amphitheater."

"Most likely. There are three cutoffs so three trails to cover."

"Okay. Who else is out?"

"Got Brian with the parents. Todd is starting at the bird blinds. Walker and I are going to take the bike trail. That's the longest."

"I'll take the amphitheater trail. We'll find them. We always do."

"Thanks, Kyler. Sorry to mess up your day off."

"No worries." She pocketed her phone. "Got two lost kids. Young. Eight and four."

"Oh, man."

She headed to the steps. "Looks like I'm hitting the trails again."

"You're coming back, though, right?"

"Of course. Don't drink all my beer."

* * *

Lexie frowned as she watched the red Jeep speed away. She glanced to the deck, seeing Mark staring after the Jeep too. She walked on, eyebrows raised.

"What's going on?"

"Kyler got called in to work. Got two lost kids."

"Oh, no."

"It happens. They always find them."

"So no Kyler today?"

"She'll be back." He eyed the bag. "Whatcha got? Tofu?"

She smiled. "No tofu. It's a bean and corn dip. And I brought some chips."

Mark put an arm around her shoulder. "Good. You want a beer?"

"Yes. Sure."

She looked back at the road that Kyler had disappeared down, noting the disappointment she felt. She let out a heavy breath, then made herself smile at Mark as she took his offered beer.

CHAPTER THIRTY-FOUR

When Kyler finished the short loop to the amphitheater, there was no sign of the kids. The bike trail intercepted it, but Jim and Walker were hiking that one. Her gaze lifted to the Skyline Drive trail. Surely they hadn't gone up there. It was way too steep and rocky for a four-year-old.

She headed in that direction, not relishing the fact that she was going to be making her second hike up there in one day. While she doubted the kids had made it this far—they'd most likely taken one of the other cutoffs—she still had to be sure. She pulled out her phone as she started up the trial.

"Yeah, Jim, it's me. No sign of them at the amphitheater or the loop. Gonna head up Skyline now."

"There's no way the little one could make it up Skyline."

"No sightings anywhere else?"

"Not yet. I've already called the sheriff, let him know what we're dealing with. He's putting together a team. If we don't find them within the hour, I'll get him out here too."

She nodded. "Well, your trail may be longer, but mine is steeper. You'll probably finish yours before I get to the top."

"Keep me posted. I'll do the same."

She took a deep breath, then trudged on up the trail, noting how quiet it was. Even though she and Lexie hadn't chatted much while they hiked, it was still nice to have company along. She was glad Lexie got a chance to see the Montezuma quail and their young. Sightings like that were always more special when there was someone to share it with.

She wondered what Lexie was doing. She would be at Mark's already, she supposed. She stopped. Would Lexie be up for a hike down Skyline? It wouldn't hurt to ask. Lexie answered on the second ring, but there were no pleasantries.

"Did you find them?"

"No. I was actually wondering if you might like to help."

"Of course. I'll do anything you need."

"Good. Go up to Skyline Drive and hike back down the trail. I'm hiking up. Chances are they didn't take this trail but it's the one I'm on. The guys are dispersed on other trails nearby."

"Okay. I'll leave right now."

"Thanks, Lexie. And tell Mark not to eat all the wings."

* * *

Lexie jogged down the trail from Mark's, back to her apartment. She kicked off her sneakers, putting on the hiking boots once again. She ran back out, only to stop and go back in to grab a water bottle from the fridge to take along. She was still tired from their morning hike, but at least she would be going downhill only.

She drove faster than the posted speed—twenty-five—hoping that a deer didn't dart out or a squirrel or something. When she got to the campground area, she turned right, following the road through the sites, past the tent area and one of the bird blinds. Past that, she saw the sign for Skyline Drive, and she turned, speeding up as the road wound around the mountain to the top.

There was another car there and two people were standing at the overlook, binoculars in hand. She passed them, taking the circle drive to the piñon pine where Kyler normally parked her Jeep.

As she stood by her car, she felt a little nervous and she wasn't sure why. Was it because she would be alone for the first time, out here among the rocks and trees? Or was she afraid she'd stumble upon the children and not know what to do? Well, yes, she knew what she would do. She'd call Kyler. Yes, Kyler was but a phone call away. What could possibly happen to her?

With that, she went in the direction of the trailhead, glancing once over to the pile of rocks where they'd share snacks earlier that morning. They'd shared a hike, they'd chatted like normal, and then they'd shared snacks—all without not even once mentioning their shared kiss.

She paused at the trailhead, taking a deep breath before retracing their steps of earlier in the day. It was very quiet, it seemed. Each step she took, she thought the sounds of her boots on the rocks were inordinately loud. She missed Kyler's comforting presence as her mind started to run away from her. What if she came upon a pack of javelinas? A mountain lion? A coyote or wolf?

Did they have wolves here?

She shook that thought away. No. No one had ever mentioned wolves. As she rounded the first bend, a rustling in the leaves beside the trail caused her to gasp and her heart leapt into her throat. She froze in place, her eyes darting along the trail, looking for movement. There, under the brush of a juniper, was a bird foraging in the leaves. He was larger than any she'd seen at the bird garden. His tail was darker than his body, but it was his bill that drew her attention. It was long and curved and it looked quite sharp as it dug among the debris there.

Wonder what it is?

She wished she could stay and watch it longer. As soon as she moved on, the bird fluttered away, landing on a low-lying limb of an oak tree. She was watching it instead of the trail and she slipped, nearly falling over. In the commotion of her righting herself, the bird disappeared, and she was alone again.

As she walked on, she could see the allure of watching birds, she supposed. This one, for instance, with its abnormally curved bill had her itching to ask Kyler what it was. But now wasn't the time for a leisurely stroll down the trail, looking for birds. She kept her attention on her footing instead, remembering how she'd nearly fallen that morning on a particularly steep part.

She stopped as the trail spilled out onto the boulder field—the large outcropping of rocks that she'd had difficulty going over with a hiking stick. She wondered how she'd fare without one. Before going down, she looked out over the canyon, noting how different it looked now with the sun nearly on top of it. This morning, the sun had still been low, the shadows more pronounced.

Again, she took a deep breath, summoning her courage as she took a tentative step on a wobbly rock. Oh, to have Kyler's hiking stick right about now. She held her arms out to her side for balance—like she'd seen Kyler do that morning—and walked on. She looked up the mountain, seeing the small ravine where the rocks seemed to have spilled from as they covered the trail and tumbled over the side into the canyon. The rocks ranged in sizes from baseballs to cantaloupes and even some as large as watermelons.

She was nearly halfway across when she looked to her left, past the little fence barrier. Something blue caught her eye. She moved carefully to the railing, nearly twisting her ankle as a rock slipped out from under her boot. If she wasn't careful, she was going to go tumbling into the canyon herself.

When she got to the railing, she realized it wasn't the sheer drop-off that it appeared. It was a sharp slope nonetheless and she braced her hand on the railing. She looked again for the flash of blue and her eyes widened.

"Oh my god," she murmured.

Her heart hammered wildly as she saw the child lying on the rocks. Several feet above, another child was making his way down. Mark had said they were eight and four. She listened, hearing crying now. She stepped as close as she dared to the railing.

"Hey!" she called, waving her arms above her head. "Up here!"

The older one—a boy, it appeared—looked up at her. "My sister fell!"

"Stay where you are!" she called back to him. "Don't go any farther."

Her hands were shaking as she pulled out her phone and she nearly dropped it in her haste to call Kyler. It was three rings before Kyler finally answered.

"I found them," she blurted out. "Please, come help me. The younger one fell, and the boy is trying to get to her. I'm afraid—"

"Lexie, calm down. How far down the trail are you?"

"Um, I'm at the boulder field. The rock outcropping."

"Jesus, they fell from there?"

"Yes. I'm not good at judging distances, but I'd guess fifty or sixty feet down." She gripped the phone tighter. "Kyler, the younger one is not moving."

"I'm just past the switchbacks. I'm a good twenty or thirty minutes from you still."

"Can you call someone?"

"Yes, I'll call Jim, but they're all out on trails too."

"What should I do? Should I go down and try to help them?"

There was a slight pause. "What do you feel comfortable doing?"

She looked at the boy who was staring up at her. Even from this distance, she could see the fear on his face. She summoned up courage she didn't know she had.

"I'll go down. He's scared to death. But Kyler, please hurry. Because I'm scared too."

"I'm on my way. You be careful."

She swallowed the lump in her throat as she put the phone into her pocket. The water bottle she'd still been clutching was squeezed tightly in her hand and she paused to take a drink, then set it down beside the trail. The kids were probably thirsty, but she knew she'd need both hands free if she was going to maneuver down the side without doing a freefall into the canyon.

The rocks were very loose near the railing and she imagined the younger child had gotten too close and had easily slipped under the lone board that served as a safety measure. She held on to one of the posts and swung her leg over the board. She took only two steps before she started slipping. She bent her knees, crouching low to use her hands to steady herself. She half-crawled, half-walked her way down, getting closer and closer to the boy.

"Hurry!" he called.

"I'm trying, kid," she murmured—right before a rock shifted under her foot and she landed hard on her ass. *Damn.*

She stayed down, scooting along toward him now. She was close enough to see the streaks of tears on his cheeks. She slid her glance to the little girl, seeing blood on her face.

"What's your name?" she asked when she was close enough.

"Jeffery."

She smiled at him. "Do you go by Jeff?"

"My daddy calls me Jeff."

She nodded. "I'm Lexie. What happened?"

"My sister fell. She's not crying anymore. I'm scared."

"Are you hurt?"

"No." His lower lip started to tremble. "We got lost."

"You're safe now, Jeffery. Help is on the way." When she got next to him, she stopped and touched his face, giving him some comfort. "You stay here. I'm going to check on her. What's her name?"

"Chrissy."

"Okay." She squeezed his arm. "Stay here."

The girl was maybe twenty feet farther away. She was on her back, her head facing downward. Lexie was almost scared to go to her. Was she dead? Had she tumbled and rolled down the hill, hitting rocks with her head? Had she broken her neck?

"Chrissy? Can you hear me?" she called.

She saw blood on rocks and expected the worst. She was shocked to see brown eyes looking at her when she scooted down to her. She smiled at the little girl.

"Hey…I'm Lexie," she said softly.

She saw the gash on the kid's forehead and gently wiped at the blood that was seeping into her eyes. One of the girl's arms was bent at an odd angle and she wondered if it was broken. She also wondered why the kid wasn't screaming her head off.

She sat next to the girl, noting the scrapes on her legs and elbows. Damn, but she had tumbled down the rocks, hadn't she? She touched the girl's face gently.

"What hurts?" Tears welled up in the girl's eyes then and Lexie thought that was probably a stupid question. She tried again. "Can you move your legs?"

One foot wiggled. "I want my mommy," she girl whispered, her voice raspy, perhaps from crying or screaming.

"I know, honey. She's on her way," she said, not knowing if that was true or not.

"Is she okay?" Jeffrey called to her.

She looked up at him. "I think so. But you stay there."

She didn't know if she should attempt to move her or not. What if something was broken? She thought back to long-ago first aid classes. If they weren't in immediate danger, don't move them.

Wasn't that the rule? But the kid was trying to sit up and Lexie stopped her.

"No, no, honey. Let's wait until help gets here."

A wail left the girl's mouth and Lexie noted that there was nothing wrong with her lungs as the wail turned into a full-fledged scream. Damn, but she was never good with kids. She'd never been around kids, really.

"Lexie?"

She jerked her head up, hearing the familiar voice. *Oh, thank god.* She got to her feet, waving at Kyler. "I'm down here."

Lexie watched in awe as Kyler nimbly hopped over the fence and—like what she supposed a mountain goat might do—scampered down across the rocks without slipping even once. Kyler stopped to say something to Jeffery, her words not loud enough to hear. Then she came down and Lexie finally dared to relax.

"You okay?"

"I'm fine, yes. This is Chrissy. I was afraid to move her."

Kyler squatted down beside the girl. "Shhh, shhh. It's okay, Chrissy. We're going to get you out of here real soon."

"My...my mommy!"

"Oh, yeah. Your mommy is waiting on you." Kyler looked up. "I think her arm is broken," she said quietly.

Lexie nodded.

Kyler took her backpack off and pulled out her first aid kit. "You got a little scratch on your head, Chrissy. I'm going to put a bandage on it, okay?"

The girl screamed and shook her head fiercely, alleviating any fears Lexie might have had that her neck was broken.

"Kyler, I think we should get her up. Save the bandage for later," she suggested.

"You may be right." Kyler shoved the kit back into her backpack. "We'll need to be careful of her arm." She handed the backpack to Lexie. "You wear this. I'll carry her up."

With surprising strength—and gentleness—Kyler cradled the little girl to her, all the while battling screams and wails. Lexie went in front of her, helping Jeffrey back up to the trail. It was slow going for them as the kid was slipping more than she was. Kyler seemed surefooted, however, and by the time they got to the railing, the girl's screams had subsided to a quiet cry.

Lexie helped Kyler over the fence, then looked up as voices were heard coming from the trail above them. She looked back to Kyler.

"Ambulance?"

Kyler shook her head. "The closest EMT is in Alpine. Jim was going to call them but I doubt they made it already. That's probably the guys with the parents."

A few moments later, three men all dressed in uniforms came hurrying down the trail. Behind them were who she assumed to be the parents. Behind them was another man, although he wasn't in uniform.

"Oh, my god! Chrissy!" the woman nearly screamed.

Lexie stepped in front of her when the woman would have ripped the child from Kyler's arms. "We think she has a broken arm."

"Oh, my god," she said again.

The man grabbed the boy into a tight bear hug which caused loud sobs from the kid as he clung to his father. That, in turn, caused the little girl to start wailing again. Soon, the parents were alternating between crying with their children and laughing with relief. Lexie met Kyler's eyes, smiling a little in all the chaos.

"I could use a beer right about now," she whispered.

CHAPTER THIRTY-FIVE

Lexie twisted the cap off the beer bottle as the red Jeep pulled up. Kyler had still been up on Skyline Drive with the others when she'd left. She'd stopped at her apartment to take a quick shower before going back to Mark's. That was nearly an hour ago. She leaned against the deck railing now, watching as Kyler got out. Their eyes met and she returned Kyler's smile.

"What did I miss?"

"You missed the Cowboys kicking the Giants' ass, that's all."

"Good. Sorry I missed it. Did you eat all my wings?"

"Mark only recently put them in the oven. Said he was waiting for you."

Kyler rested a hip against the railing too. "Thank you for helping me today. You did real good, Lexie."

"I was happy to help. I'm just so glad they're okay. The girl *is* okay, right?"

"Yeah. She let her mother tend to the wound on her head. She had scrapes and bruises all over her body, it looked like. I stayed until the EMTs got there."

"Broken arm?"

"Yeah. They took her to the hospital in Alpine."

"That was so scary. I'm sure the parents are beating themselves up."

"Yeah, they are. I'm just glad they weren't blaming the boy. He was plenty shook up himself."

"Does this happen often?"

"Not really. Once a year, maybe. I think this is the first time an ambulance has been involved though."

"You were really good with the girl. If you hadn't been there, I don't know what I would have done."

"I like kids." Then she smiled quickly. "Well, *most* kids. They come out here, they're generally curious about the animals and the birds and stuff. I try to interact with them, teach them things about the park, about nature."

"Future converts?"

Kyler laughed. "Yeah. Might make one of them a birdwatcher." She moved away then, going to the red cooler on the deck. "You want one?"

"No. I just opened this."

Kyler twisted the cap off and took a swallow. "Oh, that's good and cold." She looked over at her. "I'm beat. You?"

Lexie nodded. "Although my second hike of the day wasn't nearly as strenuous as yours. I missed having your hiking stick."

"Yeah, it comes in handy." Kyler stared at her for a moment before speaking. "Do you want to talk about last night?"

Lexie sighed. Did she? She could lie and say she hadn't given their kiss a thought all day. But as she met Kyler's eyes, she knew Kyler would know she was lying. So, she shrugged nonchalantly.

"I thought we were going to pretend it didn't happen."

"That was your suggestion, not mine."

She sighed again. "Kyler, we're not—" What? Right for each other? Well, it wasn't like Kyler was asking to marry her. In fact, she didn't even know if Kyler wanted to date her. She frowned. "What are your intentions?"

Kyler laughed out loud. "God, that is like the last thing I expected you to say."

"Okay. I'll rephrase. What do you want?"

Kyler came closer, joining her again at the railing. "It shouldn't be this hard, Lexie. I'm attracted to you. You can deny it if you want, but that kiss last night said you're attracted to me too."

She opened her mouth to do just that, but then couldn't. "Yes. I am attracted to you. But as we've already discussed, we are not each other's type. So why bother? Besides, I don't even know if I'm staying here or not."

"Whether you stay or not shouldn't have any bearing on what's happening right here and now, Lexie."

Lexie stared at her. "Oh, good lord. You're talking about sex, aren't you?"

Kyler's smile was so sweet Lexie felt herself returning it. "Well, I was kinda talking about kissing but if you want to jump right into sex, I won't complain."

Lexie laughed. "You're right. It shouldn't be this hard."

"Right. So relax. Let's enjoy the rest of the day." She looked past her to the house. "The chef is coming out."

Lexie turned, finding Mark coming through the door holding a tray loaded with chips and dips. Her stomach rumbled.

"About time you got here," he said to Kyler. "How's the kid?"

"Gonna be okay, I guess. Broken arm was the most serious injury. I doubt the family will ever forget this camping trip."

Mark shook his head. "This might be the last one they ever go on."

"Oh, I don't know. It's a learning experience. I'm going to bet that those kids never leave the campsite unattended again. The boy was plenty scared."

"Jeffrey," Lexie supplied. "But he was a brave kid, trying to get down to help his sister. When I found them, he was crawling over the rocks toward her. I told the father as much."

"Yeah, he said that. I think, all in all, he was quite proud of his son."

Lexie took a chip and scooped up a large blob of the guacamole. "I'm starving," she murmured around her bite.

"Wings will be ready by halftime. And I left the beef off half of the nachos. Just need to pop them in the microwave. We can snack on those during the game."

"Thank you."

Kyler took a chip too. "Got that meteor shower coming up. Who feels like getting up at two in the morning?"

"Is that tomorrow?" Mark asked.

"No. It's Tuesday morning." Kyler turned to her, eyebrows raised. "You feel like it?"

Lexie didn't think getting out at two in the morning sounded like much fun. "We'll see."

"It's pretty neat to watch," Mark chimed in.

"Then why don't *you* go?"

"I went last year."

"And the year before," Kyler added.

She sighed. "We'll see," she said again.

"Heard our pleasant weather is coming to an end," Mark said. "Big front coming in. Gonna be really cold and windy."

"That's what Jim said."

"Snow's in the forecast too. That would be nice."

"Snow?" Lexie asked excitedly. "Really? Like real snow?"

"We had a nice storm last year. A couple of inches. That's the most I've seen," Kyler said. "It was beautiful."

"The second year we were here," Mark said, "we had a two-day storm in January. Got almost ten inches. The locals said they'd never seen that much at once."

Lexie nodded. "I remember you telling me about that. Now that would be fun! Seeing as how I don't have to commute to work any longer."

"Well, if we get any amount of snow, I know of a great hill that we can sled on." Kyler winked at her. "Great going down. It's the walk back to the top that will kill you."

"With all the rocks around here, I wouldn't think there would be good sledding anywhere."

"It's a great trail. She took me last year." He motioned to the house. "Gonna go flip the wings. Be right back."

"Yeah. It's an old Jeep road that's been grated and scraped. No rocks. Goes down to Limpia Creek over in the canyon. It's part of a hiking trail now, but it's totally smooth. Of course, we could hike it without snow too. It's nice down there."

"But like you said, you've got to get back up."

"Well, now that you've done Skyline Drive, it'll be a piece of cake."

"My quads hurt. I probably won't be able to get out of bed in the morning."

It was an innocent line, but as their eyes met, she could see the amusement in Kyler's. Amusement and something else.

"Call me if you need help," she said quietly. "I can pop over."

"What is wrong with you?"

"Nothing."

"You're flirting with me," she accused.

"Yeah, I am." What could she say to that? She took a swallow of her beer. "So. Meteor shower?"

"Are you going to make me go?"

"I believe you asked me to take you. We were watching the sunset and you—"

"I remember. But—"

"What?"

"That was...before..."

Kyler smiled. "Before you lost your mind and kissed me?"

Lexie met her gaze. "I'm pretty sure you started it."

"Me? No, no. I think you started things."

Lexie knew it would do no good to argue. Because right then, she wasn't certain who had started the kiss.

"Wanna watch a game?"

"Sure."

When Mark came back out, Lexie relaxed, and their afternoon reverted to its familiar routine. She and Kyler chose opposite teams and again bet ten bucks on the outcome. It wasn't fair, really. She'd picked the Chiefs, leaving Kyler with the Chargers, who were a two-touchdown underdog. Nevertheless, Kyler had flashed a ten-dollar bill at her, and Lexie had agreed.

"Hate to take your money, but okay."

"I feel an upset in the making."

Kyler had no such luck with the upset, but they enjoyed the game—which was closer than two touchdowns—and ate wings at halftime. The beers relaxed Lexie, and she enjoyed the banter with Kyler, as she always did. And yes, she found herself flirting with her, as usual. She tried to stop, she really did. It was simply too much fun, especially when Kyler played along. Of course, time and again, images of the night before—images of the kiss—popped into her mind. Kyler was thinking about it too, she could tell. She'd seen her gaze drop to her lips more than once.

Oh, it was a fun afternoon and she was sorry to see it come to an end. Things were safer with Mark around. There wasn't that tension that was there between them when they were alone. It was enjoyable and carefree, the beer and the warm weather contributing too.

By the time they'd helped Mark clean up and put the TV back in the house, it was almost dark. That meant that Kyler would offer to drive her home. She panicked. No. They'd been flirting too much. They didn't need to be alone. No. So she hurried over and picked up the jacket she'd brought along.

"I should go before it's too dark to see," she said in a rush. "Had a great time, as usual." She turned to Kyler. "I guess I'll see you for the meteor shower."

"Why don't you let Kyler drop you off?"

"No, no. I can still see enough to walk," she said to Mark, glancing to the now nearly dark sky.

Kyler nodded. "Okay, but watch out for those javelinas."

She met her gaze. Damn. She'd forgotten about the mean little pig things Kyler had told her about. She blew out a breath.

"Oh. Yeah. Maybe I will ride with you then."

Mark looked at her quizzically. "Why would you want to walk through the woods in the dark? Kyler's going right by the lodge."

"I was going to walk off those last two wings you made me eat."

He laughed. "I thought you were going to take my hand off when I reached for that last one. Don't blame me."

"They were very good," she conceded. "Almost as good as my cauliflower wings."

Mark stood on the deck, watching as they went down the stairs. She and Kyler both turned to wave at him before getting in the Jeep.

It wasn't cold by any means, but she tightened the jacket around her, as if that could protect her from Kyler. She stared straight ahead, not daring to look at her.

"You can relax."

"I am relaxed."

The drive down the hill took all of two minutes, if that. When Kyler pulled to a stop beside her car, she wanted to jump out of the Jeep. She didn't, though.

"I did have a good time today," she said, as if perhaps Kyler thought otherwise.

"Me, too. The hike was fun and thanks for helping with the kids."

She nodded, finally daring to look at her. There wasn't enough light to see her eyes clearly, but from what she could see, it caused her breath to catch.

"Um...thank you for the ride."

"Anytime."

She should get out. Quickly. But still, she lingered.

"Lexie?"

"I know. I'm going."

"You don't have to. We could—"

"No." She opened the door. "So I'll see you at some ungodly hour on Monday night?"

"Two a.m., which is technically Tuesday morning."

She got out finally but looked back at her. "I'll be at your place by two. It better be worth it."

"It'll be fantastic. I'll take my work truck. Sleeping bags on the back, a couple of heavy quilts, some hot chocolate or something."

She swallowed. Sleeping bags? Quilts? She had a visual of them lying side-by-side and...

"Okay. I guess I'll see you then."

"Yeah. See you then."

She hurried inside, not trusting herself to look back. She closed the door and leaned against it, eyes closed. Damn. Should it be this hard to *not* like someone? Oh, of course she liked Kyler. It was the other part that she wished she didn't feel. She and Kyler had no future together, whether she stayed here or not. Kyler was an outdoorsy person, unassuming and down-to-earth. She was none of those things. Well, she wouldn't really call herself pretentious, would she? No. But still, Kyler wasn't her type.

She pushed away from the door. Kyler wasn't her type, no, but she was attracted to her. That made no sense at all.

The quiet knock on her door made her whip her head around as if someone had banged on it. It wasn't her mother's knock. She swallowed, hesitating.

"I know you're standing right there."

She blinked several times, then moved the few steps to the door, opening it. The look in Kyler's eyes stole her breath. She stepped inside, then closed the door behind her. It was only then that Lexie realized she hadn't turned on any lights yet. The blinds were still open on the window and the glow from the porch light sent streaks inside. Enough to see Kyler.

It didn't matter. She didn't need to see.

Last night, their kiss had been unexpected. It had been nearly frantic, heated. Hard and urgent. Tonight? Almost completely different. She felt relaxed, unhurried. In control. In control, that is, until they actually kissed, until Kyler's soft mouth moved against hers, until her lips parted for her. Kyler drew her closer and she felt her hands—moving without her permission—slide up her arms, around her shoulders.

A delicious whimper—hers—made her senses reel and she pulled Kyler even tighter, bringing their bodies impossibly close. The slow, measured kiss changed then, tongues touching, their moans blending into one. Kyler's hands slid to her hips, cupping her, pulling her flush against her. Her moan turned into a groan at the contact, and she felt what little control she had quickly slipping away.

It would be so easy. Take Kyler to her bedroom. They would make love. If their kisses were any indication, it would be fantastic. But no. Her mother would see Kyler's Jeep outside. There would be questions—lots of questions that she wasn't prepared to answer.

So she did the sensible thing and eased out of the kiss, finally pulling away. The only sound in the room was their quickly drawn breaths, nothing else. Kyler must have sensed her apprehension.

"A simple kiss, Lexie," she whispered.

At that, Lexie smiled. "Jesus, Kyler, that's your definition of simple?"

Kyler smiled too. "It started out that way. You changed it."

"Me? No, no. *You* changed it." She moved away from Kyler, her fingers brushing through her hair in a nervous gesture. "Don't you dare tell Mark we kissed. Or my mother," she added quickly.

"God, no."

She flipped on the light, chasing the shadows away. It may have been a mistake. She could see the desire in Kyler's eyes clearly now.

"We can't do this." She moved away from her.

"Are we talking about kissing or are we talking about having sex?"

Lexie felt a blush light her face. "Good lord, you just blurt it right out, don't you?"

Kyler shrugged. "I'm attracted to you."

"We can't sleep together, Kyler."

"Why not?"

"Because it'll ruin our new friendship."

"Maybe it'll make it better."

"But what if it doesn't?"

Kyler laughed. "What are you doing?"

She smiled too. "I always worry over things. Mom says I analyze stuff to death."

Kyler reached out and took her hand. Their fingers entwined easily. "I'm going to go now, Lexie. But I don't want to pretend there's nothing going on with us. Because there is."

She nodded. "I know. So what are we going to do?"

"We're going to do stuff like we have been. And we're going to kiss. And eventually we're going to make love."

Lexie's eyebrows shot up. "That's it? Simple as that?"

"I'm attracted to you. You're attracted to me. That's all." Kyler took a step closer. "I like being with you, Lexie. Out hiking, out biking. Hanging with Mark." She wiggled her eyebrows. "Kissing. All normal, natural stuff."

She nodded. "I really do like you, Kyler. Obviously, I'm attracted to you, yes."

"But?"

Lexie held her arms out. "I don't even know if I'm staying or not." She took her hand and squeezed her fingers. "I don't want you to be a factor on whether I stay or go. That's not fair."

Kyler nodded. "You're right. Your decision to stay here should be based solely on you and whether you can see yourself living up here long term. It should have nothing to do with me." She dropped her hand. "I should go."

"I'm glad you came in. We needed to talk about it."

Kyler smiled. "I came in for a kiss. Not to talk. So have a good day tomorrow. Get to bed early tomorrow night. Don't forget to set an alarm."

"The meteor shower. I'll be over at two in the freakin' morning."

Kyler leaned closer, brushing her lips across her cheek, pausing at the corner of her mouth. "Goodnight, Lexie."

Once again, Lexie closed the door and leaned against it, this time with the lights on. Perhaps it was the lights that made her see things more clearly. Because she feared she was getting in over her head. It would be so very easy to fall in love with Kyler. Wouldn't it?

She pushed away from the wall. Don't be ridiculous, she told herself. Kyler wasn't the type of person she would fall in love with. Kyler was too…too earthy, too outdoorsy. Too—

Too sweet. Too nice and charming. Too fun. Too *real*.

She sighed. Yeah, she would be easy to fall in love with.

CHAPTER THIRTY-SIX

"I can't believe I agreed to this." Lexie felt on the nightstand for her phone, silencing the annoying alarm by hitting snooze. The bedroom was dark and cold, and her head fell back to the pillow.

"One thirty in the freakin' morning," she muttered as she burrowed under the covers again. *Only an idiot would agree to this.* She needed a shower to wake up. She needed coffee. Her eyes opened. She could always call Kyler and tell her she'd changed her mind.

She'll never go for that.

With a sigh, she tossed the covers off, quickly pulling on the sweatpants that she'd removed last night. A sweatshirt followed and she shoved her feet into her fuzzy house slippers. She shuffled into the kitchen, pausing to up the heater a bit before turning on the Keurig. She yawned as she sorted through her coffee pods, finding a dark roast.

The alarm was going off again, and with a groan, she went back into the bedroom to get her phone. She eyed the bed longingly, then jerked the covers up, halfway making the bed before heading to the bathroom and a hot shower.

After she'd showered and dressed—and after two cups of coffee—she felt almost awake. She was a little excited, she admitted. She had no idea what to expect from a meteor shower. It wasn't really that, though. It was getting to see Kyler, be with her.

She hadn't spoken to her but had gotten a text yesterday afternoon, reminding her to get to bed early. And asking if she preferred coffee or hot chocolate. She'd chosen the hot chocolate, simply because she couldn't remember the last time she'd had it. Certainly not in her adult life. Besides hot chocolate, there would be sleeping bags. There would be quilts. She smiled. It could be fun. Or, if there were pillows, she might very well fall asleep.

At ten minutes until two, she was out the door. The gust of wind hit her, and she shivered. She glanced up into the sky and frowned. Where were the stars? The wind whipped around her, and she knew the forecasted cold front had come in earlier than anticipated. She paused at her car, again looking to the sky. It was totally clouded over. There would be no meteor shower.

Her shoulders sagged with disappointment. Should she go back to bed? No. After two cups of dark roast—and another for the road—there would be no going back to sleep. So should she call Kyler? Did Kyler already know the front was here? Another gust of wind nearly blew her against her car. She looked back at the door to her apartment, indecisive. Finally, she opened the car door and got inside.

She was awake. Wide awake.

She drove around the lodge and past the restaurant. She kept a watch out for the little pigs and was startled to have three deer dart out from the woods instead. She drove through the park, surprised at how familiar she was with it already. She took the little service road to Kyler's cabin. Lights were on inside and she pulled to a stop beside the Jeep. The wind was brutal when she got out and she hurried to the door. Kyler had it opened before she could knock.

"I didn't think you'd come."

Lexie went inside, rubbing her hands together for warmth. "Damn, but that wind is cold."

"Come by the heater," Kyler offered, leading her to the propane heater against the wall.

"The sky is cloudy."

"Yeah. The front is about two hours early. I'm sorry."

"Oh, well. I'm three coffee cups in of a dark roast. I didn't see the point of going back to bed." She frowned. "Or were you?"

"No. I'm on my third cup too." She set down the cup she'd been holding. "Might get snow though. We need the moisture, that's for sure."

"Snow would be fun."

"Yeah, everything will be pretty and Christmasy. I love getting out on the trails when it snows. The birds are very active. Deer come out. Everything has a sense of wonder about it. It doesn't snow every year, and when it does, it's sometimes only a dusting. If we get a good amount, the animals are as curious about it as we are."

Lexie smiled at the excitement in her voice, which only moments earlier had hinted at disappointment. She loved that about Kyler. She was disappointed that the meteor shower was clouding over but excited that perhaps they might get snow. The old Lexie, the one who had been stuck in a city, would have been content to sit inside and watch the snow from afar. She could now see the allure of getting out in it, though. If it did snow, maybe Kyler would invite her along on a trek through the woods.

"Look at us. It's two in the morning, and we're discussing the weather. What are we doing?"

"We were looking forward to each other's company," Kyler stated simply.

She supposed that was true, despite the ridiculous hour. She turned her back to the heat and looked around. It was cozy. The lights on the Christmas tree were on, the overhead light was off. She looked up, smiling as she spied mistletoe hanging on the ceiling fan.

"Was that there the other night?"

"It was. Mistletoe is a Christmas tradition. This particular one, I climbed halfway up an oak tree to snag it."

Lexie met her gaze. "And did you climb this tree before or after we met?"

Kyler laughed. "Yeah, it would have been last week."

Lexie smiled at her sweetly. "Really?"

"Really."

"So you put it up for me?"

"I did."

Their eyes held for a long moment and once again, Lexie saw everything clearly. It was two in the morning. She knew there'd be no meteor shower, yet she'd driven over anyway. At two in the morning. A part of her tried to hold on to her habits, wanting— needing—to dissect everything she was feeling right then. Put it in perspective. But only a small part. She was surprised at how easily she pushed that nagging voice aside.

She moved away from the heater, going to stand under the mistletoe. When she met Kyler's gaze again, the teasing smile she'd seen there was gone. She arched an eyebrow and so did Kyler. She nodded, answering Kyler's unasked question.

Yes, they would kiss. And yes, she knew it would lead to more. She didn't want to fight it. Perhaps because it was two in the morning and the Christmas lights were twinkling around them. Or maybe it was simply that her desire had won out over her cautiousness.

Still, Kyler hesitated. "Lexie…"

"I know it's two in the morning. Is that too early? Too late?"

Kyler took a step toward her, then stopped. "What is it we're contemplating?"

For four, five…six seconds, they stared at each other. Kyler was searching her eyes for something. Lexie wondered if maybe Kyler had changed her mind.

"You're not my type," she finally said. "And I'm not yours."

Kyler's mouth twitched in a smile. "But?

"But I'm standing under mistletoe waiting for you to kiss me."

She took another step toward her and Lexie took her hand, tugging her even closer. The kiss was fiery hot, and she tried to temper it a bit, tried not to seem so needy, so urgent. She failed totally. Mouths, lips…tongues. Hands touched, caressed…stoking the fire that was already blazing. Her heart was hammering in her chest and she couldn't seem to get enough air. She felt lightheaded and she moaned loudly when Kyler's hand cupped her breast. Yes, they were really going to do this. There was no stopping now. She didn't have the strength—or the want to—to stop.

Her jacket was shoved off and she let it fall to the floor behind her. Her hands tugged at Kyler's sweatshirt, pushing it up. Kyler whipped it over head, flinging it to the ground in one quick motion. Lexie's hands slid under the T-shirt beneath it, feeling warm skin against her fingertips. She felt Kyler tremble and it made her want to get closer, to touch more. Then her own sweatshirt was being removed. She held her arms up, letting Kyler pull it up. Their eyes met in the soft light—the Christmas tree flashing reds and greens and blues. It calmed her. She took a deep breath, feeling a little more in control now. It didn't last, however. Kyler drew her close, one hand snaking under her T-shirt, finding her breast. A thumb rubbed across her nipple and she sucked in a sharp breath, her hips moving hard against Kyler.

She was surprised she was able to walk when Kyler led her into her bedroom. Her legs felt wobbly and she held on to Kyler. It was dark and Kyler didn't bother with lights. Their fingers tangled together as they fumbled with buttons and zippers and jeans. Shirts and bras were discarded, and hands replaced clothing. Kyler's skin was like silk. She moved up her body, cupping her breasts, feeling her nipples harden as her fingers touched them.

Kyler's kiss stilled her hands and she moaned into it, her mouth opening, her tongue fighting Kyler's for control. Neither won the battle. She finally cupped Kyler's face, bringing that hot, wet mouth to her breasts. Her eyes slammed shut as her tongue teased a nipple before she sucked it into her mouth.

Then cool sheets on her heated skin, Kyler's weight on top of her, her thighs opening, letting Kyler inside. She was in a state of glorious delirium. Kyler's mouth seemed to be everywhere at once—her lips, her ear, her throat, her breasts. Gentle hands moved across her skin, from her neck to her hips, burning a path as they moved steadily and surely.

Kyler's mouth was on hers again and the sound of their moans filled the air around them. She was certain she'd not been so thoroughly kissed before, and when Kyler's touch moved lower, she arched into it, gasping as fingers slid into her wetness.

Kyler's tongue circled a nipple and Lexie held her there as Kyler's knee urged her legs apart, fingers filling her—moving inside her.

God, yes. Had she really wanted to fight this? Right at that moment, she didn't care in the least if Kyler was her type or not. It felt *good*. So she gave in to it, letting Kyler take her where she wanted, giving her free rein to do as she wanted.

CHAPTER THIRTY-SEVEN

"Stay a little longer."

Lexie snuggled against Kyler's warmth for long moment, then finally rolled over. "It's nearly five. I should go."

Kyler rolled to her side, her hand moving under the covers, across Lexie's hip. "You're not sorry, are you?"

The bedroom was still dark—the Christmas tree lights and the lamp in the living room didn't offer enough to see by. Lexie tried but couldn't read Kyler's eyes. She leaned closer, lightly kissing her on the mouth. Kyler's voice was husky from their lovemaking, and she let her lips linger, feeling her desire flame again.

"No. I can't seem to get enough of you."

Kyler smiled against her lips. "So stay. It's cold out."

"Yes. I hear the wind." She finally pulled away. "I should go, though. When Mark walks down to open the restaurant, he'll notice my car gone. I'm not ready for questions."

"He's going to take one look at me and know. I don't think we can hide it."

"I don't think I want anyone to know, Kyler. They'll all jump to conclusions, especially my mother."

Kyler sat up and touched her face gently. "We don't have to make an announcement or anything. We slept together. It's not anyone's business but ours. Let's enjoy each other and see where it goes."

She turned her head, kissing Kyler's palm. She finally nodded. "You're right. We'll just play it by ear."

She kissed her again, then got out of bed. The room was cold, and she shivered. Where were her clothes? She found her underwear, but the jeans she picked up were Kyler's, not hers. She placed them on the bed, then retrieved her own. She went into the living room, seeing her sweatshirt on the floor where Kyler had tossed it earlier. She picked it up, holding it to her as her eyes landed on the Christmas tree.

She felt almost hypnotized as she watched the blinking lights— red, green, blue, white. She'd been as aroused as she'd ever remembered being. They'd touched as if they knew each other well. She'd been so ready, so wet. She remembered holding Kyler's mouth to her breast, remembered pushing Kyler downward, her hips arching to meet that very mouth. She closed her eyes, feeling a strange fluttering in her stomach. Kyler had brought her to orgasm so quickly, she barely had time to register her mouth on her. She'd clutched Kyler's shoulders so tightly, she must have left a bruise.

Kyler had climbed back up, finding her lips again. When Lexie tasted herself there, she'd flipped them over. Her fingers had found Kyler's wetness and she'd—

"Lexie?"

She opened her eyes, blinking rapidly, the lights of the tree coming back into focus. She turned, finding Kyler standing in the doorway of her bedroom. She had on sweatpants, but her feet were bare. Her torso was bare too and her arms were wrapped around herself as if in an attempt to get warm.

Lexie dropped the sweatshirt she'd been holding. She walked purposefully back toward the bedroom, her gaze locked on Kyler's.

"Maybe I'll—" She cleared her throat. "Maybe I'll stay for a bit longer."

Kyler tugged her closer for a kiss, then led her back into the bedroom.

CHAPTER THIRTY-EIGHT

Kyler held the coffee cup between her hands, staring out as the first snowflakes started to fall. The wind was ferocious, and it blew them about, carrying them away before they landed.

"I should have stayed home." Tammy came up beside her. "We had three cancellations already. I doubt we'll have any campers for the next few days."

"There's still an RV there. I saw it this morning when I was filling the bird feeders."

"That's those folks from Abilene. Todd said they knew the storm was coming and decided to ride it out here instead of rushing home."

"I hope we get some decent snow."

"You do?"

"Sledding," she said, thinking of Lexie. "It'll be fun."

"Not in this wind. And not when the temperature is in the teens. Not fun."

Kyler looked around. "Where is everybody?"

"Brian and Todd have the day off. Jim said he'd be in later. Maybe." Tammy shrugged. "I don't know where the others are.

What's there to do in weather like this? They're probably holed up in the maintenance shed by the heater."

"Yeah, this is a great week for me to be on restroom duty. There are no campers here. At least I don't have to worry about a toilet backing up."

"So this probably isn't a good time to tell you this. The handicap shower's hot water is not working."

She frowned. "Who's used it?"

"Well, it's a big, private shower and dressing room. Mrs. Armstead—that's the lady in the RV—uses it. Went to take her evening shower yesterday and had only cold water. I got her message this morning."

Kyler blew out a breath. "Well, I guess there's nothing else to do. At least there's heat in there." She moved to top off her coffee. "I'll go take a look." She paused. "After that, I'm going back to my cabin. Call me if something comes up."

Tammy waved her away. "Don't mind me. I brought a book with me and my thick quilt. I'll pretend I'm at home, sitting by the fire."

"You should ask Jim if you can put up the self-pay signs. Like you said, the chances of getting customers today are slim."

"I'll probably do that after lunch."

She put the hood of her jacket up as she ran toward her work truck. The wind seemed to cut right through her, and she got inside and quickly slammed the door. The truck had been sitting out overnight and she knew it was pointless to put the heater on. She would be at the handicap shower long before it began to emit something other than cold air.

Oh, but once she was out on the road, the trees blocked the wind somewhat. The snow flurries whipped around her, and she slowed, taking it all in. A cloudy, dreary day—a rare treat. Their skies were usually blue and sunny. Even during the so-called rainy months of July and August, the skies were clear, save the odd thunderstorm that popped up, dumping much-needed moisture. She hoped the cloudy, snowy weather would stick around for a day or two. The north wind would die down tomorrow, and with luck, they'd get a few inches of snow. She could already envision a sled ride with Lexie. She'd love it.

She smiled. And after a sled ride, she could envision them back at her place, lounging on a comforter near the fire...hopefully naked.

For a second, she forgot about the cold as her mind flashed back to earlier that morning. Oh, yeah…she forgot all about being cold.

* * *

"That wind is strong enough to rattle the windowpanes," her mother said as she filled her coffee cup again. She took a sip, eyeing her over the top. "You've been awful quiet this morning."

"Have I?" Lexie yawned. "Getting up at one thirty in the morning will do that, I guess."

"Shame you went to all that trouble and didn't get to see the meteor shower." She sat down across from her at the desk. "Your father was up at six. Said you weren't back yet."

She tried. She really, really tried to keep the blush off her face. Yes, she did. She felt the heat of it, though, and she turned away from her mother, feigning interest in an email.

"I don't remember when I got back. We…we visited, and Kyler had made hot chocolate so we…we had that…and breakfast. She made breakfast," she lied. She hadn't eaten a thing and her stomach growled now at the thought.

"That was nice of her. What did you have?"

Oh god…really? "Umm, just toast and scrambled eggs."

"It's so nice that you two get along as well as you do. Kyler is special. She's got a good heart. Her family acts like she's not good enough, you know. They are all doctors, I think. Her sister too. They kinda look down on Kyler. But she doesn't change who she is."

She looked at her mother then. "She didn't mention that they were doctors. She did say that she had planned to go to medical school herself at one time." She rested her chin in her palm. "I know she's not close with her family. She said they only came up here one time."

"Yes. It's a shame. I'm not sure her family even knows who Kyler is."

"That is sad." Yes, it was. Kyler was nice, sweet, thoughtful. She was way better than merely *good enough*. She hated that for her. "I know she thinks of you as family."

"Oh, and we do too. We love her to death." Her mother looked at her, holding her gaze. "You like her a lot too, huh?"

She smiled. "Yes. She's been fun. She's definitely exposing me to new things."

"When I had first asked Kyler to show you around, I wondered if you could become friends. You seemed so different from each other."

"Complete opposites, I believed you called us."

"Yes. Maybe my perception of you was wrong. I certainly didn't envision you traipsing through the woods like you've been. Never thought you'd get up in the middle of the night to go stargazing, that's for sure."

"Me either."

Her mother met her gaze for a moment longer, as if she wanted to ask her something, but she must have changed her mind.

"Well, I guess we should take advantage of this lull before next week when the Christmas crowd starts coming. You want to do a practice run at payroll?"

"Sure. You think I'm ready to fly solo?"

"You took meticulous notes. I don't think you'll have a problem." She went to the coffeepot to refill her cup. "You want some?"

She was about to decline when a gust of wind did indeed rattle the panes. It made her shiver. "I guess I'll have another cup."

As she stared out of the window, she saw snow flurries blowing about. She got up, going to stand there, looking outside. Yes, the wind was fierce, whipping the trees around and scattering the snowflakes.

"Wouldn't it be wonderful to get some snow?"

Her mother came up beside her, handing her the cup of hot coffee. "It would be beautiful, wouldn't it? And so close to Christmas." Then she nudged Lexie's arm. "Let's not wish for it too much though. We would hate to have guests cancel reservations because of the weather."

No, she didn't want that. Her mother had shown her the books. One hundred percent occupancy for nearly two weeks brought in a lot of cash. Especially with the "dead" months coming up. So she wouldn't wish for a white Christmas. But they still had a week before the holiday crowds would show up. A few days of snow now wouldn't hurt things. Besides, Kyler had promised her a sled ride if they got enough.

Thoughts of Kyler made her smile. Thoughts of Kyler made her feel warm. Thoughts of them together—in bed—made her feel downright hot. She stepped away from her mother lest she feel the heat permeating from her body. Oh, yes, Kyler did that to her. She'd intended on leaving Kyler's house at five so that she'd be back before her father got up. But no. Once back in bed, she couldn't drag herself out of it again. At six, she'd still been in Kyler's arms. And at six thirty, she'd snuck into her apartment as quietly as possible, hoping that perhaps—because of the weather—her father hadn't been out to notice her absence. What she really hoped was that Mark hadn't noticed her car missing. The lights had been on in the restaurant. He'd surely been down the trail. But she wasn't going to worry about it. It had been too blissful of a morning to worry about Mark or her mother guessing how she and Kyler had spent their time.

She didn't know why she wanted to keep it a secret anyway. They'd find out soon enough. But as Kyler had said, it really wasn't their business, was it?

No, they'd slept together and it wasn't anyone's business. And they'd slept together without there being a big scene too. There'd been no lengthy discussion—unusual for her. There'd been no weighing the pros and cons—her specialty. There'd been no guilt or blame that morning. No self-reproach. No running and hiding.

Quite the opposite. She'd had to drag herself out of Kyler's bed. One more kiss. Then another. And another. She'd wanted nothing more than to stay right where she was.

It occurred to her that they hadn't really talked. Not that morning when she left, certainly. No, she'd been more interested in kissing than talking. When would they see each other again? Would it be awkward? Or would they continue what they'd started?

She frowned. What exactly had they started? Were they having an affair? A secret affair?

"Why are you frowning?"

She jerked her head up, finding her mother watching. "Nothing. Thinking."

Her mother scooted her chair around. "Do you want me to watch over you? Or would you rather try it on your own and only let me know if you hit a snag?"

"You better watch. I may not know if I hit a snag or not."

She pushed thoughts of Kyler from her mind and pulled up her notes on payroll. Time to get to work.

CHAPTER THIRTY-NINE

Kyler drove slowly along the winding park road, her eyes filled with wonder as she took in the snowy scene. They'd barely had an inch so far, but the wind had finally died down, allowing the snow to cling to branches now. Big, fluffy flakes fell, hitting the windshield of her Jeep. The clouds were thick and heavy, bringing dusk a little earlier than normal.

She was feeling a tad nervous as she pulled in at the bar. Despite the snow, there were five or six vehicles in the parking lot. She recognized the Mertz brothers' truck and Stuart's old Ford. She wondered if they ever missed a night. Before getting out, she took in the blinking Christmas lights in the windows, looking all the more festive with the snow floating around.

Her gaze slid to the bar, and there she was. Mark was leaning against it, his attention on something Lexie was telling him. Lexie had texted her earlier, asking if she wanted to "pop" over for a beer and dinner. There was nothing else to the text. No flirty innuendo. No mention of how they'd spent that morning. No mention of having a repeat. Nothing personal whatsoever. So she'd replied with a "sure" and left it at that.

Maybe Lexie was having second thoughts now. Maybe she was sorry they'd crossed that line after all. Or maybe she wanted to pretend it never happened, much like she'd attempted to do after their first kiss. She sighed, wondering if it should be this complicated.

She finally turned the engine off and paused, listening to the quiet for a moment. Then she got out, lifting her face to the sky, letting snowflakes hit her cheeks, feeling their gentle kiss as they landed on her. She smiled then, pushing her uncertainties about Lexie aside. It was too beautiful, too serene an evening to worry about that. She was a player in this game, yes, but Lexie held all the cards. If they went forward with this, it would be Lexie's decision, not hers. And if they stopped things right where they were—that was Lexie's choice too.

With that, she walked up to the porch, stopping once again to peer inside, smiling as her gaze landed on the familiar scene and familiar faces, the Christmas tree, the twinkling lights inside and out—and the snow clinging to the windowpanes. She pushed the door open, hearing the bell jingle, seeing Mark look up at her, a smile on his face.

She smiled back at him, then met Lexie's gaze in the mirror. The look there simply took her breath away. No, Lexie wasn't pretending it didn't happen. And no, she didn't appear sorry in the least. Her eyes were warm, the look she gave her had an intimacy to it, one shared between lovers. The relief she felt was palpable, and she smiled a little broader as she walked over to her.

"Hey," she said to the eyes in the mirror. Lexie nodded, then spun around on the barstool.

"Hey yourself."

Mark was already drawing her a beer. "How's the snow?"

"Looking better now that the wind has stopped."

"Stuart heard we might get five inches overnight."

"Yeah, that's what Jim said too. Wouldn't that be awesome?" She turned to Lexie. "More than enough for sledding."

Lexie nodded. "I'm game." She looked at her brother. "You?"

"Oh, yeah. That's fun. Makes you feel like a kid again." He slid the beer over to her. "This weather makes me want to cook up a big pot of chili or something."

"I've got a great vegetarian chili recipe," Lexie offered.

She and Mark groaned. "No," they said in unison.

"Venison," Kyler said.

"Mixed with beef," Mark added. "We made a good one last year. Simmered that baby most of the day."

"Since when do you eat venison?" Lexie asked.

"Since we moved up here. Phil gives us some every year. He likes to hunt, but Tammy isn't crazy about eating it, so he shares."

Lexie turned to her. "As much of a tree hugger as you are, I can't believe you'd eat a deer. Like Daisy."

"God, I'd never eat Daisy."

"Who is Daisy?"

"I throw corn out in the mornings. There's this young doe that comes by."

He laughed. "And you named her Daisy?"

"I think it's cute," Lexie said and bumped her leg with her own.

"Yeah. But maybe you're right. I wouldn't want someone to shoot and eat Daisy. Who's to say the deer that Phil gives us wasn't someone else's Daisy."

Mark shook his head. "No! Do not let her brainwash you! God, you'll be eating tofu and shit before too long."

"Look, I just want some fish." She took a swallow of beer. "When is that happening?"

"Supposed to get the grill delivered on Friday. This weather might set them back."

"Where's it being delivered from?"

"El Paso."

"Let's hope it's not delayed," Lexie said. "Like Kyler, I'm looking forward to my first fish dinner."

"Speaking of that, I'm placing my weekly food order tomorrow. If you want input, come over about ten."

Lexie nodded. "I will definitely be here." She turned to her. "What kind of fish?"

"Snapper or grouper would be my first choice."

A bell dinged from the kitchen and he went to pick up the order. Lexie leaned closer to her. "I kinda missed you today."

She smiled at her. "I kinda thought about you all day."

"Were you thinking naughty things?"

"Very naughty."

Lexie laughed. "I had to take a nap at lunch. I was exhausted."

"I only worked long enough to get a hot water heater reset, then I went back home. Slept for four hours."

"Not fair. I only got an hour and a half." She moved away when Mark came back over. "I didn't think it would be this crowded with the weather like it is."

"Oh, the regulars. The Mertz brothers and Stuart are like the post office. Nothing keeps them away." He grabbed three beer bottles from the cooler and left them again.

Lexie leaned closer, meeting her gaze. "When can I see you again?"

"You mean alone?"

"Yes, alone."

"Like maybe have a repeat of last night?"

Lexie smiled at her. "Well, it was actually this morning, but yes, a repeat."

"I could maybe be persuaded."

Lexie laughed. "That would be nice." She again moved away when Mark came back over.

"You two going to eat here tonight? Or are you cooking or something?"

"Eat here," Lexie said. "As you know, I don't have a kitchen and I doubt Kyler wants me to take over hers."

"I don't mind. That chicken you made the other night was really good. Saves me eating this fried food here." She smiled at Mark. "Sorry, but she's right. Everything on your menu is fried."

"Apparently not for long. But we're adding to, not taking away, right?"

"You're the boss," Lexie said. "I'm only offering suggestions."

"Sure. Call it that if you want."

The evening wasn't unlike others where they'd sat at the bar and shared a meal. Easy banter, good-natured teasing, and the harmless flirting that they usually did. However, whenever Mark slipped away to tend to a customer, the looks between them became steamy. The not-so-innocent touches, and the bump of knees and thighs had her squirming on the barstool by the time they'd finished their dinner—burgers.

"So you're saying this was the last veggie burger?"

"Do you want me to order some?"

"We could put it on the menu," Lexie said with a smile. "I'm sure you have people ask for veggie burgers all the time, don't you?"

"Yeah, right. *All* the time."

"Well, it was very good. Put some fresh sprouts on there and an avocado slice and it would rival those I used to get in Austin."

"Don't push your luck," he said dryly.

"How's my tab, by the way?" Kyler asked him. She normally settled up every two weeks or so.

"Not too bad. You can wait another week if you want."

"How many people run tabs?" Lexie asked.

"Oh, a few of the regulars. The Mertz brothers and Stuart, for sure. They usually pay on Saturdays when they come for dinner."

Lexie shook her head. "And they come *every* day?"

He shrugged. "None of them are married. Guess they got nothing else to do."

Much like Mark, she thought. Unless she dragged him out of here, he literally did nothing except run this bar.

"You're coming sledding with us tomorrow, right?" she coaxed.

"We'll see."

"No. You come," Lexie said firmly. "If it snows all night, you'll have no customers tomorrow."

"We'll go about nine," she said.

He finally nodded. "Okay. I'll meet you out there. If there's nothing happening here, I'll swing by, make a few runs."

"Good." She pushed her plate away. "Then I guess I'm heading out."

"Me too," Lexie said. "It's been a *long* day."

"Oh, that's right. You two were up at two-something this morning."

"Try one thirty," Lexie countered as she got up. "See you tomorrow."

"Don't forget we're ordering food tomorrow. We'll do it after sledding."

Lexie nodded. "I won't forget."

"Want a ride?" Kyler offered as they went outside. It was a lame excuse to be together. By the time she drove around the lodge and to the back, Lexie could have already walked there.

They stood off the porch, just out of the shaft of light. The Christmas lights glowed in the darkness and snow fluttered around them as their eyes met.

"It's so quiet." Lexie's gaze lifted to the sky. "Strange to look up and not see stars."

It was indeed quiet. No wind. So quiet, in fact, you could almost hear the snowflakes as they dropped to the ground. Lexie then looked back at her.

"Yes. I'll take a ride." Then she paused. "Can you stay?"

Kyler nodded but said nothing. The short drive was made in silence. When she parked, Lexie got out first, again meeting her gaze and again saying nothing. Kyler followed her inside.

When the door closed, there was no more pretense. Lexie moved into her arms and Kyler pulled her close. She moaned into the kiss as Lexie's body pressed against hers, pushing her back into the door.

"I've been thinking of this all day," Lexie murmured against her lips.

Kyler let her hands move up, cupping Lexie's breasts. Lexie's head fell back, and she put her lips against her neck, nibbling at the exposed skin. Lexie's hands at her waist pulled their hips together.

"Stay?" Lexie asked in a whisper.

Kyler moved her lips to Lexie's ear. "My Jeep...your mom..."

"Stay for a little while? An hour?"

Kyler smiled then found her mouth again. Lexie's opened, her tongue meeting her own. The rush she got from that drove out any hesitation she had about staying. She felt Lexie's fingers at the zipper of her jeans, and she shoved Lexie's sweatshirt up, urging it over her head. She pushed the bra away, her mouth settling over a nipple as Lexie moaned. Then Lexie's hand found its way inside her jeans and she jerked hard as fingers slipped through her wetness, circling her clit.

"God, you're so wet."

She was panting as Lexie touched her and she brought her mouth back to Lexie's. "Yes. Do it."

"Bed."

Lexie pulled her hand away and, with a purpose, led her into the bedroom. Kyler followed on shaky legs.

CHAPTER FORTY

Lexie stared at the snow-white trail that glistened in the morning sunlight. She turned wide eyes to Kyler.

"That's like straight downhill!"

"Not at all. It's an optical illusion," Kyler said with a teasing smile.

"Why don't I believe you?" She turned in a circle, her boots crunching on the snow. "It's so beautiful. Everything is pristine. It should be Christmas already."

"Gonna be above freezing tomorrow. The snow won't last long."

"So it'll all be long gone by Christmas?"

"Afraid so."

She looked around, taking it all in, trying to memorize the scene—the snow clinging to branches and covering rocks, the birds that landed, knocking snow off. A raucous call of a blue bird brought her attention around. What had Kyler called it?

"A scrub jay?"

Kyler smiled at her. "Dang, look at you."

"I think I would like birdwatching. I certainly like being outside. Even when it's twenty-eight degrees."

"Once we're hiking back up this hill, you'll be plenty warm."

Kyler brought out a plastic sled from the back of her Jeep. It was a bright blue and looked more like a small boat than a sled. The color was quite the contrast with the white snow.

"Where'd you get that?"

"I can't take credit for it. It was in the maintenance shed. Nobody seems to know where it came from."

"So you claimed it?"

"I did." Kyler walked to where the trail seemed to tumble over the side. "We'll have to tip it over at the end of the trail and fall off—so we don't end up in Limpia Creek."

"In the creek? Okay, so you're going to ride in the front, right?"

"No, no. To get the full experience of it, *you* need to ride in the front."

Lexie watched as Kyler's breath frosted around her as she spoke. Yes, it was twenty-eight degrees and she was outside and about to go sledding, of all things. Kyler met her gaze questioningly and she smiled at her.

"I love it." She spread her arms out. "Everything. I love it. I feel like I've been missing out. I've been living my life indoors and didn't realize how alive your senses get being outside. Everything is brighter, fresher. The air, the sky. The trees."

"The birds," Kyler added.

She laughed. "Yes. The birds." She motioned to the sled. "Okay. Let's do this. And if I end up in Limpia Creek, I'll be so pissed," she warned.

"I'll dump us before we hit the creek, but it may not be a soft landing. It's not that much snow, you know."

"Better than the creek."

Kyler placed the sled at the top of the hill, but not so far that it was pointed downward. Lexie got on, not knowing where to hold.

"Put your feet against the front and hold on to the sides."

"You have handles. Why don't I?"

"Don't know. Doesn't matter. I'll be holding on to you, not the handles."

"You will?"

"Of course."

She felt a little safer with Kyler behind her and yes, she was holding on to her. Her breast, that is. She leaned back against Kyler, smiling.

"We could skip sledding," she offered quietly. "Go to your place."

Kyler slowly removed her hand. "Have I told you how great it was last night?"

"Not since last night, no." She turned to look into her eyes. "But it was great, wasn't it?"

"Yeah. I like it a lot."

"Good. Me too." She turned a little more on the sled, enough to meet Kyler's lips in a slow, sweet kiss. Oh, yes, she liked this woman. Why did she think Kyler wasn't her type?

"You ready for me to take you on a ride?"

Lexie grinned. "Well, I'm ready for you to take me *somewhere*," she teased.

"Hold on. It'll be a thrill."

With that, Kyler pushed them down the trail and Lexie let out a scream as she was flung forward. Kyler's arms pulled her back against her and she fought against her instinct to squeeze her eyes shut as they flew across the snow-covered hill. She barely registered the cold, biting air as they barreled through it. The white snow was but a blur as they whirled along, Limpia Creek getting closer and closer. She braced herself, fearing that Kyler wouldn't get them stopped in time. Then she felt Kyler's weight shift, felt the sled lean to the left. She closed her eyes then as they tumbled into the cold, wet snow.

The landing was softer than she'd imagined—no rocks dug into her shoulder as she skidded across the snow. She finally opened her eyes, seeing the deep blue sky and nothing else.

"Was that great or what?"

She laughed then. "That was so much fun." She sat up. "Can we go again?"

Kyler stood and pulled her to her feet. "Sure we can." Then she pointed from where they'd come. "As soon as we climb back up."

Lexie looked where she pointed. The top of the hill seemed like it was miles away. "Good lord. Did we really go that far?"

She found herself holding hands with Kyler as they trudged back up the hill, pulling the sled behind them. The snow was deeper than they'd thought it would be as they sunk down several inches with each step.

"How much did we get?"

"Probably six inches."

"I took some pictures this morning. The feeders in Mom's bird garden were covered with snow and I got one of those..." She paused. "House finches?"

"Little birds with red on them?"

"Yeah. Those. Anyway, I posted it on Facebook." She stopped. "It's the first thing I've posted since I got here. I was looking through older stuff and it was all mostly things I'd been tagged in—out at bars on Sixth Street or brunch or something. This was such a contrast. Like it didn't belong."

Kyler tilted her head. "Like *you* don't belong?"

She squeezed her hand. "Like I don't belong *there*. The last thing posted was me sitting in a dark corner at a bar, holding a drink in each hand, surrounded by friends. It was my going away party. I looked at that picture this morning and—even though I was smiling—I could see how miserable I was. My eyes were lifeless. Yet, that was normal. It was just another Saturday night out on the town," she said with a wave of her hand. "It was dark and dreary. So putting the picture of the bright sun shining on the snow, the birds at the feeder—the contrast was too large to ignore.

"I feel like that, Kyler. My life was dark and dreary and depressing. Now? Now I feel light and cheery and happy. Like a weight has been lifted off. A weight I didn't know I carried." She met her gaze. "You're a big part of that, you know. Not the only part, certainly, but you've made me see things differently." She moved closer, looping her arms across Kyler's shoulders, matching her smile. "I like being with you." She kissed her gently. "I think I like everything about you. Your gentleness, your flirty side, your tree-hugger side."

"Birdwatcher?" Kyler asked hopefully.

Lexie grinned. "Especially that."

"So you're saying that I'm practically irresistible?"

Lexie laughed. "Yes. Practically. Now I can say that."

She leaned closer and kissed her again, letting Kyler pull her close. When they pulled apart, they were both smiling. Who knew having an affair would be so much fun? Without another word, they began the trek back up the hill again. She looked up to see how far they had to go, and she saw someone standing there, watching them. It was Mark. She had a moment of panic. Did he see them kiss? She pushed the panic down. So what if he did see them? It wasn't like they could keep this a secret forever. She decided she didn't want to. But when they got to the top, Mark's expression was no different than normal.

"Hey," Kyler greeted. "I didn't think you were going to show."

"Well, since my kitchen staff couldn't make it in, I figured no customers would either. I put up a sign, said I'd be back in an hour."

"Are they sanding the road yet?"

Mark shook his head. "I didn't hear any trucks. Y'all got the park closed?"

"Not officially, no. Self-pay, but I'm sure we won't have anyone come out, even after the road is sanded. Only the one RV out here. They've got the whole place to themselves. Pretty sweet deal."

Lexie pointed at the round disk he held. Pink, no less. "That's your sled?"

"Oh, yeah. This thing flies down the hill. You want to race?"

"You're on!"

Despite them having a longer, sleeker sled, Mark beat them easily. In fact, he was going so fast, he barely got stopped in time. He ended up on the bank of the creek, only a few feet from the water.

"Damn, you were fast!"

"Now that was fun!" He got up and dusted the snow from his jeans. "You should try it."

Lexie shook her head. "I think two times walking back up this hill is enough for me." She turned to Kyler. "What about you?"

Kyler shook her head. "I tried it last year."

Mark laughed. "She ended up in the creek."

"Did you really?"

"I did."

When they got back to the top of the hill, Mark was the only one who wanted another ride. They stood there watching as he sailed back down the hill, his childlike laughter carrying up to them.

"It's nice to see him being so relaxed," she said, smiling as he tumbled out at the edge of the creek again.

"You too," Kyler noted.

Lexie bumped her shoulder. "Yes, I am. I'm cold, but I'm relaxed. What a great way to spend the morning."

CHAPTER FORTY-ONE

Mark offered coffee and breakfast and they readily agreed. It had been fun, but her teeth were beginning to chatter from the cold and a hot cup of coffee sounded heavenly.

"I will attempt to make Maria's breakfast tacos. Come on back to the kitchen."

She and Kyler sat around the table in the back and sipped on coffee while Mark threw a few potatoes into the microwave.

"No way she nukes them," Kyler said.

"Sure she does. Then she crisps them up with onions in this pan," he said, holding it up. "I've watched her. I didn't pay much attention to the seasonings though. And she puts something in the eggs."

"Peppers? I've seen little green things in there," Lexie suggested.

Before long, he had onions and potatoes frying in the pan and he was whisking eggs in a bowl. An entire jalapeno had been seeded and chopped and Mark added that to the eggs.

"Too much," she said too late.

In another pan, he put four strips of bacon for him and Kyler. Lexie wrinkled up her nose. She hated the smell of bacon.

From the freezer came a package of tortillas. Kyler shook her head. "And no way she uses frozen tortillas. They taste like they're freshly made."

"These are hers. When she's got leftovers, she freezes them. They taste like fresh."

Lexie shredded some cheese for them, and Kyler found a jar of salsa. Mark topped off their coffee cups again and they sat down to their feast. After one bite, they were all reaching for water.

"Now that's some kind of spicy," Kyler said as she cleared her throat. Then she smiled. "But I like spicy."

"Maybe I put in a few too many peppers," he conceded.

"It'll warm you up, that's for sure. But it's very good." She took another bite. "Guess we didn't need that salsa."

"Can you stay and go over the food order with me?"

She nodded. "Yes. I'm looking forward to it." She turned to Kyler. "What are you going to do today?"

"I'm going to go fill all the birdfeeders and hang around and see what kind of birds pop over. Later, I'll probably go out on a trail. I love to be in the woods after a snowfall."

She met her gaze. "Can I go with you?"

"Of course. Call me when you're through with your food stuff. We'll meet up."

She looked over at Mark, seeing the faintest of smiles on his face, which she ignored. Twenty minutes later, they'd cleaned up the kitchen and Kyler had taken her leave. The smile he'd been suppressing all morning lit up his face now.

"What?" she asked.

"Told ya so."

"Told me what?"

He moved closer and touched her nose with his index finger. "Are you in love with her yet, sis?"

"Oh my god! We hardly know one another." She was sure she was blushing, but she gave him a smile. "So no, I'm not in love with her. We're just having a little fun."

"Is that all it is?"

"Yes. That's all it is. Don't think otherwise because you'll be disappointed. Besides the fact that we're both wrong for each other, I don't even know if I'm going to stay here."

"Wrong for each other?"

"She's not my type, you know that. She is so at home up here, it's ridiculous. Me? I'm at home in a city."

"I thought you liked it here."

"Oh, I do. I love it, in fact. It's given me the chance to relax and slow down and take a breath. But do I want to live here *forever*? Right now, I'd have to say no. And this is something I told Kyler— if I stay here a year, five years, whatever, I'll lose my skills. Things change so quickly in technology, if I'm not in the game, it's going to pass me by."

"So you've made up your mind?"

She heard the disappointment in his voice and she shook her head. "No, Mark. I haven't. These are just things I've been thinking about. And, of course, worrying that Mom and Dad are going to pack up and leave me here."

"Can you handle things if they do?"

"I can handle the reservations. I can do payroll. It's when something breaks that'll be the problem. It's keeping things stocked. Cleaning supplies, for instance. Toilet paper for the rooms. She's told me how she does inventory, but she's not actually walked me through it." She was starting to panic, picturing them leaving her with a wave as soon as Christmas was over. "I think this is too much for me. Too soon."

"Sis, from what Mom has told me, they wouldn't leave until February or March. They'd go to Florida for a couple of months, then come back to check on things. It's not like they plan to leave you here for six or eight months on your own."

"Regardless, it's daunting when you don't know what the hell you're doing."

"Lexie, I can help too, you know."

She met his gaze. "I'm scared, I guess. I don't want to make the wrong decision. What if I feel stagnant? I'm used to working in a fast-paced, professional environment. This is the complete opposite of that."

"Are you doing your thing again?"

"What?"

"Where you take everything apart and try to put it back together into a nice little package that fits into your life. Lexie, you worry about the silliest things."

"They are not silly," she insisted.

"Of course they are. You can have the best job in the world, but if you're not happy in your personal life…then you're not happy. Period. From what you've told me, you weren't happy in either of them in Austin. That's why coming up here appealed to you."

"You're right. I had grown stagnant in a job I used to love. And my personal life sucked." She sighed. "It's just such a big decision and I'm starting to feel pressured."

"By whom?"

"By me." He smiled at her. "I know how you are. I know how you worry over things. I know how you like to have everything analyzed before you make a decision. That's what you do. You drive yourself crazy in the meantime, but that's what you do."

"Yeah, you know me—I'm all about pros and cons."

"Maybe you should listen to your heart and not your head. Hmm?"

"That would be the fanciful thing, but it's not practical." She held her hand up. "And not a word to Mom about this. I'm nowhere near making a decision yet."

"And things with Kyler?"

"I told you, we're just…having some fun."

"An affair?"

She smiled and nodded. "We can call it that."

"Are you worried that if you get close to her, it'll have a bearing on your decision?"

He'd hit on the truth, hadn't he? "Yes. And I've told her as much." She waved her hand in the air. "I can't see that it will, anyway. It's not like we're dating or anything."

"Just having a little fun," he said, echoing her words.

"Yeah. A little holiday affair is all."

CHAPTER FORTY-TWO

Kyler found herself whistling a Christmas tune as she sanded the end of the hiking stick she was making for Lexie. She was sitting in the sunshine, having pulled a chair out from the maintenance shed. The temperature was near sixty and the snow from last week was nothing but a memory. It had lasted a good three days before it melted away as if it had never been. It was a fun three days though. She'd taken Lexie out on the trails and they'd enjoyed a hike. The deer were moving around more than usual, and they saw several groups of five to ten. There were lots of birds about and Lexie seemed to enjoy learning their names. The prize of the day was seeing a golden eagle soaring overhead. It was only her second time to see one and she'd been nearly as excited as the first time.

One night, Lexie had cooked dinner for them, and they'd eaten by the fire. They'd shared stories of high school and college, of first jobs and first loves. They'd talked and kissed and touched and talked some more.

Yesterday, she'd gone over to the bar for lunch, hoping to meet Lexie there. But their Christmas crowd was starting to trickle in at the lodge, and Lexie hadn't been able to get away. She'd enjoyed her time with Mark, though, in spite of him teasing her mercilessly.

And tonight, she had a dinner date. At the bar. For grilled fish. She'd been practically salivating all day thinking about it. Mark had the new grill installed, and they'd added a couple of things to the menu. He had warned her, however, that this would most likely be the very first fish that either Maria or Joseph had ever grilled, and she should lower her expectations.

She held up the stick, inspecting it as she ran a hand across the smooth surface. She'd hiked three trails before she found the limb she wanted to use. She'd cut it from the tree and brought it to the shed, letting it sit a day or two before starting on the sanding. It was sufficiently dry to stain and varnish, and she'd get that done in the next day or two. It was to be Lexie's Christmas gift. *Nothing quite says romance like a hiking stick.*

She froze. Romance? No, that didn't fit here, did it? They weren't dating. Well, they were, sure, but not officially. They'd talked about it the other night, in fact. An affair. A fling. No strings attached. They were both in agreement. Lexie wasn't even sure she was going to stay or not

She looked away from the hiking stick, her glance going out to the woods beyond the shed. A small boulder field was there and only a few hardy junipers had taken hold among the rocks. Farther up the hill, groups of piñon pine grew mixed with oaks. She heard the chatter of a squirrel and finally saw a bushy tail wagging on a limb. Other than that, it was quiet and still, with barely a breeze to be felt.

She sighed with contentment, noting that it felt a bit different. She loved her job, loved it up here in the Davis Mountains. She'd been content all along. But it was different now, wasn't it? Who knew having a lover would bring happiness when she didn't even know it was lacking? Not only a lover. A friend too. They were certainly both and they mingled the two aspects of their relationship easily. Even in bed, cuddling after making love, they could talk and tease—and flirt—like they did at any other time. It had been a seamless transition, going from friends to lovers.

But what if Lexie left? What if she went back to Austin? That was a real possibility, she knew. In fact, if she were placing bets—

She sighed again, this time with a bit of foreboding, as if—somewhere in the back of her mind—she knew what the outcome would be. Well, it wasn't like they were involved. They were having a little fling, that's all. A little fun, Lexie called it.

She stared absently at a tree, not really seeing it. She was starting to get involved, wasn't she? She was starting to *feel* things.

She took a deep breath, puffing out her cheeks as she blew it out. Yes, this little fling might be more than she bargained for.

CHAPTER FORTY-THREE

"I'm not sure I've ever seen anyone this excited about fish."
Kyler rubbed her hands together. "I've been dreaming of this day."

He shook his head. "I told you to lower your expectations. I don't even know what kind of seasonings they're going to use."

"Don't care."

"And the rice pilaf and vegetable medley that Lexie had in mind is only going to be a pile of white rice with some previously frozen broccoli on top."

"Don't care. I'm only here for the fish."

Lexie nudged her arm. "You're such an easy date," she teased.

"Yeah, I am."

"Okay, I'm going to agree with Mark, though. You might want to curb your excitement. I would hate for you to be disappointed."

Mark leaned his hip against the bar, holding the towel that seemed to be always in his hand. "You tell Mom yet?"

Lexie feigned ignorance. "Tell her what?"

He rolled his eyes. "About you two."

It was Kyler who spoke, not her. "Does it need an announcement? We're friends."

"With benefits," he added with a grin.

Kyler smiled too. "Damn good benefits, but still. We're friends. That should be enough."

"I agree," Lexie said. "It's not like we're going steady or anything. We're just—"

"Hanging out," Kyler finished.

"This is Mom."

She sighed. "I'm not ready to tell her. If I tell her that Kyler and I—"

"Have been having sex," he finished for her.

She rolled her eyes at him. "Then she'll think it's guaranteed that I'm staying here and that's not the case. Kyler and I have talked about this. Whether I stay or go, it has to be about me, not her. And not Mom and Dad and their plans. It's got to be about me."

Mark looked at Kyler with raised eyebrows. Kyler nodded.

"We're hanging out and having a little fun. Don't go planning a wedding."

Lexie laughed. "This is exactly why I don't want to tell Mom! She'll go crazy with the news."

And she would, she knew. Her mother adored Kyler, as did Mark. If things didn't work out here, if she ended up going back to Austin, she didn't want to be the cause of their disappointment. She and Kyler had talked about it at length the other night while lying in bed. They were in agreement—they both knew what the stakes were. Neither of them was going to get so involved that it would be devastating if she left. As Kyler said, they were simply having a little fun while she was here. If she ended up staying, then that fun would continue. If she left, well...she didn't really want to think about that right now.

No. Because it was all she could do to keep things simple between them. Simple and fun and nothing too emotional. She looked into the mirror, finding Kyler looking back at her. She returned her smile while holding her gaze. Oh, yes, she needed to keep things simple. Because it would be so easy to fall in love with her. And that was something she could not—would not—do.

"Then you two better behave."

"What are you talking about?"

He motioned behind them. Again, looking in the mirror, she saw her mother coming into the bar. She spun around on the barstool.

"I've been here a month. This is the first time I've seen you in here."

"I heard a rumor fish was on the menu." She sat down beside her. "Do you mind if I join you?"

"Of course not."

"You want a beer, Mom?"

Her mother shook her head at Mark. "You know I'm not crazy about beer. A plain Coke will do." She leaned around her to look at Kyler. "I have a favor to ask. Dale and I are going to El Paso tomorrow."

"You are?" Lexie asked.

"I told you, didn't I?" She looked back at Kyler. "We'll be gone two days, maybe three. Could you look after the bird garden for me?"

"Of course," Kyler said. "No problem."

"Thanks, dear. I didn't want to throw all that on Lexie."

"Going RV shopping?" Kyler asked.

Mark slid a glass with ice and Coke over to her. "Dad said he found a couple online that he wanted to look at."

"Yes. We're going to a dealership to look at new ones, but he found three used ones that were reasonably priced."

"Are you going to pull something, like a fifth-wheel, or are you looking at a motorhome?" Kyler asked.

"We haven't decided. We go back and forth. We like features of each of them. I think when we see the one we want, we'll know." Her mother looked at Lexie and patted her arm. "This has nothing to do with whether you stay or not. Your father has wanted to get some type of RV for years now."

She nodded and smiled but said nothing. What could she say? That she was feeling pressured? Was she? Kyler nudged her arm and gave her a subtle wink, easing some of the anxiety she felt. No, she shouldn't feel pressured. She knew that her parents had been talking about buying an RV for several years. They wouldn't be able to actually go anywhere significant unless she was here, however. While Irene could manage the office for a few days, she doubted she'd have a clue how to manage the online reservation system. She sighed. So yes, she *was* feeling pressured.

The conversation seemed to go on without her, but she was aware of Kyler's presence—the brush of her knee, the touch of a hand on her arm as she talked to Mark and her mother. If her mother noticed her silence, she didn't show it. Mark was more attuned, however, and gave her a questioning look. She answered by tapping her empty beer mug.

Despite Mark's warning that they shouldn't get too excited about their first grilled fish, Joseph did an excellent job with the seasonings. It had a bit of a Cajun flavor to it with just enough bite to make you notice, but the spice wasn't overwhelming. The blob of white rice topped with overcooked broccoli, however, left something to be desired.

"Stir-fry the rice with the broccoli and add some soy sauce or tamari or something," she suggested. "Even a frozen bag of mixed vegetables would be better."

"The fish is excellent," Kyler said. "I could eat this every day. But yeah, the rice needs something."

Her mother had taken hers with her, going to the house to eat. She had passed on the rice, saying she'd made a pasta salad to have with theirs.

"So how about you come back to the kitchen tomorrow and give Joseph some pointers on the rice," he said to her.

Lexie raised her eyebrows. "Me?"

"Yeah, you."

"Okay. He won't get offended, right?"

Mark smiled. "Are you kidding? After all this praise for the fish?"

"Okay. Deal."

"I'm thinking he could do Spanish rice and add a little more cayenne to the fish, maybe some chili powder or cumin," Kyler offered.

Lexie smiled at her. "I didn't know you could cook."

Kyler shook her head. "No, not really. But there was this Mexican restaurant down at the coast that used to serve grilled fish on top of Spanish rice. Grilled corn on the cob and some squash with it. It was great."

"That's a good idea." When Mark left to get an order, she leaned closer. "Can we go to your place?"

"Sure. You okay?"

Lexie shrugged. "I feel like talking."

Kyler nodded. "Okay."

It was as easy as that. Yes, Kyler was pretty easy about everything. Kyler didn't get too worked up about things, whereas she tended to fret and worry over them endlessly—and sometimes needlessly.

CHAPTER FORTY-FOUR

"This is nice."

Lexie smiled. "I love lying naked with you. It's freeing."

"Freeing?"

"Yes. There's nothing to hide. A symbolism, I guess. I can't hide my body from you, therefore, I can't hide anything. Freeing. I can talk to you about anything. You don't judge me. More importantly, you don't offer your opinion."

"You should tell her how you feel."

"My mother? No. She's not putting pressure on me intentionally. I don't even think it's unintentional, either. They're going about their life, regardless of what I decide to do." She wrapped her arm a little tighter around Kyler's waist. "I wish I could be like that. I'm not sure why I'm not."

"You were what? Twenty-three when they left? Maybe you felt like you needed to be extra cautious because you were in Austin without your family."

Lexie smiled. "I'd like to say that's the case, but my mother claims I've always been a bit of a worrier." She rolled onto her back, finding Kyler's hand under the covers. "I need to tell you something." She turned her head, meeting Kyler's gaze. "I'm leaving, Kyler."

There was a moment's hesitation as Kyler absorbed the news. "I see."

She closed her eyes for a moment and shook her head. "No. I mean, if I have a decision to make, I need to make it there, not here." She held her eyes, trying to read them. "Because if I stay here, and we continue doing what we're doing for the next two weeks, then I won't be making a rational decision. I'll be making an emotional one. Do you understand?"

Kyler nodded. "I understand. You don't want this to be about me. About us."

"Yes. So can we enjoy this time, these few days before Christmas? I'm going to leave right after. I was going to stay until mid-January, but I think I should go now. I've got my apartment to pack. But really, I need to be away from here—you—so I can think."

Kyler nodded. "I understand. Have you told your mother?"

"No. It's something I've been thinking about for the last few days. I think it's the best thing."

"Okay."

Lexie rolled toward her again. She could tell by the look in Kyler's eyes that she was scared. There was something else there. Something that frightened her a little. Was Kyler falling in love? For that matter, was *she* falling in love?

"I'm sorry," she whispered.

Kyler rolled onto her shoulder, facing her. "Don't, Lexie. I agree with your decision. You're right. If we continue this…this affair, then you're right. We'll get in too deep. Both of us. It's best you leave now, before that happens."

"I want to be sure, that's all. I don't want to say I'll stay, then a year from now be miserable."

"You don't have to explain to me."

She let out a relieved breath. "I knew you would react this way. I knew you would accept it." She leaned closer and softly kissed her lips. She got a rush, like she usually did when they kissed. How wonderful was it to feel this way? She closed her eyes as they kissed again. No. She didn't want to feel this way. That's why she needed to leave. If she was going to make a level-headed decision, she needed to leave. If she stayed any longer, the decision would be out of her hands.

CHAPTER FORTY-FIVE

"I understand, honey."

"Do you, Mom?"

"Yes. I had hoped, well, since you and Kyler—"

Her eyes widened. "So you know?"

"Of course I know. Why else would you be sneaking home at five thirty or six in the mornings?"

She'd never been comfortable discussing her sex life with her mother. She didn't want to start now. "Okay. But Kyler has nothing to do with the reason I'm leaving." Was that a lie?

She sat down at the desk. "What I mean is, I want to make this decision without Kyler being a factor. Do you understand, Mom?"

"I guess what you're trying to say is that you'd like to be able to say you'd be happy here whether Kyler was here or not. Right?"

"Yes. Kyler's become a friend. A good friend." She smiled a little. "And more, of course. But this is a huge decision for me. I don't want to make the wrong one. And I don't want to make it for the wrong reason."

Her mother nodded. "I understand, honey. I do. We've loved having you here, of course, but this has always been your decision."

"And I've loved being here. I really have. I've done things I never thought I would have. I've loved biking and hiking. I've hugged trees, for god's sake!"

Her mother laughed. "I wish we had a picture of that."

"Being back with you and Dad, with Mark, it made me realize how much I missed being a part of a family on a daily basis. When I leave here, I'm going to really miss that."

Her mother came closer, bending down to gather her in a tight hug. "I only want you to be happy, honey. And I know for the last year or so, you haven't been. I didn't need to be there to know that. I could hear it in your voice when we spoke." She finally released her. "You do what you need to do. If this mountain isn't for you, then it isn't for you. If you decide to stay in Austin, we'll still come visit you like we always have. Mark will too."

"Mom—"

"Honey, this is your life. Only you can decide. And I think I agree. You don't need outside influences. And yes, I'll admit, I did think that if you and Kyler…well, if you were to become involved, I thought maybe that might persuade you to stay. That was selfish on my part. And I don't only mean because it would allow your father and me some time to travel. It was selfish to want you up here with us, as a family. Because we missed that too."

"That's not selfish, Mom. I told you, I missed our family time. Seven years is a long time to be apart."

"I know. We sort of abandoned you down there, didn't we? At first we thought you'd have Mark and Mia, but then…"

Lexie stood up, stopping her mother by hugging her. "It's okay, Mom. We may have been physically apart, but I never once thought you'd abandoned me. You were a phone call away."

They stepped apart and smiled at each other. "Okay, then. So you're leaving the day after Christmas. At least the weather should be good for your drive."

"I love you, Mom."

That, of course, warranted another tight hug. "Oh, honey, I love you too."

CHAPTER FORTY-SIX

Kyler knew her gift wasn't really appropriate any longer, but she had nothing else to give. Her giftwrapping job was a little messy too, but there are only so many ways to wrap a hiking stick. None of that seemed to matter to Lexie, though. When their eyes met, she saw the misting of tears there.

"You remembered."

"I did."

"It's beautiful, Kyler. Thank you."

Lexie bent to inspect the carvings on the side. Kyler had managed to etch out a dove on one side and an eagle on the other. Eagle or hawk, it looked like either. To an expert's eyes, it probably looked like neither. Susan went over to inspect the stick as well.

"Good job, Kyler. I love the hawk."

"I think it's an eagle. And I love the dove." Then Lexie grinned. "See? I do know a bird or two."

Mark sat down beside her as more gifts were exchanged. He leaned closer, his voice low. "You okay?"

Kyler let out a heavy sigh. "I'm not sure," she said honestly. She met his gaze. "You were right all along."

"About?"

"When you said I'd love your sister." She let her gaze drift to Lexie. "It's probably good she's leaving now. I'd get in way too deep if she stayed another month."

"Have you told her?"

"No, of course not."

"I think she'll be back."

"I don't think so. There's nothing up here for her. I think she'll get back to Austin and realize just how remote we really are up here. The highlight of her stay has been a grilled fish dinner. How sad is that?"

"If we're talking food, then yeah, that might very well be true. But I'd hardly say it's the highlight of her stay, Ky." He smiled at her. "I'm going to guess the almost-meteor shower was the highlight."

She laughed quietly. "Okay, yeah. That might rank up there pretty high. I know it does for me."

Lexie looked at her and gave her a smile, almost as if she knew what they were talking about. Then she came over and surprised her by bending down to kiss her quickly on the mouth.

"I love the hiking stick."

"Good. Maybe you can get out to the greenbelt and take it for a spin."

She meant for the words to be lighthearted, teasing, but they didn't come out that way. Lexie held her gaze, her own eyes softening, but she said nothing. When she walked away, Kyler let out a breath.

"Damn. That sounded kinda spiteful, didn't it?"

"You're taking this better than I'd be."

"What am I supposed to do? Beg her to stay?"

"I would."

"No, you wouldn't. That would be selfish and you, my friend, are not selfish. Neither am I. This is her decision, not mine, not yours. Not your mother's. Hers."

He nudged her arm. "Want to get drunk tomorrow night?"

She smiled. "Not sure that will solve anything, but hell… maybe."

"Or we could go on a hike or something?"

She stared at him. "That's the first time you've offered."

He shrugged. "Maybe it's time I got out and did something."

She leaned closer, resting her shoulder against his. "Thanks, buddy."

* * *

After gifts, Susan served them brunch. She had quite a spread on the bar—a cheesy sausage and egg casserole, a vegetable quiche, crispy hash brown pancakes, fresh baked biscuits with butter and jam to go with them, a loaf of banana bread which was still warm, and tall glasses of orange juice. Kyler didn't know what to take first.

"Nice," Lexie said. "Better than a restaurant brunch, I think."

"Didn't you say your Austin brunches involved Bloody Marys?" Mark asked as he scooped a large helping of the casserole onto his plate.

"After a night out, yes. I don't miss that."

"What's the first thing you're going to do when you get back?" Susan asked.

Kyler watched as Lexie seemed to consider the question. "Honestly, I haven't even thought about it. I suppose on the drive back, I'll call Trish. Knowing her, she'll plan a dinner out with some of our friends."

"Gonna hit the gym?" Mark asked.

Lexie looked at Kyler, not Mark. "Maybe I'll hit the greenbelt and try to find a hiking trail." She returned her gaze to Mark. "But yes, I suppose I'll go to the gym at some point."

"Yeah, well I offered to go hiking with Kyler. How scary is that?"

Lexie smiled at him. "Next thing you know, you'll be on a mountain bike. I'm going to leave mine here. Why don't you try it out?"

"You're leaving it here?" Kyler asked.

"Yes. I don't have a rack for it, and I don't think I can cram it into my backseat."

Kyler was going to offer to take the front tire off, which would make it easier to "cram," but she didn't. Maybe a part of her thought that if she left the bike here, then it meant she'd be back. Of course, if she left it here, yes, Mark could use it. Getting him out on a hiking trail would be a big thing. Getting him out on a bike would be momentous.

Everyone seemed to be looking at Mark, even Dale. Mark plopped a hash brown pancake onto his plate. "You know, I think maybe I might try it out, sis." He glanced at her then. "Ky is going to need a riding partner."

Lexie's hand found her arm and squeezed it tightly. "Yes. I think that's a wonderful plan."

Susan seemed to visibly exhale, and she nodded. "Yes. Maybe that'll get you away from the restaurant more often. Irene can handle things just fine if you're gone."

"Mom, Irene is eighty."

"So? She hasn't lost a step since we moved up here. If she was stuck at her ranch by herself, I think she would waste away. Working up here gives her a purpose."

"Speaking of Irene," Mark said, "she's taking a few days off. Her granddaughter is coming to visit for a while."

"Oh, yes. She had told me she might come right after Christmas. Went through a nasty divorce this summer, Irene said." Her mother shook her head. "Her husband was abusive, to hear Irene tell it."

"Any children?" Lexie asked.

"Yes, that's what was so sad. A little boy, only two. Ended up in the hospital one time."

"It's good that she's getting away then."

"When Irene offered, she didn't think Jamie would agree. She's never been out here. In fact, it's been years since Irene has seen her. Obviously, she's never met her great-grandson." Her mother looked at Lexie. "She's probably close to your age, I guess. Of course, I don't think she's coming to live permanently. Irene thought a month or two."

"Is she from Dallas?" Mark asked.

"I believe so."

Lexie sat beside her at the table, moving her leg so that their knees were touching. Kyler smiled at her, glad for the contact. After brunch, she was going to help Lexie finish packing. Then they were going to go to her cabin and spend the rest of the day. In bed. Saying their goodbyes. Lexie wouldn't spend the night with her, though. They'd already agreed. They were going to have a simple dinner. They would make a campfire and sit out and watch the stars. Lexie would go home to sleep, though. She wanted to get away at daybreak. She had a seven-hour drive to contend with.

Then she'd be gone—back to Austin. Back to familiar things and familiar friends. And Kyler would be here, in a place she loved, with people she loved. She and Mark would go back to their old routine, Susan would invite her to dinner, Tammy and Phil would have her out to the ranch, and yes, she'd go over to Irene's and take a ride with her up to Mount Livermore. Maybe she'd make friends with Irene's granddaughter. Maybe she wouldn't miss Lexie that much.

A hand on her thigh brought her attention around and she met Lexie's gaze. Did Lexie know what she was thinking? She must. Her eyes were warm and, dared she say, loving? Yes, they were. She offered a small smile and covered Lexie's hand with her own.

It wasn't the end of the world, she told herself. Even if Lexie decided to stay in Austin, it wasn't like they'd never see each other again. Her family was here and now that she'd been here, Kyler assumed she'd come back to visit. And when she did, she could see them continuing their affair. That is, unless Lexie started seeing someone in Austin. That thought made her take in a sharp breath. So then, yeah, *that* might be the end of the world.

CHAPTER FORTY-SEVEN

Lexie stood at the window, watching a red sports car buzz through the parking lot, spewing water from the misty rain. When she saw the blur of red, for one brief—crazy—second, she thought Kyler was there. With a sigh, she spun around, taking in the clutter in her apartment. Mounds of boxes, some packed and taped, others still opened. How had she possibly accumulated this much crap?

She couldn't muster up the energy to continue packing, however. She needed to shower and dress anyway. Trish was coming by. As expected, she'd put together a dinner party at one of their favorite Mexican food places.

Trish had been ecstatic when Lexie had called her. She'd been at her apartment waiting, along with two of their friends, when Lexie arrived. Disregarding Lexie's exhaustion after her long drive, they'd whisked her away for a meal and margaritas before she'd even had a chance to unpack her car. She'd ordered her usual veggie burger and it was stuffed with fresh spinach and sprouts, a thick tomato slice, and two creamy avocado wedges. All that on a sprouted whole wheat bun. But all she could think about was Kyler's frozen veggie patties that she'd found at Potter's. A frozen patty that she'd taken to Mark's bar and had them make her a burger on a plain white bun. A burger Kyler had delivered to the lodge. No spinach, no sprouts. It had been the best burger ever, she knew now. It had been the best because of the woman who had sat across from her for their impromptu lunch date.

She blew out a heavy breath, trying to muster some enthusiasm for the night ahead. Ten or twelve people would be there. She couldn't imagine that many of them had missed her all that much, but it was an excuse for dinner and drinking, she supposed. And come Saturday—as Trish had reminded her—they were going to go down Sixth Street for barhopping. And that meant a Sunday brunch would follow.

She shoved some things around on her sofa to give her room to sit. She picked up her phone, holding it for a moment. She'd spoken to Kyler only once since she'd been back. That was to let her know she'd made it to Austin safely—this done from Trish's car so she wasn't able to chat. Of course, she'd only been back three days. Still, she'd spoken to her mother twice. Without debating it further, she called Kyler. She answered right away.

"Hey!"

"Hi. Are you busy?"

"I've got campground duty this week. Cleaning out the fire pits. So not busy, no."

Lexie pictured Kyler in her uniform, busying herself around the campsite, pausing to watch a bird if one flew by. She was right at home there, in her element. "It's raining here."

"Is it? Blue skies here. As usual. I wouldn't mind a rainy day." Kyler laughed quietly. "Why are we talking about the weather?"

Lexie sighed. "I miss you. I miss talking to you."

There was only a slight pause. "Is that all you miss?"

She gave a quiet laugh. "No. I miss other things too."

"I miss you too."

"I probably shouldn't have called."

"Why not? Friends call."

She chewed on her lower lip. "Yes, but we're not only friends." She cleared her throat. "I said I wasn't going to call, and I should stick to that. I'm sorry. I was just—" What? Missing you? Missing *there*? What?

"Lexie, you take the time you need. I'll still be here, regardless. I'm not going anywhere. Call me whenever you need to."

"Yes. I know."

"So, you went out with your friends the other night. How was it?"

"It was okay. I was too exhausted to enjoy myself, I think. Trish has a dinner party planned for tonight. And Sixth Street on Saturday, of course, and then—"

"Brunch on Sunday," Kyler finished for her.

"And brunch on Sunday." She was exhausted just thinking about all the plans she had. Normal stuff. Things she used to do every day.

"Sounds like fun."

"Does it?"

"Well, not really."

She laughed at that. "What? Too peoplely for you?"

"Well, you know the kind of crowds I'm used to."

"I know." She paused. "I guess I should let you get back to your campgrounds. It was good to hear your voice."

"You too." There was a long pause, as if they both had more to say but were afraid to. Kyler finally broke the silence. "Bye, Lexie."

She laid the phone in her lap, surprised that—if she let them—tears were threatening to fall. She got up quickly. She needed to snap out of it. She needed to do what she'd said she'd do. She would go out, be with her friends and evaluate her life. She'd do like she always did. She'd weigh out each facet, she'd list her pros and cons, she'd worry over the decision before she actually made one. And she would get her apartment packed up. That was a must. Regardless of what her decision was, she wasn't staying here.

* * *

Kyler sat down at her usual barstool, noting the emptiness of the one next to her. She turned her attention to Mark, who was looking at her with concerned eyes.

"I'm okay."

"You don't look okay."

"She called me today."

"Oh, yeah?" He took a mug from the freezer and filled it. "I thought the plan was not to call."

"It was."

"So?"

Kyler shrugged. "We talked for a minute, maybe."

"She misses you?"

"Yeah. And she's going out tonight. Dinner party. And the thing on Sixth Street on Saturday doing whatever it is they do."

"Barhopping," he supplied.

"And brunch on Sunday."

"So back to her normal routine."

"Yeah, seems like."

He leaned his elbows on the bar, getting to her eye level. "Did you fall in love with my sister?"

She sighed. "Maybe."

He smiled and stood back up. "Then have faith. Love is a special thing."

"I wouldn't know."

"I would."

She touched his hand lightly and nodded. "Yes, you would. I hope to have what you had some day. And unending love."

"Give it time."

"Time? It's been three days and I feel like it's been three months. I'm not sure how long I can go."

"What are you talking about?"

"I feel like I want to go chase after her. Tell me not to."

"You want to go to Austin and drag her back?"

"Yes. Well, you know, not *drag*." She picked up her beer. "I didn't think I'd miss her this much."

"Tomorrow's your day off, isn't it?"

"Yeah."

"Take me on a bike ride."

She jerked her head up. "Really?"

He nodded. "Yeah."

She reached across the bar and squeezed his hand. "Okay. Sure."

"Good. So quit moping around. She'll be back."

She met his gaze. "You think so?"

"I hope so. We don't need both of us up here with empty hearts."

CHAPTER FORTY-EIGHT

Lexie sat at the corner table, still nursing her first margarita. Chatter and laughter went on around her and no one seemed to notice her lack of participation. Even Trish. Lexie took the time to observe them—her friends. Nine of them. Two she'd known since college, like Trish. They were friends that she got together with occasionally, usually in a group like this. She couldn't remember if she'd ever had a one-on-one with any of them, other than Trish.

She listened to their conversations—some recounting Christmas activities but most centered on local gossip and a rehashing of old news. She'd been gone five weeks and hadn't missed a thing, apparently.

She'd been back three days and she missed plenty, though. God, yes, but she missed her. She had thought, when she left Austin, that she'd be lonely out in West Texas. Little did she know that the opposite would occur. She was around friends in a familiar place, doing familiar things, yet she was as lonely as she could ever remember being.

She let them prattle on without her as her mind drifted back to the mountains—the clear blue skies, the junipers and oaks, the rocks and stones, the bird garden, and the dark, dark skies filled with stars. And of course, the woman who walked among all those things, the woman who had taught her to love them all. The piñon pines, the doves, the red-tailed hawk…and the woman herself.

Had she fallen in love with Kyler? Or had she escaped before she lost her heart? Her assertion that she didn't want Kyler to be a factor in whether she moved or not—that wasn't really the case, was it? If she hadn't been there, if she'd never met Kyler, then she wouldn't have come to love and appreciate the things there—nature, for one. Having her parents there, Mark, that wouldn't have been enough. But Kyler taught her how to love the little things, how to love nature and look for the beauty in the simplest of things. If Kyler wasn't there, she wouldn't have the same fondness for the place, she knew that.

Didn't her feelings for Austin mirror that? She wasn't happy here. Wasn't that why she left in the first place? She wasn't happy here any longer. Being away for five weeks hadn't changed that. It reinforced it if anything. She had needed a change in her life, a new direction. That had nothing whatsoever to do with Kyler.

Then why the hell had she come back? What was she afraid of?

Someone nudged her arm. "What planet are you on?"

She blinked several times, finding Trish staring at her. "What?"

"I said your name like four times. Did you space out?"

"Yes. Sorry."

"What's wrong? You've only said a handful of words all night. And is that still your first drink?"

She tucked her hair behind both ears. "Trish, this was a mistake."

"What? Dinner?"

She shook her head. No. They couldn't have a heart-to-heart talk here. "Now's not the right time to talk. Let's enjoy the party."

"You seem to be the only one *not* enjoying it," Trish said pointedly.

"Maybe I'm tired," she lied. "I've been packing nonstop for the last two days."

"I told you I'd help on Saturday."

"Yes. We'll talk then."

She let Trish order her a second drink and she tried to focus on the group. She tried. But Kyler's face—that oftentimes smiling but sometimes serious face—kept swimming before her eyes. She gave up trying to push it away. She found herself smiling back at it.

CHAPTER FORTY-NINE

"Susan, let me help you with that." Kyler hurried over, lifting the bag of sunflower seeds out of Susan's trunk. She flung it over her shoulder and headed to the garage where the bins were kept.

"You always come at exactly the right time."

"You want me to fill them?"

"No, I filled them this morning. I just came back from Potters and the feed store." Susan lifted the lid on one of the bins and Kyler put the bag inside. "Dale heard we might get snow again."

"Yeah. New Year's Eve is supposed to be icy."

"Will you be out and about this year?"

"I volunteered to work, like normal."

Susan studied her for a moment, head tilted. "You want to sit over at the patio? Visit for a bit?"

Well, it was why she'd come over, wasn't it? To talk. She nodded. "Sure. We should enjoy the sunshine while we can."

As they walked over to the small patio, she couldn't help but glance at the door to Lexie's apartment. Susan, of course, saw her.

"Have you spoken to her?"

"The other day, briefly. You?"

"This morning. Just for a second. She was on her way to the gym."

They pulled chairs away from the table and sat down. "Yeah, when I talked to her, she had plans for a dinner party and then Sixth Street on Saturday night." She shrugged. "Not sure what all that entails."

"Hordes of young people crowded on the streets, barhopping," Susan said with a wave of her hand.

Kyler shook her head. "I have a hard time picturing Lexie in that scene."

"It's a group thing with her friend Trish. I think it's something she started doing regularly when we moved up here. I sometimes feel like we abandoned her there."

"Do you think she'll come back?" she asked bluntly.

"Oh, honey, I wish I knew. She's given no indication one way or the other. I know she's started packing her apartment. She has to be out by the end of January. She told me that Trish has offered for her to stay with her if she needs to."

Kyler sighed. "That kinda sounds like she's going to stay. As I told Mark, she'll get back into her old routines—the gym, Sixth Street, out to eat." She sighed. "It's not for everyone, living up here."

"You used to think it wasn't for you, either," Susan reminded her.

She nodded. "Took me a while to settle in, yes. Lexie was only here, what? Five, six weeks?"

"Lexie was never one to talk about her personal life with me. Never." She smiled gently at her. "Maybe you'll be more open? Fill in the blanks for me."

Kyler gave a nervous laugh. "Are you wanting to know how far we went?" She was surprised by the blush on Susan's face.

"I can guess that." She tapped her chest. "I'm talking about in here."

Kyler sighed. "We started this knowing that we were not the type of person either of us would normally date. Of course, I haven't really dated in years, but Lexie—at first—reminded me of someone I used to date. That was when I was younger, before I...I changed. My values are different now, my outlook on life has changed. My likes and dislikes are all so different now. And Lexie reminded me of her. If it had been back then, then yeah, she would have been exactly my type."

"But?"

She shrugged. "Lexie ended up being nothing like her. Lexie ended up being the type of person I'm attracted to now." She met Susan's gaze. "But I'm still me. And I'm nothing like the women Lexie dates. I don't think I quite fit into her world."

"Not down there, no. I'm not sure that's what she wants any longer, Kyler. She wasn't happy in Austin. I don't think anything there has changed, has it?"

"She's now got something to compare it to—this remote, dry, rocky mountain that we call home. It's quite the contrast. Now that she's seen it in person, she's got something to compare."

"And you think she'll get back to Austin, with its vibrant nightlife and traffic and crowds and decide she loves all of that after all?"

"She has friends there. What would she have here?"

"You came up here not knowing a soul. Do you feel like you have no friends?"

"No, of course not. But—"

"But nothing. Friends won't be the deciding factor. I know my daughter. She'll have a spreadsheet on her laptop. She'll have three columns. Pros, Cons, Comments. And she'll fill all the spaces and she'll agonize over it and try to make a decision." The she smiled. "All the while, it'll be out of her hands."

"What do you mean?"

"This decision she's about to make will have to come from of her heart, not a spreadsheet. She'll realize that as she's arguing with herself over each one. Her mind will say one thing, but her heart will say something completely different."

Kyler stared at her, searching. "You think she'll come back?" she asked hopefully.

"Lexie has always been so cautious about everything, never one to take chances. I think, this time...well, I think it'll be different. I think she fell in love. With the mountain. With you."

Kyler felt her heart tighten in her chest. "I hope you're right."

CHAPTER FIFTY

Lexie sat on the floor in the kitchen, taping up another box. Even after Cathy had gone berserk and broke most of her dishes, she still had a ton of kitchen stuff. More than one person possibly needed. Certainly more than one needed who ate out for most meals.

She leaned back against the counter, mentally going over her pros and cons once again. The pros for moving were much longer this time than they'd been before Thanksgiving. In fact, the cons were sorely lacking this time around.

She slowly shook her head, remembering how she'd agonized over them at the time—dinner dates, green smoothies, and tofu had been at the top of her con list. She rolled her eyes. Seriously? How trivial were those concerns?

She stared at the wall. She missed Kyler. She missed her far more than she'd missed anything about Austin and her friends while she'd been away. Shouldn't that tell her something? Yes, but part of her was afraid to admit what she felt. Actually, terrified would be more apt. She needed to talk it out, say it out loud. If she was looking for a friend to talk to, Kyler would be that person. However, that wouldn't be appropriate in this case.

She would talk to Trish instead, even though she wouldn't understand, she was sure. Trish assumed she'd come back with the intent to stay. And Trish was trying her best to keep her busy—out to dinner twice, lunch once. Tonight was dinner on West Sixth, then the usual parade through the bars until midnight or one. And, of course, Sunday brunch at Trudy's.

She leaned her head back against the cabinet and closed her eyes. No. She didn't feel like going out. She didn't want to be crammed together with throngs of rowdy people strolling the sidewalk while music blasted out of every bar. She felt almost claustrophobic just thinking about it.

"So don't go," she said to her empty kitchen. "Don't go."

Yeah, right. Trish certainly wouldn't understand that. Because Trish lived for Saturday nights and she most likely thought Lexie did too. Maybe, by her actions, she projected that as the truth or maybe Trish assumed. She sighed. No, she didn't feel like going. She had no excuse not to, though.

Do I need an excuse?

No. When Trish came over later for lunch—pizza—and to help her finish packing, she'd tell her she wasn't in the mood. And she'd tell her why she'd come back to Austin, she'd tell her about Kyler, and then she'd listen as Trish told her how crazy she'd be to consider leaving again.

Crazy? It really didn't seem so crazy anymore, did it?

* * *

Kyler motioned with her head to the young woman sitting at the end of the bar. "Who's the blonde?"

"Oh, that Irene's granddaughter. Jamie."

"She's attractive."

Mark nodded. "Yeah. Kinda quiet. Hardly speaks."

"Well, her asshole husband was abusive, what do you expect?"

He shrugged. "I guess. Her kid is really cute, though." He smiled. "He was running around in here earlier. Well, as fast as a two-year-old can run."

"Where is he?"

"I let them use my office. He's taking a nap. James. His name is James."

She watched as Mark's gaze slid again to the woman. She followed it, trying not to stare. The woman wasn't paying them any mind. Her attention was on a book.

"You think I should go introduce myself?" she asked.

"I'll introduce you. Come on." Kyler walked behind the barstools as Mark moved along the bar to the end. "Jamie?"

The woman looked up sharply and Kyler saw a wariness in her eyes. Damn. How badly had her husband abused her?

"This is my best friend. Kyler. She works at the state park." Jamie turned her head, nodding at her. "Hello."

"Hi, Jamie." She held her hand out and Jamie shook it briefly. "Nice to meet you."

"My grandmother has mentioned you, yes. Nice to meet you."

"You're from Dallas? I guess this is a change, huh?"

Jamie met her gaze. "A nice change."

"Gonna stay a while?"

"A few months, at least. My grandmother seems to like us being here."

"Oh, I'm sure. Irene never gets off this mountain. I know she misses not having family around."

"I had an opportunity to get away so…"

Jamie turned her attention back to her book and Kyler looked at Mark who only shrugged. "Well, I guess I'll see you around then."

Jamie looked up and smiled at her before returning to her book. A well-worn book that looked like it had been read many times before.

She went back to her normal stool, nodding when Mark drew her a beer. She kept her voice quiet when he slid the beer to her.

"She's terrified."

"You think? Of me?"

"Wonder if Irene knows what all happened. Did you see that scar above her eye?"

He nodded. "Could be from anything."

"I hope the bastard's in jail."

"It's not any of our business."

"No, I guess it's not." She took a swallow of beer. "So? Are we still going bike riding in the morning?"

"You think we can beat the front?"

She smiled at him. "Trying to chicken out?"

"Strong winds. Might get snow."

"Our Sunday will be long over with by the time the storm hits. I'm in the mood for pizza, I think."

He leaned his elbows on the table. "I want to ride. I do. But I'm afraid."

She met his gaze. "Afraid of memories?"

He nodded. "It's been almost eight years. The scene—in my mind—is not quite as fresh as it used to be."

"You're afraid it'll all come back?"

"Yeah."

"I won't push you, Mark. You do what you feel is best. But maybe, if you get on a bike, the memories that come back to you will be good ones. I mean, you used to have a lot of fun riding, didn't you? Do you ever think about *those* times? The good times?"

He stared at her for a long moment, his eyes searching. "I think about things I miss, I guess. Lexie misses her cookies. I miss our Sunday brunch...blueberry pancakes." He shook his head. "When I think of the bike, I think of that day. That's all."

She squeezed his hand. "If you don't want to ride, then we won't ride. You decide."

"Thanks, Ky."

CHAPTER FIFTY-ONE

"Where did you get all the boxes?"

"I've been hording them for months, it seems like. They were in the spare bedroom." Lexie tucked the hair behind her ears. "I've already gone through what was in there. Mostly crap that Cathy left behind." She looked at the clutter in her living room. "What the hell am I going to do with all this stuff?"

"Have you started looking for new apartments yet?"

"No." She chewed on her lower lip nervously. "Actually, I...I'm probably going back."

Trish's mouth fell open. "*What*? You can't possibly be serious."

"I am." She looked around, wondering where they could sit and talk. The only available chairs were in the kitchen. She went there, knowing the pizza they'd ordered would be arriving soon. "Let's talk."

"Oh, Lexie...no." Trish shook her head. "Why would you want to go back?"

She sat down and motioned for Trish to do the same. She was having a bit of déjà vu, she thought, as she was preparing to tell her she was leaving. Again.

"The reasons I wanted to go there in the first place haven't changed. I don't have a job and I can't afford this apartment being the main two." She rested her elbows on the table, trying to find a way to say it without hurting her feelings. "I didn't miss going out on group dinners or having lunch out or even the gym. I thought I would, but I didn't."

"But Lexie—"

She held her hand up, stopping her protest. "You would have gone stark raving mad up there. And maybe a year ago, I may have too."

"Your mother is pressuring you, isn't she?"

"Not at all." She met her gaze. "I fell in love with the place. I really did. It's quiet and slow and…and *real*." She smiled a little. "And I met someone."

At that, Trish's eyebrows shot up.

"I actually mentioned her to you before. Kyler."

"Oh my god! The birdwatcher? Are you *crazy*?"

"At first glance, I would say she was absolutely not my type. Too earthy, too outdoorsy…too gentle." She pictured Kyler's face and smiled a little more. "She taught me a lot about life and a lot about myself."

"Oh my god, I can't believe I'm hearing this. Too earthy? Let me guess. She doesn't shave. Legs and armpits both. Probably doesn't wear deodorant. Good *god*, Lexie."

At that, Lexie laughed, remembering Kyler's smooth skin. "She does shave, but that's not the point. She's very, very different from anyone I've dated before. Different from any of my friends here. She's—"

"So you're dating?"

"I guess you could call it that."

Trish shook her head disapprovingly. "So, you were sleeping with her. Good lord, Lexie."

"She's not the sole reason I want to go back, Trish. I really did love it there. Mom and Dad are there. Mark, of course. As soon as I got back here, it didn't feel right. When I was up there, I thought I would miss everything down here. I didn't. Yet when I came back, I missed everything up there like crazy." She leaned forward, meeting her gaze. "I fell in love with the place. And I think I fell in love with Kyler. It feels like home. This doesn't anymore."

Trish stared at her. "In love with her? Really?"

"Really."

"Then why did you come back?"

"Because I was scared. Scared of what I was feeling, scared to make a decision, scared it would be the wrong one. You know me..."

"Had to run the odds through a computer program, yes."

"It feels like the right decision, Trish. I don't really have any doubts anymore."

"I guess your mother is happy then."

"I haven't told her. In fact, I haven't told Kyler either."

"Because once you tell them, then it's set in stone." She nodded. "Oh, I do know you, Lexie." She smiled at her. "You've made your decision, yet you're afraid to say it out loud."

Lexie nodded. "If I tell them, then I'm going to want to be there, not here." She motioned to the living room. "And I have all of this to deal with still."

Trish grabbed her arm and squeezed. "You're really leaving? For good this time?"

"Yes, I am."

"And there's nothing I can say or do to talk you out of it?"

"I know you've tried really hard to keep me entertained this last week. I appreciate it, Trish, I do. But all those things that I thought I enjoyed doing were nothing more than busy work. The prospect of going out to Sixth Street tonight is not appealing in the least."

Trish stared at her as if she'd spoken blasphemy. "It's...it's our *thing*, Lexie."

"No. It's *your* thing. I enjoyed going when we were in college, sure. And maybe once in a while—a couple of times a year—it might be fun. But not every Saturday night. I'm sorry."

Trish stood. "So this is it? You're just throwing everything away as if it meant nothing to you? I suppose our friendship will be the same. Once you leave, I'll probably never see you again."

"I'm not going to lie, Trish. Once I leave, it may be a year before I come back to visit. We'll talk on the phone some—text—but it won't be like it's been, no."

"I didn't think you'd really do this. I was convinced that you'd hate it there, that you'd come running back."

"So was I, actually."

Trish sat down again. "Okay. I'm being selfish. I'm sorry. If this is what you want, then I need to be happy for you. So, let's figure out what we're going to do with all your stuff."

"Thank you."

"If you're not taking your furniture, put a sign down at the mailboxes. You could probably sell it all in a few days."

She nodded. "I had thought about that, yes. My clothes, I think I'll donate. I certainly won't need business suits at my new job."

Trish smiled at that. "Running a lodge. Who would have thought?"

"I know. But I love it there. And I can't wait to get back."

"So, come out with us tonight. One last time. Dinner first, then bars. One last time, Lexie. Please?"

She looked around her cluttered apartment, knowing she and Trish could have it all boxed up this afternoon. What else was she going to do tonight?

"Okay. One last time."

Trish clapped. "Great. Because I need a date."

"A date? What happened to...what was his name? The guy with the beard."

"Jacob. No. But Aaron will be there, and he's been asking me out. He's not my type at all. He's got tattoos all over both arms. Can you imagine my mother if I brought him home?"

She laughed. "I remember in college, your mother always warned you to stay clear of tattoos."

The doorbell rang, signaling lunch and they spent the next hour eating pizza and drinking beer, reminiscing about past exploits, and sharing many laughs. They both seemed to know this was their goodbye. When they saw each other again, whether a year from now or longer, things would be different. But that was okay. This was a new chapter in her life, and she'd make new friends. She wouldn't ever forget the fun times she and Trish had had, going all the way back to their freshman year in college...but things would change.

And she was ready.

CHAPTER FIFTY-TWO

"Are you sure?"

Mark nodded. "I think so."

"You look ridiculous in Lexie's helmet, by the way. It's too small."

Mark gave her a glance. "That's what you're concerned about? Who's going to see me, Ky? A deer?"

She wheeled her bike closer to where he stood. He was holding Lexie's bike by the handlebars, but he had yet to attempt to get on the thing. She saw fear in his eyes.

"Are you sure?" she asked again.

"Yeah. Let's take it for a spin." He got on then and she saw him visibly swallow. "But go slow."

They didn't speak as they wound around the restaurant and onto the park road. It wasn't until they were past the picnic area before she dared to turn and look at him. Tears were streaming down his face.

"Oh, man," she murmured.

He shook his head. "I'm okay."

She rode on, glancing at him from time to time, seeing him wipe tears off his cheek, only to have them run down again. When she got to the first road that went to one of the tent camping areas, she turned. She found an empty campsite and stopped. Mark was nearly sobbing then, and she let her bike fall to the ground, going to him. She held his bike while he got off and she put it down beside hers.

He covered his face, as if hiding his tears. She took his hand, urging him down. They sat there on the rocky ground, leaning against trees. She didn't say anything, she just held his hand while he cried. A few moments later, the sobs turned to laughter. She frowned as he leaned his head back against the tree, wiping his tears and laughing at the same time.

"God, Ky…I needed that."

She scooted closer to him until they were touching, but she still didn't say anything.

"When I think of Mia, I think of that day. That's how I see her. Always." He turned to look at her, his eyes still damp with tears. "It was like, as soon as I was on the bike, I remembered all the fun we used to have. All the good things—the good times—that I'd pushed to the very back of my mind, so far hidden that I didn't even remember them anymore. I got on the bike and I felt…I felt free, Ky. Everything came rushing back at once."

She leaned against his shoulder, feeling the relief that he must surely be feeling.

"I hung on to my grief, that's all. I let everything else go." He turned to look at her. "I hated life. I hated everything and everybody. I felt cheated." He gave her a smile. "Then you walked into my bar."

She smiled back at him but kept quiet, wanting him to talk, not her.

"She was pregnant. I was going to be a dad. I was going to have a son." He swallowed again and fresh tears sprang to his eyes. "I blamed myself. She was six months along. I shouldn't have let her go riding. I should have made her stop." Then he shook his head. "That's what I thought I should have done. That was my guilt. But she loved to ride more than I did, I think. There would have been a horrible fight had I even suggested she not ride anymore." He leaned back against the tree, looking up into the sky again. "We had a nursery all fixed up. I couldn't even go in there. I couldn't do much of anything. Lexie came and stayed with me for a couple of weeks. Then Mom and Dad asked me to come up here with them. I didn't even think twice. I wanted to leave Austin—and my memories—behind."

He turned to her then. "And that's what I did." He motioned to the bikes on the ground. "That was like a time machine. The wind on my face, the blur of the trees—how many miles had Mia and I ridden?" He smiled again. "Good memories that I'd forgotten." He pressed closer against her shoulder. "Thank you for making me do this."

"It was your decision, but okay, I'll take the credit," she said with a smile. "Next thing you know, you'll be hiking."

He wiped his nose with the sleeve of his shirt. "I think I'd like that. It was fun to get out and do something."

"We should plan a hike. Maybe ask Irene's granddaughter to go."

"Jamie?" He shook his head. "I imagine she pretty much hates men now. Or she's scared of them."

"Yeah, no doubt. But you're a damn nice guy, Mark. Might do her good to have a male friend who is gentle and kind. She'd probably like to get out and do something too."

"When she comes with Irene to the bar, she just sits at the end of the bar and reads. I try not to bother her."

She stood up and held her hand out to him. "Invite her for a hike. We can take an easy trail. Now come on. Let's take a spin around the park. We've got football on the agenda."

CHAPTER FIFTY-THREE

Lexie pushed the food around on her plate, listening to the others as they laughed about their exploits from the previous night. Their group had started out with twelve. By the time they'd hit the last bar of the night, there were only five left. Trish was not one of the five. She'd met some guy at their second bar and had disappeared. And judging by the look on her face this morning, she'd had way too much to drink last night and if she had to guess, she doubted Trish had slept in her own bed.

If this was to be her last Sunday brunch after a night out on Sixth Street, she would be happy to see it come to an end. She wasn't sure why she'd even come. Well, the prospect of cheesy migas and Trudy's famous Bloody Mary had sounded good. She glanced at the drink, which she'd only taken a few sips of, then ate another forkful of eggs.

She'd already answered the handful of questions directed her way. Questions and comments. Comments like "I could never leave Austin" or "What in the world are you going to do out there?" Or this, from Janine. "I'd have to be pretty desperate to move way out to West Texas. I hear it's absolutely desolate there." She would admit that the drive out was pretty barren. She remembered how excited she was when she finally saw a tree. But up on the mountain was completely different. While barren and rocky in spots, it was still teeming with life. And she couldn't wait to get back to it.

She had called Kyler yesterday, before dinner. It went to voice mail and she'd left only a brief message, telling her she was on her way to Sixth Street and had simply wanted to hear her voice. Kyler had returned her call sometime during the night, leaving an equally brief message, saying she hoped she'd enjoyed her night out on the town and mentioned plans she and Mark had for a bike ride. A bike ride this morning, in fact. She wondered how that had gone. Actually, she wondered if Mark had really gone through with it. If he had, maybe it would be a turning point for him.

She glanced at her watch. It was a little after eleven. Were they getting ready for their football party now? What would they have today? Frozen pizza? Or maybe since she wasn't there, they'd grill a steak or something. With a sigh, she turned her attention to the conversations around her, but in the back of her mind, she was wishing she was on Mark's deck instead of here.

Actually, she wished she was back at her apartment, sorting through her kitchen boxes, deciding what she'd take with her and what she'd get rid of. And she wanted to call her mother. She wanted to tell someone her news, someone who would be excited for her. Unlike her friends here. Their reaction ran the gamut from a disinterested shrug to utter disbelief.

Kyler would be excited too, she knew, but she wanted them both to be alone when she told her. She'd call her later tonight, after football.

"Lexie?"

She looked toward Trish. "Hmm?"

"What do you think?"

She frowned. "About what?"

"Did you not hear any of that conversation?"

She sighed. "I'm sorry. No. What?"

"Joni says I should color my hair. Red. What do you think?"

"Red?" She blinked at her and smiled. "Sure. Why not?"

CHAPTER FIFTY-FOUR

Kyler heard the boards creak as she walked—tiptoed—across the deck. She paused at the door, looking overhead into the sky. The storm had blown in later than expected, but it was there now, in full force. The moon was nearly full, but the clouds obscured it. The wind was shaking the trees and she listened as the limb of a piñon pine brushed against the railing. The temperature had dropped into the twenties and she had no business being out. As she watched, the first flakes of snow drifted about. She stared at them for a long moment, thinking she should just go back home.

Instead, she slipped her key into the lock, quietly turning the doorknob. She went inside, letting her eyes adjust to the darkness. It was warmer inside and she saw the glowing embers of Mark's earlier fire. She moved toward his bedroom door. It was ajar and she pushed it open. She smiled as she listened to his light snoring. Then she went up to the bed, shaking his shoulder. He jumped.

"What the hell?"

"Shhh. It's me."

He rubbed his face. "Why are you whispering?"

"Oh. I don't know," she said in a normal voice. "Get up."

"What time is it?"

"Umm…I don't know. Late. Or early."

He leaned up on an elbow. "What the hell are you doing?"

"Get up. Let's go."

"Go where?"

"Austin."

He lay back down. "No. We're not going to Austin."

"Come on," she nearly whined. "She left me a voice mail."

He sat up again. "And? What did she say this time?"

"She said she wanted to talk. In private. That can't be good. That means she's not coming back, right?"

He lay back down with a sigh. "Ky, really?"

"We've done nothing but leave voice mails. She called me while I was in the shower tonight. I called her back. Nothing."

"And what exactly did she say?"

Kyler fumbled with her phone. "Here. I'll play it for you. Listen." She swallowed as Lexie's voice filled the quiet room.

"Hi…it's me. I wanted to talk to you, but I wanted to do it in private. Thought you'd be back from Mark's by now. I've got a late dinner date so I'm heading out. Maybe we can talk tomorrow morning." A pause. *"I miss you, Kyler."*

"So from that you gather that she's not coming back? She said she missed you."

"She also said that we needed to talk. That can't be good."

"Have you been drinking?"

Kyler sighed. "Maybe."

"Have you been to bed?"

"No."

Mark took her phone, looking at the time. "Jesus, it's two in the morning, Ky." He moved the covers back on the bed. "Come on. Get some sleep."

"I'm pretty sure I'm in love with her."

"Yeah. I'm pretty sure you are too. Come on. Get in."

"What if she doesn't come back?"

"Then she'd be crazy. And I don't think my sister is crazy."

Kyler shuffled around to the other side of the bed. She kicked off her jeans and got under the covers. "If we left now, we could be there by ten."

She heard him sigh. "Storm. Snow. You've been drinking. We're not going to Austin."

She rolled toward him. "If I get my heart broken, will you take care of me?"

Another sigh. "You're being pathetic."

She smiled. "I know. I'm all grown up now. I can handle a broken heart."

"Then what are you doing in my bed?"

"I knew you'd talk me out of going." She waited while he rolled toward her too. "You're a good friend, Mark. Thank you."

"You're welcome."

"I love you."

"Love you too."

She smiled in the darkness. "We probably shouldn't tell anyone we slept together."

"You think?"

* * *

Lexie was pouring her first cup of coffee when her phone rang. Seeing as it was barely five o'clock, she knew it wouldn't be any of her friends here. She smiled when she saw Mark's name.

"Good morning," she answered cheerfully.

"Good. You're up."

"I am. What's wrong?"

"You need to come back. Like now. Today. Because she's going to drive me crazy."

She laughed lightly. "I guess you're talking about Kyler and not Mom."

"What's with you leaving cryptic voice mails? She's convinced you're not coming back."

She frowned. "Why are you whispering?"

"Because there's a woman in my bed and it's too cold to go out on the deck."

"Oh my god! You *slept* with someone? Who? Who? Tell me!"

"Sis…Kyler is in my bed."

She actually stopped breathing as she held the phone tightly. "*What?* You slept with Kyler? Kyler slept with…with *you?*" She squeezed her eyes shut, feeling all sorts of emotions slam into her.

"What are you talking about? No, we didn't sleep together! Well, yes, technically we did. She broke into the house at two this morning, wanting me to take her to Austin."

She finally dared to breathe again. "So she, like, spent the night there?"

"Yes. Good lord, did you think we had sex? Besides the fact that Kyler is gay, she's my best friend. She's like you—a sister. God."

She shook her head, trying to clear it. "Okay, okay. So what happened?"

"She's lovesick. Pathetic. She's actually whining. She wanted me to go to Austin with her. So you need to come back. And soon." He paused. "You *are* coming back, right?"

She smiled into the phone. "I am. I've been trying to tell her, but we keep missing each other. I called Mom last night and told her."

"And she didn't tell me? What's with that?"

"I asked her not to. I didn't want Kyler to find out second or thirdhand. I wanted to tell her myself."

"Then let's do it. Right now."

She heard him walking, then heard muffled voices before a familiar sleepy voice sounded in her ear.

"Lexie? Is that you?"

"Hey, sweetie. Whatcha doing?"

Kyler cleared her throat. "I guess you know where I am."

Lexie laughed. "Had a sleepover, I hear."

"Did he tell you why?"

"He did."

"He can't keep anything to himself," Kyler muttered.

"The two of you are too cute, you know that? Were you really going to drive to Austin this morning?"

"I was. It was stupid. I know this decision is about you, not me. I was…I was lonely, and I missed you. And your message, well, I figured it meant you weren't coming back, and I panicked."

"Why did you panic?"

"Because I want you to come back. Selfish, I know."

"So I should tell you that I've made a decision, I guess." There was a long pause and she knew she shouldn't be toying with Kyler this way. "Do you know what it is?"

Another pause. "I figured once you got back there, you'd realize how much you missed it, missed all the things you used to do."

"Yes. I thought the same thing. The opposite happened, Kyler. I missed you. But I also missed…*there*. I missed the mountain. I missed the bird garden. I missed the trees and the stars that we looked at at night. I missed all of that. But you, Kyler, I missed you the most. I didn't miss *here*."

"So...you're going to come home?"

She smiled at Kyler's choice of words. It was true what they say. Home is where the heart is. "I'm coming home."

She heard Kyler's relieved laugh and she smiled too. Yes, she was going back, going back home.

CHAPTER FIFTY-FIVE

"Show me a constellation."

Kyler shook her head. "You show me one."

The sunset had been spectacular, as usual, but that's not why they'd come up to Skyline Drive. They'd missed the sun setting, only getting there in time to watch the red colors streak out along the horizon behind Mount Livermore. No, they'd come to see the crescent moon—four days old—as it paired up with Venus, the evening star on this cold February night. She stared at the moon, seeing the bright star beside it. Lexie's Venus.

"Venus is in the constellation Aquarius this time of year."

Kyler raised her eyebrows. "How do you know that?"

"I read it in your book this morning. I don't know all the stars that make up Aquarius, though, so that shouldn't count as showing you a constellation."

She drew Lexie into her arms and kissed her. "I love that you like this stuff."

"Well, I credit Venus for us falling in love."

"You do?"

"Uh-huh. That very first time we watched the sunset. Afterward, you showed me Orion—the hunter. And then Ursa Minor—the Little Dipper."

"Or what else is it called?"

"Little Bear." Lexie looped her arms around her neck. "And then you pointed out Venus. And I thought it was all so romantic and I wanted to kiss you right then."

Kyler gave a teasing gasp. "Kiss me? We were only friends. Friends don't kiss."

"I know. I kept telling myself that, but I wanted to do it anyway." Lexie kissed her then—a long, slow, drawn-out kiss that left her breathless. "I'm not cold any longer."

Kyler smiled and pulled her closer. "After that kiss, I guess not." She cupped her from behind and held their hips together. "We can be home in two minutes."

Lexie laughed. "You'll have to wait. We're having company for dinner, remember?"

"Oh, yeah. Mark's coming over."

"And I invited Jamie, remember?"

"Uh-huh. Are you playing matchmaker?"

"Of course not. But Jamie is finally opening up. You know, at first, she would hardly speak to anyone. Plus, this gives her a break from her son and gives Irene some alone time with him."

"You like her?"

"I do. She seemed so fragile. Broken. She came up here to heal, I think."

"Like Mark did."

"Yes. And he is pretty much back to normal. I knew he would love to ride with us. It's so nice to see him this free again."

"Yeah, it is." Kyler took her hand and led her to the Jeep. "So what's for dinner?"

"Something simple. Tacos."

"Sounds good."

"Roasted cauliflower and chickpea tacos."

Kyler frowned. "Huh?"

"You'll love it. They're very spicy."

"No beef?"

"Nope."

"Chicken?" she asked hopefully.

"Nope. There is cheese and guacamole involved though."

She groaned as they walked back to the Jeep. "I've lost like six pounds since you've been cooking for me."

Lexie laughed. "Do not blame that on my cooking!"

They paused at the Jeep, looking up into the dark sky. The stars were right on top of them, twinkling and dancing over their heads. Lexie squeezed her hand tightly.

"I love you."

Kyler's gaze moved across the stars, finding the dipper, then the North Star. She smiled, then turned to Lexie.

"I've loved living up here on this mountain. It never occurred to me that something was missing. Not until you. You fill up all the spaces, Lexie. You make me so happy. I never thought I could love like this."

Lexie moved closer and kissed her deeply, passionately, leaving no room for questions. Lexie loved her. "Come on. Let's go home."

Bella Books, Inc.

Women. Books. Even Better Together.

P.O. Box 10543
Tallahassee, FL 32302

Phone: 800-729-4992
www.bellabooks.com